Dear Bad Boy

Kelsey McCluskey

D1265394

Contents

♥

To the friends who attended my many
many breakdowns over this novel...
Thank you.
My ever-suffering husband, I'm sorry.
But also thank you.
And finally, to the little demon who lives inside
of my head telling me that I can't do it.
Thank you.
I did it.

Aster Stone Carlisle

I t's a curious thing, love. Some fight for it, where others merely settle. Many can't see it when it's standing right in front of them.

If it's so curious, then why is it one of the most commonly used words in the English language, or any language for that matter. The easiest and hardest words to say.

I don't have an opinion because to open yourself to love is to feel, and I don't think I've done that in years...

Dad storms into the kitchen slamming his briefcase down on the table, "what's that god awful smell?" He grunts, heading right for the decanter on the island.

"Dinner, I made some pasta." I shrug pulling out another plate, if I set some out for him then maybe he'll eat. Line his stomach a little. But I can tell by the haze in his eyes that he already did, with miniatures on the plane.

Slumping himself down at the table by the window he looks up at me through his Glenfiddich eyes, and for a second I could have sworn I saw his disappointment in me waver.

"You settled on a school yet?" His voice lured me into a sense of false security, it was calm and interested. He wanted to know about me for once.

"I uh...I'm leaning towards UCLA. The theatre prog—"

"Theatre." He scoffs shaking his head, "why? And why are you going so far away? What's wrong with the schools here?"

This is where he demented me. My soul purpose in life to stay here and be ignored by him. But as long as I'm here. Even when he isn't.

I used to think it was better with dad here, dreading being alone in this big house on the outskirts of town. But this summer something has changed in him. I sometimes wonder if it's because I remind him of my mother. It would explain why he drinks more and picks faults wherever he can find them so now I look forward to him going away. Now I beg to be alone.

That was until I met Aster.

Lying in bed, drifting in and out of a dreamy haziness, I am startled by a rhythmic tapping on my bedroom window. What the hell? I get out of bed, stumbling in the darkness of my room, "Ouch! For fucks sake!" I groan through gritted teeth, stubbing my toe on the dresser by my window. The faint tapping continues, my heart beating in rhythm as I pull the blind up slowly, revealing the hooded figure sitting on the sill of my window.

Rolling my eyes, it's him...again..."Carlisle, you know this is inappropriate right?" I slide open my window, inadvertently stepping aside to let him in, all too familiar butterflies dance around in my stomach at the sight of him.

He slithers through the gap, pulling down his hood. He pushes his light brown hair back from his face, the cool blue of his eyes threatening to drown me as he curls the corners of his mouth.

"Shut up. I need a place to crash." He starts removing his sneakers and hoodie, exposing his muscular torso.

Looking at that body makes it harder for me to force him to leave. Did I ever really want him to? I hear the faintest of noises coming from downstairs, reminding me that my dad is within ear shot."Stone, you can't stay here again. If my dad finds you, we're both dead." I hush, drawing my eyes at him exasperated, frustrated. He has me flustered.I toss his hoodie and shoes back at him as he sits on the edge of my bed, licking his lips he smiles arrogantly at me, my entire body vibrating. I'm unsure if it's the fear of being caught, or the desire to be ridden into the sunset by him, but my hands shake violently.

"I'll be outta here by mornin', wasn't a problem on Wednesday." He smirks. He makes me frustratingly weak.

I heave a sigh, "my dad's home this weekend. And I thought it was a one off, Stone!"

"I know...I saw his car."

He had made his first appearance last Wednesday, with some excuse about being locked out or some shit like that. Eighteen years we have been sort of neighbours and this summer is the first time I have ever encountered him. Now here he is wreaking havoc in my very boring little life.

I longed for conversation with him, I wanted him to tell me all about Harvard, to learn more about him. But all he wanted to do was touch me.

If I were completely honest with myself... I wanted that too.

"Listen," he stands up, walking towards me towering intimidatingly above, with each step closer I take a step away, eventually falling into my dresser, knocking over perfume and picture frames. I turn around to stop them from crashing any louder, bracing their fall. I feel him pressed against my back, "Stop fucking whining, you won't even know I'm here." his hot breath lingers in my ear.

His nose runs along my ear lobe, before nestling in my messy hair, I feel his tongue trace down my neck, sending shivers up my spine, I squeeze my thighs together trying to stop the knot beneath my jersey shorts.

"Stone?" My voice quivers in anticipation.

He kisses the nape of my neck, "Mhmm?" Thrusting himself forward his stiff bulge parting me..I can't remember what I was going to say, I'm lost in the thrill of him. Feeling his heavy breaths against my skin rippling me with goosebumps.

His hand reaches slowly around, sliding inside my tank top cupping my breast, massaging it firmly, rolling my stiff nipple between his thumb and index finger.I involuntarily throw my head back resting it on his chest, he brings his mouth down to my shoulder biting firmly, grinding himself against my back.

Fuck."You want this." Stone nibbles my earlobe.

Yes, I want this.

Still manipulating my nipple, he takes his free hand sliding it down inside my shorts, reaching between my legs, parting my dripping slit with his fingers, circling around my clit gently, swirling two thick digits around in my juices, "uhh..." I let out a sordid moan, his fingers slide into core curling as he pumps them in and out. He brings them to his mouth tasting me. I hear the faintest of groans coming from his throat, he thrashes them back into my slick teasing my entrance as he works ferociously on my pearled nerves.He pulls out his fingers, bringing them up to my mouth, forcing me to taste myself, a hungry groan escapes my lips..."Beg for it." He whispers in my ear.I squeak, famished. Imagining his hardened cock pumping me, "p...please..." I moan as he edges his fingers further inside my tight core, my walls tighten around them impatiently waiting for him to grant me my ardent release.

A knock at the door startles us both, Stone retracts his fingers abruptly. I grip the sides of my dresser trying to gather myself.

"Eva, what are you doing in there? What's with the banging?""Nothing dad, I just stubbed my toe g...going to the bathroom." Stumbling over the words as I pant in fear and pleasure."Alright...be more careful." Dad's footsteps pace down the hall as he leaves.

Stone races to the window slipping away, leaving me breathless, gasping for more.

I chuckle to myself, the arrogant son of a bitch was scared of my dad.

I pull the window closed taking long deep breaths to compose myself, I catch the faintest glimpse of Stone as he disappears into the darkness of our estate.

What now?

What Did He Do?

"No Griffin, I'm sorry... I haven't seen the boy...It's been months. Yes Griffin...of course I will ask her, but I don't think they are...they aren't friends." Dad paces around the kitchen holding the phone away from his ear as Griffin Falconer, Stones grandfather, shouts on the other end. I take a seat at the breakfast table, trying to hide my guilt, as flashbacks of Stone's hot breath on my neck, with his fingers buried deep penetrate my mind.

"Eva!!" Dad shouts, I snap my head round. Panicking I answer, "What?"

"Have you seen Stone Carlisle recently? He didn't go home last night." He asks hanging up the phone. *Fuck*. "No, I haven't. He's probably off on a bender." I shovel eggs into my mouth, so I can't tell any more lies or incriminate myself. If dad finds out I've let Stone crash here when he's away on business trips, he'll kill me, or worse force me to go to college in Boston and live here at home with him. It was only the one time, and last night doesn't count because he left after...

Dad told Griffin the truth, Stone and I aren't friends, when he came home from college on summer vacation, I ran into him at the lake on our estate. He barely remembered my name, despite us being neighbours for 18 years. His mother and father couldn't control him, so they sent him to live with Griffin, but he can't control him either, or maybe he doesn't want to. Griffin is a very famous author, he has written a series of true crime novels. You'd never know it though, he lives a quiet life and the few interactions I have ever had with him he seemed like a sweet man. Our houses are the only ones on a very secluded estate just outside of town, accessed by a long tree lined gravel road. There must be an acre of flat grass that separates our large houses, but dad likes to keep himself to himself and I guess I'm like that too. Or I was, until I met Stone. I wonder where he has gone? Why he had to crash here in the first place, is beyond me. Stone is nineteen, an adult at college. I'm convinced that there is a big fat trust fund behind him, one that's more than capable of renting an apartment for him to live at.

Dad sits across the table from me, sliding over a nice hot cup of coffee, "Eva, I don't want you near that boy. He's bad news." He nods assertively.

"Sure dad, whatever." I mumbled through a mouth full of eggs, "I don't even really know him." I wash them away with the strong coffee.

"Griffin made a deal with the District Attorney, he has to stay with Griffin within the estate, or he'll go to jail." Choking on the coffee, I take a napkin wiping it as it runs down my nose, "Jail?" I repeat. "Yes...so if you see him, you go in the opposite direction y'hear?" He slams down his cup.

"Like I said dad, I don't know him." My heart races. Jail? What did he do to warrant house arrest? It just shows how far Griffin's millions can stretch when it comes to keeping family out of prison. He really must be powerful.

From what I remember about Stone at school, he has always been arrogant, volatile, and often violent.So what did he do? My mind races as I trudge upstairs to my bedroom.I couldn't imagine Stone in jail, swapping his Gucci sneakers for government issue plims oles.He probably got into a bar fight, took it too far.

Closing my bedroom door I drink the glass of water by my bed, swirling it around my mouth trying to rid the coffee and morning breath taste from my mouth. Spitting it down the sink in my ensuite bathroom. I give my teeth a vigorous brush, and hop in the shower letting the hot water beat down on my body.

I run my hands over my breasts as I lather up under the hot spray of the shower, running my hand between my legs replaying the memory of Stones thick fingers inside my slit, the juices from last night linger in my folds as I massage myself gently, pings of pleasure shooting through my body. My core pulses with hunger. After our startling interruption I couldn't bring myself to finish what Stone had started. The moment had gone when my heart took a terrified leap out of my chest and into my stomach. I close my eyes, day dreaming about Stones hardened cock resting on the cusp of my opening, nudging my clit. Fresh juices seep onto my lips. I reach for the shower head...I am blissfully deep in my passionate daydream, when I feel a hand reach around my waist pulling me forward, a tongue parts my slit, lapping my glistening folds. At first I am so drunk in the need for a release that I don't quite realise that this isn't the work of my vivid imagination...This is the work of someone else, someone real...My eyes snap open, hands shaking with fear, afraid to look down at the intruder between my legs, I can't help but let out a guttural moan as *his* tongue swirls around my swollen nub. Stone lifts me, hooking my legs over his shoulders as he pins me against the tiled wall of my shower, moaning aggressively, devouring my core, licking every inch of me. "Say my name." He growls, darting his tongue in and out of my opening. "S...Stone..." his name falters from my lips. He pulls me further, his face buried inside me as he works relentlessly to give me what I so desperately want, *need*. My heart races, body convulsing as my climax builds to its highest point. I try to be silent but it is useless, "Fuck!" I squeak. He sniggers "Do you want to cum?" His pace slows, and he flicks his tongue lightly on my clit, "beg for it." His tongue barely touching me. "P...please...I'm begging you," I mewl trying to grind on his face, my orgasm resting impatiently on the cusp. Fiercely he picks up the pace, fervently licking every inch of me, manipulating my engorged clit with his teeth, "fuck!" I moan in excessive pleasure, unable to contain myself, "fuck!" I grip the back of his head pulling him in further, "fuck!" , the aching coil in my core comes undone, coating his face. I try to catch my breath, Stone unhooks my legs bringing me down from his shoulders. He plants me down on the floor of the shower, as he washes himself quickly under the stream of water, his solid length dangles in my face, pre cum seeping from the tip, I lean forward to lick the tip tasting him. "No." He pushes me back, leaving the cubicle. He grabs a towel drying himself quickly, tossing it on the bathroom floor. Where is he going? My legs shake as I jump up, grabbing a towel and race into my bedroom.

"Where are you going?" I ask.

He thrusts his leg into his jeans jumping as he pulls them up, "see you around." He husks heading back towards *his* entrance.

I stand rooted to the damp carpet, completely dumbfounded by what just happened.

The window slides shut, and Stone disappears. Again.

Maybe This Is What I Need

♥

Aster,

That sounds weird, doesn't it? Definitely not calling you Aster. Stone. You can't keep coming around here. Especially when my dad's home. Scrap that. You can't come here period. It's really inappropriate. We've never even had a conversation. You don't know me. I don't know you. Hell, I don't know myself. Please leave me alone.

Eva.

I slam my laptop closed; I look across the estate at Griffin Falconers mansion. Afraid of what might happen if I stay in this room, but still, I don't lock my window. I desperately I want to go outside and wander the estate, but chances are I'll bump into Stone, the way he makes me feel is indescribable. He's like a drug, I know I shouldn't have tried it, shouldn't want it, but now that I've had a little taste, I'm addicted, but I'll do anything to try and stay away. I don't have any friends here, everyone from school thought I was weird. The shy rich girl, which I guess I am, or was. This means I don't have anyone to invite out, to occupy my corrupted mind. I'm lonely. Isolated. But I can't spend a full summer inside these four walls waiting for the devil.

I pop my iPod into the back pocket of my black denim shorts, and begin the mile long walk into town. Cutting through the trees to avoid the Stone mansion.

Its stiflingly warm in town, at least on the walk from the estate I had been shielded from the sun by the thick cover of trees. There's a tiny little cafe in the square that sells the most amazing ice-cold homemade lemonade, so I head there first before the record store.

"Afternoon, what can I get ya?" A middle aged rotund man stands behind the counter, a welcoming smile spread from ear to ear. It's sad really, I have lived here my whole life, been in here a thousand times but never once learned his name. His smile is infectious, I can't help but feel happy here, "just a bottle of house lemonade please." He nods politely, and walks over to the refrigerator, grabbing a ice cold bottle from the back .As he rings up the register my eyes wander around the quaint little cafe, landing on a **'Help Wanted'** poster. I begin to wonder, maybe this is what I need...Maybe this would give me purpose, and keep my idle hands busy. I've never had a job before, I've never needed one.

"Excuse me, Mr...?" I ask nervously. He chuckles heartily "Roger. Just call me Roger!"

I blush a little, trying to gather my words, "Excuse me... Roger. I was wondering about the sign..." I point to it sheepishly.

"You want a job honey? You should be spending your summer with your friends. Not workin' in here!"

I look down, shuffling my feet. Tears form in the back of my eyes, "I don't have any friends." Admitting anxiously to the large stranger. He heaves a sympathetic sigh. "Alright sweetie, you got experience?"

"No."

He rolls his eyes. "You know anything about dealing with the public?"

I bite my lip, embarrassed by my lack of know how. "No."

He lets out a jolly guffaw. "Where d'ya live missy?" I hesitate for a moment, Rogers kind eyes encourage me to be truthful, making me feel completely at ease. "I...uh...Earls Gate." I smile shyly at him, his mouth hangs open a little. "Right next to the Stone mansion, you're the Miller girl? You sure you wanna work here little lady?" I nod enthusiastically, hoping that he'll take a chance on me, "I'm sure, and I'll work really hard, I promise."

Roger gave me a strawberry pie to take home to dad as a 'welcome' gift. I walk down the dirt track road to my house, a spring in my step. Finally taking charge of my own life, doing something for me. Proud of myself for plucking up the courage to put myself out there. "What's in the box?" The firm voice comes from behind the big oak tree that marks the border from Earls Gate to the Stone Estate. Stone steps round from behind it, hands in his slacks pocket. Startled, I stand in silence my heart pounding inside my chest, He glides sinuously towards me, his ice blue eyes penetrating my soul as I stand frozen in intimidation. He creeps behind me, "I got your message." His nose brushes my hair as he circles round, he slides his hand into my back pocket, takes out my cell phone and presses digits into it, he snaps it shut and slowly slides it back in. I shudder in fear. Taking the box out of my hand, he opens it his eyes widen at the fresh strawberry glaze, he delves two fingers in, scooping the dripping red topping out and bringing it into his perfectly shaped lips. "Tastes almost as good as you." He smiles devilishly. Wiping some of the excess of his bottom lip, he parts my mouth with his thumb, inserting it into my mouth. The salty taste of his skin electrifies my nerves. He leans into me, breathing heavily in my ear. "Don't ever call me *Aster* again." He licks my lips harshly, his fingers wrapped firmly in my dark blonde hair holding my head in place while I try to pull away in disgust.

"Stone! You leave that girl alone y'hear!?" Griffins booming voice comes from the steps of the mansion that dominates in the distance. "I'll be seeing you, Eva." He swirls my name in his mouth, taking cruel steps away from me.

Storming into the kitchen I slam down the box on the kitchen counter. Dad opens it eagerly, "shit! What happened to the pie?" He asks disappointedly.

"Dropped it." I lie, my hands shaking uncontrollably.

How can a man I barely know, a man I can hardly tolerate hold such power over me? When I encounter him, I am weak.

Is That You?

♥

"**E**va darlin', you have worked here for 3 weeks now, without a single day off. Please, go home and take tomorrow off." Roger tries to usher me out the door of the cafe. A huge crowd of my old classmate's pile in, spinning on my heel I catch Rogers panicked gaze, he rolls his eyes at me. "Well shit." He laughs heartedly, looking at me helplessly. I grab my apron off the table, putting it back on pretending to be exasperated with having to work on, but I'm actually not. I love it here.

The ex-jocks and cheerleaders bark orders, sharing cakes and milkshakes. They begin to get pretty rowdy, throwing shakes everywhere, Roger tries his best to keep them at bay, but they have zero respect. I bend over scooping up fries and rubbish from the floor. "Hey!" A voice from behind startles me, as I turn to see the owner I lose my balance, falling on my ass, "Weren't you in my AP English class?" Jake Chapman, the handsome school football star towers above me, his bright smile slipping as he guiltily kneels next to me, picking up a glass and setting it on the table above. I'm surprised he recognised me; I've always just floated through school invisible, always under the radar. Never anything special. "Yeah, I think so." I clear my throat nervously as he takes my elbow helping me up off the ground. One of the 'peaked in high school' cheerleaders cries, "EW! Look...Jake picked some trash off the floor!" As I stand dusting myself off, she turns away from me, I throw up my middle finger at her back. Jake hands me the broom that leans against the wall, "you live up by the Stone estate. Next door to Stone Carlisle, right?" *How does he know where I live?* He never bothered me in high school, why is he starting now? Shrugging my shoulders, "Sure." I reply dryly. "He's a cool guy." Jake nudges me, raising his eyebrows suspiciously. My heart falls into my stomach, call it paranoia, call it instinct but it feels like he knows something that he should not.

The sun begins to set behind the cover of the trees on the dirt track, I keep replaying over in my head the look that Jake gave me, I'll be so fucking angry if Stone has been blabbing! I pull out my cell phone remembering that he input his number. I had forgotten all about it. I wonder what he put himself in as...I scroll down the phone book searching for the new entry, I didn't have to scroll far, I only have 10 numbers.

A.S.C

There it sat, in all its temptation. But I'm too fucking chicken to do anything about it. It's been peaceful without him, dry... but peaceful. So I stuff my cell into my back pocket.

I walk up to my front door, fumbling around in my purse looking for my keys. Dads gone away to Illinois for the week to work, so I've had the place to myself, been able to sing loudly enjoying dancing in my underwear. Eating things out of the fridge without his judgmental watchful eye mentally counting every calorie.

Jumping into the shower washing away the sweat of the hot working day I lather up, quickly shaving my legs, I wet my hair not bothering to wash it, I'll take care of that on my day off tomorrow. I grab a towel off the rail, drying myself before sliding into some grey sweat shorts and a white tank top, popping my cell into the pocket. I have a quick look at myself in the mirror, noticing the unfamiliar content little smile that has moved in on my face.

Something bangs downstairs, and I freeze listening intently for another, as my heart rate begins to pick up. Nothing... not a sound. I chuckle inwardly, exhaling with relief. But then I hear footsteps. I pause again. It's definitely footsteps. Someone is in here. I walk out of my room slowly, silently. Maybe dad come home early. "Dad?" I shout leaning over the banister looking down the staircase. A hooded figure stands at the bottom, not moving. It looks up. I gasp running into dad's room. It's probably Stone. Dear god let it be Stone. The intruder doesn't make their way upstairs. Stupidly, really fucking stupidly I crawl back out onto the landing to investigate. The figure stands on the middle step covered by darkness. He doesn't see me. But I see him, well just the shape of him. Petrified, I hide in my dad's closet, pulling out my cell phone I dial, "What?" His deep voice mumbles quietly. My voice courses in fear, "Um...S...Stone," a terrified whimper ripples through my lips, "is that you?" "What the fuck are you talking about? Yes it's me. You called me. Now wh..." he snaps at me angrily, I cut him off before he finishes. "No," I clamp my hand over my mouth concealing my strangled sob, "is that you, in my house?" The call goes silent as he hangs up, my heart sinks into my stomach, curling up in a ball on the floor of the closet, I begin to rock back and forth.

Tyres screech outside the house, I crawl out from the floor of dads closet to the bay window, I jump up, looking out the window to see Stone scrambling out of his BMW. He bursts through the front door, but the backdoor slams shut. My body convulses in fear, making my way back to the top of the stairs. Stone holds up his hands at the bottom, leaning over to flick the light switch. "It's me! Its Stone." He takes the stairs two at a time, leaning down to look at me, I nod as tears and snot run down my face. "Whoever it is, they've gone." He takes off his black Prada zipper and drapes it over my shoulders. "Who was it?" I shiver as the adrenaline leaves my body. He shakes his head, walking me to his car. He sits me down in the front seat, goes back into the house, locking all the doors and windows. He gets back in the car speeding along the gravel road to the Stone Mansion.

Griffin stands at the door with his arms folded shaking his head in Stones direction, "what's going on, Stone?" Stone opens the passenger door, "someone broke into Eva's house. She's staying here tonight." Griffin throws his hands up in despair. I swing my legs out of the car, pressing my bare feet onto the loose stone driveway, I wince as they dig into my feet. Griffin lifts his cane waving it in my direction, "help the girl will ya, Stone?" He saunters round the front of the car scooping me up in his arms. Carrying me effortlessly into the house.

I lie on the sofa in the lounge, dozing lightly. Griffin had offered me a bedroom but I declined, I didn't want to put him to any more trouble. My eyes snap open at the sound of the old house creaking in the gentle breeze. I'm drawn to Stone sitting in the arm chair, his chin resting on his hand. He licks his lips fervently. Getting up he walks slowly over to me, I sit up and he kneels in front of me. The silence between us thickens. Taking his finger he runs it from my ankle up the inside of my leg, when he gets to my knees he parts them, I allow my legs to fall open. Exposing my bare self beneath my shorts, the glow of the moonlight shining through the break in the drapes. He brings his finger up to my slit, running it inside resting it gently on my clit. I inhale sharply as the pleasure takes over. Wetness pools in my heated core, pulsating in anticipation. Stone brings his mouth up to mine licking my bottom lip, "are you a virgin?" He whispers softly, before thrusting his middle finger inside me. I gasp in gratification, "no." He smiles coyly, pulling out his finger licking it hungrily. He stands up, sniggering. Leaving the room abruptly.

Grounded

"**A**nd you didn't even think to lock the door when you came in?!" Dad paces the kitchen angrily, "it's completely irresponsible, Eva!" He slams a glass down the counter causing me to jump out if my skin, I open my mouth to try and explain but dad won't even listen, "And Stone of all people?! Why didn't you call the cops? What were you thinking?" He screams, I try to speak but he interrupts me "You know what don't answer that. You are grounded."

I laugh in disbelief shaking my head, walking around the counter to drink some of the scotch that lies there, "I'm eighteen, you can't ground me!!" Rage fills his face, and he charges towards me, "the hell I can't! You will *not* leave this house." My mouth falls open, tears of panic fill my eyes... "B... but what about my job?" He sighs, "work & home. That's it." Leaving the kitchen, taking the bottle of scotch with him. I had every intention of rebelling against him, in my mind I told him that he couldn't control me but, in the end, I just do as I am told. The reality is, it isn't worth arguing with him especially when he has been drinking. Oh yeah, his drinking. That's been getting progressively worse. I want to say it started when mom left, but I can't really remember. Maybe its why she left. I guess we'll never know because we never talk about it.

It's been an unusually quiet Saturday in the cafe, Roger went home leaving me to close, giving me permission to close early. It feels nice to be trusted, Roger is always so pleasant. I never feel like a burden when I'm here, it's the opposite. He makes me feel needed, wanted. We talk about music and movies, I know him better than I know my own father, and he knows me.

After cleaning up for the evening I sit behind the counter, listening to my iPod, willing 5pm to roll round.

"What are you doing in here?" His voice cool and seductive as he takes out my earphones. Startled, I blush. Stone sits on one of the stools in front of me. His piercing blue eyes raking up and down my body, I feel exposed. "I work here. What are you doing here, thought you were under house arrest?" I grab a bottle of lemonade from the fridge and offer it to him, he declines with a wave of his hand. "I had an appointment." He washes over the questions vaguely. Lifting a cherry out one of the jars he puts it into his mouth, popping with his teeth. He takes out the stone and sets it down. Putting the stem in his mouth. Never taking his eyes from mine, making me feel uncomfortable, yet utterly mesmerised, the slight twitching of his jaw the only movement from him, he takes my hand guiding it to his mouth; his lips brush the centre and he places the perfectly tied stem in the middle of it with a raise of his brow. He stands up to leave, leaning in to me, and for a solitary moment I thought he was going to kiss my cheek, but instead he pressed his lips against my ear and whispered, "this is beneath you." The bell above the door chimes as he exits, once again.

I lock up and sit in the passenger seat of dad's car. He doesn't speak to me. He hasn't spoken to me since he grounded me two weeks ago, I have never felt so isolated. I stare at the stalk in my hand, bringing it to my mouth carefully tracing the outline of my lips. I can't help but glance out of the window at the Falconer Mansion as we drive past, I'm not sure why, but I do it every time.

I go straight to my room, I can't for the silence between dad and I to end any longer, I won't even try. After my shower I walk into my bedroom, my cold face warmed the continuous stream of tears that fall with exile. I stare at myself in the mirror, naked. Scrutinising my body once again.

The reflection of Stone sitting on the end of my bed doesn't even startle me, numbly I walk over to him, mentally yearning for him to explore me. Wanting to be used by him. He pulls me by the wrists, wrapping his hands around my waist, guiding me closer to him. He places a gentle kiss on my naval, lightly squeezing the roundness of my seat. My head falters in defeat resting my cheek in his hair, the smell of his cologne intoxicates me. He runs his large hands up the inside of my legs, resting in the crevice of my thighs, he ushers me forward, brushing his lips against my pubic mound, parting my slit with his tongue, I gasp in pleasure, but I take an involuntary step back. "No." I tremble. His brow furrowed he stands towering above me, "No?" He takes a step towards me leaning over, I quiver in fear, he reaches onto my dresser and touches the cherry stalk, tilting his head in confusion. His chest moves in and out his breathing quickens, placing his hands either side of my face he crashes his lips to mine, he slips his tongue into my mouth massaging it forcefully, my taste still lingering on.

I kiss him back, gripping his hair. A shiver runs through me, Stone lifts me onto his clothed body, hooking my legs around him. I grab the hem of his white t-shirt, lifting it to pull over his head. He grabs my hands stopping me abruptly, "Are you saying yes?" He asks bluntly. I nod kissing his chin as I fight with the zipper on his pants. He releases his hard cock, stroking his length fervently as he takes my breast into his mouth furiously manipulating my nipple. I feel the heat building in my core, he lets go of his cock and swirls 2 thick fingers deep inside me, playing around inside my juices. I groan in delirium as he circles my swollen clit angrily. "I want you inside me." I pant in a frenzied bliss. Spreading my legs further apart, he slides his throbbing cock into my slick entrance. He stretches me out, touching my walls, "Stone," I whimper as I bite into his shoulder. His eyes roll into the back of his head, unable to control the look of pure ecstasy as the passion fills us. I rock back and forth greedily, working myself into orgasm, convulsing sordidly as my fluttering walls grip onto him in climax. He lifts me off hastily expelling himself over my stomach. Stone stands up, and walks into the bathroom, bringing out a towel, he wipes me clean. Lifting his t-shirt off the floor, he puts it over my head and pulls my arms through the sleeves. Grabbing the back of my head he brings my mouth to his, kissing me ferociously. I pull away, walking to my dresser I take out a pair of underwear, sliding them on. I glance over at Stone who stands with his pants still at his ankles, turn my back on him and leave, walking downstairs to get a glass of water. I don't even close the door, part of me wants my dad to see him there, then maybe he will take notice of me, talk to me. Get to know me.

The Roof

My heart sinks at the emptiness of my room, did I really want him to leave? Walking over to the window to close the drapes, I see Stone sitting on the roof. Fuck.

Sliding out of the window, I reluctantly take a seat next to him. "I don't want a girlfriend." He snaps staring ahead blankly. I scoff back, "I don't want a boyfriend." Shocked by my own truth. "You can't change me." He looks ahead arrogantly. "You can't break me." My voice shudders,

He turns round, his brow furrowed "I don't want to break you." His voice laced with a sudden concern. "You can't fix me either." I stare numbly into the tree line, barely visible under the stars.

"Oh!" My back arches and my eyes snap open as the space between my leg's twitches in ecstasy.

I reach down raising the duvet to find Stone nestled down there, eating me out.

"Wh... what are you doing in here?" I beg.

He hooks his arms around my legs pulling me deeper into him, lapping around my folds hungrily, sucking firmly on my nerves. His tongue moves downwards darting into my opening, the intensity causing me to reel forward, jutting his face further into me. I grab his head pulling him up to meet me, I sweep his tawny hair away from his face, he crashes his mouth into mine the salty taste of my juices melting in our kisses.

I wrap my leg around him, forcing him onto his back, I slowly trail my tongue down the curves of his muscles, feeling his stiff cock bobbing between my breasts as I take my time enjoying the sounds of his anticipated moan echoing around my room, I grind my sopping core on his leg, he snaps a glance at me smirking at my kink. Finally, my mouth reaches the tip of his tumescent cock, begging to be sucked as pre cum seeps from the tip. I run my tongue from the base up the entire length, wriggling it on his nerve centre, repeating the motion a few more times.

"Yes." Stone groans, delirious. I love the way he responds to my touches, the praise making me feel like I am worth something to someone.

My tongue climbs to the top again, this time I wrap my lips around the head of his cock and suck, releasing him with a pop, he leans forward in rapture placing his hand on the back my head taking a fistful of my hair, attempting to guide my mouth onto his shaft, I let him take me down and I swallow his entirety without gagging. Quickly he realises I don't need help; he relaxes his grip resting his hands behind his head.

I work his dick sucking in strokes, tasting every inch of him, I feel his throb inside my throat as he sits on the brink of climax. His breathing quickens.

"Enough." He asserts, placing his hands under my arms pulling me up, his face still glistening from the coat of my orgasm. I guide myself onto his cock, it hits my sweet spot immediately, brushing my cervix with the head.

We both moan in synchronised gratification.

He sits up, lifting me off then slamming me down as hard as possible onto his length.

"Fuck!" I gasp as the force takes my breath away.

I bite into his shoulder in thrill, he rocks me back taking my breast into his mouth biting gently on my nipple, the pressure of his pelvis tantalising my clit bringing me closer to the finish.

A squeal of intoxication jumps out of my body as Stone flips me round in a flash, pummeling me into the mattress, he pounds my core hard and fast, his cock slides in and out with ease with each shuddering thrust I lose myself in euphoria.

He wraps his arms underneath me, bringing me into his chest, he peppers kisses up my neck trailing his tongue upwards along my jaw, taking my lips in his. Winding his tongue inside my mouth, sending my core wild.

My walls grip around his cock milking him, he fills me full of cum pumping me forcefully, with his last thrust I scream out as I'm completely taken over by orgasmic contentment.

Stone slides his arm underneath me, and I rest my head on his chest, the warm mess of us dripping out, soaking my sheets.

He kisses me on the top of the head, his nose lingering my hair, "Good morning." This feeling is alien to me, to us. We don't do this. We fuck, then he leaves. I'm not going to complain, it's nice to have someone want to be around me.

The bell above the cafe door dings loudly, I snap my head up to see Jake Chapman strolling through the door, a wide smile plastered across his face.

He sits on a stool in front of me, "Hey Eva!" he nudges my shoulder with his fist, "when can you take a break?"

I heave a frustrated sigh, "whenever I want." He smiles playfully reacting to my blunt reply.

"C'mon Eva, you don't have any friends. I can be your friend!" He gently punches my shoulder again.

A hand wraps around his wrist forcing him to the ground, Stone towers above him. Holding him down with his boot pressed firmly on Jakes forearm.

"You hit her again I'll snap your fucking arm." He grits angrily through his teeth.

"Fuck!" I yell, my heart pounding. I jump over the counter, pushing my hands against Stone's shoulder, "Stone, stop! I seethe, pushing him away.

He glowers at me through his glassy blue eyes, sneering in my face, he slides a small box into my apron before lifting his boot from Jakes arm.

I crouch down helping him up, falling back against the counter as he lunges forward "what the fuck Carlisle?!" He shouts after him as Stone storms out slamming the door behind him.

The cafe falls silent, the atmosphere thick and dense.

Jake flashes me a worrying glance before he scrambles out, embarrassed.

All eyes fall on me as I attempt to compose myself, tears building in my eyes.

The Box

"What the fuck was that Stone?!" I stand in the middle of his bedroom, unzipping my jeans shimming them down my legs, "Are you fucking insane?!" I tap the side of my head vigorously.

Stone runs towards me, shoving me hard against the wall, my eyes widen with fear, as his face fills with rage hanging millimeters from mine...

"He laid a hand on you." A Neanderthalic growl rumbles in his throat.

I push him away from me, "Kinda like the way you are now?" I grab my t-shirt from the chair in the corner and begin to get dressed.

"Where are you going?" He grabs my arm and forces me against the door with thud, he reaches down tracing the crease of my core with his finger, "we've got unfinished business, open your legs." He kicks my feet apart, forcing his hand inside my lace panties, he takes his middle finger and slides it inside my folds, gently rubbing my clit.

My breathing becomes shaky as I succumb to the pleasure.

Stone brushes my ear with his lips, "He put his hands on what's mine." His hot breath sending shivers up my spine.

He swirls the wetness from my folds around, inserting another finger inside my slit, spreading my lips wide.

"Stop!" I hiss through the humming pleasure.

But he doesn't, he keeps going...manipulating, my clit, sucking and biting on my neck.

Panting as he brings me to the brink "Please, stop!".

With one motion he hooks my leg up around his hip, sliding a finger into my opening he works in and out with vigor, unable to contain my orgasm I gush coating his hand.

He drops me to the floor, "Go to the bed, now."

"No." I whimper, "I'm tired." I crawl over to collect my things.

Stone crouches beside me lifting my chin with his finger, "We're not finished." He sneers.

I am defeated. I want him, of course I do. I'd do anything to make him happy.

"Okay." I sigh.

I crawl onto his bed, lying flat on my back, waiting for him to lie on top of me, closing my eyes as tears flow out of them filling my ears like wells. I turn my head to the side to look for him, but he doesn't come near. He sits on a chair in the corner of the room. His lips pressed together harshly, his chest moves in and out as his breathing deepens. His gaze never falters.

Our eyes stay locked barely blinking.

I must have fallen asleep, my eyes snap open at the buzzing of my cell phone on the floor. Scrambling off the bed disoriented I fumble around searching for it, finding it under my jeans.

Fuck.

Its dad.

"...uh...hi dad!" My voice shakes in panic.

"Where the fuck are you? The cafe is in darkness, its 10:30!!" He yells.

Fuck fuck fuck.

Stone comes out of his bathroom, sits in front of me and whispers, "You are at the movies, with Jake."

I nod while my heart pounds like a fist banging against the wall of my chest.

"I... erm...I'm at the movies with Jake Chapman, didn't you get my message?" I lie through my teeth, hushing my voice.

I catch a look of disappointment in Stones eyes as he stands up and heads into the shower.

"Straight home after."

Sighing in relief, "Yes, of course dad." A little sob of panic escapes my lips.

I step into the shower still wearing my underwear, Stone stands naked under the stream of scalding water. His back red, face barely flinching at the heat sears his skin.

I pull him out from the spray, his body tensing he glowers at me.

I step up on my tip toes, "thank you."

Kissing his cheek lightly.

"No." His voice harsh and deep.

I kiss him again on the other cheek.

He clears his throat, "I said no."

I shiver, as I hesitantly press my lips to his, trailing my tongue along his cupids bow.

"No!" He screams, shoving me against the shower cubicle.

I race out in fear, dripping water over the tiled floor, causing me to slip bashing my elbow on the hard floor, I let out a shuddering gasp. Trying to catch my breath and steady myself on my feet, Stones arms wrap round me helping me up.

I shake him off, "let me go." An agonising moan ripples through me.

He hands me my clothes sheepishly; I get dressed quickly and shamefully in the corner of his bedroom.

Dads asleep on the sofa, a bottle of Percocet sits on the side table next to a glass of scotch.

Whimpering quietly, I try to straighten out my arm to reach for the pills, taking two into my mouth washing them back with what's left of the scotch.

My entire body aches as I climb up to my bedroom.

My phone buzzes in my pocket and I think to myself, 'I'll check it later'.

ASC: Did you look in the box?

The message flashes on the screen as I collapse onto my bed, exhausted and medicated.

How did I get here?

The sun shines through my window straining my eyes, my head feels like it's going to explode. But it's not a hangover, I feel groggy and sick. I reach for the bottle of water on the side table, my hand quivering in pain, the harsh light of the morning exposing my sins.

I make a feeble attempt to sit up, every inch of me aches. My elbow is swollen, and the deep bruise that surrounds it throbs mercilessly.

Fuck.

I reach for my cell, dialing Rogers number.

"Roger," my voice croaks, "I'm really sorry, but I don't think I can come in today..." I wince as I try to straighten up, "no... I'm fine...well I had an accident.... I slipped on the bathroom floor...I'm sorry to let you down..." I whimper trying to gasp back my pain, "I will...thank you."

After hanging up I see a message from Stone.

The box?

That's right!

I slide off the bed, that's when I realise, I am still completely clothed, making a mental note to never take Percocet again.

The box...

There's no box here.

I pick up my cell again and call Stone...

"What?"

"It's me, I can't find the box." My voice croaks.

He sighs heftily "You gotta be shittin' me..." I hear him shuffling around his bedroom.

I wince as I move around painfully, trying to retrace my heavily medicated steps.

"It's here," he huffs, "I'll leave by the tree, pick it up before work." His tone is so dry.

Inhaling sharply as I climb back into bed, "I'll get it later, I'm not working today."

I hang up abruptly.

I manoeuvre into the bathroom to use the toilet; I strip myself and stare at my body in the mirror. My elbow is tender and swollen, my knees are bruised, and I have a bruise on my neck where Stones mouth had been.

I go back into my bedroom, Stone sits on the window ledge, almost sulking. I'd usually find him sitting on the edge of my bed, "your dad's car is gone." His eyes fall on my knees.

"Mh-mm, he's gone to San Francisco for work." I nod climbing onto the bed, trying to conceal my pain. "He left this morning I think." I groan wearily.

He tosses a box over to me 'Plan B', "I thought...well...take it."

Smart, we have been having A LOT of unprotected sex.

"You didn't think there was a ring in there did you?" He sniggers, raising his eyebrow in my direction.

I take the tablet, wishing that it was something stronger. Cyanide maybe.

Stone rushes over to me urgently placing a finger under my elbow, "shit, Eva! You need to go to the ER!"

Is he insane?!

I throw my un-injured arm up, "I can't go, because the insurance and credit cards are billed to my dad!"

I lie down in bed, exasperated and still groggy.

"Get up." Stone mumbles

I start to weep, tired and aching.

"I'll put it on my credit card, Griffin won't care. Now move!" He helps me out of bed, taking the stairs slowly. The aches on my body begin to ease with the movement, but my elbow remains the same.

I sit patiently waiting on one of the ER beds, Stone paces around the cubicle running his hands over his head, messing up his already untidy hair.

A nurse opens the curtain and walks round the bed sitting on the stool next to me. She glares at him, gazing at me with concern she glances at my chart.

"Uhhh...okay... Sir, Imma have to ask you to wait outside..." she raises an eyebrow at him threateningly.

His nostrils flare and he strides towards her, "I'm going nowhere!" Gritting through his teeth as he walks round other side of the bed.

She sets the chart down and reaches over to the phone, shaking her head angrily, "security, ER...bed 4." She smirks at him.

"Stone!! Get outta here..." I hiss, my eyes widen hoping that he will see sense.

He storms towards the curtain, "coffee?" He looks back at me, his brows knitted together almost looking concerned. I send him a reassuring nod.

The nurse pulls back the sheets, and looks at my knees, a small twitch in her eye speaking a thousand words, as her eyes fall on the mouth shaped bruise on my shoulder, "sweetie...did he do this to you?" She asked the question so bluntly.

I shake my head softly, if I protest too much she won't believe me, "no, well...no...uhm, well yes but...I uh...it was when...we um...I liked it." I stumble and my cheeks flush, face burning as I admit to a complete stranger that it's all part of a sexual encounter.

But there's more to it than that.

It's complicated.

Toxic.

And I am living for it.

"But this," she lifts my arm, "did he do this?"

I snap my head round to her, "NO!" A low growl comes from within, "he didn't do anything! Ugh! I didn't even want to come here, he made me!!" I start ripping the hospital gown off and reach for my top, "is it broken?" I hiss at her pointing to my elbow.

She heaves a sigh, "no. It is not broken, just badly bruised." She lays the chart down.

"So, I can go?" Exasperated with the entire situation.

She bobs her head in defeat, "sure thing honey, I'll go get your meds then you can go." Tutting as she closes the curtain.

I lie back on the bed, closing my eyes wondering how the hell have I found myself in this situation, what happened to me. The invisible girl, who roamed through life unnoticed even by her parent, the girl who lost her virginity at summer camp and told no one because it was the most mundane experience of her mundane existence.

So, someone please explain to me, how did I get here?

Stone swings into the cubicle he slides me a cup of coffee, kissing my cheek softly allowing his lips to linger for a moment forgetting himself for just a second, he snaps away covering his face with his hands.

I inhale deeply, "I uh...Stone?"

"What?" He groans

My hands shake, I'm so nervous.

I gulp anxiously, "Why were you on house arrest?" I have to ask, but part of me doesn't want to know the answer.

I blink, and somehow, he is sat right in front of me.

"I am going to tell you everything, and then don't bring it up again. I mean it Eva...not another word about it. Y'hear?!"

I can't speak, I am ferociously terrified.

Have I just opened Pandoras box?

I Believe Him

"Okay." My lip quivers in fear of what he's about to tell me.

He takes a deep breath letting it out slowly, raggedly rippling through his lips. Looking closely, I can see his waterline fill, but only a little.

"I...uh..." the curtain of the cubicle swings open suddenly, Stone sits bolt upright clearing his throat rapidly.

The nurse hands me a white paper bag, "don't take these on an empty stomach, you should start to heal in a couple of days." She presses her hand on mine, turning to Stone, "please take better care of her."

Stone growls at her with his eyes, and we rush out to the front desk. He hands over a platinum credit card, rapping his fingers on the desk impatiently, snatching it back we make our way to his BMW.

We sit in the hospital car park, the silence between us deafening. The only sound comes from the nervous breaths that thicken the atmosphere.

Stone breaks our silence with a solemn change of tone. He was no longer arrogant and cocky, he was almost defeated, "there was a girl, Taylor. I met her in the college bar." He tightens his grip on the steering wheel, "she tried to get into my pants, but I wasn't interested...she was hot but...there was something crazy about her eyes. I wasn't feeling it." He stares blankly ahead, but I can't tear my eyes away, seeing him vulnerable like this.

He swallows harshly, and I fixate on the masculine bump on his throat as he continues, "she said I... but I didn't. She told everyone that I... raped her. I didn't!" He bangs the wheel; I jump out of my skin.

He snaps his head around to meet his eyes with mine, "I' am a lot of things. I am everything they say I am and more, but I am NOT that." His eyes widen with anger, I nod trying to reassure him but my body shakes with fear, and a little bit of doubt.

"The cops gathered evidence and statements, and it was my word against hers, but she fucked up her boyfriend tried to blackmail me. So, I kicked he shit outta him. Griffin, he uh... struck a deal with the DA to keep me out of jail, but I had to do a month house arrest. I didn't do that to her I swear to you, but I woulda killed him."

I fight back vomit, unsure if its relief or panic or just a general overload of information. But I believed him.

I take a seat on the sofa, enjoying the change of scenery. I can spend time here when dads gone. Stone sits on the armchair across from me, staring at the TV as he flicks through the channels.

I raise myself up from my seat, his head jerks round to me, "what? Where are you going?" His lips purse suspiciously.

"I'm going to make some tea, do you want some?" I simper gently, trying to put him at ease.

He stands, ushering me back to my seat, "I'll make it, sit down." I slump back into the sofa.

Is this what...? Is this what a relationship with Stone could look like?

An exasperated laugh escapes me.

Fuck up Eva, this is nothing more than a situationship.But it's nice to pretend.

"What's so funny?" Stone hands me a cup, I inhale the steam allowing the smell of the lemon calm me.

Stone doesn't sit back in the armchair; he sits next to me. He pulls my feet onto his lap, rubbing them gently.

My heart begins to race, my palms sweat.

I try to suppress a groan as my elbow throbs, Stone pops one of the pills out of the blister pack and slides over to me. He pops it into my mouth, lifting the tea to my lips. I swallow it nervously.

He kisses me softly, passionately sliding his tongue gently into my mouth.

"Mmmm," the sound of my lustful whine, causes the corners of his mouth to twitch.

He pulls away from me, I take my other arm and grip his sweater, bringing him back to me.

I take his lips into mine, and our tongues fight against each other, he wraps his fingers in my hair holding me as he places beautifully wet kisses on my cheeks, along my jawline and down to my neck, he breathes deeply as he laces his tongue along my collarbone.

He brings his eyes up to meet mine seeking permission, I crinkle the corners of mine with a smile, "yes." I whisper.

He slides his arms underneath my body carrying me up the stairs to my room, he could have had me on the sofa. I would let him have me anywhere.

Stone lies me on my bed, he climbs on top of me careful of where he places his weight, he smooths hair away from my face with his perfect hand, kissing my neck again, reaching up for a nibble on my ear lobe. The sensation so electric I jerk in pleasure.

He kisses my shoulder all around the bruise left by him, "I'm sorry." He hums quietly.

"Don't be, I liked it." I kiss his forehead, the taste of the natural oils on his skin salty on my lips.

"Do you like this?" He slides down my tank top, exposing my breast nipple hard and begging to be sucked. He takes it into his mouth flicking it with his tongue, playing with it.

I let out a yelp of excitement as he takes his hand and slides it into my panties, spreading my sopping slit with his vast fingers, "and this?" He smirks, looking up with my breast still bobbing in his mouth.

He rubs my clit slowly with his index finger while he slides his middle one closer to my opening, gently teasing in and out. Arching my back in ecstasy I reach fumbling around for his cock, he takes his hands, one dripping wet and puts my arms at my side, "stay there." He purrs, kissing his way down my body, leaving hot grazes of his lips on every inch of me.

He removes my underwear slowly, raising my legs up and kissing my mound. Parting me with his tongue, "OH!" I squeal. He laps my juices like his life depended on it, sucking on every part, his tongue darting in and out licking the length of me.

Panting in ecstasy as I try to contain my orgasm, I grab his head with one hand, "please Stone. Now...".

He removes his pants swiftly, clambering back on top of me taking position between my legs, I reach down and grab his long, thick, hard cock, guiding him inside me. As the pleasure grapples us I sit up leaning against his chest, he holds me onto him effortlessly, thrusting me as his length reaches deep inside me, the pressure on my clit from his body causes my walls to contract tightly round his cock. He moans in my ear with intensity, reaching up to crash his lips onto mine.

Something was different this time.

Rocking my waist back and forth on him as he supports my weight his eyes roll in the back of his head. The pace quickens as we are intoxicated by one another. He jerks me harder, each movement bringing me closer to the finish. His mouth open, resting on mine we crash our bodies together, he pumps me sordidly, climax happening simultaneously, my clit twitching as we fall in a heap onto the bed, his cock remains inside me as my walls contract delirious with satisfaction.

We lie together naked, our bodies stuck together with passion, I rest my head on his chest and he kisses the top of it perfectly.

I close my eyes; feeling his lips brush my cheek as she shuffles out from underneath me.

I open them watching him get dressed, his gaze catches mine.

"I guess this is it?" My lip trembles almost undetected.

A heavy sigh falls from his chest, "I guess so."

He leaves through the bedroom door, I listen as the sound of his footsteps disappear down the stairs, A single tear rolls down my cheek as the front door closes behind him, and a painful sob bursts from my throat at the sound of the door being locked and when the keys are pushed through the letter box, clattering on the floor, I wail into my pillow.

I guess this is it.

The Kindness of Strangers

♥

E very morning when I wake, I look to my windowsill half expecting him to be there, and half wishing.

When I come out of the shower, I look for him at the end of my bed. I pass the oak tree, willing him to be lurking behind it, nothing.

Then one day, I just stopped looking, stopped wishing, stopped hoping.

"Oh Eva, I can't believe it's your last day. What a breath of fresh air you have been. When you walked through that door 10 weeks ago begging me for a job, I never for a minute thought that when it was time for you to leave you would take a piece of my heart with you. So raise a glass to Eva Miller." Rogers eyes fill with tears as he gives me a light squeeze, the diners raise their sodas and milkshakes in my honor.

My last shift.

I can't believe it.

Being in this place is the happiest I have been in a long time.

I choke back tears.

Grateful of the love given by strangers.

"Excuse me miss." A voice booms from behind me, I spin round trying to disguise my blotchy face with my hand.

Oh shit.

"Griffin...I...urr...Mr Falconer sir..." I stumble over the surprise of his presence.

His eyes wander around the cafe, "it's a wonderful thing to be thought as highly of as you are in this town." He smiles kindly at you, slipping a hundred-dollar bill into the tip jar.

My mouth twitches uncomfortably, wanting to ask the question desperately.

Almost as though he can read my mind, "he attends all his classes and is still using his credit card, although I haven't heard from him personally." He raises an eyebrow at you, taking a cherry out of the jar, he winces at the sweetness spitting it into his handkerchief, and stuffs it into his pocket.

The bell above the door dings, Jake Chapman appears at the counter.

I acknowledge him with a smile.

"Ready to go Eva?"

Shuffling my feet uncomfortably I reach over the counter and give his hand a squeeze, "I'll meet you in the car, I want to say goodbye."

Jake kisses me lightly on the cheek, making his way outside.

"It was so nice to see you Griffin, I um..."

I can't find the right words to say, all that comes out if my mouth is, "thank you."

I grab my bag, and wave goodbye to everyone.

Just as the door closes behind me, "Eva?" Griffin shouts after me.

My eyes wide with curiosity, I pace towards him.

"He loved you the only way he knew how," he simpers.

It was like a dagger to the heart.

I smirk, shaking my head "with all due respect Griffin, what we had wasn't love." A tear falls down my cheek, as I prepare to walk away.

Griffin grabs my hand pulling me back, "let people see you Eva, don't hide underneath that cloak." He taps the side of my head softly, "perhaps you'll come see me at Christmas?"

Pursing my lips, trying to stem the emotion I nod.

I sit in the front seat of Jakes truck, ready to take him home to meet dad. Griffin's words resound in my head.

Jake reaches over squeezing my thigh, "you ready?"

I stare out of the window my mind spinning off course.

"Eva?" He squeezes again

I snap my head around faking a smile, "sure! I'm ready."

I wasn't, not at all.

All I ever wanted was for my dad to be happy with the person I am, for him to be proud of me, to treat me as someone he liked even remotely. So, when he asked to meet Jake after I fabricated our 'date' I decided to give Jake a chance.

It's only been 2 weeks but we are hitting it off, we've had a few nice kisses but between football training and work we haven't gone any further than some heavy petting in the backseat of his truck.

We walk into the kitchen hand in hand, it makes me uncomfortable.

Dad stands behind the counter in the middle of the kitchen pouring himself a scotch, I can tell by the haze over his eyes that it's not his first glass.

Fuck.

He's progressively getting worse.

"Dad, this is Jake Chapman. Jake, this is my dad. Uhh... we're going to my room..." I pull him away, but before I get to the door dad shouts after us, "hold on a minute! This is the first boyfriend that you've had, I wanna get to know him. Sit down Jake..."

I grab a couple of beers from the fridge setting one down in front of Jake, I lean against the fridge as dad is friendly towards him, laughing and joking. Finding out all about him, asking questions about his likes and dislikes, his life.

He now knows more about Jake Chapman than he knows about his own daughter.

Behaving as though he likes him more than me.

Dad checks his watch, "shit! I've got a call with Hong Kong in 5 minutes. You kids behave! Have a good night, Jake, hope to see you more often." He slaps him playfully on the shoulder.

Brushing passed me knocking me forward, dad stumbles towards the study, "don't fuck this up." He hisses under his breath. How could I stop myself from fucking this up, when everything I touch turns to shit? When the last person I gave my heart to, fucked me then left me.

Jake follows me upstairs to my room; he looks around at all my stuff. Lifting picture frames off my dresser smiling kindly at my youth. He saunters over to my window, gazing out into the distance as the sun sets behind the trees.

"That the Falconer mansion?" He quizzes

I reach round my back unclipping my bra, "mhmm..."

He opens the window wide hanging out to get a better look, "that Carlisle guys fucked up. Were you like friends? I... mean I never saw you together at school." He turns around seeing me standing in nothing but my thong, my arms covering my breasts, "what're you doing?"

He closes the window softly, walking towards me the bulge in his pants growing with each step.

I don't say a word.

Images of Stone taking me against the dresser flash across my mind, I try to push them out. I want Jake to have me now.

He stands before me, his green eyes meeting mine.

I place my hands on his hips, undoing his jeans, freeing his meaty cock which throbs furiously at the sight of me. Wrapping my hand around it firmly, I begin sliding it back and forth, "ohh yes!" Jake groans in my ear, he ushers me towards the bed as I grip his dick.

He pulls my thong to the side, thrusting his cock deep inside me, pulling out slightly to spit on my sex. I'm not quite ready for him.

He plunges in, hammering me into the mattress.

His head bowed watching himself roam in and out of my core.

I lie numbly, letting him have his fill of me.

After seconds he pulls out shuddering, exploding over my breasts like some sort of porn star.

He lies next to me, his semi hard cock waving in the air, "wow...just wow..." kissing my cheek.

He leans up, "did you come?" His eye eager to please.

Another fake smile falters from my mouth, "sure." I kiss him back gently.

Getting up from my bed I turn and say, "I'm gonna go for a shower."

I toss him the TV remote.

I turn the temperature up as high as I can barely tolerate and sob into the stream as it batters down upon me, stripping my skin in all its sorrow.

Hello, You.

I hold my cell tightly between my ear and my shoulder fumbling around in my bag for the keys to my apartment.

"Shit!" You sit on the floor of the hallway.

"What is it, Eva? Is everything okay?" Jake calls out, his voice awakes with worry.

"I lost my fucking keys, so now I'll have to wake the super to let me in."

There's an awkward silence, I can hear Jake whispering, "Jake, if you're with someone we can call later." trying my best not to sound annoyed, because I'm not with him.

"Your dad wants to know if you'll make it home for Thanksgiving." He sighs nervously. I pull the cellphone away from my face clenching my jaw as I pull back a string of frustrated screams. Thanksgiving is tomorrow, how drunk is he that he thinks I'll be able to make it back in 16 hours. And since when did they start hanging out, he's got his claws into Jake, God only knows what he will be filling Jakes head with.

"No, like I told him last week, I can't do both. I'll be home for Christmas and New Year's."

Ending the call abruptly I decide against waking the Super and instead walk back to the library.

Why would Jake want to hang out with my dad in the first place, what doesn't he have friends at college? Who am I to judge, I've been in LA for 6 weeks and I haven't spoken to a single person except the guy who owns my building, the barista in Starbucks and the librarian. I've been writing with Griffin back and forth; he sent me some flowers before I left and asked me to stay in contact. I didn't think he would want to email so I put pen to paper and wrote to him instead. Words come easier with pen and paper.

I walk down the humid streets of LA, I fucking hate it here. It's too hot... and too big and I just don't like it.

I only picked UCLA to get as far away from home as possible, I got into Harvard...I just didn't tell dad because then I would be stuck at home with him, and honestly, I'd rather pick out my eyelashes one by one.

Juilliard is my dream, but NYC that's where mom is, and I didn't need the heartbreak of crossing her in the streets. Would I even know her if I did?

I had this ideal that because I had lived my life in Massachusetts under the radar, that I would thrive in college, but it seems I'm just as invisible no matter where I go.

The library sits in darkness the modern steel doors locked, not a security guard in sight.

"Arghhhhhhhhhhhh!!!" I scream at the absolute top of my lungs, rasping my voice. My throat aching.

I sit down in the Starbucks round the corner, lying my head on the table, glancing at my cell 8:45pm, there is a message from Jake.

Hey babe!

God, I hate it when he calls me babe.

Watching football with ur dad. Going to crash in ur room.

Miss u so much babe.

Luv u

How attracted are you supposed to be to your boyfriend? Because lately, Jakes been giving me the 'ick'. It's not his fault, maybe its because my dad loves him so much. Maybe it's the distance...no its not that because I was feeling this way before I left. I just cant make myself feel anything for him. He doesn't thrill me. I tried breaking it off with him...

"I just think long distance is going to be difficult Jake, and I want you to be..."

He slammed his hands down on the steering wheel,

"Be what? Eva...be WHAT?!"

My heart races, his anger giving me a little thrill, "I want you to be able to enjoy college, meet other girls."

His head spun; eyes wide with rage "is it you that wants to meet other people? Do you want to go to LA and slut it up?"

"No... it's just uh..." I didn't know what to say...I just didn't want to be in a relationship, with anyone.

So, I didn't say anything else.

I went to my room with him, and when he bent me over on my bed and thrust his himself into me, I let him spit on me, readying me up. I sobbed silently into my pillow as I pretended not to notice that he was videoing himself pulsing in and out of me. I turned a blind eye when he sneakily snapped photos of me in the shower, and I sat idly by and listened to my dad and him ridicule me over dinner.

I gulp a coffee down quickly, my stomach rumbling uncontrollably, I get up and make my way back to the barista.

"Hi, can I...uh...have another...and a blueberry muffin please..." I smile politely sliding my empty mug over to her.

She places the muffin on a plate in front of me I take a little off the top and shove it into my mouth, the sweetness allowing me to escape my anxiety but only for a moment.

"Hello you."

The voice creeps over my shoulder, the familiarity of his woody scent fills my nose even over the smell of the coffee.

My heart somersaults inside my chest, I didn't know it could do that.

I turn slowly to see Stone towering above me, his white Hugo Boss t-shirt clings to the contours of his perfectly sculpted torso, he takes his wallet out of the pocket of his black jeans, swiping his card on the machine paying for my coffee and cake.

"What are you doing out here in LA?" He sips his espresso, his eyes meeting mine for a second before falling to the text message that lies open on my cell.

"I go here," I stutter, "I mean UCLA, I go there." A nervous chuckle escapes my mouth.

"You gonna reply?" He raises his eyebrow.

"Excuse me?" Lost in his presence I forget myself for a moment,

"Your boyfriend 'luvs' you. You gonna reply?" He shakes my cell playfully in my face.

I snap it out of his hand, shakily typing my reply:

Ok. See you in a month.

I silence my cell and stuff it into my bag, "what brings you to LA, Stone?"

His ray bans tucked into the crew neck of his shirt dangle as he leans across the table, he reaches slowly taking a piece of my muffin and popping it into his mouth, as he swallows the bite, I gulp imitating him involuntarily.

"Winter sun." taking another piece he presses it to my lips parting them gently, he slides it into my mouth.

He leans his head on his hand as a devilish smile twitches across his face.

I'm Weak

"Why winter sun, why not go home for Thanksgiving?" I ask shyly as Stone studies my face with his ocean eyes.

"What have I got to go back to?" He scoffs, dipping his finger into the froth of my coffee and sucking it off, licking his lips making every hair on my body stand up.

"You have Griffin,"

"He's going to my parents, and we both know that I'm not welcome there. Wait... why aren't you home for Thanksgiving?"

I throw a smile his way, his eyes search mine and all I want to do is dive across the table and kiss him, just a little taste of what we had, if I could bottle the feeling of lust, I had for him I would, and I would inhale it every minute of every day.

"I have an exam next week, SHIT! I got to go..."

I race out of the coffee shop by now it's dark, bolting across the street to the library hoping that a security guard or someone will be there by now to let me look for my keys.

I search around campus but there is no sign of anyone, its eerily quiet. Everyone has gone home for Thanksgiving. Maybe I should have gone home too. Then I wouldn't be left wandering the streets of LA aimlessly.

Pressing my head against the wall I breathe out an infuriated groan. Can't I do anything right?

A hand reaches over my shoulder, grasping my breast I gasp holding my breath too scared to breathe. In my head the words 'scream' resound, but when I try to open my mouth, sound won't come out. Turning around slowly as fear creeps over me, rendering me useless, I raise my head to see the attacker.

A shuddered breath falters. Relief washing over my entirety.

"Stone!" I punch him in the chest, "you asshole! You scared the shit out of me!"

He smirks holding up my bag, "you left this."

Honestly, I could wipe that smirk off his face with my fist, but I don't...

I lunge towards him, colliding my mouth with his wrapping my hand around the back of his head, pulling him into me.

He lifts me off the ground hooking my legs around his waist taking my tongue with his, our teeth clash as the passion builds and the taste of him fills my body with a euphoric high. I pull away for a moment remembering Jake as guilt creeps inside me, but when Stone presses me against the wall panting deeply, he gazes into my eyes, simpering as he moves in to ghost his lips on my neck, moving upwards nibbling lightly on my ear lobe.

"Stone." I moan softly.

He trails his lips down my collarbone "Mhmm?"

"I can't." I sigh, full of defeat.

I know that I am a lot of things, I am not a good person, but this isn't me.

"You can't, but I can." He sets me down; his lips never leave my body.

Should I be doing this?

No.

Do I want to?

Yes.

I'm weak.

I'm wet.

Soaking wet.

Stone kicks my legs apart, "stand completely still." His deep voice sends shivers rippling up my spine, my clit throbs as he slowly unzips my jeans, sliding his hand inside my underwear, parting my slick slit with his middle finger he runs it around my opening, the juices flowing around it as he runs it back up to my clit, manipulating it savagely.

"Oh fuck." I moan in ecstasy, "fuck...fuck...fuck..." he presses his mouth on mine muffling my cries, "silence." He asserts, his voice echoing in my mouth.

He moves away from my mouth, slowly getting to his knees, "spread them." He pushes my legs apart. Stones nuzzles the top of my mound with his nose, rolling his eyes in the back of his head, sliding his tongue between my dripping lips running it hungrily into my core, darting it deep inside me, taking in my creaminess lapping up every bit of me.

I try not to make a sound, but involuntary squeaks softly escape my lips.

My clit twitches, Stone sucks it harshly I grab the back of his head pushing him deeper into me, he works further down back to my hole, sliding his tongue back lightly flicking my ass, the new sensation sending every nerve in my body wild.

He runs his tongue back, deep into me scooping the fresh juices that seep out covering his face. He licks his lips, before thrusting his tongue into my mouth, forcing my juices to fold with his saliva

I hear him unzipping his trousers, releasing his meaty cock as I reach my hand down to grab hold, he pins my arm against the wall.

"You 'can't'." A smug smile rests on his face, "I'm going to have a little taste of what's still mine." He places the tip of his cock inside my pink slit resting it firmly on my clit as it pulses longingly against him.

"You are still mine aren't you, Eva?" He moves his length inside my lips gliding against my core, teasing the entrance.

"Well...?" He lightly dips into my hole, the smacking of his cock in the wetness of my sex, enrapturing me.

The pleasure intensifies, I want him deep inside me. I want his entire length filling me up, I want to overflow with his hot sperm.

"I'm still yours." I whimper into his open mouth as he pants heavily.

"Good girl." He thrusts inside me taking my breath away as his touches my walls. Bouncing me up onto his hips he bobs me up and down on his cock, I constrict around him, gripping him as he brings me down hard.

The scratch of the wall behind me irritates my skin but adds to the height of my pleasure.

"Say you're mine." Stone huffs as he heaves his cock into my core.

"I'm yours!" My orgasm grows inside me, resting on the cusp, waiting to be released.

With each ferocious pulse into me, Stone groans ready to come too.

"Not yet baby." He whispers in my ear, as my voice quivers.

I bite his bottom lip as he groans sordidly into my mouth.

"Are you mine?" Mewling back.

The question sends him into nirvana, with one final colossal pump his cock pulsates inside me filling me to the brim with his hot cum, he thrusts me into oblivion as I ride the high of my orgasm, my own gush coating his length.

We huff together lost in our euphoric state of, fucking.

Connect

S tone leans against me, pinning me against the wall we pant in unison our eyes locked together.

He kisses me softly, a bead of sweat seeps into my mouth.

I shuffle myself, pulling him out of me my hand coated in us.

"That's never happening again Stone." I pull up my jeans zipping them quickly, remembering where we are...outside the fucking library.

He stands behind me fixing himself, "never say never." He sniggers.

I spin on my heel to face him, "I mean it. I have a boyfriend."

A smug smile sits on his face, "do you love him?"

"Do you love me?" I bite back.

He steps towards me harshly, "don't ask me that." growling with ferocity.

"Why! Why can't I ask you that? What's the big deal Stone, it's a simple yes or no question."

I don't even wait for the answer, I snatch my bag and make off towards my apartment.

"Eva!" He cries after me.

Jesus.

"Fuck off, Carlisle." I keep walking, not looking back, my cell beeps from within my bag.

I pull it out to check my messages 4 missed calls from Jake and one from my dad.

"...Jake, hi...sorry I was...yeah I know but...Jake please don't sh...yes...I'm sorry. Tell dad I'm sorry too...no you do not need to come out here! Jake! Please....stop calling me that..."

Stone catches up, snatching the cell out of my hand.

"Really Eva? He's not good enough for you, he doesn't deserve you." He wipes away my tears with his thumb.

"Is that so?" I scoff, "Then who is Stone? Is it you?" reaching for the cell as it rings again,

"Dad...I'm sorry...I dropped my cell. No... I'm going home now...I'll wake the super, he'll let me in... yeah I know...I fucked up...it won't happen again...".

Stone follows behind me as I sob silently on the walk to my apartment, "what happened?" He calls behind me.

"I left my keys in the library, I'll have to ask the super to let me in." I whimper.

Stone jogs a little to catch up, "so, what's the big deal?"

"The 'big deal' is that it's another item added to the list of things that Eva can't do right." I hiccup on the tears and sobs, unable to control them any longer. Allowing it all to flow freely.

"I'm such a failure, no matter what...I can't make anyone love me. My own mother, the one person who was genetically designed to love me couldn't even do it, and don't even get me started on my father. And you! You just come in and out of my life like I'm some sort of fucking train station. Do you love me Stone, Stone...do you love me?" I plead through a river of snot and tears.

He grabs my arms shaking me, "it's not that simple Eva!" He glowers at me.

"Why?" My voice weakens in despair.

"I don't love anyone. No one." He releases me, turning around he walks away, leaving me alone once again.

I decide not to go straight home, I need some air...some time to think, so I take the long way through the park, it's so peaceful...

"Max!?" I pound on the super's door "Max!? I'm really sorry to wake you, its Eva from 8B... It's just I left my keys at school."

The door swings open, "Eva, its 12:30 am... It's fucking Thanksgiving tomorrow. I gotta be up at 5am... move your ass..." he trudges reluctantly up the stairs to the 5th floor, I follow behind him sheepishly, trying not to make a sound.

"Fucking hell, he yours?" Stone is slumped on the ground outside my door with his eyes shut, lightly sleeping.

"That's the million-dollar question." I mumble kicking his Gucci sneaker, "Stone, Aster Stone Carlisle! Wake up!"

His eyes snap open, he jumps to his feet.

"Who the fuck are you?!" He edges up to Max, towering above him a deep growl comes from inside him.

"Stone!" I yell mortified pushing him away from Max, "stop it! He owns the building ...he's letting me in is all."

Stone reaches around me glaring at Max while he opens my door, "you sure that's all he planned to do?"

"Will you please stop being such a fucking asshole!" Get in, I shove him through the open door into my apartment.

I go back out to the hallway, "Max!" I call after him, he walks cautiously back towards me searching behind me for any sign of Stone, "I'm sorry about that, he has...issues."

Max puts his hand on my shoulder, "the guys a jerk Eva. Happy Thanksgiving." He turns back around leaving me embarrassed.

"Are you fucking kidding me Stone, what the fuck! Not every guy is trying to fuck me." I slap him on his chest,

Sneering at me he throws my hand away, "you'd be surprised."

I throw my arms up exasperated with his attitude, "what are you doing here? I thought you had fucked off. Wait...how did you find me?"

He holds up a letter that I sent Griffin a few weeks ago, "I lied...I knew you would be here. I had to...I...FUCK!" he takes his fist and puts it through the dry wall, instantly bursting his knuckles open

"Stone!"

I jump out of my skin terrified of him, but it thrills me all the same. His eyes are wide with rage, his lips pressed together in an angry thin line, his skin vibrating.

I grab a dish towel from the kitchen wrapping it around his hand.

"I had to see you." He sighs in my ear as I clean up his hand, "Griffin gave me your letter...you sounded so..." he opens the letter, "'I can't connect to anything, not to this life and certainly not that one.'" Quoting my words back to me.

"I can't give you what you want Eva." His eyes search mine for validation.

I grab some ice from the freezer wrapping it in the towel and press it onto his fist.

"Do you love me?" I ask him for the very last time.

He grabs the back of my head pulling me in to him, kissing me passionately, he pulls away for a moment studying my face.

"I don't love anyone." He murmurs.

Thanksgiving

"When I said you could stay, I meant on the couch." I roll my eyes as he props himself on the pillow, eyebrow raised and that famous Stone smirk hinting out the corners of his mouth.

How can he go from such ferocious passion mixed with complex feelings to this, oozing sophistication and arrogance in a matter of minutes?

I'd kick him out if I didn't think he'd sneak back in, or that I'd miss him too much.

"Couch! Now!" I hiss at him he wiggles his eyebrows up and down, his attempt to entice you into bed, "not happening again Stone. What I did was wrong...I'm a cheater." I shun myself, grabbing the blanket off the bottom of the bed tucking a pillow under my arm.

"Eva...please..." he pats the bed.

I'm so fucking weak.

I throw the pillow at his head and jump next to him, "nothing is going to happen y'hear, Stone. I'm warning you," I kiss the tip of his nose without even realising I was going to do it, "no funny business."

"Whatever you say." He grabs my head, pulling my mouth to his nibbling my bottom lip.

Why couldn't it be like this all the time?

Why couldn't he tell me that he loves me or at the very least say he wants me.

Do I love him though?

If this is love, then why is it so hard? Why does it hurt so much?

We lie together in the bed exhausted both physically and emotionally, Stone slides his arm underneath my neck pulling me closer to him the rhythmic beat of his heart soothing me to sleep.

It occurred to me that I had never seen him smile, well not like this.

Stone works around the tiny kitchen in my apartment, "Happy Thanksgiving." He beams at me, it's all very unsettling, because this is a side of him, I didn't even knew existed.

Except...

I think I did.

"Happy Thanksgiving. What're you doing in there?" I sit down at the tiny breakfast bar rubbing the sleep from my eyes.

Stone sets down a cup of coffee in front of me its aroma instantly waking me up, "I went to the market, we are having Thanksgiving together...I got everything except a turkey...so I substituted it for chicken, but I think that's..." I get up and walk round the counter making my way to him reaching up to kiss him softly, he leans down kissing me back, "...I uh...can't remember what I was going to say."

Panic rushes over me...I run across the apartment grabbing my cell out of my bag...

"What?!" He yells

I press the cell to my ear, "Hello 911? yes...Stone, Stone Carlisle is lost for words...definitely an imposter..." You snap it closed giggling as his nostrils flare exasperated with me.

"I really thought something was wrong..." he runs towards me snapping a pair of tongs chasing me, "I couldn't resist!" I scream running away from him, he grabs my legs pulling me to the ground gently nipping my backside with them.

Lying in a heap on the floor panting in unison, he rolls onto his side looking deep into my eyes.

"What?" My mouth twists uncomfortably.

He exhales slowly, the smile running away from his face, "Does he tell you that you're beautiful?"

"Who?" I frown.

"Jake...does he know how lucky he is?" His voice is almost pleading.

I sit up bringing my knees into my chest, "Stone, you've really ruined the mood."

"I didn't mean to...I just...never mind. Forget I mentioned it." He waffles, his uncharacteristic vulnerability filling the room with a thick smog.

I can't have this type of conversation with him, it makes my skin itch and every feeling I have recoil. Why can't we go back to playing house, pretending that we are the happy family that never had. Before the stark reality of life comes crashing back, pushing us apart once more.

We sit down together at the breakfast bar Stone fills out two large glasses of red wine, and we tuck into the most delicious roast chicken dinner with all the trimmings, it's the most wholesome meal I've had since I moved here.

"Well...what's the verdict?" He turns his whole body to face me.

I finish chewing my last piece of food covering my mouth with my hand, "honestly Stone, I think you've found your calling."

He leans into me clasping either side of my face between his warm hands, I try my best to contain the smile that wants to burst from my face as my heart slows to a halt wondering what he is going to do, preparing for our last kiss, knowing that this perfect day will have to end at some point. And I will have to deal with whatever comes after him.

Still holding my face, he slides down off the stool and inches his mouth to mine, licking my lips...every nerve in my body electrifies.

"I'm gonna wash up." He kissed my forehead and starts gathering plates, filling the sink.

I sneak in in-front of him and begin washing handing him the things to dry, we stood comfortably in each other's silence doing a mundane everyday task.

I don't know what made me do it, but I couldn't help myself...I flick a little of the soapy dish water at Stone as he puts dried plates into the cupboard, when he spins around, I was terrified for a minute, I didn't know how he would take it.

He trudges over to the sink, dipping his hand into the water and flicks some back at me. I do it back to him just as he turns back to the dried dishes, he lets out a mighty guffaw as he swoops me up throwing me over his shoulder. He slaps my backside playfully heading towards the bathroom, turning the shower on as I kick and laugh protesting.

I love this.

Setting me down outside the shower he kisses my neck before reaching his mouth up to my ear, "behave..." he whispers softly sending shivers throughout me...

He undresses me slowly, lifting me and placing my naked body under the warm stream of water.

I watch as he strips himself, his hand wraps around his pulsing cock working himself, my hand slides down between my thighs to my heated core, rubbing my clit gently, preparing myself for him.

He steps in beside me, tilting my head back under the water taking my nipple into his mouth, using his legs to spread mine apart, as he slides his entire length inside me, but he doesn't pump me he rests it there... contracting myself around him longing to be filled.

"Is this what you want Eva?" He pulls himself out of me teasing my opening with his tip, edging it inside and taking it away from me.

"Fuck me, Stone." I gasp in anticipation into his mouth.

He lifts me against the tiled wall sliding his throbbing cock deep into my core, crashing it against my cervix, his tongue wrapped around mine as he pummels me powerfully into a sexed haze.

Every inch of him fills me as I twitch in delirium, "I'm coming, Stone." I tried to hold it back, but I couldn't.

"Come for me, Eva." he pulses inside me, the pressure of his cum shooting through my core sends me over the edge and the most euphoric toe curling, back arching orgasm expels out of me as I gush everything I had over his cock.

Stone crashes his lips onto mine parting them with his tongue and we kiss, we kiss for what felt like hours.

We kissed as we lathered each other up in soap...

Our mouths never parting as we dried or got dressed.

We sat on the sofa, our fingertips brushing together as we watched TV, Stones perfectly sculpted lips ghosted against the top of my arm every other second. It was like he couldn't get enough of me.I couldn't get enough of him. I felt my eyes closing softly as I drifted off to sleep, his lips lightly pressed against mine as he covered me with a blanket.

Closing the door behind him as he left.

Revenge Porn

"I'm so glad your home babe." Jake cuddles into me closely, my body goes ridged but I try to loosen up for him letting him kiss my cheek in front of all his friends.

It seems like the whole town is here. I don't want to be here.

My dad talks business in the study with the other high earning stockbrokers, while 'the kids' get drunk in the kitchen.

My eyes search the vast crowd looking for him, it's been almost 4 weeks since Thanksgiving and I've heard nothing from, Stone, it was the perfect day but all its done is left my heart longing for more.

Guilt washes over me as I recall Stones hands lacing mine, his soft lips caressing my body, his laugh resounds in my head like a song.

Someone nudges me, reluctantly bringing me out of my daydream, "Eva?"

"Sorry, I was in a daze." I search for the owner of the voice.

"You're being really rude." Jake hisses through his teeth squeezing my wrist a little.

"I was just saying, LA must be fuckin' tight!" Jakes friend, Toby, slaps my shoulder handing me a blue plastic cup filled with beer, "But you gotta miss our boy here," he hands one to Jake as well, "He is KILLING it at Bay Path." He sings.

How the hell did I end up here? If I'm to listen to this bullshit I'm going to need a stronger drink.

"I'm going to use the bathroom," I flicker a smile at Jake, he leans down ferociously bashing his lips onto mine forcing his tongue inside my mouth the taste of stale beer swirling around, I pull away, but he holds onto my bottom lip with his teeth drawing a little blood, eventually releasing me.

As I walk away, I hear his friends congratulating him, I turn around for a second to watch him as he pulls out his cell phone, "Watch this..." he giggles like a frat boy showing them some bullshit sports video.

"Ohh send me that!" Toby unable to contain his excitement pulls out his phone, the rest of the crowd join in.

I weave my way through the clusters of crowds gathered around the house, nodding, and smiling as people make eye contact as they let me through.

I spot a bottle of red wine on a table swiping it I sneak into the bathroom and gulp it as quickly as I can, the first taste causing an almighty shudder through my body, but by the time I get to the last drop its rich fruitiness is moreish.

I stash the empty bottle in the shower, washing my hands in the sink I look up to the mirror.

Who is she?

I don't think I've ever known who she is.

But then does anyone know who they truly are?

Are we all a different person based on who we're with?

The Eva with Stone has a voice, I wouldn't let him away with half of the things that I let Jake do.

But why do I let Stone away with away with making me feel like he cares, then pulling the rug from under me. Leaving me alone yet again.

I open the bathroom door my dad stands outside waiting, rolling his eyes at the sight of me exhuming obvious disappointment, "Hi dad."

"Eva, where's Jake?"

"Kitchen, I think." Shrugging my shoulders as I hang on his every word, wishfully waiting on some praise or indication that he acknowledges my existence as his daughter and stops treating me like a stranger.

"He's a great guy. Don't fuck it up." He slams the bathroom door in my face.

A hollow laugh escapes me.

If I didn't laugh, I'd cry.

"Hi." I walk back into the kitchen kissing Jake on the cheek, his eyes are blurry with alcohol.

I suppose mine are too.

"Can we talk babe?" He kisses my neck before pulling me out of the kitchen.

He pushes me into the only quiet corner of the house, kissing me fast and hard. I try to slow his pace, but he just slops kisses all over me, running his hands up and down my bare arms causing the heat of friction to build, stinging them.

He shoves his hand down the front of my top pinching my nipple furiously, "Ouch!" I yelp.

Jake moves my hands away from my side pinning both above my head, he takes his free hand and lifts my dress.

"Not here Jake," I hide my fear behind a false giggle.

"Shut up." He shoves his hand inside my panties, panting as his cock grows.

He slides his finger inside my slit trying to fumble his way to my clit.

"Not here I said, too many people around. Wait till we get back to mine." I plead with him.

He starts to grind himself against me as he works inside my lips, but I don't want this.

"Its good baby, let's just do it." His hot breath lingers around my face.

"I said no!"

Jake sniggers as he thrusts a finger inside me, "Come for me baby."

I try to pull my arms free, but his strength has me pinned.

"Jake, please stop." I whine.

Why is he doing this?

I said no, I'm sure I said it. Did I say it out loud? "Stop, please. I said no, Jake." I sob quietly.

"She said stop."

Oh, thank god.

Stone towers above us, he grabs Jake by the scruff of his neck trailing him away from me.

"Carlisle. This got nothin' to do with you! That there is my girlfriend." He tries to take a drunken swing at Stone, but he steps out the way dodging it.

Jake drunkenly falls to the floor alerting the crowd the commotion.

Oh shit.

"Whats going on here Eva?" My dad lifts Jake up from the ground, he stares at me with hatred in his eyes.

"I... uh...and Stone and uh..." I'm mortified. The whole party stands in silence gawping at me. What do I say?

"He's drunk, he can't even walk straight. Take him home!" Stone scoffs sophisticatedly sipping his scotch, saving me from any more embarrassment.

Dad helps Jake out of the party, and I'm left alone to gather my things. Stone stands with his back to me covering me he whispers over his shoulder, "fix your dress." Scorning through his blue eyes.

My dad and Jake leave the party in a cab forgetting me, I find myself back in the kitchen having to make excuses for myself, "I left my purse." Is the best I could come up with.

I can sense the judgemental stares as I search for my belongings. Jakes cell sits on the counter, I reach for it, but Toby's hand grabs my wrist, "he was sending me something, can you wait a minute till it's done?"

Sure, I tilt my head suspiciously. Opening the cell to see what was being sent.

My heart sinks into my stomach, it's a video. I can tell by the thumbnail that it's a video of me, it's a video of me being bent over the bed while Jakes cock pulsing inside of me.

Here it was being sent to all his friends. Like some sort of fucking revenge porn.

My face burns as I look around the room, Jakes friends twist their mouths trying to stop themselves laughing.

I run, pushing my way through the crowd.

Wiping my tears away my fingers black with mascara.

Why did he do this?

"Still crying?" Stone stands outside on the wrap around porch, a cigar in one hand and a scotch in the other.

"Fuck off Stone." I can't not tonight, I storm away down the steps, going over on my ankle a little when I reach the bottom step.

Excellent.

A red corvette pulls up the gravel drive, a blonde-haired bimbo sitting in the driver's seat, "you ready to go baby?" She calls out to Stone.

"Wait a second Jodi!" He snaps.

Stone walks down the stairs inching past you, "You really know how to pick em Eva. That guys a dick." He hisses as jealousy laces his tongue.

I turn my head slowly making eye contact with him, Jodi presses the horn impatiently, "You better go, *baby*." I reply coldly.

"Merry Christmas Eva." He whispers as he leaves me standing on the gravel.

Christmas Eve

"I said its over!" I scream through stuttered sobs.

Jake sits on the windowsill his head hung in shame, "I'm sorry. I don't know what I... what I was thinking. I was drunk," he gets up making his way across to me, his arms extended out reaching for me. I hate him.

"I don't accept your apology. Now leave." I open my bedroom door for him, "get out!!!" I scream.

"I'm not going anywhere till we talk about it!" He roars back at me.

Dad runs to the top of the stairs, "What's going on up here Eva?"

"Nothing. Jakes leaving, and he won't be back." My nostrils flared in anger watching Jake gather his things from my room, heading sheepishly towards the landing.

"Jake, don't break up with her. She's difficult I know, but she'll come around man." Dad slaps him on the shoulder.

"It's not me Mr Miller, it's her. She's breaking up with me."

Dad whips back around to me, a look in his eye that chills me to the bone. With just slightest haze to them. I feel so helpless against them, how am I supposed to defend myself when they are both too drunk to listen. Imagine thinking that my dad would protect me from this, or at the very least have my back. "I'll sort this Jake, don't worry." Dad gives him a wink.

He trudges towards me banging his hip on the banister, "It's time to home, Jake." He hisses.

My heart beats so fast, scared of my own father.

His poisonous tongue ready to bring me down.

"Are you outta your god damn mind Eva!?" He slams his fist down on my dresser, "You really think you can do better than him? He's got a great football career ahead of him. He can get you out of my house for good. He loves you! Why I'll never know, but he does."

I can't even fight my tears, I let them flow freely because what's the point in trying anymore?

"Dad, Jake isn't everything you make him out to be..." I wipe snot away from my nose, "he's not a good guy."

"What do you know about being good?" He scoffs back at me.

"Well, you sure as shit never showed me!" I take a fearful step back as his face reddens with anger.

"Do you know he has been videoing me...videoing us...on his cell phone, having sex," my dad winces because no father wants to think of his daughter that way, even one as shitty as him.

"He sent it to all his friends, but of course no one could see him, only me! Do you know how humiliating this is for me?" Tears fall off my chin, my eyes blurred with emotion.

"That's what boys do." His bluntness knocks the wind right out of me, my mouth gaping at his apathy.

"W... what did you say?" I bend over weakly trying to gather myself, is this really happening?

He stumbles over to my bed letting it hold him in place, "you should think about why everyone leaves. It's you...you know. You push people away, force them to leave...they can't stand to be near you, God Eva, you are worthless. Always so difficult. Its why your mother left..."

"Don't. Don't you dare blame that on me." I gasp horrified, I knew he had a sharp tongue, but I never knew it could cut me so deeply.

Moving closer to me as I back away eventually falling onto the sill, he leans in menacingly...his finger stretched centimetres from my nose,

"She left me because of you...she hated YOU!" His spit flies everywhere as he seethes.

"No dad, she left me because of you!!" I scream back at him, he takes the back of his hand off the side of my jaw, "get out my fucking room before I call the cops!" I shove him, I shove him harder than I ever thought I'd be able. He falters backwards out the threshold of my door, and I slam it behind him. Sliding down the other side sobbing into my knees, I close my eyes drifting into a catatonic pit of despair.

"I heard screaming." My head whips up, Stone sits on my windowsill.

How long have I been slumped here?

He walks over to me lifting my defeated body off the ground he moves my hair away from my face, wiping my tears and snot away with his hands.

I try to hide pulling away from him, fighting him.

"What happened to your face?" He growls, his nostrils flare waiting for my answer.

"He...he...hit me." I stutter, "my dad he uh..."

Stone pushes me aside trying to open the door, "I'll kill him."

I scramble to hold the door closed, "please Stone, please don't. You'll only make everything worse!" Pleading with him, my voice panicked.

"Please Stone...Aster?" He whips his head round, grabbing my face, "Don't call me that."

"Just stop." I try composing myself.

He nods sensing my urgency.

"Fuck." I sob.

"Fuck? Fuck what?" His brows knit together searching my face for answers.

"Fuck!" I lay a punch into the wall, he grabs my wrist stopping the next one being landed, "fuck!" I pound his chest, tears falling down my face once more.

He lets me beat him, my feeble fists ricocheting and in one violent movement I reach up trying to crash my lips to his.

"No." He pushes me away.

I shove him against the wall fumbling with his belt and zipper, trying to free him. He grabs my wrists stopping my hands clumsily sliding inside the waistband, "I said no." He stifles a moan

My heart sinks.

"No? What do you mean 'no'? Now you don't want me?" I stare into his eyes, silently pleading with him to take me. After what feels like an eternity neither one of us has moved a muscle and I resign myself to rejection. The only thing I've ever been good for is fucking, and now he won't even do that. Turning away so he doesn't see the defeated tears that sting my eyes, I decide that wallowing in my own self-pity alone in the bathroom is the only place for me, I'm almost at the door I feel his hand wrap around my wrist pulling me back, his mouth meets mine.

He wants me.

Finally.

"Let's just lie down Eva, you've had a rough day." He takes off his shirt and lies in bed, why is he being all fluff?

I slide off my clothes and walk nakedly towards my dresser, remembering the first time he slid his fingers inside me.

I push the perfume bottles and picture frames onto the floor, hoisting myself onto the dresser spreading my legs for him, showing him all of me.

My juices drip onto the wood below me as I slowly trail my hand down inside my glistening pink slit.

I rub my clit perfectly, in a way that would have me gushing in seconds.

Stone licks his lips watching me take my finger in and out of my opening.

His cock throbbing underneath the sheets I bite my lip as he wraps his hand around, pumping slowly.

"You really going to leave me to do this all by myself?" I slide my wet finger into my mouth and then back between my folds, groaning as the desire builds inside of me.

Stone saunters to me hand wrapped around his thick greedy cock working it slowly but powerfully.

He falls to his knees lining his mouth up with my core, eyes wide with delight, he dives in lapping my juices teasing my clit between his teeth switching between sucking and biting the motion forces my head back in luscious pleasure. I run my hands through his hair, pulling him further he drinks me hungrily licking every inch of me as I gush onto him.

"Take me Stone." I beg as he slowly gets off his knees, I reach my hand out for his shaft grabbing hold of it, rubbing the pre cum around his tip, playing with its glisten between my finger and thumb, I taste its salty goodness feverishly.

His cock glides between my folds, taunting my opening nudging my clit with his seeping tip.

He looks to the side of foot distracted for a moment, lifting the cherry stalk into his hand a speck of a smile peeks out of the corner of his mouth.

I slide my hand between my legs and guide his throbbing meaty cock into me, stretching me wide.

A little sting of pain causing my skin to electrify.

He lifts my body up and bobs me onto him, sliding me on and off his cock with ease.

We fall to the bed, and I straddle him, my hips buck as I grind myself along his shaft. The sound of my juices smacking on his length sending us into orbit.

I lift myself off dancing my slick opening on the tip relishing in his want. His eyes roll into the back of his head as he begs for release.

I thrust myself down hard onto him touching my cervix. Stone sits up holding me as we move in motion together, rolling my hips on his obedient cock, as his neatly trimmed pubic hair rubs gently against my clit.

"F... fuck." He groans deeply into my breasts.

I grab his hand and place it around my throat, begging him to squeeze, "I'm not going to do that." He dips deeply into my gushing wetness, "I'm never going to do that." He breathes into my ear, "I'll never hurt you." He bucks my core, "I love you." He moans, into my chest. I give into my orgasm allowing it to ripple through me, its shivering debilitating splendour drips down my thighs surrounding Stones cock in creaminess, as my walls contract, gripping him, milking his enormous length as he pumps his hot delicious cum deep inside me, spelling out onto the bed below us.

We collapse together in a sexed haze panting into one another.

His calming cock still buried inside me sticky with lust, I rest my head on his chest. He nestles his nose in my hair, the awkward silence filling the room.

The three words I longed to hear from him floating around threatening to be swallowed by regret.

"I meant what I said Eva, I love you." He whispers, kissing my forehead.

"Nobody loves me, Stone." I reach down the side of the bed pulling on his t-shirt I slide my panties up, shuffling my feet. Waiting for him to disappear.

He puts his boxer shorts on and takes a sip of a bottle of water I have by the bed.

What is he doing?

He lifts the perfume bottles and picture frames from the floor and arranges them on my dresser, taking the cherry stalk in his hand again, placing it down in front of the Chanel No.5.

"You can leave," I turn away from him, hiding my humiliation as the haze of fucking settles and the feelings begin to flood me.

His big arms wrap around my body, "I'm not going anywhere until you feel safe."

I turn around to look at him, just to make sure he is real... "I'd do anything to make you happy Stone. I could lie down here, and you could do anything you want to me, anything."

Stones brows furrow in worry, "Will you stop trying to make me happy, and just be happy yourself?" He cradles my face between his hands, "do you love me?" His eyes searching mine for answers.

"Do we even know what love is, Stone?" Tears trickle down my face.

How could we? No one has ever shown us.

Christmas Day Part 1

"You forgot to leave." I groan turning round in my bed to see Stone propped up on a pillow.

His mouth corners into a little smile, "Merry Christmas."

He stretches out on the bed sliding down under the covers his mouth meeting mine softly.

"Shit...it's Christmas." I pull away.

My heart is heavy as the memories of last night flood in. My jaw aches where the back of dad's hand crashed against it, I massage it gently trying to ease the pain when Stone grabs my chin turning my head round. His nostrils flare inhaling deeply a guttural growl builds inside his chest.

"It's not worth it Stone honestly. Let it go. I'm leaving the day after tomorrow..." I feel myself start to well up, "and I won't be back."

His gaze whips to meet mine, "never coming back huh?" Taking his finger, he traces the contour of my cupids bow, he squeezes my face between his cupped hands pressing his lips on mine, lingering for a moment before he slips his tongue inside.

I melt giving into him biting his bottom lip gently, he moans devilishly in my mouth hooking my legs over his hip. I can feel his stiff cock bulge through his boxer short I press my pelvis against him, yearning for him to fill me.

"Fuck!" He sighs lifting his vibrating cell phone from the table and placing it to his ear.

"What?" He growls.

I take the opportunity to slide down underneath the sheets, freeing his cock and wrapping my lips around the tip, flicking the head with my tongue.

"...uh...yeah Griffin...uhm no I uh...I went for a run really EARLY..."he shouts in pleasure as I thrust his pulsing cock deep into my throat, "I'll be there...I'll get a shower at the GYM...mine is open on Christmas...FUCK! No... not you...I went over on my ankle...I gotta go." He hangs up the cell abruptly and grabs hold of my hair.

"Sit on it." He moans loudly.

I work Stone, sucking and licking his entire shaft, feeling the fire building inside of me.

He bucks his hips thrusting himself into my throat deeper, I grip my mouth hard onto him sucking with force, "Eva. Fuck." His legs quiver as he tries to lift my head off him, but I push myself deeper is milky load expelling down my throat.

"You can thank me later." I get out of bed and head towards the bathroom leaving Stone wide eyed and panting on the bed, running his hands through his hair in exhilaration.

"What're you going to do today?" Stone kisses my wet forehead as he steps into the shower beside me, he reaches for the soap and lathers himself up.

I can't take my eyes off him, remembering the first few encounters we had, and how much he has changed. How much I have changed.

"Eva?" He leans down matching my eye level, "what's your plans."

"Oh...um...I'll stay here watch a movie. I don't plan on going downstairs at all..." my lip trembles in disappointment. I always loved the idea of Christmas; I relished in hearing about other family's traditions.

We have never done anything remotely special; dad would give me my gifts that were signed by his secretary, we'd have breakfast, watch TV and then we'd have Chinese food for dinner, he'd get drunk and cry about mom leaving and I would go to bed.

I feel the stings in the corner of my eyes as the painful memories take hold. Are they painful? Or are they just there. A constant reminder of the failure I am as a daughter. The piss poor excuse of a nuclear family we could have been.

Poor little rich girl hiding her tears from the intimidating rich boy from next door.

I turn away so Stone doesn't see me cry again.

"That's settled then...you're coming with me." He clears his throat.

Who is this man standing before me?

Where is the boy who used to treat me like a sex object? Have the tables turned, is it me who treats him like one now.

"With you where Stone?" I run my face under the stream of water washing away the sadness that pained my eyes.

He turns off the water and hands me a towel from the rail, "To Griffins. He's having a party; my parents will be there...so I need someone on my side. Will you be on my side?" He kisses and nibbles the sweet spot on my neck, my eyes rolling in the back of my head he knows I can't say no when he does this.

I stare at myself in the mirror, my black sequin shift dress skimming nicely over my body, my feet slid into a pair of black suede court heels, which I already regret wearing.

My long brown hair bounces around my face, which has been painted and repainted about twelve times since I decided to go with Stone.

As I glide a deep 'biker bitch' red onto my lips I look at Stone in the mirror as he fixes his hair, imagining if this is what it would be like if we were actually together, getting ready for family gatherings admiring one another.

My mind drifting to a 'what if?' state.

What if this was our apartment, what if we were 't raised by toxic parents. What if, we were happy.

I suppress the thought quickly.

This'll all be over by tomorrow.

I give myself a final once over, Stones slides in next to me wrapping his arm around my waist, smiling lovingly at our reflection.

Who is she?

I've never seen her before.

"You go out the window, I'll go downstairs and out the front door." Grabbing my bag off the side table I head out my room door, "shit!" I run back for the little bag of gifts I stashed in my wardrobe.

Stone stands in the middle of the room faffing with his belt, "everything okay?" His head hangs.

"Yeah...aren't you gonna go?"

He sighs, "I was waiting to see if everything was okay with your dad...I wanted to be here in case y'know."

I run over to him, "Go...its 2:15! I'll meet you there in 10 minutes." Pecking him on the cheek.

There was no sign of dad, I think he is sleeping in the lounge. I place his gift on the credenza by the front door, his red Prada tie, and a bottle of aged malt whiskey. What do you buy someone you barely know?

I turn on the lamp before I leave, hating the idea of him waking from his drunken slumber in darkness.

He's still my dad after all.

"Come in Miss Miller!" Alma, Griffin's housekeeper yells loudly, "thank god you're here, go save Stone...he's been getting a hard time, sweetie." Whispering in my ear as she takes my coat.

Stone storms out of the lounge his face blushing, "hey! Merry Christmas." He leans in hugging me awkwardly.

Griffin rushes out after him swinging his cane, "Eva Miller! Thank you for keeping your promise, how's your father?" He winks at me, kissing both my cheeks, "you remember my daughter Angela, Stones mother."

"Oh sure, its lovely to meet you again." I fall into a half curtsy.

Why the fuck did I do that?

Can I die now?

A tall, sophisticated woman stands just behind Griffin, "Oh look...its 'the gym'..." she scowls.

"Fuck off Angela!" Stone yells, "don't be rude to my g... I mean Grandads guest."

She raises an eyebrow and takes a long drag from her cigarette.

"Come meet the rest of the family Eva." Griffin links my arm, "you look wonderful dear."

I offer a simpering smile, blushing as I am introduced around the family.

Alma shoves a glass of champagne into my hand, "there's plenty more where that came from."

I nod thankfully taking a huge gulp, Stone tops it up instantly.

"How's the uh...ankle son?" Stone's father Richard asks sarcastically, throwing a raised eyebrow in my direction.

"Fine." Stone snaps, throwing back his drink.

Stones cousin Meg stands in front of me, her eyes sizing me up, she's around the same age maybe a little younger.

"So, you guys fucking or what?"

Griffin gasps, "Megan Falconer!"

"Oh, we're all thinking it, why else would she be here?" She inhales her e-cigarette blowing the vapour in my face.

"She is here because I asked her as my guest," Griffin slams down his cane and the room falls silent, "Now, I won't have any more comments y'hear? You will all make Eva feel welcome. Stone...fill her out a drink...she looks like she could use it."

He wasn't wrong.

Christmas Day Part 2

I wash my hands in the sink looking up in the mirror at my reflection, god I am so drunk. Maybe it's time to lay off the booze and stick to water.

I reapply some powder where my face has gotten shiny and fix my lipstick.

I am trying so hard to impress them trying to be perfect for Stone, his perfect little guest.

Except I'm not his guest. I'm Griffins.

Oh fuck. What am I doing?

I inhale deeply, trying to centre myself before anxiety takes over and my mind implodes with the pressure of overthinking.

It's nice to take a little breather, when you aren't used to a large family and a lot of noise it can be daunting, my mind over stimulated by the various conversations all happening at once

A light knock at the door startles me, "one second!"

"It's me, let me in." Stone calls from the other side.

I unlock it letting him in, he sits on the toilet and lights up a joint.

"What the fuck are you doing?" I panic, his whole family are out there, and he wants to sit in the downstairs toilet and spark up?

"Calm down, its Griffins...it 'medicinal'." His fingers hang in air quotes, "they've brought out the brandy, which means its serious conversation time."

He holds out the joint, his mouth twisting irresistibly.

I give in.

He holds it as I take a drag, the smoke swirling around my mouth burning my throat causing saliva to build inside my cheeks, trying my best not to splutter everywhere, I spit into the sink and take a swirl of mouth wash from the medicine cabinet.

An endearing chuckle bursts from Stone, he reaches out grabbing my wrist and pulling me onto his lap. He nuzzles my neck biting and nibbling gently, I rest my nose on the top of his head intoxicated by him. His hands roam up and down my thighs underneath my dress.

His fingers slide my thong to the side as he runs one inside my moistening slit, "stop." I pull away trying to fix myself.

"Whatever you say." He takes another drag of the joint before lifting the seat and flushing it down the toilet. He looks pissed.

"Hey," I grab his arm as he walks towards the bathroom door pulling him back, "I... um...want to. Just not right now, not with your family out there. They already have the preconception that I am some big slut."

Stone brushes his lips softly on the back of my hand, "okay."

"So Stone, how's college?" Richard walks around the coffee table setting himself down on the arm of the sofa.

Stone sighs deeply rolling his eyes, "it's fine Dick, why'd you ask?"

Richard smirks shaking his head in disapproval, "oh...why were flights to LAX charged to the credit card?"

Stones nostrils flare in preparation for the Spanish Inquisition.

"Respectfully Richard, what does Stones college experience have to do with charges to LA on the credit card that you gave to him?" The room falls silent, my eyes widen. Fuck. Did I say that out loud?

Fucking champagne.

Fuck.

"Respectfully, Eva, is it?" He kneels in front of me, "Forgive me, I never waste my time learning the names of my son's latest notches. I've often thought of installing a revolving door to his bedroom."

A deep thundering growl comes from within Stones chest, he stands fists clenched. I place my hand on his chest feeling the rise and fall of his breaths as the rage builds.

"Well, that would have been a good idea, had you actually raised him instead of shipping him off to Griffins because you couldn't finish what you started, Dick."

I swipe my bag from the side table, "Griffin, thank you for a wonderful day but I think I've out stayed my welcome."

Griffin lets out a mighty guffaw, "Eva, sweetheart you could never out stay your welcome." He claps his hands in jest, pointing at Richard who stands with his mouth hanging open in disgust.

"I don't know what you see in her Stone, please tell me this is just some 'friends with benefits' arrangement, and dear god tell me you are using protection. The last thing we need is to be tied to her for the rest of our lives."

I stand at the door waiting for Alma to bring me my coat, listening to every word. They haven't had a nice thing to say about anyone the whole evening. It must be exhausting living such a negative life.

But if they are talking shit about me, then at least they are leaving Stone alone.

"Enough!" I hear Stone roar, "I won't hear another shitty thing said about Eva." He slams his glass down, his voice quivers.

"What is it son?" I hear Griffin's cane shuffling along the hardwood floor, "tell us..."

Alma stands by my side slowly manoeuvring me into doorway of the lounge, where we stand observing undetected.

"You don't know her. When you talk about her like that it hurts me." He pounds his chest, "just stop." He bites his trembling lip.

His parents stand scoffing at one another ignoring their only sons' emotions, but Griffin rests his hand on Stones shoulder, comforting him.

"Tell us, Stone..."

Stone grabs the bottle of brandy that sits on the table gulping it greedily, his eyes flitting around the room at unsympathetic stares.

"No." He turns matching my gaze as I stand at the door, tears streaming down my face.

"Let's go, Stone." I simper.

Alma hands him his coat, "here you are, Stone."

I swipe an unopened bottle of champagne from the ice bucket that sits by Angela.

"I'm taking this." Sauntering out hand in hand with Stone, "wait!" I run back in, kissing Griffin on the cheek, "thank you."

We stand underneath my window, "there is no fucking way Stone...I can't climb up there!"

He laughs lifting me onto the trellis, "sure you can. You go first and I'll enjoy the view." Twitching his eyebrow.

"I can't!!" I let go dramatically falling onto him, knocking us to the ground, we roll around the sopping grass laughing till our sides ache.

"I'll meet you up there." I slide my tongue into his mouth, he takes hold of my bottom lip moaning deeply into me.

"Unless...?"

"No Eva, I've had more than enough encounters with toxic parents for one evening." He begins to climb the trellis to my window effortlessly.

The house was deadly silent, dads present still sat on the credenza, I snuck in as quietly as possible up to my room.

I slide through the door seeing Stone sitting on the end of my bed, "hi." He gets up, and preys towards me.

His lips meet mine, wrapping his arms around my body unzipping my dress slowly. I slide it down, and unclip my bra exposing bare breasts, Stone takes my hardened nipple into his mouth flicking it hungrily with his tongue as I fumble with his zipper, releasing him from his pants. The passion builds, our breathing speeds, he pushed my thong to the side lifting me against the wall, my legs tangle around him he begins ramming himself inside.

"Fuck!" I moan sordidly into his neck.

I relish in the heat of his body pressed against mine, the taste of alcohol on our breath feverishly intoxicating.

Stone glides in and out of me with ease, fitting together perfectly.

"Eva!" Jakes voice calls from outside my door.

Stone clamps his hand over my mouth, "shh." He whispers, dipping in and out of my core.

The door handle squeaks as its pressed down.

I push Stones hand away, "fuck off Jake! We broke up. Leave!"

I fight with Stone for him to put me down.

"I... I just want to talk." He shouts through the crack in the door.

I kiss Stones lips as he sets me down, handing me a hoodie that lies on the floor.

"I'll be down in a minute," I try to compose myself, "Be right back." I stand at the door as Stone pulls up his pants.

"I'm coming with you." He clears his throat.

If anyone see's Stone, it'll only make matters worse. I can fix this, all of this I can get rid of Jake, hopefully smooth things over with my dad and put him to bed. Then its back to college the day after tomorrow and start my new life. Alone.

"Just stay here. I'll only be gone a minute." I nod urgently.

I get to the landing Jake stands at the bottom of the stairs swaying incoherently.

"Please go Jake."

My dad steps out from behind him, "hear the boy out."

Oh my god. Are they for real?

I am so sick of this.

Am I invisible?!

Do my opinions and wishes not matter?

What about my feelings?

"No! Jake what you done was disgusting not to mention illegal!" I start to sob with rage, "you sent videos of me to all your friends. It's totally unforgivable."

"He done what?" Stone stands behind me growling with anger.

"What the fuck is Carlisle doing here?" Jake screams charging up the stairs.

My dad falls into the credenza lifting the bottle of malt up smashing it against the wall, the brown liquor running into the electrical socket, the lights flicker on and off, darkness ensues the only break of light coming in from the porch lamp.

Jake stands on the middle stair staring through the darkness. A cold shiver excites my body, I tilt my head, is this DeJa'Vu. I've done this before.

Stone wasn't here. I was alone.

This has happened before.

"It's you." My heart falls into my stomach as the realisation takes hold.

He takes a step towards me.

"You were in here...that night. The break in, the night I called Stone for help...it was you."

Before he even gets the chance to answer Stone charges towards him gripping Jake by the throat throwing him down the stairs. He falls to the ground, Stone raises his fists beginning to beat him into a pulp, my dad tries to pull him off but Stone grabs him by the shirt launching him to the side.

"Stone!!!" I scream at the top of my lungs, racing down the steps to them. My throat rips as I shriek as loudly as I can.

I get behind him trying to catch his arms as he pulls them back, his elbow thrusts back ready to gear up for another blow, but it connects with my face instead, my nose crunching under the force.

"Fuck!!" I gasp, blood splutters everywhere as I try to catch my breath.

"Eva!" Stone clambers off Jake rushing to my side, "I'm sorry, I didn't...fuck...I...I... I'm sorry." He tilts my head backwards, "fuck its broken." His lip trembles.

"Get away from her!" My dad's voice booms.

Stone holds me tighter, "I'm so sorry Eva. I love you. Please forgive me." He pleads.

Jake rolls onto his side spitting blood onto the hardwood floor, he groans as he tries to sit.

My head spins, white spots floating around my vision, I'm aware of everything but I couldn't speak even if I wanted to.

Blue flashing lights circle the house.

"Police! Open the door!!" The pounding echoes throughout the house.

Deceit

"Alright sweetheart that should heal in 2 to 3 weeks, it's a clean break. The cops will come and talk to you..." the doctor hangs his face in front of mine, "Miss Miller?" Clicking his fingers, "Eva?"

The tears that well in my lower lash line build and fall perpetually soaking my face.

"...I understand." My feeble voice scratches my throat.

The Doctor exits through the curtain, adjusting it to give me privacy.

How did this happen? We were so happy...for 5 minutes...but happy, nonetheless.

I replay the entire evening over in my mind, wishing that I had some sort of time machine, isn't there someone out there that can rewind the night to let us start again.

"I'm the mother!" A shrill voice belts from the reception.

My heart jumps.

Mom?

Angela Carlisle storms through the curtain, "I didn't say I was her mother." She mutters pulling up a chair.

I feel stupid. Of course, it wouldn't be my mother.

I try to control my breathing but it's impossible, my chest pounds in fear, waiting like a child for her to speak. Preparing to be belittled. Angela takes her glasses off, cleaning them with a handkerchief from her purse.

As her gaze falls on my face a slight wince hides in the furrow of her brow, nervously I scrape some of the crusted blood from my chin.

"He's been arrested..." she shakes her head.

"He who? Which one? Jake?"

She scoffs her lips pursing as she holds back a sob, "Stone."

My whole body is consumed by lead, the periphery of my vision becoming darker with each short, panicked breath. I try to stifle a whimper unsuccessfully.

"What about the others?" Bile builds inside my sinking gut.

Before she is able to answer me a policewoman steps in, "would it be okay if we had that chat now Miss Miller?"

Angela wipes away a tear from the corner of her eye, "I was just leaving." She storms away leaving me with my unanswered questions in purgatory. The weight of the unknown rendering me paralysed.

"Miss Miller, we have Mr. Carlisle arrested for the assault...but we need to go over a few details with you before we continue pressing charges."

I nod my head nervously, the only movement I can muster.

"You are in a relationship with Mr. Jacob Chapman, is that correct?" Her pen resting on her pocket notebook ready to scribble information.

"Jake?"

"Yes, Mr. Chapman. He is your boyfriend?" She repeats.

"Can I see him?" My lip trembles, Stones balled fists connecting with Jakes face shivers across my mind, the noise of the gurgling blood being spluttered on the hardwood floor causes me to tense my entire form.

"After you answer my questions...I'll take you to see him." She rests her hand on mine, "how about that?"

"Okay..." I inhale deeply, "Jake and Stone got into a disagreement, I guess Jake didn't like it that I went to Griffin's for Christmas." Twiddling my thumbs, trying to strategically piece together the events.

"Mhmm...and you got hit?" She points to my nose and black eyes with her pen.

"I got in the way trying to split up the fight." Stones elbow crashing against my face flashes in my eyes.

"Okay...your father is down at the station." She stands ready to leave.

"Giving a statement?" I'm ashamed to admit that I totally forgot that dad had been there. He was useless anyway.

"He'll be there until Monday..." the cop looks at me sheepishly.

So, he's sleeping it off.

Best place for him.

It means I have until Monday to get my shit together and get the fuck out of Massachusetts.

"Miss Miller, are you okay? Do you need me to get the doctor...Miss Miller?" The officer places a gentle hand on my own snapping me out of the torment of my own mind. My dad's words are echoing 'they can't stand to be near you, you're worthless' he's right, isn't he?

"Miss Miller, would it make you feel better, safer for me to take you to see him?"

The officer stands beside me outside of the room where he lies sleeping, "it looks worse than it is...fractured eye sockets, broken jaw and some missing teeth...but he'll live."

"I'm sorry, he's not taking visitors at this time." A nurse whispers softly barely audible over the beeping machines.

"This is his girlfriend, she's pretty shaken up." She leans into the nurse, "you think we can make an exception?"

The nurse agrees to allow me in for 5 minutes, I go in alone while the officer watches from outside.

I choke back sobs as I lean in kissing Jakes forehead lightly, trying to be gentle with his wounds.

"J... Jake?" I squeeze his hand, his eyes flicker at the sound of my voice.

A pained smile corners his mouth.

"I know you can't talk, but I just wanted to tell you..." I lean in brushing my lips to his ear.

"I have your cell phone in my purse, I've seen all of the videos and photographs you took, and they date back to before we were dating," my hushed voice eerily calm as I fight for Stone.

"And the photos you took from inside then locker room at school, that's classed as child pornography. That's 10 years minimum." I hear him hold his breath in shame.

"...so, I am telling you now...you drop the charges against Stone, or I'm handing this cell phone over to the police."

His eyes are wide with fear as he mumbles incoherently, "drop the charges. Make this go away for him, or I will ruin you." I kiss him on the cheek applying too much pressure.

He fucking deserves it.

The nurse taps the window lightly, times up.

I wipe away my false show of emotion as the officer wraps her sympathetic arm around me.

"He'll be alright honey." The nurse pats my hand.

She and the cop share a patronising smirk to one another.

My role played to perfection.

Fight

I can't even remember how I got here...

I only realised I was home when I opened the front door to the scene of the many many crimes.

Evidence lying shattered on the hardwood floor, the smell of whiskey filling the air.

I tiptoe over the broken glass being careful not to cut myself, the sight of the room makes me sick to my stomach.

Do normal families find themselves in situations like this?

Too numb to cry any more I look around the empty house, cold and loveless.

Forgetting myself for a moment, I step in a puddle of stickiness.

Blood, mine? Jakes? Dads? Stones?

I try not to slip as I head toward the kitchen, the last thing I need is another injury.

I heave myself up, my eyes fall on the bag of gifts sitting by the refrigerator, that's right...it's Christmas.

Well...not anymore, but it's still the holidays.

Sitting on the kitchen counter with my feet in the sink I run the tap over my bare feet, washing the clots of blood down the drain.

I catch a glimpse of myself in the reflection of the faucet. Holy shit.

My eyes blackened; blood crusted around my nostrils.

I'm a mess.

Did I go to the hospital like this?

I turn off the water and pat my feet dry with a dish towel.

Did I go to the hospital wearing nothing but a thong and a grey hoodie? How completely mortifying.

I chuckle.

I chuckle a little louder.

The chuckle turns into hearty laughter that I can't control, the kind of sad bellyache laughter.

Because if I don't laugh, I'll cry.

And I'm so exhausted with crying.

I just can't do it anymore.

Is life this difficult for everyone or just me?

I snigger at myself, my pity party for one.

Allowing the last laugh to falter through my lips I heave a sigh composing myself. Fighting a losing battle against tears.

"What's so funny?"

My head snaps round to see Stone stand by the sliding door.

Oh, thank god.

I wipe away tears and slide down from the counter, "hi." I take a step towards him.

He puts his hand out to stopping me from coming any closer.

His eyes glance around the room, falling on anything but my face.

"When did you get home?" I open the fridge not because I wanted anything, but for something to do.

I grab two beers and slide one over to him.

He shakes his head.

"Did you just get home now?" I look at his outfit, grey sweatpants and a sweatshirt, it's so un-Stone.

I follow his gaze to the bloody footprints on the floor, "I uhh...stepped in it...out there."

He bobs his head like he is in a trance.

"S.. Stone?" I walk toward him my hand trembling as I reach out to touch his as it hangs by his side. I just wanted him to know that he wasn't alone. All the words I wanted to say were suddenly gone and all I had to offer was this. I looked at our fingers as I intertwined mine with his own, he doesn't flinch.

I exhale slowly pressing my forehead into his chest, why won't he speak to me?

"Stone?" My pleading voice cracks under the weight of silence.

"Mhmm." If a faltered groan is all he can bear right now, then that's what I'll accept.

I look up at him trying to catch his eye. I need to see him and not just his presence, I need to look into his eyes.

He stares blankly ahead. His catatonic state striking me with fear.

"Tea?" I pull away gently. Fucking tea, is this all I have to offer at a time like this?

As I pull away Stone grips my hand tightly pulling me back allowing his eyes to fall on my face. Tears flow down his cheeks, he studies my face using his free hand to tilt my head, getting a better look at my monstrous face.

"I... I did this." His eyes widen he bites his lip trying to stop it from quivering.

I shake my head, "no...it was my fault. I got in the way." I can feel him shutting me out, I'm losing him.

"Every time you get hurt its because of me..." he lets go of my hand; everything just feels so...so empty.

My entire body breaks out in a cold sweat, my lungs fight for breath as my heart cracks open leaving it raw.

A sudden rush of rage bursts from within, "NO!"

"No?"

"No, Stone." I inhale deeply, I'm not about to let him go without a fight. I will fight for us. I will fight for him, "did you ever stop and think that maybe I'm the reason I get hurt? You...Jake and my d... dad." I bang my fist on the counter, the sound echoes through the house, "who's the common denominator? Me!"

It is me.

"Stone, Stone Carlisle...if you are willing to take a chance on me, then I'm willing to —"

He cuts me off abruptly, "I'm not."

My heart falls into my stomach, I clutch my chest.

"Please don't say it Stone," I try my best to hold the tears back, but I can't they cascade down my cheeks, "if you're going to leave me again why did you even bother coming here?"

He stands sheepishly staring at me through his furrowed brows, his mouth twitching into a solemn frown, "I... we can't keep doing this, Eva,"

I always loved the way he said my name, but this time I resented it. I want it back. He's taken more from me than I ever gave him. They all have.

"Stone...I l..."

"No." The familiar growl rumbles in his chest.

"Yes Stone! Let me...l—"

He rushes forward to me wrapping his hands in my hair his cheeks flushed with emotion, jutting his face forward to crash his lips to mine he hesitates instead he presses his lips gently against me, I melt into him.

I'm so weak. I would do anything to have him, just to keep him a little longer. If I can do this with him in-spite of the crushing pain, then maybe he'll stay.

The Lake

It's the first day of summer vacation I can't quite believe that high school is over, I'm out in the world now as an adult it's so daunting.

Dad left for San Francisco yesterday leaving me alone again. At least he made it for graduation, he never showed up for anything before, so I was surprised to see him there in the auditorium. I think he was disappointed that I didn't make Valedictorian, I always stayed under the radar. Never had any friends. No one wants to be friends with the quiet little rich girl who never found a place to fit in.

I lie with my knees raised on one of the old deck chairs at the side of the lake that sits by our house, the sun beats harshly down on my skin which is barely covered by my black bikini. I always enjoy the peacefulness of it here. But the peacefulness was short lived as a shadow casts over me.

"Who are you?" I open my eyes to see Stone Carlisle towering over me.

I slide my sunglasses on to my head, "Eva Miller, your grandfathers neighbour for the last 18 years."

What a dick! He knows exactly who I am.

Just like I know exactly who he is, the arrogant asshole who acts as though he's king of the world and that there are girls throwing themselves at him.

He seriously thinks he's all that, but he's not. He's not even that attractive, well I suppose in some lights maybe.

"Is this half of the lake yours? I thought it was Griffins." He smirks coyly his eyebrow raised as he sits on the end of the wooden sun bed.

Our families were never one for socialising, the usual obligatory Christmas card passed back and forth every year, and when my mom left Griffin sent his housekeeper Alma over with food. Other than that, there has been little to no contact with our neighbours, or anyone in town for that matter. I suspect they think dads too stuck up, and I'm just invisible. But now that schools over its time for me to reinvent myself, time for me to grow up and find out who I really am, that is if Stone would get off my towel.

I get off the sun bed tugging at my towel, "well I guess I'll be going, Aster." I grunt as he sneers from the corner of his mouth.

"Call me Stone, it's my middle name..." he lifts my denim shorts from the pebbled shore and hands them to me, "I hate being called, Aster."

I snatch the shorts from his hands and shimmy my way into them. I try to control the flustered sting that spreads across my cheeks as he eyeballs me pulling them over my butt.

He hooks a finger in one of the belt loops and stands trailing them slowly up, "wh... what're you doing?!" I take a step away from him tripping over the bed, he grabs the front of my bikini top breaking my fall.

"Watch where you're going will you," he pulls me forward looking at my partially exposed breast, "wouldn't want that incredible body of yours getting injured."

I bat away his hand and try to gather my things, "fuck off will you!" I try to conceal my embarrassment, but I'm not even sure that's what it is, he is so...enthralling, my heart pounds deeply inside my chest. I'm surprised he can't hear it.

"Why are you in such a hurry Eva." His voice is smooth like velvet the way his tongue rolls over my name sends shivers up my spine, I am rooted to the ground my pink pouty lips rest parted slightly. Stone traces them lightly with his finger, a sharp almost silent gasp shoots into my chest as I try to control myself from trembling with an arousal of nerves. Is it nerves or is it arousal? Oh god, it might be both.

Heat builds inside me.

Am I sweating?

I turn my head to the side and rest my cheek on my shoulder in an attempt to break eye contact with Stones intimidating stare, the smell of the sun lingers on my skin like salted caramel.

He places a finger under my chin and turns my face back to him, brushing his mouth against my cheek as he brings it to my ear, "would you like to taste me?" He trails his tongue down my neck caressing my collarbone with his lips, "can I taste you?" He whispers softly as he licks my jawline slowly making his way to my lips where he stops at the corner of my mouth. His one hand placed on the small of my back, the other resting in the waistband of my bikini bottoms.

Say something Eva.

Say no.

Say yes.

Fucking hell, speak.

He skims the top of mound, just above my opening. Half a millimetre and his finger could glide inside me with ease.

His finger twitches down resting lightly on my slit, unable to control the squeaking gulp that emits from my throat. It appears that I have forgotten how to breathe.

I can feel my core wetting with each passing second.

I want him but I don't.

"I'll be seeing you, Eva." He removes his hand and lips from my body, leaving the space cold and me fervently yearning for more, but before I can gather my thoughts and process what just happened, he disappears into the wooded area that shields the lake.

Leaving me infatuated, gasping for breath.

Raw

We stand pressed together in the kitchen, lost in the haze of confusion. His hands linked with mine as the sun sets and the room is awoken with the flickering garden lights.

Our words hang in unspoken unity.

Unable to linger in this catatonic state of limbo any longer I look up to him, "Stone..."

"Mhmm?" He mumbles.

"Could you hold me?"

He wraps his large arms around me.

I allow myself to melt into him, yearning to be a part of him. I stand on my tip toes reaching up, brushing my lips on his jaw.

I feel his ridged frame release, and he brings his mouth to mine.

Our tongues meet massaging together, he must be able to feel my heartbeat...it's pounding loudly inside my chest. I want him, I need him.

He sweeps me up and I wrap my legs around him, he tries to be so gentle with me. My face aches with every tiny movement but I don't care. This is all I have ever wanted. To be loved by someone as deeply as he loves me. And I know he loves me. I can feel it in my bones.

"Stone..." I pant through our kisses, "I want to go to bed..."

He nods walking with me attached to him carrying me upstairs to my bedroom forgetting for just a moment that our whole world had gone to shit.

He sits down on the edge of my bed I stay entangled around him sitting on his lap, content but too afraid to let go. With his eyes closed he plants soft kisses all over my face taking care not to touch my injury.

But all of me is tender, and try as I might, I can't contain the pained groans that escape me.

His eyes snap open, "I'm sorry," he pulls back, "I can't." He turns is head away from me.

The pain of him is all I have left to hold onto.

Without him I have nothing, without him I am nothing.

"Stone..." slowly I slide from his lap standing in front of him, he places his hands either side of my hips looking up at me his defeated eyes wailing, "please don't leave me." I plead keeping my voice strong, but the breaking quiver trails off at the end exposing my every insecurity.

"I... I should be begging you not to leave..." he presses his forehead against my stomach.

Why can't it just be easy, why did it have to start off this way?

Is love always supposed to be this hard?

"Stone. I love you."

He stands, "don't say it if you don't mean it."

Of course, I mean it. I was infatuated with him from the moment I met him, it was potent infatuation that unwittingly coerced me into allowing him through my window that very first night.

I have never felt more seen or more alive than I every time he sets his eyes on me.

"Do you still love me?"

His mouth presses against mine gently before pulling away, "I adore you. I didn't want to fall in love with you, I didn't want to love anyone. You infected me."

"Are you FUCKING INSANE?!"

My eyes spring open at the roar of voices coming from downstairs, I look across the bed to the empty space left by Stone.

"...there is no way! I will not allow it!" My dad's voices echoes through the house.

I slide on a pair of sweatpants from a pile of unwashed clothes that lie on the floor.

"Preston...listen to the boy."

Griffin?

I creep downstairs trying to be silent enough to eavesdrop hovering just outside the kitchen door.

I see Griffin sitting on a chair with his cane resting by his legs, Stone paces around the kitchen furiously, and my dad who looks exhausted is stood leaning against the counter.

My dad juts forward towards Stone throwing his hand out inviting him to continue, "she can't stay here with you. You don't deserve he-"

"And I suppose you do?" Dad cuts him off, "how long have you been fucking my daughter?" He stabs his finger into Stones chest.

I can hear him growl, I clamp my hand over my mouth muffling my breaths, "Presto n..." Griffin mutters tapping his cane on the tiled floor.

Stone appears at the door opening it for me as I step into the room, I offer a small, concerned smile.

Nervous and confused seeing these 3 men together.

Griffins' brows knit together as he studies my face, for a second I almost forgot I had been injured.

Dad stands with his head hung shamefully unable to look at me direct.

"What's going on in here, why you are all shouting?" I walk to Stone, standing by his side. He puts arm around my waist. With a small movement he pulls me in closely, causing dads lip to curl in disgust.

Griffin stands from his chair, walking towards me his cane tucked under his arm. For the first time I realise that it was purely cosmetic, to give him a more commanding presence in a room where his elderly stature could be easily looked over. He leans down meeting my eyes, "Stone would like you to attend Harvard with him, you certainly have the grades and I have pull with the dean." A gentle smile peers from the corner of his mouth, "Stone has an apartment near campus for you both."

My mouth hangs open, I'm utterly dumbfounded.

"W... what?"

Dad storms forward pushing me away from them both, "you do as I tell you! You will stay here with me. Get a job at my office where I can keep an eye on you," he spits at me, "stay away from that thug!" He grabs my shoulders shaking me violently, "they aren't your family! I am!!"

Stone grabs his arm pulling him back from me, throwing him against the refrigerator.

Griffin sweeps me into him holding my trembling body tight.

"Tell me...tell me that you love me dad!" I sigh through a river of tears, the room falls quiet the only sound coming from my shuddered sobs, "tell me that it's not my fault mom left...face the truth, it was you!"

I stand waiting, he stands in complete silence unable to form any words wearing a cold blank expression. The old wounds on my heart crack open leaving me agonised and raw.

"Just what I thought." I shake my head in knowing disbelief.

I've had enough.

"And on that note, I'll be leaving. I'm not going with anyone, I'm better off alone." I try to leave but a large firm hand grabs my wrist pulling me back.

Griffin tucks a lock of my hair behind my ear, "you'll never be alone." He slides a thick piece of paper into my hand, I grasp it tightly the edges jabbing into my palms.

Stone turns to my dad his eyes wide with anger, "why can't you just love her? She's so easy to love...it's like breathing."

New Year's Eve

"Where are you gonna go Eva?" Stone hovers in my doorway as I throw things into a hold all.

I move around my room, trying to remember what I'll need, "Manhattan." I mumble.

Stone stares at me perplexed, "Manhattan?"

I shove the piece of paper Griffin gave me into his hand, "Emily Catherine Miller, East 64th Street, NY." He reads it aloud.

The wind blows an icy blast through the streets, cutting us in two. It's got to be below zero here.

I grab Stone's wrist to check his watch, 7:48pm.

We stand together at the bottom of a huge brown stone townhouse. I count and recount the stairs, eight.

Eight steps to see the woman who birthed me, who cared for me for my first 10 years before she gave up on me.

"You gonna go in?" Stone slides his hand inside mine, gripping it tight. I glance down at our entwined fingers.

I need this. I can't do this without him.

"No. I don't think I am. I'm scared." I start to nibble the skin around my nails, Stone grabs my other hand turning me round to face him. He leans down into me, "do you want me to go first?" I shake my head, "let's just go back to the hotel and try again tomorrow."

But before I can pull his hand and drag us away from the steps, "excuse me..." a man pushes past us walking up the steps, he turns back "can I help you?" He asks Stone.

"Uhh...we uh..." Stone clears his throat, "we're looking for Emily." It occurred to me in that moment that I didn't even know my own mother's maiden name, and that she may have remarried.

The man opens the heavy front door, "Em...! Ya better come out here... there's ah couple of kids here for ya!"

Stone scoffs arrogantly, "fucking kids." He mutters under his breath.

A tallish woman comes to the door her brown hair specked with grey tied neatly in a bun at the nape of her neck, she is dressed beautifully in a black sparkled polo neck which is tucked into a leather pleated midi skirt, and a pair of black court heels.

A confused smile is plastered across her face, "you guys lost or somethin'?"

Holy shit.

It's her.

The man looks at Stone as the words hang static in the air, no one looks at me. I'm invisible.

Stone gently nudges me forward to the bottom of the stoop "This here is—"

"Eva, right?" The man peers round attempting to catch my gaze, "I'd know those eyes anywhere..." he touches my cheek smiling sweetly, but I pull away sharply thudding into Stone who stands right behind me.

"You, okay?" He whispers in my ear.

No. No I am not.

Emily takes a few steps down the stairs, her eyes wide but underneath her beautifully painted face her skin is white with shock.

"Eva...what are you doing h... does your father know?" Her eyes flicker in panic.

I can't speak, nausea bubbles inside me burning my throat.

"Mr. Miller is no longer part of Eva's life, he —"

"Stone. No." I cut him off, she hasn't earned the right to know. She didn't even recognise me. She hasn't earned the right.

"Stone...you're the Falconer boy?" Emily's brows furrow her mouth twisted into a frown as she stares through me coldly.

"Carlisle, but yes...I'm Griffins grandson." He wraps his arm around my waist, "I'm Eva's boyfriend." He said with pride pulling me in.

Emily bobs her head; the once crisp air is pulled down by the heavy tar of awkwardness created by this pathetic family reunion.

She doesn't want me here.

"It was nice seeing you, but we are entertaining for New Year's Eve." She walks backwards up the steps her hand trembling.

"Em!" The man shouts after her but she closes the door abruptly.

I can't anymore. I feel numb.

Stone pulls me inside his camel-coloured coat, "hey...she's in shock. She just didn't expect it alright." He kisses the top of my head.

I don't cry. I feel empty.

I feel a warm hand on my back, "listen sweetheart...come back tomorrow. My family is Scottish we have a big party on New Year's Day, I want you both to come. Okay?"

Stone nods, "sorry, we didn't get your name?"

"Oh shit, Robert!" He extends his hand Stone shakes it firmly, "Eva...it's really good to meet ya, you'll come back tomorrow wont ya?"

"Sure." I agree because I hate saying no.

"Alright, you kids have a good night!" Robert disappears into the house.

"I'm sorry." He mouths to Stone.

I hear Stones voice inside his chest, "hmm" rumbles acknowledging the apology.

We walk through the cold streets of New York, Stone tried to hail us a cab countless times but NYC on NYE...you got more chance of drawing blood from a stone.

So, we walk in the blistering cold...

For a moment I felt like I was going to wallow and tear up, but something changed.

I was undoubtedly hurt by Emily's coldness towards me, but something was different with me.

So, I don't cry.

I laugh... I laugh at Stones ridiculous muttering as he complains about the smell of the city.

How can people live here? Repeated over and over as he pinches his nose and splutters every time we walk over a drain.

"Can you get a colonoscopy for your lungs? If so, I am going to need one." He covers his mouth with his expensive cashmere scarf, draping some over my face as well, "cover yourself. Fucking disgusting shitty city."

"Stone...?" I stare at myself in the mirror as I wipe away my makeup. The bruising under my eyes yellowing slightly, my nose still swollen and bruised but its easily concealed.

"Mhmm?" He slides his arms undermine from behind pressing his bare body against mine he kisses my shoulder nibbling lightly on my skin.

He runs his fingers under my bra strap snapping it playfully.

"You told them you were my boyfriend." I turn myself round to face him, he leans down kissing my forehead lifting me onto the edge of the bathroom counter.

"I did." He trails sweet kisses down my cheek finally leading to my neck, I let out a pleasurable whimper.

"Did you mean it?" Here it is...the moment of truth...

The way he answers this will either make or break me. And I'm not sure there's enough glue in the world to put me back together.

"If you'll have me." He kisses my throat running his tongue along my collarbone down to chest lingering his lips above my breasts.

I gasp at the pleasure of his lips brushing over me, but mostly I am breathless by the simplicity in which he says it. No wait, it's not that. It's that he's actually asking me to be his. I'm wanted, I'm not invisible. Not to him.

"Always." I say with adoration, allowing my heart to open fully.

He rushes his mouth to mine it was a bruising kiss, fast paced and exciting.

The taste of his tongue as it massages mine is irresistibly intoxicating, I relish in his saliva, addicted to him.

His hands roam my body as he moves his mouth to my breast taking my hardened nipple into his mouth, licking, and sucking it hungrily.

Heat building between my thighs as he spreads my legs pulling my panties to the side with his long thick finger, he runs it teasingly up and down my slick slit parting me ever so slightly.

I break our kiss to attach my mouth to his neck biting and sucking his salty skin, I lace his jaw with kisses bring myself to his ear I brush my lips gently against it, "fuck me, Stone."

He pulls away from me raising that damn eyebrow smirking at me, the gesture orgasm inducing all by itself.

He slides my leg out of one side of my blush laced thong and falls to his knees delving his face into my dripping core, exploring my folds with his tongue every tantalising movement releasing pure ecstasy through my veins, his teeth nibble furiously on my clit I gasp in rapture my hips buck forward pushing me further onto his face, he grabs them pulling me deeper onto him.

I don't want to cum not yet, I want this to last forever. I raise my foot pressing it against Stones shoulder and kick him away from me, he lands on the floor of the bathroom, I slide off the counter and saunter towards him planting my feet on the ground either side of his head. I slip my thong off my other leg and drop it onto his face, my exposed wet mound lingers for the taking, he grips my thong tightly in one fist reaching up with his other hand trying touch my glistening lips ready to insert his fingers, but I kick his hand away and sashay towards the bedroom.

I turn to see Stone still lying on the tiled floor, cock bursting through his Calvin Kleins begging to be released, he is biting his fist in the raptured vision of me.

"Well...?" I slither onto the bed spreading my legs wide, Stones scrambles from the floor tucking the blush lace into his waistband. His eyes wide with delight as he watches my fingers dance over my clit, scooping the moistness and trailing my fingers to my mouth, relishing my own taste.

"Eva...you're killing me." He groans in anticipation.

He clambers onto the bed freeing his massive pulsating cock, the purple head lustrous with pre cum.

"On your back." I command, his eyes rolling in the back of his head as he obeys.

I edge up onto his face and clamp my sex onto his mouth driving myself back and forth grinding on him as he munches my weeping folds with his invading tongue. A hitched breath ripples through my lips and I raise myself from him, he grabs my thighs trying to hold me in position, I slap his hands away pinning them beside him.

I crawl down to his aching dick, feathering it from base to tip with my tongue, enveloped in the saltiness of his pre cum that seeps in anticipation, I fill my throat with his silky shaft, sucking firmly trying to milk him. He groans deeply as I devour him greedily. I can tell by his breathing that he is going to explode. I stop abruptly. Glancing up at him he laughs in anticipation, biting his bottom lip as I glide myself onto his length with ease. Slamming myself on to the base as the tip brushes my cervix blushed with the sloshing sound of flushing juices which coat his entire cock. I rock back and forth gliding on his shaft, enthralled by the control I have over him. Raising myself off, and bobbing my opening on his tip, his mouth hanging open in a mix of pleasure and awe impatiently waiting for me to grant him gratification.

"My turn." He growls, flipping me onto the mattress.

I try to fight him for control, but he pins my hands above my head, slamming his cock into my sodden core. Ravishing me, pummelling me hard into the bed. He lets go of my hands as he thrusts himself into me ferociously each slam hitching my breath the perfect of pain and pleasure. He turns me on my side spreading my legs wide, his meaty cock stretching me to the brink. I scream out in pleasure, ready to expel everywhere feeling my climax peak inside me. He reaches for my thong that lies on the bed beside us and stuffs it into my mouth with force, the sordid kink sending me over the edge as he batters me. I can't hold it back anymore, I gasp for breath through the most explosive, toe-curling back arching and vagina bursting can't help but scream your lungs out orgasm. Stone snatches the panties out of my mouth and attaches his lips onto mine, our mouths open as I scream his name.

Juices gush from inside my walls contracting around Stones cock gripping hold, squeezing him, as I writhe around in the aftershocks of my climatic haze he moans devilishly his pelvis twitching, I latch my mouth onto his shoulder biting down hard as my clit throbs in delirium, Stone pounds into me, his breathing shudders, pumping me full to the brim. Collapsing beside me on the bed, we pant in unison trying to catch our breath.

FIVE.... FOUR... THREE... TWO...ONE!!!
HAPPY NEW YEAR!!!!!

We hear the crowds in the streets scream welcoming in the new year.

Stone slides his hand underneath me pulling me in closely to him, "Happy New Year." His tongue slips into my mouth, my first ever New Year's kiss.

New Year's Day Part 1

♥

I try my best to pry open my eyes, my head pounds while my mind races a million mile an hour trying to piece together the night before.

Stone and I consumed the entire contents of the mini bar and ordered a bottle of champagne from room service. Its New Years after all.

But the hangover is real.

I think back to the conversation or lack there of with Emily, I can't help but think that there was more to it than what was scratched from the surface.

Did I really just stand there in silence?

Thank god for Stone.

Shit!

Robert invited us for a Scottish inspired New Years Day party, I wasn't aware that it was something people celebrated unless they were continuing the party from the night before.

Grabbing my cell from the bed side table I search google; Scottish New Years

What the hell is a steak pie?

Stone groans softly next to me, "mmm good morning..."

He rubs his temples, thrashing his hand around the bed searching for something.

"Morning," I hand him a bottle of water.

A sigh of relief ripples through his lips before he gulps the entire bottle in one.

He leaves a trail of wet kisses on the small of my back sending shivers up my spine as I swing my legs off the end of the bed.

"Stone...?" I simper nervously, handing him another bottle.

"Eva?" He glugs it quickly knocking himself out of breath.

"What do you wear to a traditional Scottish New Years Day Party?" He throws his head back dramatically, "Argh! I fucking forgot about that!"

He rolls out of the bed, "you coming?" Purring as he heads towards the shower.

I wish we could stay here forever.

He shoves me against the wall of the shower, his hand entangled in my hair as he bites and kisses my throat, intense desire builds deeply between my legs longing to be touched, I slide my hand down to my nook to give my throbbing clit what it wants but Stone grabs my hands, pinning them above my head.

"Not your job." He smirks at me.

Oh that smirk will be the death of me.

He nibbles my bottom lip fervently, "oh fuck Stone." I pant in anticipation.

I need him to be inside me.

He drops to his knees spreading my legs as wide as he can, he wants me stretched.

Stone runs his hands up the inside of my thighs parting my lustrous lips. He delves into me running his tongue inside my folds, teasing my clit between his teeth. "Fuck Stone..." I grip his head pushing him further into my mound, his tongue darts furiously in every direction and try as I might, I can't contain my orgasm. I jut forward expelling my juices, coating his entire face. He throws his head back laughing proudly while I am left panting in ecstasy.

"Mmy t...turn..." I stutter trying to compose myself through flustered breaths, reaching for his cock.

"that one was for free," he nibbles my ear lob, "you'll see me alright tonight." he smacks my backside playfully ushering me to move from the stream of water.

I wrap my arms around him, brushing my face along the freckles on his back.

I love him.

"Eva!" He grabs my quivering hand, "you look amazing. Stop fidgeting!" Stone pins my arms by my side. I take a sharp shuddering inhale of air trying to focus through the nausea that has been fertilising the bile in my gut.

We stand side by side looking in the mirror...I give myself one final look over.

I want to be perfect.

I need it.

I tug at my emerald green silk skirt, my black chiffon blouse which has been tucked in and out a thousand times is bursting at the second button...I guess I've put on a little weight since the last time I wore this.

Stone undoes the button, "a little cleavage never hurt anyone...you're not a nun. Its trendy."

He has always been interested in fashion, his outfits always clean and crisp. Never in your face about it though.

He plants a kiss on my neck.

He stands tall next to me, his dark blue jeans hang perfectly on his strong legs, his white shirt caresses his torso immaculately.

I blush. He is so handsome.

I slip my feet into black stilettos putting a leg onto the chaise lounges at the foot of the bed I spread some Chanel No5 moisturiser onto my bare legs.

I put the other leg up ready to lather it but Stone's hands replace mine and he does it for me instead. Rubbing the excess cream on his neck.

We stand one more time staring at each other, "flawless." He whispers kissing the top of my head.

Stone knocks on the huge varnished townhouse door, offering me an encouraging smile.

"It's going to be okay...but if at any time you want to leave just say the word and we'll go."

I can't say anything, a sharp furious nod is all I can muster.

He squeezes my hand 3 times, "I love you." He hums into my ear softly.

I hear laughter from inside the house, as footsteps get louder as they approach. The door swings open.

Oh fuck.

New Year's Day Part 2

Oh fuck, oh fuck, oh fuck.

I've changed my mind.

Robert answers the door with a huge smile spread cheek to cheek. He sets down a glass of scotch on a side table in the entryway.

"Eva!" He pulls me into an uncomfortably tight embrace, his green checked shirt smells of a musty cologne, expensive no doubt. The grand house is bustling with laughter and commotion.

He cups my face between his hands, "happy new year sweetheart." I blush intensely as he kisses each of my cheeks, and when he finally lets me go I step behind Stone shielding myself for a moment, taking a second to calm from the overwhelmingness of...family?

He pulls Stone into a hug slapping his back enthusiastically, "Aster! Happy new year!" I can't help but laugh internally, I don't think I've ever seen Stone hug any one much less someone he met yesterday.

Stone pulls away smiling awkwardly, "I...uh...call me Stone. Its my middle name." He reaches out shaking Roberts hand.

Why can't I speak? Its like I've forgotten how.

"Em!!" Robert bellows over the loud murmur of conversations happening in various rooms, "Eva's here honey!"

Oh fuck, I want to die. Please let there be an explosion or a sinkhole. Just get me out of this.

Stone slides his coat off and hands it to Roger who is gesturing for me to remove mine. Looks like I'm staying.

Stone helps me out of my coat and passes it to him.

I feel bare, like it was some sort of security blanket. Now every part of me is exposed for the world to gawp at.

Emily walks troublesomely out of the kitchen, "Hello." Her lips part sheepishly, the house falls into an awkward silence as she makes her way towards us.

She holds a large glass of deep red wine in one hand her other rests on her slender hip.

She looks so elegant wearing green checked trousers, the fabric matching Roberts shirt, cute. She has a black chiffon blouse tucked in neatly. Her dark hair scraped high into a bun, she looks like Audrey Hepburn.

She is effortlessly beautiful.

I feel out of place.

Stones eyes burn into me willing me to speak.

If I could I would. But I feel myself shutting down.

I can't do this.

I never thought I'd say this...but I want to go home.

"Happy New Year...Ms uh..." Stone stumbles not wanting to be impolite.

"Mrs, Anderson but Emilys fine." She dips her head.

Wait...do I call her Mrs Anderson, Emily or Mom?

"Happy new year Eva." She forces herself towards me holding me rigidly in an unenthusiastic hug.

"Happy new year Emily." I croak anxiously, the party falls into awkward silence.

I pull away from the embrace, Stone's hand grips mine, squeezing lightly three times.

Emily's brow furrows as she offers me a guilty smile, her eyes flitting around unable to make eye contact with me.

They both lead us into the bustling lounge, I allow my eyes to search the room quickly as I look for anyone remotely resembling grandparents, hoping that maybe mine will be here.

I'm not entirely sure if I've ever met mine from Emily's side, and dads parents died when I was a baby. Maybe things would have been different if I had them.

"Hey guys, this is Eva!" Robert introduces me to a room full of faceless strangers, each one jumping to their feet and pulling me in for a kiss on the cheek and a tight hug.

"This is Stone my uh..." He wraps his arm around my waist, "my boyfriend."

Its his turn to be attacked by hugs and kisses.

He accepts each one, and returns the greetings graciously.

Where has my bad boy gone?

How is he so good at this?

Emily thrusts a glass of champagne into my hand she stands by my side for a moment before I'm passed around and introduced to strangers whose names I can't retain. I smile, nod and say 'thank you', answering their questions about college. I lose sight of Stone, my anchor. My throat begins to tighten as the room overwhelms me.

I neck my glass of champagne in panic and search around of another, unable to locate one so I use this as my excuse to leave the room.

Standing in the hallway I push through ragged panicked breaths my fingertips white as I grip on to the credenza, holding it for support.

My gaze falls on the countless picture frames filled with idyllic family photos, smiles and laughter spilling out of each one. Each one happier than than the next. Emily's happy family.

And there nestled in the back is me.

I must be seven years old, my eyes beaming with delight standing by her side. Emilys arm draped over me as she smiles proudly.

I lift the frame to get a closer look.

"We went strawberry picking that day." The downcast voice from behind startles me, "you ate more on the way round than we put in the basket. Prest...your father was terrified you'd puke in the new car." Emily takes the frame from my hand, wiping a little dust from the glass before placing it back into its place.

"Why can't I remember this day?" I ask, my voice thick with emotion.

She shrugs her shoulders letting out a long sigh, "how long have you and Stone been an item?" Her eyes wander into the kitchen and I unwittingly follow her gaze to see him drinking a scotch with Robert, both deep in conversation.

"Not long, we've been hanging out since last summer." I lie, not wanting to divulge the gritty details with this stranger.

She nods studying my face, "and this." She points to the yellowing bruise under my eyes and my nose, "how did you get this?" I thought I had done a decent job of concealing it, obviously not.

I'm not even sure how to answer the question, but before I can come up with a lie or fabrication I blurt out... "oh this is nothing...I got in the way of a fight between Stone and my..."

"Your father?" She cuts me off.

"My ex." My brows knit together, why would she assume dad had done this?

She stands her eyes glazed over with tears, I actually feel sympathy for her. I take a step towards her, I don't know why but I wanted to comfort her, as I walk closer she steps away from me.

It cracked me open, raw.

"Why are you here Eva?" Her lips pressed together in a thin line, "and I don't mean at this party, I mean why have you come into my life?"

Her words cut me deep, laced with her resentful tone.

"Back." Stone growls deeply sliding himself between us. I hadn't noticed him coming from the kitchen.

Emilys lip curls in disgust, "excuse me?"

Stone brings his eyes to meet hers his chest moving in and out as his breathing intensifies, "you said 'come into my life' and I think you meant 'back' because you were there for some of her life, before you abandoned her and left her with Preston, while you lived an entirely new life here in this shitty city." The sound from the party falls silent as they listen intently.

I watch numbly as Stone pushes her against the wall, "I'm not sure why Eva came here I don't think she even knows, but she is your daughter!" He spits, his body vibrating in anger, "she raised herself and you should be thankful that she did. I wouldn't want her turning into a hateful bitch like you."

His hands grip her shoulders as he slams her body hard against the wall, "enough!" Robert roars pulling Stone away, his fist clenched harshly as he raises his arm ready to meet Stone's face.

My chest tightens, I've seen this before. I know how it ends. I still have the bruises.

"STOP!!!" I scream at the top of my lungs the word scratching my throat, but I can't move.

The colour from the room starts to fade, my legs can barely hold me up.

I clamber my way to the front door racing down the steps onto the empty street, the icy wind howls around my ears and my body rattles uncontrollably.

"Eva wait!" Emily grabs my shoulder spinning me around to face her, "I'm sorry...I've been so harsh. But I'm happy here, and I have to put myself first. You're an adult now, you don't need me. So respectfully please just leave me alone."

I wasn't able to control what came out of my mouth next but as I watched Stone being thrown out of the house by Robert I burst into uncontrollable laughter, "you fucking selfish bitch!" I squeal, "you're right I have everything I need. That doesn't include you. You are such a...such a CUNT!" And by no choice of my own I take my hand a draw it across her cheek, the loud slapping noise echoing through the street.

Stone runs towards me throwing my coat over my shoulder, "you good?" He cups my face studying my expression.

He turns to face Emily who stands with her hand pressed against her scarlet cheek, her eyes hang wide with shock.

I slide my hands into the sleeves of my jacket, "fucking fantastic, lets get the fuck out of here."

Love In An Elevator

Barely a word was uttered between us the entire walk home. Stone wanted to take a cab but I wanted to walk, I could have walked and never stopped. I could have walked until the soles of my shoes were worn thin and the gravel ripped my feet to shreds.

I wonder what happened to the Emily in the photograph, the woman whose arm was so lovingly draped over her daughter. What made her so cruel?

We make it to the hotel it's a little after 8pm I slide off my shoes while we wait on the elevator. My stomach rumbles a little too loudly but I'm too tired to be embarrassed.

"we'll order some room service." Stone leans down to plant a kiss on my shoulder, I nod

The metal doors open slowly, and we heave our emotionally exhausted bodies inside, Stone presses 16 for our floor. The elegantly silent metal box shudders for a second and we move in a smooth motion.

This time Stones stomach growls, "I'm actually really disappointed that we never got to find out what a steak pie was." I whine, twisting my mouth to the side to conceal my smile.

"I'll get Alma to make you one." Stone answers back completely straight faced.

"Stone..."

His face falls into concern, "Mhmm?"

"Fuck me."

I reach up to grab his face pulling him down to meet me, taking his tongue into my mouth as our lips crash together into a bruising kiss. I nibble his lip harshly and he groans sordidly into my mouth. Stone hikes up my skirt pulling my thong to the side he thrusts a finger into my slick slit bringing juices up to my clit and swirls them around, "so fucking wet." He breathes into my ear, as I fumble with his belt ready to release his stiff cock. He brings his mouth to my neck biting firmly on my sweet spot and I feel him springing free, he hooks my legs around his waist pinning me against the wall of the moving elevator, he charges himself inside me my walls grip around him tightly. I run my hands through his hair as he pounds me into the wall. Each thrust hitching my breath, the ecstasy of him grinding me threatening to push me into a quick orgasm, the thrill of the public ride the catalyst that will send me over the edge.

"Fuck Stone...harder please. Fuck me." I pant through delirium; he grins devilishly as he pummels me harder sending a painfully indulgent sharpness shooting inside my throbbing core. A high that I will chase for the rest of my life.

The elevator dings at the 9th floor. "Shut up." Stone whispers harshly as he clamps his hand over my mouth, my climax sitting on the cusp, one motion from his body will expel it from me. I want him still because when I come, I want it to be an explosion as he grinds me into a pulp.

The doors slide open, thankfully there is no one there, he reaches his arm out to press the button to close the door, and before they have sealed he has resumed bashing into my sopping folds.

"You going to come Eva?" He purrs in my ear, his lips brushing the sweet spot just below. He thrusts a hand down between my legs, he pinches my clit between his thumb and index finger while his cock pulses inside me resisting his own climax. His hips jut as I writhe in a carnal pleasure, "hold on..." his voice quivers, "stop moving." He rubs my clit menacingly. I contract my walls around his twitching cock he smashes his lips onto mine, "stop moving," he moans into my mouth. I relish in the thrall of keeping him on the edge, slowly tightening the muscles in me, my orgasm teetering patiently waiting until I've had my fun with him. I glance at the digits above the doors, 14... I take his bottom lip and bite harshly, "fuck Eva...you are everything." He moans into my mouth. I roll my hips against him allowing myself to give over to a cataclysmic orgasm, I feel myself gush down my thighs as I grip like a vice onto him, milking him. A bead of sweat drops off the end of his nose and onto my lips the salty taste of him lingering in my mouth.

"Fuuuuck EVA..." his pelvis convulses as he explodes his load inside me, spilling out the sides and dripping down my inner thighs mixed with my own fluid.

16...

The doors slide open and Stone sets me down on the ground, his hands cup either side of my face our bodies press together as his lips brush mine. I can taste his breath and I am addicted to it.

My phone chimes just as we arrive at our room it's not a number I recognise, Stone's brow furrows shaking his head, "no clue."

"Me either..." shrugging my shoulders, I ignore the call.

But it rings again almost right away, "hello?" I answer politely as Stone nuzzles my neck in the door way, we fall through the door as I listen to the silence on the other end of the, "helloo?" The door closes behind us, and Stone disappears up my skirt swirling digits around my swollen core, "bYYeE then!" I squeak as he presses a thumb against my hyper sensitive clit.

"Its Emily." The downcast voice croaks.

Stone heard it too instantly stopped what he was doing and reappeared.

"Okay..." I gasp in shock.

"Meet me tomorrow, I'll text you the address...give me a chance to...to explain. Please?" She begs pathetically, "just us." Her voice a little commanding.

Shit.

"Okay." I half heartedly agree.

Shit.

Emily

"Are you sure this is a good idea? I don't like this one bit." Stone paces anxiously around the room while I tie the laces on my sneakers. There's a hint of anger in his voice.

My stomach churns and watching him walk a trench into the floor isn't making it any better.

"You should have said 'Fuck you Emily' and hung up," he spits her name like fire.

Of course I would have loved to have told her to fuck off, but I need answers and he doesn't understand that. His family have always been upfront about their feelings towards one another and they have always been there in some way or another, even when they were absent. My mother abandoned me when I was 10 years old, I haven't seen or heard from this woman in a decade, and when my life was falling apart with the only family I had Griffin sent me a life line he gave me the chance to find her.

Last night was a mistake, I should have declined Roberts invitation and asked to meet with her privately, I see this now. Last night was all my fault. Shes giving me a chance to fix things. I need this.

Stone slams his fist down on the dresser causing me to jump, "Fuck it! I'm coming with you."

"No you aren't, Stone, this is about me and my mother. I'll call you when its over." I charge out of the room waiting to hear the door slam behind me, fucking safety doors. I turn to see if it has closed but instead I see Stone standing holding it open, his worrisome eyes burn into me.

"I don't know what to say Eva," he shuffles sheepishly.

I shrug my shoulders, I don't know what the correct etiquette is in this situation either. What possible words of wisdom could he bestow on me

He lets out a defeated breath walking slowly towards me, his brows knitted together the crease between them deepening as tries to force an encouraging smile.

I offer him a soft smirk, "wish me luck I suppose."

He wraps his big arms around me squeezing me tight, "the door just locked behind me didn't it?" sighing heavily.

I nod laughing way harder than I would normally, the nerves taking over me entirely.

"Stupendous." He kicks the door irritated

Emily is already sitting in a booth in the diner, I'd hoped I would have arrived first to let my nerves settle not that it would have made an iota of a difference.

"Hello Eva, thank you for meeting me." Emily sips a coffee as I slide into the seat across from her.

My heart pounds harshly inside my chest I can hear its rapid rhythmic thud echo in my ears. I am conscious of my quick breaths; I do my best to try and slow them but my body won't allow it. It's in panic mode. I am in panic mode.

I clear my throat, "thanks for...um...calling I uh guess." I study her face carefully to see if I left a mark on her cheek, which I didn't. She unwittingly studies mine in return and I remember I forgot to cover my bruises.

We sit in a bone crunchingly awkward silence for a few minutes both waiting for the other to speak, neither one of us having the courage. Just as I think she was about to open her mouth a waitress interrupts refilling her coffee, "Can I getcha anything doll?" I decline politely by shaking my head.

Emily sips her fresh cup uneasily glancing out the window avoiding eye contact with me once again. So I guess I'm going to be the first to speak.

"You said on the phone that you wanted a chance to explain...here's your chance Emily." She winces as her name rolls out of my mouth. Almost as though she's hurt at my monosyllabic manner.

She takes a long deep breath inwards exhaling slowly through her nose as she presses her lips into a harsh line, "Your father and I were high school sweethearts, we fell in love and we got married young. I was only twenty years old when I had you." She picks at her nails nervously spouting old information, "and when I did everything changed and he became controlling but oddly he ignored me unless it suited him to nit-pick about everything. He was so focused on being this image of a perfect family, but he never put in the effort to be one. And one day I couldn't take it anymore, so I left." She looks down at the table, tears glisten in her eyes, "I left you."

She looks up at me shamefully tilting her head to the side, it wasn't until she passed me a napkin that I realised my face was soaked with tears, "was he ever violent with you?" regretting asking the question the instant the words fell out of my mouth.

"God no! He just thought he could be in charge of everything. Making snide remarks about my weight and the food that I ate, who I spoke to in the supermarket, what I wore, watched, listened to. He never laid a hand on me." She gasps suddenly clamping her hand over her mouth, "did he do that to you?" she points to my face, her eyes wide with fear.

"I already explained what happened, he's a drunk but he would never hurt me. Not physically anyway." Shaking my head, not wanting dad to be incriminated for anything more than what he's actually done.

I decide I'm done. I've heard all I needed to.

I am not the victim here, she is. She is the victim of her own bad choices, I was just collateral damage in the war between her and my father. And thats okay.

At least now I can repair what they broke.

"Eva?" Her heavy eyes search mine, "i'm sorry I wasn't able to be your mother." She blows emotion through her lips, as though a weight had been lifted from her.

She needed to say that more than I needed to hear it.

"Its okay." I reach my hand across and squeeze hers reassuringly.

A sympathetic smile creeps across her face, "do you think we could..."

"No." I cut her off, "I think we're done." Drying my eyes on my sleeve I raise myself up from the booth placing myself above her I plant a kiss on her cheek.

"Goodbye, mom."

I turn on my heel and leave the diner, never looking back.

Something inside me felt different. I felt lighter somehow. A small part of me felt bad for dad, what made him the way he was with mom, and me?

Talking with Emily obviously freed her from guilt and it made me feel better too.

Dad had raised me the best he knew how, alone. But someone raised him to be this way. Could I help him? And even if I couldn't help him, talking with him might help me.

I'll have to convince Stone first.

Is this growing up?

The Status Quo

"I didn't expect you to come home, when you left I thought you were gone for good."
Dad gets out of his office chair taking slow solemn steps towards me as I fidget in the
doorway.

Stone sets down my small case, "I'm gonna leave you two to talk. I'll be at Griffins." He
pecks my cheek before leaving.

Dad and I stare at one another for a few moments, he looks different. Its only been a
week but he looks so old.

"Coffee?" A sad smile twitches in the corner of his mouth.

"Sure." We make our way into the kitchen; he lets me go first through the door.

Mechanically I start fidgeting around the kitchen rinsing a single plate and coffee mug
that sit lonely in the sink, I quickly dry them and put them away in their place. I go into
the fridge to get the creamer out for the coffee, and as I close the door my dad is behind
it. Frightening me with his red face. I can't read his expression. I don't know what to do.
I take a step backwards putting the kitchen island between us.

"Dad are you...is everything?" my voice quivers as he walks around my barricade, he
reaches out his arm and I flinch my eyes screwed shut in fear. He flicks the switch on the
coffee machine behind me and it begins to whirr. I open my eyes to see a look of defeat
strewn across his face, "sorry." I whisper guiltily my cheeks flushing.

"I think we need to talk don't we, sweetheart?" even his voice has changed.

What is his game?

He's never called me that. But he is right, we do need to talk.

"I'm sorry for everything Eva, you have every right to me furious with me. I...I..." he
looks down into his mug sadness clouding his eyes, "I had no right to treat you the way I

did, I wish I could blame it on your mother and the alcohol but the that would be weak of me. I just hope one day you can forgive me." his voice breaks and I try my hardest to stop myself from crying, but the tears flood my eyes and when I blink, they fall perpetually soaking my cheeks.

I look into his dark eyes framed with guilt, tears drip from his chin and falter onto the table I watch him wipe his damp drawn in cheeks. The man who tore me down so many times, made me feel less than worthless, reduced to this pathetic shell of a human.

"I do forgive you dad..." he smiles softly at me and his shoulders relax he reaches out his hand for me to hold I take it for a second, "I forgive you." I pull mine back resting it under my chin, "But I will never forget it. You treated me like an asset not a daughter. You cared about nothing except yourself and the little mask you put on for the world to see...and you hid me under there with you. You thought it was okay for Jake to use me and humiliate me, just as long as you looked good. Your daughter dating the big football star was more important than how happy she was." His mouth hangs open, all colour drained from his face.

"Wh...what are you saying Eva?" his voice cracks under the scornful weight of my courage.

I raise myself up from the table.

"What I'm saying, Preston... is that I wish you a nice life, but it will be one without me in it."

I open my purse and slide my platinum credit card across the table to him alongside my key. I gather myself internally and make my way to the stairs lugging my overnight bag up to my room with me.

"Stone Carlisle will never give you what you want Eva...He'll either end up in prison or dead. If you want a rich life Eva...this life, then you are better off here with me." He stands at the bottom of the stairs desperation spitting out like flames.

I feel sorry for him, he doesn't understand. That all I ever wanted was his time, I have never been interested in his money, all I have ever wanted from any one was love and affection.

"I couldn't care less about a 'rich life' dad. I only ever wanted love."

I hold myself together long enough to make it into my room closing the door firmly behind me, I slide down to the floor, choking on muffled sobs. What did I expect? He was never going to be the father I so desperately needed him to be. I should be proud of myself for being so strong, for growing and moving on from him. But here I am crying on my bedroom floor again because of something my dad said. The way his silver tongue could cut me raw, and he never saw it. I wasn't about to let him start now. I pick myself up off the floor, as I have done a million and one times before.

I begin throwing things into my hold-all. Just the basics, clothes, underwear, makeup and jewellery. I stare at the picture frames that sit on my dresser dad and I posing in Cape Verde when we went on vacation, I think I'm about 13 here. Yet it never occurred to me before now that I don't have actual memories of the time we spent there. I know we were there, but I cannot for the life of me recall a single memory.

I lift the almost empty bottle of perfume that sits next to the frame and underneath it, is the cherry stalk that Stone devilishly tied with his tongue, he knew exactly what he was doing to me that day. A smile hides in the corner of my sad mouth remembering how exhilarating it felt to run about in secret with Stone but it is far out weighed by being loved by him. I trace my cupids bow with the stalk recalling what it felt like to wish he would bruise my lips with his, and now I can have them whenever I want

I think back to Thanksgiving and blush at us standing in the kit...

Wait...

Thanksgiving was 5 weeks ago...

Oh fuck no.

"I was about to send out a search party, how'd it go?" Stone takes the bags from my hands and tosses them on to the floor in the entry way, "I cant even tell you how hard it was not going over there..." he looks down at me his eyes searching my face for an answer, "Eva...are you- "

I suppress the ball of bile that sits in my throat, "we need to talk."

Stones brows knit together and he nods ferociously.

I stare blankly ahead as I sit on the edge of his bed, I hear Griffin shuffling around in the room below. Alma knocked the door about 10 minutes ago to let us know that dinner would be at six. I'm certain she knew what was wrong with us she studied our panicked faces, lingering a little longer than she usually would.

"Well...?" Stone snaps at me like its all my fault.

"Well what?" I growl back.

He throws an exasperated hand out towards the box that sits next to me, and I glance down not wanting to look at it for too long because if I cant see it then it isn't there. I can bury my head in the sand and pretend that it does not exist. I'm only 19, I still get excited over a stupid cherry stalk. I'm not ready for this, am I?

Two Minutes

I lock myself in Stones bathroom unravelling the clear plastic wrapper on the pregnancy test. I'm not even surprised it came to this.

"Do you know what to do?" Stone snaps on the other side of the door.

"Its not that difficult Stone, you pee on a stick and wait." I snipe back and place it between my legs as I let my stream wash over it.

Fuck.

I place the little blue cap on the end of the stick and wash my hands, looking at myself in the mirror.

What a mess Eva, you've made such a mess.

This isn't what I want. I haven't even lived my own life yet, I am in no position to bring another into the world. I feel my stomach, turning to the side to push it out I run my hands over. Fuck.

"Let me in." Stone growls as he ferociously wrestles with the door handle trying to force himself in.

I open it slowly; I already know how this is going to go.

Grabbing the test out of my hand he studies it meticulously, "Now what?" his eyes widen with exasperation.

"Now we wait." I sigh, "and in two minutes we'll know." Tears flow down my cheeks. I don't want this.

Stone paces around the bathroom breathing deeply, he doesn't want this either. Who can blame him. He's about to turn 21, we're so young, barely adults. "I guess we'll get married then." He sits on the ground, throwing his head into his hands. I'm almost convinced I heard him sob.

"Stone...I don't want to get married. I'm only nineteen." Its not that I don't love him, but I'm not one hundred percent sure of us. I mean look at me, look at the bruises around my eyes. I've just let the only family I had go... I am about to start a life on my own, albeit I have Stone, but for how long? How long until he finds himself bored of me; the thrill of the chase gone. How long until the novelty of me wears off. When I'm fat and tired and have puke in my hair. Will he still love me then? Will I love me? Because I'm not even sure I love myself now.

"You think I want this Eva? How the fuck could you let this happen!" He throws his hands in the air, getting to his feet he charges towards me.

His face burns with anger as he towers above me, "Oh my god Stone, you really think that I wanted this? You think that I done this all on my own. Are you fucking dense?" I seethe back, my entire body shaking with rage.

We're just a couple of kids, we lived this sham of a relationship on a whim. Now we're about to bring an innocent child into this reckless life.

"I'm not giving up Harvard. I'm almost done." He leans over the sink splashing some cold water on his face, "You'll have to stay here with Griffin. Alma will help raise it." He takes some water and swirls it around his mouth.

He's right. The man never has to give anything up, I'll sacrifice my body, my mind and now my life for this little being inside of me. I'll do it all, and he'll come home on the weekends. Its simple, Eva is gone.

I blow away the continuous stream of tears that fall onto my lips, "What about me?" I sniffle trying to make my words clear, "When do I get to do what I want?" the image of my dreams slowly disappearing. Realistically I wouldn't have had one any way. I ran away from dad's money. The only way I was going to be able to achieve anything and I stupidly gave it back. So maybe this is what happens when you cut your nose off to spite your face, you get given a little lifeline, but it comes with conditions. You can live with luxury, and you can have a family and safety, but you can't have dreams or aspirations.

"You'll be taken care of, what more could you want Eva? When you make mistakes like this you must accept the consequences."

Why is this only my fault?

"You did this too Stone." I whimper, watching him slowly leave me. The way he used to look at me disappearing with each passing second.

He scoffs nodding his head in agreement.

I look at the stick that sits on the cistern, nausea washes over me and I vomit into the toilet. Stone doesn't move, not a muscle. He stares at the stick. The reality of our situation now at the fore front of our minds. The relationship faltering before us.

I hand him the pregnancy test, "its negative."

"Its negative." he repeats, relieved.

I gather myself, leaving Stone staring at the stick in the bathroom.

He follows me into the bedroom watching me slip on my coat and shoes, leaning against the door frame, using it as a crutch to stop his defeated body from crumbling.

"What now?" he asks sheepishly.

"Goodbye, Stone."

This time I leave, too afraid to look back.

It's Been Seven Years

Its been a long hard seven years. If it hadn't been for the kindness of Griffin I don't think I'd have achieved anything. I attended and graduated Juilliard despite the crippling fear of running into my mother, which incidentally never happened the entire time I lived in the city. A few years ago Griffin asked me if my father could contact me, and of course I said yes. After everything he is still my father, although I have only saw him twice in the three years we have reconciled. I suspect my father paid Griffin back for Juilliard, he is too proud not to.

I haven't seen or heard from Stone since the pregnancy scare. When I left, I left for good. I hear he is doing well...still spending Griffin's money; but he graduated Harvard and went into journalism, so at least he has income of his own. I don't hold any hard feelings over him, we were so young, too young in fact, and too dumb to understand love.

The curtain closes the applause of the audience drifts to hustling as they leave the theatre. I can't help but breathe a sigh of relief, six weeks of back-to-back shows done. Being the leading lady on an off Broadway show that has taken New York by storm is exhausting. Its not that I'm ungrateful for the opportunity, but I am dead on my feet. Now its time for my vacation. Autumn in Massachusetts, before winter auditions start.

"Miss Miller," My assistant Lacey hands me a bunch of roses, "These came again." She smirks, a childish giggle erupting from her lips.

I love Lacey, she has been my saving grace. I really hope my next assistant will be as adorably naïve and patient as she has been, because I'm ashamed to admit I've been a tyrant, all work and no play. No time for fun.

I shake my head, "Lacey, they are from my dad." They are always from my dad. He has sent a bunch of roses every night for the last six weeks. My apartment is overflowing with them. But its nice that he thinks of me. I think of him, I'll pop in and see him on my way through.

Lacey dances around excitedly, "That's not why I'm laughing! There's a man here Miss Miller."

"I told you twelve weeks ago on the first day of rehearsal call me Eva." I peak out of the gap in the curtain. There is no one in the seats, just a few stragglers waiting to exit the theatre, "there is no one there Lacey, did he give a name?"

She nods ferociously, "Yeah and he's really cute."

"Lace, the suspense is killing me..." Maybe it is time for a little fun. Lacey rummages through her pockets searching for something.

"He was really tall, he had dark hair and blue eyes...he uh...shit...he was maybe the same age as you," She opens scraps of paper shaking her head and tossing them on the ground, "Maybe a little older, thirty maybe."

OH MY GOD! She has never once been this disorganised and usually I am not one to snap but fucking hell the anticipation is taking over me.

"Lacey!" I yell, blushing as my fellow actors quieten down and their eyes burn into me.

"I have it! Sorry I have it...uhh a Mr Chapman...Mr Jake Chapman." My face must have drained of all colour the minute she said his name a cold and uncomfortable sweat took over my body. My legs become heavy and weak, I stumble from side to side shakily. Someone thrusts a chair underneath my body and forced me to sit down.

I can hear the drone of voices around me but it's like I am stuck under water, gasping for breath as my chest tightens, my throat closing over.

Why is *he* here? I can't breathe.

What does he want?

Is he going to try and sabotage my career? Oh god I'm going to vomit.

Why is my nose wet, I lift my heavy hand up to my face and wipe away a trickle of blood. Some one, I think it was Lacey tilts my head back and pinches my nose at the top.

"Give her some room!" Joseph the director barges through pushing everyone back.

A familiar figure lingers behind him.

He's here.

"That was very theatrical Eva, pun intended." He hands me a bottle of water examining my dressing room.

I'm completely dumbfounded. What is happening. Its been so long since we saw each other, no contact whatsoever and the way we left things, it felt final.

So it begs the question, "What are you doing here, Stone?"

He sits on my dressing table that infuriating famous smirk spread across his face, "I was in town, thought I'd check out the famous play Griffin keeps banging on about." He picks up my bra that hangs on the chair beside him swinging it around.

"Real mature," I grab it from him, "and you thought it would be what...funny to use Jake's name?" I ask coldly folding my arms across my chest, trying to hold myself together.

"Relax, it was a joke. Don't get so fucking pissy about it." He scoffs playing with the bottle of perfume that sits on top of my bag.

I honestly thought I had let it all go and I'm not sure if it's the panic of thinking that Jake had followed me, or if its Stone being here but I'm transported back and I'm nineteen all over again. The wounds reopened and weeping. My heart uncovered and vulnerable as he simpers at me through his ocean eyes.

I spent the last seven years throwing myself into work and school trying my best to distract myself from the pain of missing him, I was so deep in trying to forget that I ended up doing just that. Unprepared for the moment when we would meet again, naively thinking that it would never happen. Innocently neglecting reality, all the searing torture brought back to the surface.

His eyes burn into me and I can do nothing but stare back, biting the inside of my cheek as my chest moves deeply up and down. He steps towards me, and I step back, he takes another and as I try to avoid him, I trip over my dressing rail falling backwards into the costumes. Of course, he catches me with one swoop. Pulling me tightly into his chest, his musky scent filling my nose as I will myself to fight against him, but I can't. When it comes to Stone, I'm weak. His nose brushes my ear, I can hear his shuddered breaths exposing his own vulnerabilities. He inhales slowly lacing my neck with his lips as he brings his mouth up feathering his tongue along my jaw, I can't move. I'm useless as the desire builds inside me stronger than the will to fight him. It's been seven years. What now?

Envelope

"Tell me you want this..." Stone breathes into my ear the tickle of his lips excites me as they brush against my skin and electrify my every nerve. His fingers slow dancing along my hip, he snakes his arms around me ready to lift my body onto him as soon as he has permission.

"...I...I...can't," I whimper, trying my best to be strong, going over the reasons why we broke up and why I can't give in and fall back into his arms. Coming up empty.

He traces my lips with his tongue, lingering for the approval that I wish I couldn't give him, but I'm so incredibly feeble that I foolishly allow my lips to part. He takes this as consent and slips his tongue into my mouth, massaging mine gently at first picking up the pace with each passing moment. How is it that he can taste exactly the same, he's the drug I didn't know I was reliant on, the thing I didn't know I craved until I had it in my grasp again.

"Fuck Stone," I moan feverishly, his hand slowly moves up my inner thigh his thumb grazing my moistening underwear. He continues to bruise my lips with his, his breath like sweet nectar, I inhale him like life support. Joining his kiss, as I melt into him. I can feel his stiffness built inside his jeans pressing against my hip begging for release, I turn myself around leaning my head back onto Stones shoulder, he feathers his lips along mine, pulling down the loose strap exposing my breast, sliding his hand into my underwear parting my slick slit with his thick finger I let out a sordid moan. I hadn't realised how much I longed to feel the touch of a man, especially this one. One hand works on my opening relishing in my sopping core and the other manipulates my nipple. He brings juices up to my clit swirling them around deliciously, the ecstasy of my orgasm sitting on the cusp of expulsion.

"I've missed your wet fucking pussy, Eva." He growls in my ear as his fingers thrash around me, "I need to be inside you." He begins fumbling with his trousers, I hike up my skirt as he bends me over my dressing table, thrusting his solid length into me. His hand rests on my shoulder gripping gently for support I reach for his hand and bring it to my throat forcing him to apply pressure, while I run my fingers around my decadently drenched slit feeling him pulsating inside me as I reach down further into my nook.

"Fuck me hard Stone," my hoarse voice begging to be pummelled viciously, his throbbing penis stretching me wide and with each vigorous pound his head brushes against my g spot and I can't contain the squeal of sinful moans that escape my lips. My legs shudder under the weight of my cataclysmic orgasm threatening to erupt but I try my best to hold back, not wanting the thrill of this to end. Stone lifts my leg onto the chair next to me spreading my core wide and tight, I see in the reflection of the mirror his eyes rolling in the back of his head, "I'm going to come Eva," he hammers deeply, harder than he ever has before. I can't hold onto my climax any longer and as my walls contract around him a gush of juices forces his cock out of my core, and he expels himself all over me, my skin swimming in a coat of our mixed juices.

My legs are numb, and I collapse face first onto the dresser, barely holding myself up, my anatomy glistening, exposed to the world, but I am too exhausted to care.

Stone cleans himself up with a tissue and tucks himself back into his pants. I decide its time to move, and I turn myself round facing him once again. His all-consuming eyes ardently searching my face for something. I am surprised he's still here.

"Eva Miller." He sneers over my name his eyes eagerly looking over my body as he bites his bottom lip.

Why did I let him fuck me? I am so weak. I should have chased him out of here. He reaches into his back pocket, handing me an envelope with my name beautifully scrawled across the thick, embossed cream paper. "What's this?" I say aloud as I open it. It's an invitation to Griffin's 80th birthday, which so happens to be when I'm in town. Of course, I'll go how could I not after everything he has done for me.

"Thank you, tell him I'll be there." a smile corners my lips.

"Good, see you then." Stone grabs his coat from the stand and without so much as a look back, he leaves me.

I clean myself up the evidence of us running down my inner thighs, aching as I move around the dressing room gathering my things to leave.

"Miss Miller?" Lacey knocks the door blushingly.

"Come in Lace," I shout out, smiling awkwardly as she enters my pit of despair.

She throws herself onto my body wrapping her weepy arms around my neck, I cannot help but be self consciously aware of the smell of sex that fills the room, can she smell it? Can she tell that something wretched has just finished in here?

"Are you okay Miss Miller?" I watch as the tears build in her eyes, nostalgically jealous of her youth.

I nod, "Totally fine." I lie, "just a little dehydrated I think." In more ways than one.

Lacey's tears tumble down her face as I hand her an envelope stuffed with cash, a bonus for putting up with my tyranny. I try my best to act normal, but less than 3 minutes ago I was being bent over the very desk that Lacey has just rested her hand on.

"Please consider me as your assistant in any future projects Miss Miller, it's been a pleasure to work for you. I'll miss you so much!" she wipes away snot and tears.

I find it hard to focus on anything other than what has just happened with Stone, I am still trying to process it.

"This has been my dream job," she continues while I zone out, I nod every so often.

"Of course, Lacey. But only if you call me Eva." I pull her in for a hug, and over her shoulder I see Stones signature paisley patterned scarf peeking out from under the clothes rail.

Growing Up

"Well, if it isn't the biggest brightest star in New York City! To what do we owe the pleasure?" Roger bounces towards me grinning like a cheshire cat he pulls me in for the warmest hug, and suddenly I feel at home.

Returning his wide grin I set myself down on one of the stools at the counter, "I had a craving for the best lemonade in Massachusetts, and I wanted to see my old friend." I pat the back of his hand looking at the jolly man who took a chance on me when I felt at my lowest. His once thick mop of dark brown hair now speckled with flicks of grey and white matching his bushy beard.

I love it here.

"How long you in town for Eva?" Roger asks as he slides over the chilled bottle, "glass?"

I wave my hand reaching for a straw from the glass cylinder on the counter, "mmmm..." my eyes roll into the back of my head as the flavour zings around my mouth, "just a few weeks before winter auditions start, I thought I'd swing by before going to visit my dad. My gaze falls on the jar of cherries that sit neatly next to the register, suddenly my mind is dominated by memories of Stone's lips brushing the palm of my hand as he placed the stalk there with his mouth, hearing the clatter of stools when he tried to choke out Jake, God...sometimes I wish I'd had let him. This little place that I love so much, teaming with the memories of my angsty adolescence.

"Eva?" Roger clears his throat grabbing my attention.

I offer him an apologetic smile my cheeks flushed with embarrassment at my momentary lapse, "sorry Roger, you were saying?"

"I only asked if you were staying at your fathers?" His eyebrow arches, he's concerned. Of course, he is.

It's a small town, word got around about the catastrophe that was Christmas. The Falconers, Chapmans and Millers are well known and highly thought of families in town, it was a great scandal. Roger and I always kept in contact, he and his wife Sophie even came out to Manhattan to see a matinee performance, in some ways he was more of a father to me than Preston.

I shake my head trying to disguise the dull ache that's now spreading through my body, "I'm gonna book in at the motel—"

"Absolutely not...you are staying with us and I wont hear another word about it!!" Roger cuts me off, taking the spare key off his bunch.

It was so lovely of him...to have someone actually want me was like Tylenol for the soul.

It took some convincing, and a little white lie but I managed to decline his offer. I've gotten so used to being alone, it sometimes hurts more to be surrounded by people. I'm not even sure who the real me is any more. I paint on so many faces to disguise myself, using the camouflage as protection, I truly believe I've lost sight of who I am.

There isn't much to talk about with dad, not that we ever had much of a relationship but it's worse now, it's almost derelict. There's not much left to salvage

"I uh...I wondered if you had a partner?" Dad shuffles around the kitchen nervously trying to make small talk as he fills out two glasses of red wine.

I was a little disappointed to see that he was still drinking.

Shaking my head as I stifle a pathetic laugh, "no... definitely not. Too busy!" I gulp the wine as flashbacks of Stone bore their way into my mind.

"What about you dad...have you met anyone?" I regret the question as soon as it left my mouth. He'd only ever had one girlfriend that I recall and after she met me it fizzled out.

His mouth corners into a smile, "As a matter of fact..."

Oh fuck.

"I have, you know Alma? Griffins housekeeper." He blushes into his glass of red.

NO! Shit a brick. My mouth hangs open my eyes gaping wide.

"No way! Alma? Seriously. Alma? Alma. Alma?"

I choke on my wine trying not to picture them together.

Dads eyes scrunch together obviously dissatisfied with my reaction, "are you quite fucking finished?" He snaps defensively.

"I'm sorry," I look across at him sheepishly, but a part of me was happy that he was able to display some emotion towards me even if it was brash.

He puts his hands up releasing himself from the strain of awkwardness.

He tells me they've been dating for a few months, and I'm the first person he's told. They don't go out much, they enjoy cooking together and watching movies. It's nice to hear that he has someone, and that he has the ability to feel something for someone.

I wonder what that's like, I haven't had a connection with anyone for seven years. It's lonely trying to keep yourself busy.

Before I know it, it's midnight and we've drank two bottles of red wine, we laughed about the few good memories we have and glossed over the shit. I can't dredge it up anymore. I've had to try and let it go. Holding the grudge is back breaking, being so angry all the time as wore me down to the quick. But we both know it will never be normal, whatever that is.

"Fuck!" Realising that I haven't called ahead to the motel I pull out my cell and dial the number, "Hi I'm looking to book a room...around five nights?...from tonight...oh I see...well okay...I'll see you tomorrow...take care."

Shit. I slam my cell on the table.

"Eva, your room is exactly the way you left it. You are more than welcome to stay here for as long as you need." Dad gets up and rinses the glasses in the sink.

"It's just for tonight, thank you.

He wasn't lying, it was exactly the way I left it. Its a little stuffy so I make my way to the window struggling at first to slide it open but when it finally does, I can't stop myself from looking out to the Falconer mansion, its lights twinkling in the distance.

I brush my teeth ridding my mouth of the bitter red wine taste, heading to my drawers to see if I left some pyjamas. Running my hand over the smooth wood. How can an inanimate piece of furniture hold so many feelings? Like the emotions are engrained into the fibres.

My pinkie finger brushes against something out of place, the cherry stalk, dried and frail. I lift it carefully gently tracing the outline of my lips, it's not as soft as it once was, but it stirs the same feelings. I place it back on the dresser, I could never part with it. The little token of emotion, the match that started our fire.

I choke on a little sob as I look at myself in the mirror. I don't even recognise her anymore. Little lines have formed in the corners of my eyes, when I close them, I see my younger self dancing around the room.

I remember the first time Stone startled me by sitting on my window sill, how I protested that he shouldn't have been there, but it would have devastated me if he left, and of course the bitter sting of tears when he did. Because he always left. I never actually had him. He always belonged to himself, and that was okay. I just wish I could have been as strong. I would have let him do anything to me.

I open my eyes tears forming in corners threatening with all their might to cascade down my cheeks. This room representing so much sadness, but there was also more love felt in this room than most experience in a lifetime. At least I was lucky to have loved. And he loved me back, in his own way he loved me too. Just not enough.

The wind outside my window howls, blowing the drapes around ferociously I turn around from the dresser to go over and close it.

I wasn't even startled by him, I half expected it.

"Hello you." He purrs from the sill.

We're Adults Now

♥

"Well, if it isn't Massachusetts favourite fuck boy." I lean over him closing the window the cold air creating a draft which in turn is causing my bedroom door to rattle irritatingly.

Stone's mouth hangs open, "fuck boy? Ouch!" He clutches his chest dramatically.

"How was the climb?" I point to the trellis smirking at the beads of sweat formed on his brow.

He runs his hands through his hair which is neatly slicked back, "why'd you ask?" He arches that damn eyebrow.

"Well, you're an old man now...is it still as easy as before?" I turn my back on him scrunching my eyes shut trying to push him away, I need him and that's the problem. I've had a taste and now I'm an addict again. Addicted to the pain he leaves behind. I steal myself, ready for the inevitable disappointment of his absence. I inhale deeply and turn on my heel almost pirouetting around, falling clumsily into his familiar chest and he catches me, like he always does... or did. I miss this version of him, of us. What is it about this bedroom that turns us back into teenagers? My fingers grip his chiselled torso smoothing over the contours of his adult body, different but somehow the same.

"Will you be at the party tomorrow?" hHt stirring heat inside me, I wish I could resist him, but he comes in here with his face and his bad boy attitude, and I need him. Just one more taste.

He slides his hand into the waistband of my shorts, my heart races rapidly and I try to slow my breathing, we've danced this dance a thousand times. I try to be stronger than my craving. His fingers feather themselves into my moistening slit, "Please don't." I quiver.

He chuckles, "You want this Eva, you're already wet."

I roll my head back and he attaches his lips to my neck biting firmly, I wish I had control over the primal moan that escaped me, but it took me by surprise. Stone delves two fingers deep inside my folds relishing in my weakness as my legs shake, he brings juices up to my engorged clit, working them furiously around, my back arching pushing me deeper into him. He walks me backwards towards the dresser, pulling out his hand from inside me and lifts me up placing me on the wood, in one quick motion he removes my shorts, peppering his tongue from my inner thighs down to my ankles. Kneeling before me, he lifts my legs planting my feet firmly on the dresser my core spread wide glistening in the harsh bedroom light. The vulnerability starts to take over me, but I think I like it. I enjoy him looking at me like this.

Slowly reaching up wrapping his hands around my seat pulling me closer, he dives into me immediately sucking my pearled clit, the euphoric sensation sends me thrusting backwards knocking my head on the wall behind me.

"Fuck Stone..." I breathe out as he glides his tongue ferociously around never coming up for air, and just as I am about to cum my core twitching around his mouth, he halts. Standing he begins fumbling around with his belt, he smirks as I pant for breath at the delayed gratification, my own fingers dancing around instinctively wanting to finish myself off. He swats them away, "Stop it."

He releases his cock lustrous and unyielding; he grabs my hips plunging himself deep inside me forgetting himself for a second, he lets out a sordid moan and his eyes roll in the back of his head. He pulls me from the dresser, and I wrap my legs around him, never parting. His arms snake around me holding tightly as I grind myself on him, he intertwines his fingers in my hair pulling my face down to meet his, bruising my lips with an intimate kiss. "Stone...I'm coming." I squeak trying to hold back.

"Come for me Eva," He drapes me onto the bed cupping my face between his hands, his brow furrows as he pulses deep inside me he presses his forehead onto mine, when he pulls back something behind his eyes changes. I gasp for air as I ride the high of my orgasm, Stone simultaneously lets go of his spend inside me, his breaths are deep and vicious as he pulls himself out.

He lies next to me a tear sits in the outer corner of his eye, one small movement away from spilling down the side of his cheek, almost mistaken for a bead of sweat. Inhaling sharply, he wipes it before it falters.

"I uh...I'll see you tomorrow." He makes his way to the window, his ocean eyes looking down evading mine.

"Just go out the front door Stone, we're adults now." I hold open my bedroom door flicking my head to the side gesturing him to leave. I scoff as he gathers himself.

He sighs defeatedly, "I'm...I'm...s...sorry." Walking sheepishly down the stairs.

"Fuck off Stone." I mumbled through strengthened tears, he's never apologised to me before, so why the sudden change of heart. I let him do this to me, hell I even enjoyed it. I used him as much as he used me. I knew what he was, and I knew he couldn't give me the perfect life, so I let him destroy me instead. I am as much to blame as him. I should be the one apologising. Why did I ever think this was love?

Such stupid fucking kids.

Alma opens the door to greet me, "Eva! Your father told me he told you, I'm so happy the cats finally out of the bag." She gushes nervously, taking my coat and purse as she shows me into the unchanged familiar Falconer mansion. Alma's hands shake as she begins to show me into the noisy lounge, "Alma..." I whisper comfortingly, "I'm so happy for you both." I force a smile, unsure who I am trying to calm more.

She nods returning my smile leading me through the grand door, Griffin jumps up from his chair clapping as he beams at me. I love this man. He is everything I could have wanted in a grandparent; warm and wise.

"Eva!" he pulls me into a loving embrace squeezing me a little too tightly, "I'm so glad you're here!"

I look around the room as the Carlisle/Falconers exchange a glance of unmistakable invidiousness with one another, "no one else got that kind of welcome." Meg, Stone's cousin grumbles into her mother's ear.

"Well the prodigal grand daughter has returned." Angela walks towards me arm stretched handing me a glass of champagne, wearing the same smug smile that her son sports all too often. Speaking of, I look around the room for Stone, finding him sitting silently in the corner of the room nursing a glass of scotch in one hand, his chin resting on the other. The sparkle of blue darkened in his eyes. He doesn't even leave the chair to greet me. He acknowledges me with a scathing nod as he downs his scotch in one.

I am sandwiched between the arm of the sofa and Meg, who absolutely reeks of weed. She disappears outside every so often, with her boyfriend Lucas, who is the most tolerable out the two. He sits on his cell phone barely looking up and as the conversations spiral around the room, while I try my best to keep up, smiling and nodding along. I am thankful to be sat next to the champagne bucket, topping my glass up before its even empty. Stone hasn't looked at me, not once. I try my best to keep my eyes away from him but it's near impossible, treating me like this has left me feeling empty. Something is missing, and I need this hole gone. I need him to have me or leave me.

I excuse myself and head into the bathroom, staring at myself in the mirror, incoherently swaying, reminding myself to slow down on the champagne. Waiting on the coveted knock, the cynical symmetry of that nostalgic Christmas Day playfulness overshadowed by the bitter silence. But the knock never comes. We really are adults now.

I open the door to leave, stumbling out I crash into his familiar chest, he glances around for witnesses before forcing me back in. Stone drives his lips onto mine harshly our teeth clashing.

"What the fuck are you doing, you ignore me all afternoon and now you wanna shove me in here and kiss me?" I grit through my teeth keeping my voice hushed not wanting to cause a scene.

"Shut up and kiss me back Eva. Kiss me back." He lunges forward violently pressing his lips to mine, my tongue parting his lips as we breathe each other in feverishly, he lifts me onto the sink snaking his hands up my thighs under my skirt running a finger around the elastic of my underwear stopping when he reaches my opening. He slides the lace to the side grinning smugly at my wetness, he reaches into his pocket bringing out a little clear bag filled with a white substance, with the finger he had resting on my clit he dips into the bag his eyes meeting mine, I am frozen with shock. He latches his mouth to mine again, rubbing the cocaine onto my bundle of nerves, passionately working it around with my juices. The sting of the obscene mixture of emotions causing me to moan lewdly, Stone clamps his free hand across my mouth. Laughing explicitly. He dips the tip of his tongue into the powder, sinking down to my gushing folds he flicks my clit with his powdered tongue, I am unable to control myself and I expel myself coating his face.

Taking a second to breath and process what just happened I am awash with shame.

I kick him away angrily, "What game are you playing Stone?" He wipes his face with the back of his sleeve, making me grimace in disgust. "You weren't complaining three seconds ago were you Eva?" He shoves me out of the way pouring the cocaine onto the edge of the sink, pulling a pre rolled 50 dollar bill out and begins snorting.

"Fucking hell Stone," I suppress the bile and disappointment bubbling like acid in my stomach.

He looks up at me his an arrogant smile cornered as he offers the bill to me.

Not a chance in hell. No way. My heart shatters. Is he really so broken that he has resorted to this, can I fix him? If I leave him here alone will it be something more, is this the gateway to his demise?

"Why Stone?"

"Why not Eva?"

As I leave the bathroom trying my best not to tear up but Alma steps in front of me, a freshly opened bottle of Moët in one hand and a tissue in the other. I grab both and take my seat back in the lounge and drop the bottle into the empty bucket.

"Just in time Eva," Richard takes my hand pulling me back to my feet, there's someone here you should meet. I push my tongue around my mouth trying to stave the desperate sob that sits in the back of my throat, Richard pushes me in front of a tall brunette, she was thin and effortlessly beautiful her skin was strikingly sun-kissed.

"Louisa, this is Eva Miller. Griffin's favourite grand child." Angela throws her head back in laughter, the family all join in cackling at the inside joke.

"I'm sorry, I'm confused...I thought Meg was the only grand daughter." Louisa offers her hand out and I take hold shaking it pathetically.

"Ignore them, Eva grew up in the house across the lawn." Stone groans pushing me to the side taking place beside her, "They are jealous because Griffin likes her better than all of us."

"Can you blame me? Eva is the only one who writes." Griffin pecks me lightly on the cheek.

I don't understand, what is happening right now?

"Louisa is Stone's fiancée, Eva." Christine, Megs mother smirks grabbing Louisa's hand and shoving her perfectly polished nails in my face, the large square diamond decorating her to perfection. And as Stone wraps his arm around her waist I am unable to hold onto the bile any longer, throwing up onto the ice that has just been freshly replaced.

The Scarf

I race out onto the patio inhaling deeply as the pain constricts around my heart choking it to death, clutching my chest as I gasp through my laboured breathing trying to stave the pained sobs. I want to wail, scream, shout but the only thing I can do is sob. How could he have done this to us, both of us.

Louisa...

engaged?

To be married...

All while Stone had me in my dressing room, my bedroom and just now in the family bathroom. Why?

I hate him, more than anything in the world, I despise him. After everything that's happened in the past, this is the worst, and it has come from the one person I loved the most. I never thought he could hurt me like this...except...I think I did.

That poor woman, she stood there so proudly with her fucking perfect hand thrust in my face. She was as clueless as me. I stood there like a deer in the headlights, frozen. Mortified.

Heartbroken.

"Are...are you...you, okay?" Meg's uninterested voice comes from behind me, her face exposed by the heat of a cigarette.

I needed to be alone, but of course Griffin would send someone to check on me. But why did I think it would be Stone? Why did I hope?

"I'm f...f...fine, Meg." I snatch the cigarette out of her hand, hesitantly putting it to my lips. Exhaling sharply before I take a long drag of the disgusting stick. It burns my throat, and I remember why I never took up the habit as I cough and splutter expelling my guts onto the slabbed patio.

She raises her eyebrow in dispute, "Sure." She scoffs walking back into the party.

"When?" I call after her looking for answers, that truthfully, I'm not sure I need to know.

Meg turns slowly sighing sympathetically as her head tilts to the side, "We met Louisa," she grimaces apologetically as I wince at her name, "We um met her at Easter, they met in Panama in January. Stone was covering some story over there, she worked as a receptionist at the hotel he was staying at...they started dating right away. They got engaged in New York on top of the Empire State building in August."

The everlasting stream of tears engrain their salt on my cheeks, searing themselves like a brand. Another tattoo of pain left by him.

"Wh...when in August, Meg?" she shuffles her shoulders, contorting her face baffled.

"I don't see what difference it makes-"

"When Meg?!" I yell out indignantly desperate for more answers.

She pulls out her cell phone frantically scrolling through social media, "The second...it was the second of August." She slowly turns the cell around showing me a picture of them standing together, Louisa's face, streamed with blissful tears, Stones infamous smirk lingering behind her. His scarf, the very one I have stuffed in my purse draped around them both shielding them from the breeze.

I gasp clamping my hand over my mouth, my legs give way and I falter to the damp patio floor. "Eva?" Meg rushes over eyes wide with concern, as she reaches out to pull me from the ground.

"Tell them...tell them I've gone home...that I drank too much champagne and I'm sick. I'm sorry Meg but I have to leave." A fragmented laugh forces itself out through strangled sobs, "I can't be here," I blow tears and snot from my lips "tell G...Griffin that I'm sorry. I'll make it up to him." I scramble to my feet trying my best to gather myself, steading my shaking legs before descending the slippery stone steps, stumbling onto the gravel tripping as I rush off across the estate trying to get away, determined to be anywhere but here. Running blindly over the disappearing ground, my shoes sink into the damp grass.

Fuck this.

I kick them off.

All the while the tears perpetually run down my face.

I make it to the tree, the one that marked the border from him to me, throwing myself on it, gripping it for support the bark burying its way under my nails, the pleasurable sting relieving my heart of the deep-rooted throb that threatens to rip me apart. I close my eyes wishing to wake up from this nightmare...cursing the day we spoke. Clawing my skin.

The lake glistens in the moonlight, the water calmly rippling in the soft wind. The tears have run out, I am emotionally dehydrated. There's nothing left of me. What the hell did I do to deserve this?

Edging closer to the water the tide nips my toes like sharp needles, I step in closing my eyes tightly, inhaling deeply as the water threatens to sweep me away.

Please...take me away.

Get him away from me.

I rid myself of my clothes, exposed to the moonlight I crouch down into the water. Involuntary breaths fighting against the bitter cold as I fully submerge myself in the water. My lungs fight against me, traitorous organs. I come to the surface running my hands over my face, cleansing myself of him.

As I lay back floating in the calmness of the current, being comforted by the rhythmic sway of water, it was short lived...

"Eva!" Stone wades his way through the water, struggling to part the water as he comes to wreck my peace once more.

Dragging me from my moment of tranquility he pulls me to the shore.

He takes off his coat wrapping it around me pulling me deep into his chest trying to warm me, but I'm not cold.

"Are you out of your fucking mind?! I...I thought you were fucking dead." He bends over trying to catch his breath, I try not to focus on his words. All I hear is the sound of the water falling onto the pebbled shore.

Stone lifts my coat from the ground and places it around my shoulders, I can't even look at him.

"I brought your purse; Alma couldn't find you." The wind picks up the inevitable chill in the air blows leaves around us, he wraps his arms around his body protecting his own warmth.

I open my purse and pull out his scarf, I press it to my nose inhaling it deeply like I have so many times before, "You left this in my dressing room, I've had it since my last performance, y'know when you came to see me in New York. The very same night you asked another woman to marry you." I thrust it into his hands.

"I'm sorry," he sighs closing his eyes regretfully.

I shake my head in disbelief, "You made me the other woman Stone, that poor girl..." I can't even say her name, "You don't deserve her. You don't deserve anyone. I... I truly, and honestly wish I had never laid eyes on you Stone. I wish I could wake up and be eighteen again and have the strength to walk away from you. Because I'd rather have lived an isolated existence than ever have known you! You ruin everything. Everything you touch desiccates." He reaches his hand out to touch my face, "No!" I slap it away, "I hate you Aster Stone Carlisle. I fucking despise you."

"Eva, p...p...please," he stutters pathetically, this time its his face soaked with tears. Reduced to a crumbling mess.

"Forget you know me, forget you know my name." I grab my things, tossing his coat at his feet.

I want nothing from him.

I leave him at the side of the lake, taking one last look at the man who ripped the beating heart from my chest and made me watch as it faltered.

I prepared myself for the consumption of heartbreak, as I walked away that night, I readied myself for the unescapable vortex of misery and despair.

Two months... I'll allow myself two months.

But as it turned out there wasn't time for hopelessness.

Because life had already begun preparing another barricade for me to push through...

The Hurdle

Alma and I take turns caring for dad, the cancer has spread quickly throughout his entire body, he wasn't even given a fighting chance. The diagnoses was fairly quick, I suppose it helps when you have really good insurance and you can afford the best doctors but unfortunately money and science can only carry you so far. That's the thing about cancer, it's classless. It doesn't discriminate. So now all we can do is make him comfortable.

I stand leaning against the door frame of his bedroom watching as Alma snuggles in beside him most likely watching Great British Bake Off, they laugh together ignoring the beeping of the machine that keeps dad hydrated and the other one clicking as it administers his medication. I wish they had more time.

Griffin visits on a Wednesday and reads pages from the financial section in The Times, dad loves it. I must admit I do too, once a week a snippet from the paper will be slid under my door with open auditions circled on it, but I promised myself I would use what little time we have left with dad to rebuild our relationship, if this has shown us anything it's that family is everything and he's all I have.

It's been 4 months since Griffin's birthday party, and it seems that for once Stone done as he was told, he's forgotten me. I just wish I could forget him, but instead I find myself listening intently to conversations between Griffin and Alma to see if there is any indication that they have wed, I search every news paper looking for wedding announcements but so far there has been nothing, there is no doubt in my mind that I will find out soon enough, the prestigious affair will be thrust under my nose.

"Good afternoon my sweet girl," Griffin leans down kissing me sweetly on the cheek a newspaper tucked under his arm just like any normal Wednesday, but something is different about him today as he shuffles into to the kitchen instead of heading straight upstairs.

"Before I read to your father I thought we might talk. About Stone..."

Oh shit.

I grip the marble countertop harshly, trying to steady myself. I wasn't prepared for it... hearing his name. It made my heart stop.

I sigh deeply, "Mhmm."

"I know he hurt you, and while I don't condone what he has done to you, he has himself, been suffering too. Stone's been a shell of the man we used to know. He has thrown himself into work, he doesn't visit. He...uh...he doesn't call me like he used to..." his once powerful voice cracks under the emotion stirring something inside of me.

"What do you expect me to do, Griffin?"

He gets up from his chair wiping his lone tear away on a crisp white handkerchief, "I will never fully understand what happened between you but if you could find it in your heart to forgive-"

"No." I slam my fist down on the marble, "You don't get to ask me to do that Griffin, I love you but no. He doesn't deserve my forgiveness, what he has done to me, to Louisa, its inexcusable!" I throw my hands up in exasperation, he glances at the floor avoiding eye contact, "Are they still together Griffin?" I try to stave the desperation in my voice.

He shuffles himself off the seat and heads towards the stairs, I guess that's my answer.

"He may not deserve forgiveness, but he needs it." He presses his lips into a sorrowful thin line, dipping his head he disappears to dad's room.

Alma appears from the living room having heard the entire conversation, she places her hand gently on my shoulder giving it a reassuring light squeeze before pulling me into an embrace, "what about what I needed?" I whimper into her body.

"I know," she shushes me swaying my defeated body, "I know."

"Eva," Dad's voice croaks startling me, I must have dosed off. I slide off the windowsill panicked, rushing to his side, I start fussing with the machines making sure they are still doing their job. His hand reaches out grabbing my wrist, "stop...its okay. I want to talk." He smiles gently sliding himself across the bed to make space for me to sit.

My heart thuds deeply, what is happening?

"Do you need some water?" I pass him his cup my hand on his back supporting him as he leans forward to drink through the straw. I can feel every bump and curve in his spine as the cancer eats its way through his flesh and organs.

He points to the newspaper that rests next to the jug of water, "Hand me that will you?"

He opens a page up in the back, "There's an audition in New York tomorrow, and I think it would be perfect for you." Red circles are spread across the page, he lifts his pen tapping one of them repeatedly.

I had always assumed it was Griffin that had been posting snippets under my door, but it was dad and Alma all along.

"Oh great, I'll think about it." Every part of me wants to, is desperate to but I can't leave him.

"Go...get the train tomorrow morning, you'll be home by evening...Alma will be here." I can hear the frustration in his voice, "I don't want you to give up on your dreams because of me Eva, I've already done so much to hurt you. Don't do it for me though, do it for yourself."

This is his way of apologising, of making amends. I have to grant him at least that, even though I forgave him a long time ago.

"Okay." I simper, swallowing the painful lump swelling in my throat.

He shoots forward in excitement, "Really? You'll go!?" he laughs clapping his hands breathlessly.

"Alright sick note, lie back." I push him back onto his pillows, a wash of colour hides behind the peakiness of his illness.

I'll go, and not just because it will make him happy but because it will make me happy too. And after my conversation with Griffin this afternoon, I need to do something for me.

"Alma!!" he shouts from the bed banging his cup on the tray making as much racket as possible.

Alma comes bounding into the bedroom with the same panicked look on her face that I had, when her eyes fall on him sitting with a smile spread from ear to ear, she bends over doubled in two trying to catch her breath. I know exactly how she is feeling but I can't help myself and join laughing with dad. The laughter wasn't soft, it was hearty side-splitting hysterics, the kind thats aches your ribs. The angrier Alma gets the harder we laugh, her nostrils flare as she starts fussing with the machines but hidden in her scorn is a smile, it doesn't take her long to join in.

"Eva is going to the audition..." dad nods happily, Alma spins throwing her arms around me.

"that's wonderful," she cups my face between her hands, "I'll drive you."

"No, you have to be here for dad. I'll get the train."

We all bob our heads in agreement.

The Audition

I stand on the stage, the harsh theatre lights bringing my vulnerabilities to the surface. Sweat building on my brow as I try to steady my breathing. Thankfully the director knew me from my previous show, but that doesn't guarantee me the part. It doesn't make it any easier, because they have higher expectations of 'experienced' performers.

"Ready when you are Miss Miller." The director calls through his mic.

I dip my head respectfully; I can do this.

I hand my sheet music to the pianist; he tilts his head smiling. He likes this song. Leaning into his ear, "ritardando please."

"like this?" he tickles the keys of the grand piano softly, the immediate sound of the melody calming me.

I smile softly at him, "perfect."

The director and others around him share an admiring glance between them.

Inhaling deeply I allow myself to be taken over by the music, my anxious mind emptying the theatre, its just me and the music.

"Someone to hold you too close,
Someone to hurt you too deep,
Some one to sit in your chair
And ruin your sleep

Someone to need you too much,
Someone to know you too well,
Someone to pull you up short

To put you through hell."

It wasn't until I was finished that I felt the anguish in my throat, my face soaked with tears, that I realised how truly lost I was in the song. I can tell by the pain that all my training went out of the window, I sang from the soul but more than likely it wasn't my best performance. When the lights are dimmed the director is wiping away his own tears, the pianist hands me my sheet music his eyes blood shot from emotion, but his head bobs and the smile cornered in his mouth is somewhat ambiguous.

Fuck. No one has said a single word. Was it good, bad, or worse? Are they just so happy its over?

"Eva?" the director calls, and I walk to the edge the stage rolling and unrolling my sheet music, "may I call you Eva?"

"Of course sir," my mouth twitches anxiously.

He looks down at his notes, "Trained in Juilliard," he mumbles.

Oh fuck, I bet he's thinking 'Trained in Juilliard, and just butchered one of the most influential songs in Broadway history.'

"Eva, why did you choose this song?" He sits back down resting his hand on his chin.

My legs shudder underneath me, I was not prepared to be asked questions about song choice. Usually you audition and then the director shouts 'NEXT!'. Its all very degrading. I inhale sharply trying to fabricate an answer that he will want to hear, "please sit Miss Miller." The assistant points to the edge of the stage, and I set myself down dangling my legs over the edge.

"The song Eva...what does it mean to you?"

I hadn't thought about it, I had never given it an analysis. I just love it.

So I tell them that, "I have always loved the song as a child, but now that I'm older I understand it. I feel it deeper."

"you understand the true meaning of it?" He asks gently.

"I do sir, but with all due respect the idea of music is that its open to your own interpretation." He nods along and the pianists mouth twitches again.

"You didn't perform the song in the traditional sense... so what was your interpretation. What did your character feel?" he scribbles on his page.

An inadvertent gasp surprises its way out of my mouth as I try to fight back a sob.

"I guess she is begging for love, I guess I'm admitting that I know love and relationships are hard and that I will accept being hurt because its part and parcel of love, but I want it in spite of that. Being alive is only worth it if you have someone to be alive with." Tears build in my eyes again and I fight my hardest to stop them falling, not wanting to cause myself any more embarrassment.

"Who or what were you thinking of during your performance?"

"I wasn't," I lie, "I just got lost in it all, but if I had to guess I'd say my father, at this moment he's at the forefront of my my mind." He nods acknowledging my situation, it's all there in black and white. The reason I've been having a career break.

"Miss Miller, thank you for your time. We'll be in touch." He smiles waving his hand signalling the next hopeful aspiring star.

I gather myself walking from the stage.

"one last thing Eva," he calls after me alarming the young girl who has taken my place on the stage, I turn on my heel and face him once again.

"whomever you were really singing about, doesn't deserve to hurt you like they have. But I for one am glad that they did. That was most honest and raw adaptations of that song I have ever in my 32 years of theatre had the pleasure of enjoying."

I can't say a single thing. I look at the pianist who nods in complete agreement.

I knew there and then that I didn't get the part. I put too much of myself and my emotion into it, it wasn't what they were looking for, but the praise was like the key to unlocking my cell of despair.

As I exit the theatre my cell pings;

I hear you're in NYC.

Can you meet for lunch?

Word travels fast, my happiness was short lived.

"Please sit down," Angela Carlisle's harsh mouth twitches into an oily smile, "How did your audition go?" she asks dryly as she sits in her chair, ordering two glasses of chardonnay from the waiter.

These fucking people and their fucking games...never in my life will I trust another Carlisle.

"What do you want Angela," I fold my arms preparing myself for the next bout of bullshit, is she here to plead for forgiveness for her dear son? I didn't even think she cared that much about us to fight for it.

She smiles at the waiter as he sets down our glasses, she takes a huge gulp. Hold on, is she nervous? I let my glass sit untouched as she finishes her, I enjoy watching her squirm.

Which in reality is extensively petty of me, but I don't care.

"He can't marry her Eva." She blurts.

"Are you fucking kidding me right now Angela?" a spark of rage is ignited in my veins and suddenly my blood burns as I get up to leave.

She holds her hands up apologetically, "Hear me out Eva, please." Her hand gestures to my empty seat, and I reluctantly sit back down.

"She is not the one for him, they aren't in love. Well maybe she is but Stone certainly is not." As much as I hate to admit, hearing that he is about to trap himself miserably is difficult to swallow. However, I feel sorrier for Louisa because she thinks he loves her and that is worse, and I would know.

I heave a heavy sigh as she tries to burden me with her dysfunctional family shit.

"Angela, no offence but this has nothing to do with me. Stone and I weren't together very long, and we broke up seven years ago. I really can't help."

"Cut the shit Eva." She snaps across the table trying to keep her voice as hushed as possible so as not to cause a scene, "The whole family knows you were sneaking around together behind Louisa's back."

Before she can even finish speaking, I lean in across the table not caring whether the others can hear us or not, "No...you cut the fucking shit Angela. I didn't know a single thing about Louisa until Griffin's party. I was fucking ambushed by you and your husband yet again. What your son did to me and that poor woman was deplorable. But coming here and asking me to break up their engagement is worse." I didn't mean to go on a rant but I couldn't help myself. Angela Carlisle brought out a part of my personality I didn't know existed.

"I'll pay you." She mumbles low enough just for me to hear.

"You'll pay me, to end your son's engagement?"

She nods, "I'll pay a lot."

"Oh my god, you really are deluded! I can't with this fucking family." I throw my hands in the air.

Angela stands up abruptly inching herself into my face her finger pointed right at me, "Listen you little shit, none of this would be happening if it weren't for you."

I swat her hand away and she sits back down in her chair, "Are you scared in case the whole thing ends in an expensive divorce and—"

Her expression doesn't change, she stares blankly at me.

"Oh my god...thats it isn't it? You're not worried about your sons happiness. All you care about is having to part with your millions. Wow! Mother of the year." I slide on my coat and bag preparing to leave.

"I'm trying to do you a favour in the process." Angela finally opens her mouth, "don't think for a minute that we don't know."

"Know what?"

"That you're in love with him."

I roll my eyes, "Fuck you Angela." I scoff as I exit the restaurant.

I walk to Grand Central Station but what Angela said replays in my mind like a broken record, skipping over the same part again and again. Is he really miserable? Hell mend him if he is because I can't save him. I can't fix him. He's not my problem any more.

"That you're in love with him." The way she spat those words, how can you be in love with evil?

He's not evil I take that back...he's just...he's not a good guy.

Except sometimes he is.

Fuck.

Somehow I end up taking a wrong turn, perhaps its muscle memory because here I am outside my old apartment where I spent so many nights on the fire escape running lines. Probably the happiest I've been was the time I spent in that tiny little shitty place, because I was alone.

The nostalgia sparks a smile and breathe deeply trying to hold onto that feeling, and head back off in the direction of the station. Admittedly I could have rode the subway, but I needed to walk to clear my head.

As I approach the station I see them, Stone and Louisa. Her arm looped in his, shes laughing her perfect white teeth gleaming as she throws her head back. Stone looks as though he is in a trance, his face stoic, not reacting to a single thing she is saying.

I try to duck my self amongst the busy people in front of me, doing my best to conceal myself from them. I need to stay out of sight.

"Is that Eva?" I hear her thick accent over the hustle and bustle, the way she says my name makes me want to throw myself in front of a bus...

Stone pushes his way through the crowd calling my name, "Eva! What are you doing here?"

Oh what fresh hell is this?

Can't I catch a fucking break?

See...this what happens when I leave the house.

I shuffle my feet sheepishly, "Hi. I had an audition. I'm heading home now." Why did I tell them that?

Stone dips his head trying to make eye contact with me, but I can't look at him. So I do the next painful thing and look at her instead.

"We're going to Griffins, I have my car I'll give you a ride." He puts his hand on my back trying to turn me around in the direction they are going.

"No thank you. I have my ticket." I shrug him off trying to writhe myself away from his touch.

"We were just in the city picking out some things for the wedding, its very stressful." Louisa giggles as she flicks her hair behind her shoulder, she looks down at me, "Oh my god! I love your shoes!" She kneels down to get a better look. Stones brow furrows as he tilts his head and I allow our eyes to meet.

"Are you still taking drugs?" I blurt out nastily only loud enough for Stone to hear, the corner of his mouth turns up and he shakes his head, "No." He mouths.

Louisa stands back up abruptly after fussing over my feet, "Are you sure we can't give you a ride? It just seems so silly that we are all going to the same place."

"No thank you, I like to ride the train." I bow my head respectfully and ready myself to walk away.

"I'll see you tonight?" Stone grabs my wrist, I pull it away quickly and walk away from him leaving him standing obstructing the flow of traffic as bodies nudge and shove him.

Time And Regret

Why does this damn train have to move so slow? I swear its going backwards. Music blares through my headphones but I can't even concentrate on the melodies that play, Stones face lingers in my mind, his voice resounding in my ears, 'I'll see you tonight.' Why did he have to say that? I didn't sound like a threat, but my heart felt it that way.

Fuck him and his beautiful fiancée.

I drum my fingers repetitively on the table in front of me, I must be irritating the man sitting across from me as he sighs heavily, rolling his eyes in disgust. He groans audibly causing some of the other passengers to glance in my direction.

"Look dude," I lean over the table menacingly, "if I could stop I would, alright!" I yell, a little too loudly.

It was the truth though, if I had the ability to stop myself from being this anxious over the fear that Stone Carlisle had once again planted in my head, damn right I would. But I don't because I am useless when it comes to him.

The man raises his eyebrows at me waiting for me to finish, I throw my arms up exasperated. He raises off his seat grabbing his baggage and trudges off down the carriage to find another seat. Passengers whisper intently to one another about the crazy table tapping lady.

After what felt like a thousand hours the train pulls into my station, I race off hoping to find Alma waiting on me, but she's late.

FUCK!!

My heart thumping deeply in my chest the audible boom pounding in my ears I decide that I can't hang about here, standing still is making me feel worse. I need to walk; I need to go somewhere. I can't be here alone with my thoughts. I leave the station car park and head west towards the town, spotting in the distance the café light flickering. So, I make my way to Roger's, hoping that he'll be around, he's always good at advice and in general just good at listening. You can bare your entire soul and when you are finished you have all the answers without him having to even say a word.

Just as I get to the door, I remember to text Alma;

At Café meet me outside.

Slipping my cell back into my pocket I reach for the handle ready to head inside,

"Eva...what are you doing here?" a chilling voice sends shivers down my spine, I turn slowly to see Jake Chapman towering above me, my throat dries up and suddenly I'm paralysed with fear. He simpers softly pushing the door to the café open, holding it waiting for me to go inside, inside with him.

"J...J...Jake." I stutter trying to compose myself, of course it was Jake. Who else was it going to be? Just when I thought this day couldn't get any worse.

"Hi Roger, just two bottles of lemonade and a slice of cherry pie please to go please." Jake leans against the counter his sheepish gaze falling on my idle face, I don't even know how to emote anymore. This day has been too much, and now this... now Jake.

"The wife still giving you grief there Jakey boy?" Roger slides a paper bag over to him, "Eva darlin' I didn't notice you there. What can I getcha?" His eyes flitting between us suspiciously as he rings up the register.

"Hey Roger, nothing for me thanks. Just waiting on Alma." My tired legs can't hold me up any longer and I sit on one of the stools and pull out my cell praying for a reply, but its empty.

Wait... "wife?"

"You caught that huh?" Jake laughs nervously tugging at his dark green jacket.

"Listen Eva, I owe you an apology... and I know that I don't deserve your forgiveness, but after having my daughter I realised the way I treated you was...inexplicable. It was awful, and...and well I just wanted to say I'm sorry."

I never thought about what would happen if I ever ran into Jake again so it never gave me a chance imagine scenarios in my head, not that they would have been any use, because realistically who actually reads from a script when the inevitable moment does arise? So here I am like a deer in the headlights unprepared.

I nod, because it's all I can do. I have nothing left in me.

"Okay." Is all I can manage.

I check my cell again, just to try and stave off the awkwardness. Jake grabs the bag from the counter and heads to the door hesitating for a second, "Do you need a ride, Eva?"

I shudder as a cold rush of air blow through, "I uhh...no I don't think...no. Maybe...I don't know."

I know I should have said no, but I need to get home and nail my window shut. Alma hasn't text me back...I am shit out of options.

Roger grabs my wrist, "If you hang around for an hour or so I can drive ya." His touch on my wrist almost brings me back into the moment, it gets me out of my over thinking brain and allows me a clearer mind to make more fucking stupid decisions.

"I'll be okay," I pat the back of his hand and get up from the stool, "Jake!" I call after him, "Can I get a ride to the border of the estate?"

We walk suffocated by awkward silence to his truck, I am still unable to pinpoint my feelings. It's almost as though I have no control of my body or emotions, like I'm some sort of pre-programmed machine.

Just as I'm about to place my foot on the step of Jakes truck a hand grabs my shoulder, "What the fuck are you doing?" Stone pulls me down from the step causing me to stumble grazing my knee on the gravel.

"Carlisle." Jakes voice quivers in fear as he holds his hands up in protest. Stone growls at him as he lifts me off the ground, "Get your fucking hands off me!" I seethe through my teeth, shoving him away from me as I stand dusting myself down.

"Eva, you aren't answering your calls." Stone grabs my bag searching through it holding it high as I jump around trying to grab it from him.

Jake reluctantly steps forward sighing as he prepares himself to get involved, "Stone, give it back. I was only giving Eva a ride." he shuffles his feet nervously.

I stop jumping as Stone pulls out my cell rolling his eyes defeatedly, "I don't answer *your* calls Stone, you know that. Now fuck off!"

His face changes, and I stare for a minute trying to work out what emotion his face is expressing.

"Stone?" My heart falls into my stomach, "What is it?"

His mouth pouts in sadness, his eyes full of pain.

"Your cell is on flight mode." He hands it over to me, "We've been trying to call you, Griffin and Alma..."

I start fumbling around with settings, my breathing speeding up frantically, "I put it on flight mode when I went for lunch with your moth-" He tilts his head furrowing his brow.

When my phone connects back to the network messages and missed calls start flooding in.

"Stone...wh...is...what is all th-this?" I scroll through the messages, listening to half voicemails of sad panicked voices.

His mouth sort of twitches as he forces back a sob, "I'll take you home." He reaches out his hand to grab mine I pull it back turning around to make sense of the numerous texts.

"Eva, please." Placing both his hands on my shoulders he turns me around, the telling break in his voice shattering my heart. It was the deep sadness surrounding my name that gave it away. Because I couldn't read the messages, they were so unbelievably cryptic and the well of tears that blurred my vision made it impossible to see, so once again I had to rely on him.

"Tell me Stone... please." My body convulses as bile threatens to heave itself from my guts.

"He's gone Eva, I'm sorry." A sharp breath ripples out of his mouth blowing a stream of tears off his lips, "I'm sorry." He repeats, pulling my limp body into his chest.

"This is your fault." I whisper into his torso, staining his powder blue shirt with my mascara, "Its all your fault," I slap his chest with the palm of my hand, balling it into a fist I bang him again, this time harder and repetitively "It's all your fault!!"

He stands taking every anguished punch supporting my devastated body with his arms.

I look up at him, his bottom lip quivering as he looks down, "We had more time Stone, we were supposed to have more time."

He smooths away a strand of hair from my face, "I know, but it was his time."

"But I wanted more time, I needed more time. We were just getting to know each other." Stone leads me to his car, holding open the door as I slide into the passenger seat.

"He's in there sweetheart." Alma stands outside dad's bedroom door and wraps her arms around me. I shrug her off, I don't want anyone to touch me.

I hesitate for a moment before going into his room. Wrestling with the thought of regret.

He was so happy this morning before I left for my audition, we sang together the first time I ever heard him sing. I always assumed I got my talent from Emily, but it was him all along. Wouldn't it be nice to have this as my last image? Will I regret seeing his body?

We needed more time.

But when they commit him to the ground, when it is too late to change my mind will I regret not looking at him one last time?

I wanted more time.

"You don't have to do anything you don't want to do." Stone slides his hand inside mine, and instinctively I pull it away gripping the door handle. I turn the knob slowly and push myself into the bedroom, for a moment it was to get away from him, but once I was in, I realised it was because I needed to see my dad one last time. To thank him for the last few months. To forgive him fully for our past, and to free myself from the vice of pain that I held deeply in my chest for countless years.

I try to smile through shuddered breaths, tears eternally falling down my face, his body lies peacefully on his bed. A small whimsical smile etched on his thin lips. I smooth his dark grey hair into a side shed and press my lips onto his cool forehead, wiping my faltered tears off his sunken cheek.

He's gone.

I turn to exit the room; intrusive weepy faces are gathered outside. Alma sobs onto Griffin's shoulder, a nurse rubs her back. Stone has his back to me, I didn't mean to, but I walk right to him and press my face into it, he turns around inside my embrace and pulls me tighter.

"I don't have a dad anymore." I gasp.

Stones big arms hold me at the top of the landing, supporting my weight as my knees give way, I cry in breathtaking sobs. I can feel his chest twitch as he cries with me.

"Lets give her some time Stone." Louisa tries her best to pull us apart, "Lets go."

Stone clears his throat, "I think I'll stay a little longer, you go." He grunts.

I hadn't realised she was here.

"Just go." I allow her to break us, turning away from them I am met with Griffin who gently puts his hand on my face rubbing my damp cheek with his thumb, a solemn simper hidden in the corner of his mouth.

"I'll come by tomorrow, I'm sorry my sweet girl."

Once everyone has left Alma and I sit with him waiting until the coroner comes.

We sit in silence, weeping every so often in broken sorrow.

Alma never lets go of his hand.

They deserved more time.

I Don't Want it

A faint tapping on the kitchen bi fold door startles me, I set down my mug of tea and pull up the blind to find Stone standing sheepishly on the other side of the glass. We stare at each other for a second as my hand lingers on the lock trying to make the decision, not knowing who to listen to...my head or my heart. Useless because, both are saying, 'Pull down the blind and walk away'.

I unlock the door and slide it open for him, I have been making a lot of mistakes lately and this is only another one to add to the long list.

He drags in a blast of cold air with him causing my body to shudder underneath the wave of anxiety that presses down firmly on my chest. I am numb from the sadness, I allowed myself a final expulsion of sobs when the coroner wheeled dads body out of the front door. I promised myself that I wouldn't cry anymore. I'm just so tired.

He places his hand on my cheek and I lean into it, remembering the smell of his skin, longing for it.

I wish we could go back to before, before all the lies and deception. When it was just us, teenagers sneaking around.

"I saw the kitchen light on, I wanted to check on you." His thumb runs softly over my cheek, I cover his hand with mine. I know I shouldn't have but I couldn't help it, his touch was so comforting.

"You broke my heart." I whisper, Stone drops his hand from my cheek and stuffs it into his pocket letting out a sharp sigh as he stares past me guiltily avoiding eye contact.

I don't know why I said it, it wasn't like he didn't already know. I made myself very clear, but the words were out before I even thought about them.

"I don't think this is the right time to get into all this Eva, I just think-" he doesn't finish, instead he just looks at me. His ocean eyes burning into me, the familiar look. I know what's about to happen and I don't have the strength to stop it.

But the dramatic lunge never came, he didn't run to me. He stood frozen in front of me.

"You should go, Stone. Go back to your fiancée." I simper sadly, unable to form her name in my mouth, not that any of this is her fault, but I just can't.

He doesn't fight for me, and with a simple nod he walks to the door, I follow behind him to lock up as he leaves, but before he disappears into the darkness, he turns in a swift motion leaning into me cupping my face between his hands attaching his lips to mine. I inhale his breath like I need it to go on living, and the tears that I had begged to stop well in my eyes slowly trickling down my cheeks once more. Betraying my wishes.

I pull away remembering our situation, trying to be rational about my exposed vulnerability in the moment. Stone presses his lips against my forehead, and I lose myself in him again wrapping my arms around his waist soothed by his rhythmic breathing.

He breaks our moment silently and slips through the door, "Stone!" I call after him trying to keep my voice hushed, "If you invite me to that wedding, I will set your house on fire."

"Please don't Eva..." Stones pained eyes brought forward by the contrast of the darkness behind him and the light of the kitchen in front.

"Don't...s-set your house on fire?" I scoff.

He shakes his head defeated, "Don't hate me."

"I don't have the strength to hate you, Stone," I answer immediately almost as though the answer was prepared.

He takes a slow small step towards me, his mouth twitches his unspoken words hanging in the air swirling us around in a vortex of torment.

"You're exhausted...try and get some sleep, I'll come by in the morning." He dips his head and disappears into the vast darkness the twinkling lights of the Falconer mansion guiding him away.

I lie groggily staring at the ceiling, my entire body aching, I feel useless, run down. Like I could close my eyes and sleep forever. Except I didn't get any sleep, not one hour. Alma couldn't bring herself to sleep in dad's room, so she spent the night cleaning every inch of the house and between the ferocious scrubbing and sobbing I didn't manage to shut an eye. I sat on the sofa staring into the sadness, when I offered to help with the cleaning she ushered me out of the room.

I take a quick shower and get dressed, sweats thats all I can bring myself to wear. Its not like I'm going anywhere.

I can't believe he's gone, and I wasn't here. My mind was so consumed by Stone, as usual. I am irrevocably stuck within his thrall, and he doesn't even know it.

When I finally emerge from my room I hear the familiar voices of Stone, Griffin and Alma coming from dads study. I make my way down to find them seated with Jason Wiseman, dads attorney.

Its too soon.

He hasn't been dead twenty-four hours yet. Why do we have to deal with this now.

Griffin sets me down while Stone stands awkwardly in the corner avoiding eye contact with me.

Mr Wiseman opens a embossed envelope breaking the wax seal on the back, "in Prestons final days we talked and worked closely with one another on his last will and testament. He wanted to ensure all his affairs were in order, and he wanted it done quickly. As soon as he passed." He bows his head respectfully at me.

Even dead he had to be in complete control of everything.

"Lets get right to it shall we..." he offers me a kind smile, I can't help but feel overwhelmed he must have sensed it, Griffin taps my shoulder reassuringly.

"We can leave if it would make you more comfortable Eva."

I snap my head round, "No! Please don't go." I grab his hand and hold it on my shoulder.

Griffin chuckles softly, "okay my darling, we'll stay."

Wiseman reads everything off of the thick cream paper, and if I am completely honest I zoned out. I didn't need to hear it. I don't care, I'd give it all back just to have another twenty-four hours with him, we were just getting to know one another. We were becoming friends.

"Does every one have a clear understanding? I mean its pretty simple, Preston didn't want it complicated. Miss Miller, do you have any questions?" He asks as he preemptively closes his expensive briefcase.

I shake my head, "Can someone dumb it down for me?" I look at Stone, worry written across his face, "Can you explain what I have to do?"

He walks over and kneels in front of me taking my hands in his, a comforting smile forces itself across his lips, "You don't have to do anything, he left everything to you. Alma has been taken care of." You glance at her and she nods sadly, her face permanently blotched.

"I don't want it." I blurt out in a haze of tears.

Stone holds my face, "What?"

"I don't want any of it, I don't even want to be here. Give it all to Alma." I turn to her, "Please take it all, I don't need it and you deserve so much more."

I wake up on the sofa at dusk, how did I get here?

Sitting myself up I look across at Stone sleeping on the armchair, "Hi sweetie." Alma whispers softly from behind me.

"What happened?" I try to clear my throat but my voice is hoarse, and when I swallow it feels like shards of glass are scraping the inside, Alma hands me two white pills and a glass of water.

"You passed out, I think you were just so overwhelmed by everything. How do you feel?" She places her hand on my forehead wincing at the touch, "You have a fever, take off the blanket for now."

I nod doing as I'm told, I get up and drape the shawl over Stone.

I wish I didn't do it, but I kiss him on the lips as he breathes heavily in his deep sleep. It was an instinctive action that I had no control over, like my lips had muscle memory.

"You two always did have something special." Alma pulls me away settling me back onto the sofa.

"I always wondered what his life would have been if it weren't for you." She brushes my hair behind my ears.

"Alma?"

"Mhmm."

"I meant what I said, I don't want any of it. You deserve to have it all. I have enough." I finish sipping my water unable to take my eyes off Stone.

Alma smiles gently as she watches me watch him, "I'm not going to do that Eva, that is your dads legacy and he left it for you, he worked hard for you."

She pushes me back slowly lying me back forcing me to sleep, "I don't want to be alone any more, Alma." I whimper.

My eyes force themselves shut.

"You wont be." A voice echoes in my ears.

Could It Get Any Worse Than This?

"Whats that smell?" My nose twitches as I saunter into the kitchen spotting Alma at the sink washing out the coffee pot.

She points to the medicine on the counter, "For your throat, drink the honey and lemon tea too."

I turn around to the kitchen table ready to take my usual seat by the bi fold door, where I would secretly look out across the estate to the Falconer mansion. Why is she here?

I lose all strength in my hands and drop my mug onto the tiled floor, the cup and its contents obliterating everywhere.

"Good morning Eva! I brought you some fresh cinnamon buns from the adorable cafe in town."

I scramble to the floor picking up the broken pieces, "Eva! You are sick, get up! I'll clean this mess away in no time!" Alma rushes over helping me off of the ground. I sit shamefully across from Louisa.

"You're sick? Thats so funny...so is Stone. He has tonsillitis or something." She slides over the box of baked goods opening the lid offering me one.

I decline with a wave of my hand, Alma clears her throat, "No thank you, Louisa, I don't feel like eating."

I fixate my gaze on her perfectly manicured hand.

Her large brown eyes bore into my soul forcing me into a vice of guilt.

"Me either, not with the wedding so close. I can't risk not fitting into my dress!" She giggles as she snaps the box closed moving it to the side of the table.

We sit uncomfortably for a few moments, Alma fusses in and out of the kitchen answering phone calls and generally just trying to keep herself busy.

"Were you and Stone always close?" Louisa blurts out the question all nonchalant.

Fuck.

How do I answer this?

"We uhm...w-we were uhm..." I struggle to find the words. Do I lie or tell her the truth? Do I tell her that he is a cheating scumbag? What do I do here...help!

He's been so different these last few days, but doesn't he always do this?

What he did was inexcusable right? RIGHT?!

She reaches across the table and takes hold of my hand, "I know its very scary losing a parent but you will always have us, Stone and I...you are like a sister to him. Therefore you are almost like my sister in law."

Gross.

I wish I could have corrected her, I wasn't a sister to him we were lovers. We were in love. Anyone with a brain could see that.

Now I'm ripping her apart and thats not fair, its not her fault she didn't ask for any of this.

I have to let it go.

Just as I'm about to say, "Sure sounds great!" Alma interrupts us, "I'm sorry Louisa, we have an appointment at the funeral parlour. Will you please excuse us."

Thank fuck for Alma.

"Alma...do I have to be here?" I shuffle around the funeral directors office, "just tell me where and when I don't need to know the rest." I can't hear it any more.

Its painful enough that he's gone, but having to be constantly reminded in all the little details its too much. I can't do it any more.

Alma exchanges worried glances with undertaker, "sure...do you want to wait in the car?" She asks cautiously.

I shake my head, "I'm gonna walk. I need the fresh air."

"But your sick, honey." She gets up from her seat.

"I feel much better, I'm going to grab some lemonade and walk."

Alma nods acceptingly and I leave the parlour turning left onto the main street.

"Hello you."

I spin frantically on my heel to face the voice behind me, Stone.

"Oh, hi." I look down at his hands, holding a pharmacy bag.

He lifts it up, "Antibiotics, I have tonsillitis apparently."

I gulp painfully swallowing what feels like a million tiny needles, great.

"And here I thought your immune system would have been ironclad." I raise my eyebrow smirking at his offended expression.

"When's the funeral?" He asks softly, a sad smile hanging on by a thread.

"Friday, I thought I'd have more time." Stones eyes widen and his cheeks flush.

I start to panic, do I have something on my face? I wipe my nose incase theres dried snot stuck to the end.

Then I realise, I look like shit. He's shocked with how awful I look, and he's figured out the math. I'm sick, I kissed him when he was asleep and now he's sick. He knows.

But something in his eyes tells me that its not that either, "I uh...my uh..." he stutters nervously.

"Spit it out, Stone." I spit at him.

He sighs heavily the blue sparkle in his eye falters, "I'm getting married on Friday."

"Don't." I gasp, trying my best to think before I speak. Which has evidently become impossible these last few days.

Stone steps backwards away from me, "Don't what?"

I bend over trying to catch my breath, my already shattered heart slicing away at the cavity of my chest walls.

"Don't marry her." Is what I wanted to say, but instead what I managed to squeak out was, "Don't worry about it."

I blow away my tears as I power walk across the street away from him, "Eva!" He calls my name and despite attempting to use all my strength to keep going I stop and turn back to look at him. He jogs towards me crossing the busy road, not bothering to look where he is going.

"Eva, tell me you don't want me to marry her. Say the words and its off, its done." His mouth presses into a thin line as his eyes search mine for an answer.

Of course I don't want him to marry her! He's a Harvard graduate for crying out loud, how can he be so fucking dense?

"That's the thing Stone, if you don't want to marry her then don't! I shouldn't need to be your excuse," I sniffle back my emotion, "It's your life."

He lunges towards me crashing his lips to mine for a second I give in allowing myself to melt into him, "Stop!" I push him away, "You can't keep cheating on your fiancee, it's not right."

I brush him off trying to shake my hand free from his, "You're right." He pulls away from me sheepishly.

"Goodbye, Eva." He storms off down the street fumbling around with the keys to his BMW.

Three Times, Four Times

"Alma! Alma!" I run around the house frantically shouting her name, somehow the house seems larger, no matter how fast I move my legs I don't seem to be getting anywhere, feeling like I'm wading through tar.

When I stop to take a breath panting through the foggy feverish headache thats brewing, I hear her soft sobs coming from dads room, I must have missed her before because there she is, sat on the floor of his walk in his favourite suit draped over her lap.

"I'm sorry." She wipes away her tears lifting herself off the soft plush barely touched carpet.

I shake my head dismissing her apology, "Why did you pick Friday, Alma?" I didn't mean to come across insensitive but I couldn't hold back any longer, I had to know.

She lays his perfectly pressed suit on the bed, a sad smile twitching in the corner of her mouth, "I have to drop this off tomorrow." She whispers to herself.

"Alma...why Friday?"

"What is it now Eva?!" She snaps uncharacteristically, rushing to my side immediately, "I'm sorry, please forgive me." She rubs my shoulders comfortingly, I shrug her off. I'm irritated with her, cant she sense the urgency in my voice. Doesn't she see me falling apart?

Of course not, because she's falling apart too.

"What is it sweetheart?" She lays her hand gently on my cheek her brows furrowed with worry.

"I had just wondered why Friday? But its okay Alma...I guess I'm being pedantic." I walk towards the door, its not important...not in the grand scheme of things, well maybe it is but only to me.

I know I should have been focused on the grief of burying my father today, but my thoughts were consumed by fictional images of Louisa floating down the aisle to Stone. My Stone.

Its 10am and the funeral car arrives at the house, Alma's sister flew in to support her so she didn't have to be alone.

I don't have anyone. I'm alone.

We sit in silence in the back seat as the car travels slowly along the gravel road that links our estate. I look out at the mansion, wondering how he is feeling. Is he nervous, is he happy? Is he happier with her than he was with me?

We were so young, and now we're grown up.

He has Louisa, and I'm alone.

I stand staring out of Griffins study window hoping for a glance of her, just one glance. I had this image in my head of her running up the grass verge begging me not to marry Louisa, asking me to take her instead. If I thought that she really truly loved me, then I would. I'd give it all up for a chance to start over with her.

Its time for me to settle down, and what Louisa and I have is special. I love her.

Just not the way I love *her*.

I watch as the black funeral car pulls into the estate, I wonder if she's okay. Wincing at the image of her, tears streaming down her face as she slides her feet into her shoes. Having to do all of this alone.

A tap on my shoulder comes startling me, "These are for you son. I'm so proud of the man you have become." Griffin hands me a small box, a pair of platinum cuff links twinkle inside.

"Thank you, Griffin." I offer him a smile.

He stands tall matching my gaze as I turn back to the window, the funeral car pulling back up the gravel. I'm not sure if I imagined her, or if I could actually see but she was alone in that car. Weeping, by herself.

A sharp pain strikes my chest and as much as I want to look away and pretend that it isn't there I can't. I can't tear my eyes away not even for a second.

"It's a sad day for Eva," Griffin passive aggressively hums, "Poor thing, I wish I could be there for her." He taps his cane on the ground glancing up at me.

Fuck it.

"I'll be back Grandpa." I throw on my suit jacket, untying my bowtie I hand it to him.

Not a fucking chance am I going to let her go through this alone, without me there. Even if I sit in the church and she doesn't see me, at least I will have been there for her.

I have to be there.

Griffins eyes widen with pride, "Go boy, you'll make it back." He slaps my back handing me the keys to my car.

I can't move.

Making it out of the car was easy, I thought that would have been the hardest part.

But everyone is inside, it seems like the whole town is in there and I can't make it down the aisle.

"Eva...?" Alma hushes trying to pull me down to the front of the church, but I'm frozen still.

Roger slides out of a pugh, he whispers inaudibly in Alma's ear and she nods whimpering softly as she finds her way to her seat at the front.

"C'mon darlin', lets go sit." He places his hand on the middle of my back trying to push me down but I'm a dead weight. I can't move. If I could I would. Even though I don't want to.

So I stay, hiding behind a pillar. Faceless faces staring at me, whispering about me and the spectacle I'm causing.

The minister begins the service.

While I hide myself.

He begins talking about dads younger years, growing up in the 70's, making nostalgic jokes about his hair styles and fashion choices. He knew him.

I take a small step closer, the sound of my heel on the wooden floor stopping the service for a millisecond as everyone turns to have a quick gawp at me.

The minister continues drawing the attention away from my unintended dramatic display of emotion.

I'm angry with myself, I didn't know half of what he is saying. The stories he is telling about my father, people nod in agreement, sniffling between sad bursts of laughter about his antics as a teenager.

I wish I knew him better.

"He has left behind a beautiful daughter, Eva..." the congregation turn to look at me again, I move closer my face perpetually soaked by a river of tears, "I am under strict instructions to read this to Eva; I wish we could have had more time darling, I will spend my eternity cherishing the time we were able to reclaim." I throw my hand up halting him, shaking my head as my heart is wrenched.

I want the rest to be private. I want this to be a private moment between me and my dad.

He holds out the paper for me to take, my arm desperately wanting to reach for it. But I can't move.

So I stare catatonically ahead.

I'm at my breaking point.

Just when I think that I might implode a hand slides into mine, I look down at our fingers intertwine gripping tightly. I look up, Stone's eyes brimmed with tears, a painful lump in my throat swells. "You can do this," his lips brush my ear, "We can do this together, you're not alone." He walks with me down to the very front of the church, sliding into a pugh beside me, never letting go of my hand.

He gently squeezes it three times.

I firmly squeeze back four.

Don't Marry Her

"Would you like to ride back with us Stone?" Alma clasps her hands around his face, her thankful expression speaking the thousand unspoken words that drift around us.

He shakes his head, "sorry no, I brought my own car," he gestures towards his BMW parked in the lot, "I could drive you home, Eva, that is if you want to." He simpers sorrowfully, looking down at my hand as it grips onto his too afraid to let go.

"I'd like that."

He holds open the passenger door for me and I slide into the leather seat, looking up at him as he lingers by the door.

A soft smile corners his mouth, "Eva, as much as I don't want you to, you need to let go."

I choke back a bursting sob, "Okay."

"Of my hand, so I can get in the car." The smile falls from his face and I release him from my vice.

Just as we approach the estate he takes the little slip road that leads us to our lake. We sit in silence looking out at the water. Stone doesn't stop the engine keeping the car warm.

"How do you feel?" He traces the steering wheel with his finger.

"Emotionally tapped out." I un-clip my seatbelt and turn my body round to face him, "Remember Thanksgiving?"

His cheeks redden as a smile forces its way across his face, "That was a good day."

"That was my favourite day." Tears build in the back of my eyes.

I want him to drive us away, far away from here. I want to drive with him to the ends of the earth, I'm just not sure he wants to do that with me.

"Don't marry her, Stone." I plead with him softly, if I don't say it I'll regret it for the rest of my life. He asked me to ask him not to, so here I am...practically begging him.

He heaves a long heavy sigh, "It's not that simple Eva, I want to be everything for you and I want to do the same for her."

I slide myself onto his lap forcing my lips onto his before the inevitable 'but' comes, I expected him to push me away but instead he held my head and kissed me intensely, his tongue slips inside my mouth massaging mine ferociously. I throw my head back in ecstasy content with being back where I belong, even if its going to be short lived, he attaches his mouth to my neck slowly lacing his tongue up to my ear, I squirm at the heat building inside me I feel the stiffness of his bulge beneath his pants press against my slit. I grind myself on his lap, his lips brushing my ear as he lets out a sordid groan. I flick my head to catch his mouth with mine, taking his bottom lip between my teeth biting down harshly watching his eyes smirk at me.

Stone runs his hands up my thighs pulling me deeper onto his lap, kissing every inch of my neck and face fervently, we roll together the desire to be a part of one another now the only way to end to our infidelity.

We aren't thinking, instead we're behaving like feral animals tearing into one another. He hikes my skirt up around my waist before ripping my pantyhose apart at the seam, he thrusts his hand down sliding my underwear to the side. Using a thick finger to part my slit wide gliding it into my wetness manipulating my pearled clit.

An untamed gasp howls from my throat at the sensation, I shove my hand down undoing his leather belt releasing his aching length through the zipper, he grabs my behind lifting me up and slides me down ferociously down on to it, my breath hitched as the carnal movement combines the perfect combination of pain and pleasure.

I cycle my hips on him grinding erotically, we pant sordidly into one another's mouths our climaxes building. I place my hands on either side of Stones face my eyes locked into his as we move together in a series of lewd motions, I kiss his forehead tasting the salt of his brow. One final thrust of my hips pushes my orgasm to the edge and my walls tighten around him gripping him, holding him deeply inside me as I twitch in ecstasy, I feel him shudder inside releasing his load.

We don't separate instead we stay glued together, I rest my head on his shoulder. A continuous stream of tears falls down my cheeks soaking his jacket, "What now, Stone?" My breath catches as I choke back sobs. He ignores me, his hand perpetually smoothing my hair keeping his eyes closed.

"She's pregnant isn't she?"

Stone releases a slow heavy sigh, "She told me two days ago." Tears begin to tumble down my face.

I sit up on his lap looking him dead in the eyes, "Well then...I guess you have to marry her." I wanted him to say no, but the thought of her being abandoned with a child pained me.

"I want to be with you Eva, but I have to do right by her. I have to do something right." I felt the pain in his voice, he too was lost.

I wanted so badly to save him like he saved me, but what could I do? What could we do?

"Well you best go get married." I try my hardest to be strong, strong for him.

A tap comes at the window of the car, we jump separating. Stone does his zipper up and I pull down my skirt. Through the condensation on the window I can make out the slender figure of Angela Carlisle, Stone rolls down the window.

She stands hand on hip leaning in with a seedy smirk plastered across her face, "Stone dear, you're getting married in thirty minutes. The cars are here." She scoffs at me, throwing a handkerchief onto his lap, "Clean yourself up."

"I have to go." His eyes filled with fear and sorrow.

I nod doing my best to hold back my heartbroken sobs, "I know."

Stone and his mother leave on foot, and I drive his car back to my house. The only way I can describe how I feel is utterly devastated, but I can't cry any more. I' am unable to shed a single tear. I think somewhere deep down I knew I would lose him because I never really had him.

I must be a horrible person but I no longer feel guilty for what we have done to Louisa, I don't have it in me to care. I've lost so much of myself to all these people that I had to take something for myself, and I took a little bit of my Stone.

Our sinister act of infidelity will live on in my mind as a precious memory.

Our subtle hand squeezes will be forever engrained in the fibre of my bones.

Two Years Later

♥

"Good morning, Miss Miller, there is a woman here to see you." My assistant Lacey hovers in the doorway of my dressing room.

I get up from my stool making sure to tie my robe, not wanting to flash anyone unnecessarily and make my way to the foyer.

When I see her I'm breathless like I've had all the wind punched out of me, I gasp subtly trying not to be dramatic, "Angela..." I smile awkwardly keeping my composure as best I can.

"I was in the city to do some shopping and saw your name in lights," She smirks sarcastically at me, "I thought I'd check out tonight's show, and bring you these." She steps forward handing me a bunch of red roses. My heart twists painfully inside my chest.

I keep waiting for the other shoe to drop, I want so badly to ask for Stone but I promised myself that I would keep him locked away in my memory.

"Thank you Angela," I lean in kissing her cool cheek respectfully, "Lacey, could you please make sure Mrs Carlisle receives champagne at the interval?"

"Absolutely, Miss Miller." She nods writing it down on her iPad checking Angelas seat, the most expensive in the theatre.

Angela thanks Lacey with a gracious smile, "I heard you're selling the house, Eva."

Word travels fast I only put in an enquiry a week ago, "I am, it seems silly keeping it when I live here. Alma moved to be closer to her sister. It's too big for just me."

Her face shifts, she knows it's the sensible thing to do.

"So when are you back in town?" she pulls out her cell phone opening the calendar.

Why is she so interested in me all of a sudden?

My eyes venture to my watch, hoping that she'll take the not so subtle hint that I am ready for this to be over and I would like to leave, but she doesn't and she lingers waiting for me to answer, "I...uh...I'm there next week to meet the realtor."

"Which day?" She arches her eyebrow swiping the screen of her cell.

What game is she playing this time?

I look at Lacey who is standing within ear shot waiting for instructions from me, "Lace...what day am I going to Boston?" she smiles gently and begins swiping her own screen fumbling around nervously.

"Wednesday the 12th of November, Bulfinch." She announces her wide eyes waiting for the next task, I hand her the extravagant bunch of roses and she offers me a sad smile knowing the sentimental value they hold for me.

"Well that settled then, we're having a party for Griffin to celebrate his latest book. It's his last one, he's retiring now."

These fucking Carlisle's and their ambushing parties. I haven't spoken to a single one of them since the day of my dad's funeral. Even Griffin, and I don't feel guilty about it, not one bit.

"I don't think so Angela, it's inappropriate. I should think you of all people would understand." I try to appeal to her better nature if she even has one that is.

What makes her think that I would want to go, or that Stone would want me to be there. What about her daughter in law and grandchild, why would she put them through this? Because she didn't want it in the first place, that's why. She lives for the drama, perhaps she will write a book about it too.

She stuffs her cell back into her Birkin bag, "Well I've done my part. I extended my invitation. Balls in your court Eva."

She looks around the foyer of the theatre as the crowd piles in, "Is Richard with you?" I enquire trying to change the subject, ready to order more champagne for them not that either of them deserves it, but I'm nice like that.

She scoffs adjusting her sophisticated glasses on her face shaking her head, "I suspect he's off with his mistress."

What?

"You think Stone is the only Falconer/Carlisle that's ever had a bit on the side? You really are terribly naïve Eva."

"I'm sorry Angela, so you understand why I can't go." I look down at my feet, poor Angela. The unexpected information giving me a little insight into her marriage and why she was so cold.

"Don't pity me, you really think that you were the 'other woman'? No, that title goes to everyone who came after you."

"Miss Miller, are you sure you want to sell?" Oliver, the realtor walks around the kitchen admiring the impressive structure, "Its so sleek and modern, your father really built this?" he scribbles on his clipboard.

I nod admiring it myself, its cold emptiness causing me to shiver involuntarily.

"He designed everything right down to the sockets, but its too big for me. I don't have a family and I spend most of my time in Manhattan."

I really don't think he should be trying to talk me out of selling, the commission he'll pull in on this will be substantial.

"Well, I would look to market it at around offers over 1.8 million. You'd be looking at 1.6 after fees and commission. Does that sound about right?"

Its hard to think that someone else would be living here and the thought of someone tearing it apart to make it their own stings, but that's life.

Maybe they'll find some happiness here.

"I really think it'll sell quickly." He flicks the page on the forms, "Oh that's right what about the lake? The deed to the house doesn't include your half of the lake. That still belongs to the Falconer mansion, but we have a letter of comfort signed by both parties here saying that it was shared equally between the two families. Informally, half of it belongs to you, should you wish to include it you would need to purchase it legally from a Mr Griffin Falconer?"

I stare out across the estate at our lake, only visible through the barren autumn trees. I should have said yes right away, I could afford to buy it from Griffin, even though I know he would gift it to me for a dollar to avoid the tax, but something deep inside me halted me from making the decision.

"I'm not sure Oliver, can I get back to you on that?"

He scribbles once again, "Will I hold off on marketing the property until you decide?"

I shake my head, "No, I need it gone. We'll figure something out. Don't mention the lake just yet."

I slide into my old room, still exactly the way I left it only its covered in dust sheets. I pull them off and make up my old bed, if I'm going to be here for the week I'm sure as shit going to be comfortable.

You Don't Know?

♥

"Hey!" A hushed voice comes from outside my window, I jump up from my bed not quite sure if my mind is playing tricks on me or not, my heart hammers in my chest as I slowly climb off to peer out of the window, "Its me...its Stone," The hooded figure becomes more visible.

Why is he here?

Still trying to gather myself I slide open the window, "Let me in!" He whispers as he pushes through the gap.

He stands towering above me his arching his eyebrow, "I need a place to crash." He unzips his hoodie and places on the back of the chair at my dresser.

"You can't crash here!" I gasp shoving his hoodie back at him.

If my dad gets wind of this I'm finished!

He takes his thumb and traces my lips, "Why not? We could be friends you know."

Brushing his mouth against my ear he whispers, "Maybe even one day we could be lovers." He slowly trails his hand down my arm and laces a finger around my waistband.

My eyes dart open I haven't dreamt of Stone in so long, being in this place a pebbles throw away from Griffins has obviously stirred something inside of me. I check the time, 04:58am, I doubt I'll be able to fall back asleep so I head downstairs and set up my computer, I sit in front of it with a large mug of coffee and begin opening an abundance of unanswered emails, thankfully none of any importance. Except...there nestled amongst the magazine subscriptions and money off coupons is the subject title, 'I'm sorry'.

My shoulders heave as bile stirs inside me and hesitantly I open it:

Dearest Eva,

I was so sorry to hear about Preston.

I only wish I had heard sooner, and then

perhaps I would have been able to

attend the funeral.

If you ever need anything,

please call.

Emily

It was sent the week after his funeral, how has it taken me two years to see this? For a small moment I feel awful and that maybe I should reach out, but then coldly I hit 'delete' and watch it disappear from my screen.

I must have fallen asleep after that, I wake up startled with the shrill ringing of my cell phone.

Its the realtor, "Hi...sure...not a problem at all. I can be at your office in an hour or so. See you then."

After signing some papers in the realtors office in Boston I decide to grab a coffee, its nice having some time for myself. What I didn't expect was the sting in my chest as I opened my laptop in Starbucks and there it was my house, my home. Except it wasn't any more, and it hadn't been for a long time. It was prepped and primmed with a pretty little bow on top just waiting to entice someone to buy it, a family to love it in a way that I was never able to, but what if they rip it apart, and the thought of that utterly tore me apart.

So I sit audibly sobbing into my flat white, unable to contain the whimpers that escaped my lips.

A hand is placed on my shoulder, "Eva?"

I wipe away my tears looking up to its owner, Louisa stands above me, "I thought that was you, are you okay?." Her head tilts to the side.

"I'm fine, I-I just...I'm fine." I shrug her hand away, I can't bear her touch.

I tried so hard not to look for it, but my eyes inadvertently looked for her rings. Her hand lain bare.

My eyes flit from her hand to her face and back again.

"Oh..." she rubs her ring finger, "Oh..." she scoffs, "You don't know do you?" Her mouth twists from a concerned to a self satisfied grin, she folds her arms across her chest.

Wiping snot and tears on the back of my sleeve I stand to meet her gaze, refusing to allow her to look down on me, "Know what?" I query trying to stop it sounding like I was begging for answers.

She tucked her hair behind her ear, "I'll let him tell you." She twitches her nose sardonically, chuckling to herself as she leaves me standing wide eyed like a deer in the headlights.

No.

I run after her, "Louisa! Tell me!" We stand in the pouring rain staring at each other, Louisa is shielded by an umbrella while I allow myself to be soaked to the skin.

Rolling her beautiful eyes patronisingly she takes a step forward, "We never got married."

I feel like I've been struck in the chest by a hammer, my heart stops.

"A...and...the...the b-baby?"

"There was no fucking baby! I would have said anything to keep him from you." She spins on her heel and heads in the opposite direction.

It isn't enough, so I follow her down the street shivering in the rain, "Tell me what happened Louisa, tell me everything now." I plead with her.

"Go ask your precious Stone and his meddling mother. God knows I never stood a chance," she storms towards me in a rage, "I could have had everything and then you took it from me." Her hand crashes against my cheek in a loud echoing slap.

"I'm sorry." I wheeze through the sting on my cheek.

Louisa runs off and this time I don't follow her.

What we did to her was unforgivable.

But we both lost because she didn't have my Stone, and neither did I.

He didn't come running for me, he let me be. He left me.

I pull out my cell and dial Alma's number, "Alma, did you know that Stone never married Louisa?" My voice rasps as I choke back tears, "You didn't? Are you sure? No, I'm fine. I have to go."

In our small town just outside of Boston, where everyone knows everything about everybody especially our two prestigious families how could this have gone under the radar?

Then it hit me, like a tonne of bricks.

He was hurt.

To: ASC
Stone...I'm sorry.
I'm so sorry.

I hit send and almost immediately the symbol appears under my message as he types back.

From: ASC
Me too.
See you tonight?

Fuck Off Angela

♥

"Hi," I open the front door, "I didn't expect to see you until tonight." Stone stands on the porch, a drop of rain hangs off the end of his nose. I think it's the first time he's ever knocked on the door and not slid through my window.

I show him inside, his eyes hovering around at the boxes stacked around the hallway, "I thought it would be better if we talked before the party, because y'know..."

"Your mother." I grin softly finishing his sentence as I grab us some beers from the fridge.

He sits down at the breakfast bar twisting the cap, gulping it down in one, "Got anything stronger?"

I dip my head and disappear into dads study, standing with my hand hovering over the glass decanter filled with some sort of scotch. I take a moment to myself to breathe. Stone is back, here in my life. But the sparkle of blue that once glistened in his arrogant eyes is gone, replaced with pain. He's defeated.

Composing myself I saunter back into the kitchen waving the scotch, a grateful smile flickers across his face. We half heartedly clink our glasses together, "To the truth." He looks down sorrowful.

Oh boy.

I don't want to press him, so we drink three glasses in silence. He occasionally looks up at me, sending me a sad wink or a soft sigh.

My eyes never falter from him, my stomach churns agonising over him.

Finally he speaks up, "When I left you in my car, Angela took me back to Griffin's ." He gulps before inhaling sharply, "The cars hadn't arrived yet, but the place was deserted, she lead me round the back to the kitchen...a-and thats when I saw Louisa..."

I hang on his every word, desperate for the answers. Slowly sipping my drink waiting for the punch line.

He pours himself another scotch swallowing it in one. "Bent over the counter...in her wedding dress...fucking Griffin's gardener."

I spit my drink out spraying it over Stone, bursting into uncontrolled hysterics, "The gardener?"

He chuckles trying his best to hold back his laughter, "The gardener." He pours himself another drink as he continues to bob heartily.

I'm pretty sure it was the alcohols fault and I really wished I could have stopped it but the involuntary chortle continued, "Like a fucking porn star?" I wipe away my tears trying to collect myself.

Stone nods, "Like fuckin' Jenna Jameson."

Scotch flies down my nose stinging my nostrils, "I'm sorry. I'm so sorry Stone."

Taking slow breathes trying to stop the uncontrollable laughter I walk round to dry him with a dish towel, slowly dabbing his face, "And the baby?"

His voice quivers in an attempt to stifle his chuckles, "There never was one." He looks down at the empty decanter, "I really wanted there to be one, I thought being a dad would be my chance, no...my reason to change." Tears fill his eyes and I pull his head into me, to see him broken bruises me painfully. Like repeatedly banging into the corner of a desk.

I drop the dish towel and gently brush his hair away from his forehead, "You don't need to change Stone, I-I think you're perfect." It was definitely the whiskey talking but what I wholeheartedly meant what I said next, "Perfect for me that is." He grabs my hand, stopping it from touching him and in that moment I looked into his eyes and realised he didn't love me any more, scalding tears falter down my face, searing my cheeks.

Nothing he could do now would cauterise this wound.

"I uhh I better get cleaned up for the party." And by cleaned up I meant sobered up.

I left him in the kitchen staring into his empty glass, and I sobbed...I sobbed and it felt like it would last forever.

I've cried enough tears over this man to fill our lake twice.

I lock myself in my bathroom, looking in the mirror seeing a grown woman staring back at me. Twenty nine years old and still heartbroken over the bad boy next door. "You never gave yourself a chance." I say to her coldly.

I wash up, hoping that by the time I'm done Stone will have left and we can forget I ever opened my mouth and just exchange awkward glances at the party instead.

But that would be too easy, right?

There he is, sat on the end of my bed.

"What now Eva?" He bites his bottom lip nervously.

I just don't have the strength to fight for us any more, "You tell me Stone." I shrug waiting for the answers, hanging on every unspoken word.

"I'm just not ready to start something new," His honesty strikes me like a dagger.

"What about something old?" I turn away from him, choking back a pained sob.

I see the reflection of him in the mirror, something about the way he moves has changed. He breathes deeply getting off the bed and walks to me.

Please don't touch me.

He places both hands on my shoulders, turning me slowly, "If we were meant to be together, wouldn't we be by now?" He presses his forehead against mine, "I could have you right now, but it wouldn't be fair to you, Eva."

"We've burst our banks." I whisper softly.

He dips his head lingering his gaze on me, "what?"

I shake my head dismissing my statement, "Nothing."

After Stone left I made sure to leave an hour or so before turning up at Griffin's, I was greeted by the man himself with bear hug, "thank you my girl, I wasn't sure if you would make it."

Griffins new housekeeper takes my coat and bag before offering me some champagne, I politely decline. I'm not here for pleasure, this is purely business now.

"Griffin, I need to speak with you. Could we...in private?"

His face changes sensing the seriousness in my voice, "absolutely, my study?" I nod as he shows me the way.

I don't wish to see any of the Falconer/Carlisles, I want in and out swiftly. In a rush to get this done I take out the manilla envelope that is tucked under my arm.

Griffin sits in his commanding chair behind the old oak desk, "what can I do for you?"

I sigh then inhale sharply, "I want to buy my half of the lake." I blurt out not wasting any time, "I know it's already been gifted to my family by you but in order to sell it along with the house I need to purchase it legally from you."

"Hmmm." He looks over the paperwork, nodding occasionally. Grabbing a post-it from a stack which sit underneath a baseball he scribbles on it, turns it over and slides it across to me.

'$1 and a yearly lunch date with me.'

I look up at him, his head tilted to the side smirking at me with his piercing blue eyes, Stones eyes.

"I'm going to make a lot of money from the sale of the house, more so now with the lake. Why don't we say, $100,000 and two lunches and two dinners a year?"

He laughs heartily, "My girl someone should teach you how to negotiate! You are awful at this." He reaches out his hand I place mine in his, "I have more money than I'll ever know what to do with, it will all end up going to them," he throws his head to the side gesturing to his moronic family in the other room, "I will take the four meals and the dollar, to avoid the gift tax of course. Do we have a deal?"

I walk around the desk to him, leaning down I peck him softly on the cheek.

I tuck a dollar into his shirt pocket and we both sign the papers with an expensive fountain pen.

"Whats going on?" Stone stands in the doorway.

"Eva and I had some private business to conduct, son." Griffin tucks the papers back into the envelope and slides them to me.

Stone snatches the envelope out of my hand tearing it open furiously, "You're selling the house?!" I grab them back and head for the door, "Yes I am, I'm selling my house."

"Bathroom, now." He growls at grabbing hold of my arm trailing me into the downstairs toilet, almost yanking my arm out of its socket.

He slams the door behind us and sits me down on the toilet seat, "Will you think about this for a minute."

"It's all I've thought about for two years Stone, I don't want it." He runs his hands desperately through his hair, "Why are you so mad?" I get up to leave and he pushes me back down.

"What about us Eva?" Is he serious?

I let out an exasperated groan, "Were you there in that room?"

"No you and Griffin-"

Inhaling sharply I stand shoving him against the sink, "Not that fucking room you moron! My room!"

I open the door and storm out of the bathroom, Stone's family standing in the foyer whispering to one another in hushed tones, Griffin's housekeeper hurriedly brings me my coat and bag.

"So thats it Eva? Just like that you're leaving...leaving me?" Stone calls after me his face red with rage, eyes blurred with tears.

I can tell by the way he turns from his family that he is embarrassed at his honest display of emotion.

I can't do this any more.

"Stone, you paved the way for leaving. Like you said, if we were meant to be together then we'd be together, and we're not. You're not ready and I can't put my life on hold waiting for you to grow up and realise that I'm the one!"

Angela Carlisle steps forward, "If I may-"

"Oh fuck off, Angela!" I scream at her, hearing Griffins mighty guffaw in the background.

Stone chases me outside on to the gravel driveway, "Eva, please."

"I love you Aster Stone Carlisle, I probably always will. Maybe one day we'll fall back into each others arms, but I can't wait for you to fight for me." I lean up kissing his lips softly tasting the salt of his tears.

And that would be the last time I ever saw Stone Carlisle.

Yeah right.

Ambushed At The Airport

Eighty three hours, eighty three hours and it was gone. That's all the time it has taken for my house to not longer be my house. All the memories are boxed up, the good and the bad. Oliver had told me it would sell quick but I didn't think it would have been this fast, I thought I'd have more time.

I had to go to Boston to sign a few papers that irritatingly couldn't be signed via email or fax.

Still unable to face the train I decide uneconomically to catch a flight instead.

I hate JFK airport, no not hate... I loathe it. Its so busy, and even when you don't have baggage you feel like you queue for hours on end. Which is ridiculous for an hour long flight.

I decide that this deserves a drink, not to celebrate but to drown my sorrows.

"Just a glass of red wine please." I simper at the bar tender, airports don't actually have time zones. Every hour is drinking hour.

He slides across the wine list, "what kind?" Never in my life have I felt so uncultured, and in an airport no less.

"She'll have the Cabernet Sauvignon." I snap my head round already aware of the owner of the platinum card that's slid across the bar, "hi."

Stone sits smugly in the stool next to me, "we'll take the bottle."

"As you wish sir."

You have got to be kidding me.

"I can choose and buy my own wine, Aster." The bar tender shrugs, he's already swiped the card. His eyes flit from Stones face to mine uncomfortable under our blanket of awkwardness.

"Don't call me that, Eva." He grunts taking a sip, "where are you flying to?"

I can't believe this, where do I have to move to avoid crashing into him?

Tell me...because I'll move there.

"Its absolutely none of your business, Stone." His eyebrow arches as he snatches my plane ticket reading over it.

"So home then, maybe I could persuade the flight attendants to let us sit together."

I honestly couldn't think of anything worse, and I mean that.

At least I thought that for around five seconds, until I saw them over Stone's shoulder walking towards us awkwardly smiling, giving me a limp wave.

Emily and Robert.

Fucking hell.

What sort of evil person was I in a previous life? Why can't I just buy myself a red wine and drink it peacefully. Why can't these people just leave me alone?

"You have got to be fucking kidding me." I whine glugging down the painfully hearty drink.

Before Stone can turn his head to look Emily and Robert close in on us.

"Hello, Eva," Emily shuffles uncomfortably in front of us, "Stone." She dips her head towards him.

My throat dries up and I can't begin to think of the words to form. I hate this day.

Emily links her arm with Robert's as they exchange tense glances.

Stone fills my glass up and I take another mouth full.

She glances at my hand, "I thought you two would be married by now." Widening her eyes towards him, the shock of her statement causes me to choke red wine shoots down my nose.

If only she knew.

Part of me thinks Robert knew, I'm pretty sure I seen him try and mentally remove Emily's foot from her mouth.

The bar tender slides me a napkin and I clean myself up, eternally grateful that I chose to wear black.

"Not yet, we're too busy at the moment. Isn't that right, sweetheart." Stone pats the back of my hand winking at me softly.

What the-

I can't cope with this.

I glance down at my wrist inwardly pleading for time to hurry up, please let my flight be now.

"What are you doing with yourselves?" Robert tries to cut through the thorny atmosphere.

Stone clears his throat, "Eva is just finished a show on Broadway, isn't that right?" He nudges me gently, trying to encourage me to speak but apparently I'm mute. Words wont come.

I nod in agreement.

"Is that right? I didn't know you were theatre oriented." Emily pats me on the shoulder, "we never really liked the theatre."

Stone furrows his brow, "she's amazing very highly commended. All the big theatre companies want you, don't they?"

Never thought I would be grateful for Stone, but here I am thankful that I am not alone with these people.

However, given the choice none of them would be here.

"Well thats nice I suppose, you'll be getting too old for it soon. Then you'll have to get a real job." Her giggle sparks anger inside of me and it takes all my strength not to slap her across the face, again.

Robert senses it I'm sure because again he buffers with a subject change, "where are you kids off to?" He speaks directly to me making uncomfortable eye contact, and I have no option but to speak.

"Boston." I stand up reaching down for my purse, Emily hands it to me politely.

She tucks a lock of hair behind my ear, it was so intrusive, "I was so sorry to hear about Preston, Eva." Resting her hand on my cheek.

"I know, I read your email." I bat her hand away.

She stuffs it into her pocket, "I'd imagine you will be thinking of starting a family, filling all of those rooms in that big house."

Why can't they take the hint I don't want them here.

Any of them. Including Stone.

"I've sold the house Emily, I'm going back to sign some papers and then I'll be done with Boston." I drink the rest of Stones wine before abruptly leaving the three of them standing awkwardly in the airport bar.

"Eva!" Emily runs after me her shrill voice cutting through me like glass.

"What...what is it?"

She doesn't know where to look, I actually think she expected me to keep going.

"I wanted to-" she shuffles her feet hesitantly.

Fuck this.

"You wanted to what? So far all you've done is insult my career and make Stone uncomfortable. Please leave me alone."

Robert and Stone approach us cautiously, "Emily, did you know that Stone here is going to Syria to cover the-"

I felt like all of the oxygen was sucked out of the room, my lungs fighting to keep me alive. Everything in the periphery of my vision disappears into darkness.

"What?" I interrupt, frantically grabbing Stone's face between my hands, "you're going where?"

Emily and Robert fade into the background as I stare deeply into his eyes, in this moment no one else exists. The whole world disappears while my world threatens to crumble before my eyes.

Suddenly nothing else matters.

All that matters is that I might lose him, again. Before I've really been allowed to have him.

"I'm covering the conflict over there, its a huge deal it could really make my career." His eyes stay locked into mine I don't let go of his face.

"I don't want you to go." A burst of sobs squeals from my lips, and he takes my face between his hands.

"I'll be gone six months, then maybe..."

He glances down at his watch, "we're going to miss our flight."

Operation: Make Him Stay

♥

"How much will it take for you not to go?" I lean over the airplane seat stretching across the passenger next to me.

Stone shakes his head, "It's not about the money, I want to make something of myself." He hushes back gritting through his teeth.

Not about the money. He wants to make something of himself. He's a Falconer/Carlisle for christ sake.

"Stone! You're a Carlisle. You are Griffin Falconers favourite grandson you were born 'something'," the man next to me shuffles underneath my weight ushering me back to my seat, "Don't do this, please don't do this." I practically beg.

The man next to me turns to Stone, "would you like to switch seats?"

Stone buckles in next to me, "I'm sorry Eva-" he brushes hair away from my face.

"Don't you ever get tired of saying you're sorry?"

I knew saying that was a mistake as soon as the words left my mouth, he sighs heavily as we ascend into the air.

I've got one hour and five minutes to convince him not to go.

I dance my fingers along his forearm, "Now I'm sorry." I whisper brushing my lips against his ear.

"Do you want coffee?" He adjusts himself I can see the shape of him growing beneath his jeans, and it excites me.

"I want you." I breathe, just as I'm about to conceal his stiffened length with my coat and slide my hand inside his pants, the flight attendant comes around with the drinks menu, "I'll have two of those tiny bottles of red wine, and he'll have two teeeeny tiny bottles of scotch."

Because if I get him drunk then maybe I can get him to give up on going to a fucking war zone.

After passing us our drinks the flight attendant moves further up the cabin. I nuzzle into his neck inhaling his cologne and the smell of his skin. The smell of Stone.

He grabs my hand, "enough." He growls pushing it away. I screw open one of the bottles of wine, swallowing it in one and repeat the motion with the second.

"Will you stop trying to join the mile high club," He looks around at the busy plane, "its 9:30 in the morning, we'll be landing in thirty five minutes."

I fold my arms across my chest, slumping back into my seat.

"We'll talk more when we get off," he necks his scotch, "and then I'll fuck you."

He slides his hand up my leg resting it on my inner thigh, why did I have to wear jeans?

I don't even remember getting from the airport to my house, all I remember is crashing through the front door...

Stone yanks my jeans down throwing them across the floor, too impatient to wait he slides my underwear to the side and delves into my already moistened slit, taking my clit between his teeth, he tears into me ferociously.

I grab either side of his head pulling him up to meet me I bruise my lips against his tasting myself on him, "I fucking missed you so much." He drives two fingers deep inside me furiously pumping them in the way he knows sends me into orbit. He twists and curls them pulling me deeper into euphoria.

I grab his hand and pull out his fingers bringing them to my mouth, sucking on them relishing in my juices. His eyes roll in the back of his head and he rips open my blouse exposing my black lace bralette my perfectly pebbled nipples stretching through the fabric, "who were you wearing this for, huh?" He pulls it down exposing my breasts taking one into his mouth as he lifts me onto his hip carrying me upstairs to my bedroom.

He lays me down on the carpet, he stands in front of me undoing his belt and zipper freeing his meaty cock, kneeling before him I take his solid length into my mouth grabbing his seat and pushing him to the back of my throat gagging just a little, moaning around his cock, "fuck Eva...fuuuuck." He pants. I slam him into my mouth, sucking and releasing with a pop feeling him pulse and twitch inside.

He crawls on top of me trailing his tongue from my neck to my core, taking my swollen clit into his mouth grinding it between his teeth as hard as he can savouring my squeals as I gush coating his face in me.

He rests his lustrous cock between my slit, the throbbing tip feathering around my opening, "fuck me Stone, fuck me hard."

A devilish smile corners his mouth and he slams himself deep inside brushing my cervix, hitting my g spot rapidly. I struggle to catch my breath through the ecstasy of the multiple orgasms that fire through me like bullets one right after the other.

"On your back," I breathlessly call out, and of course he obliges right away.

I slide myself on to him slowly rocking back and forth gaining the momentum to fuck his brains out, he thrusts himself forward I can see him trying not to come, I enjoy having the control over his explosion. I roll my hips furiously in the way that drives him crazy, bucking myself.

He sits up wrapping his arms around my body slamming us together, I squeeze my legs tightening myself preparing to milk him. My walls constrict and hold him inside me as he pulses his seed deep inside my core, drawing out yet another climax out of me.

Stone presses his lips against mine slipping his tongue into my mouth, "I've missed fucking you."

"Please don't go, Stone." I try to contain my sobs.

I know we aren't together the thought of him being so far away and in danger no less breaks my heart.

"Eva..." he sighs defeatedly.

"I know you want to, I know you think you have to but please stay here with me." I roll onto my side and stare into his eyes hoping that my tears will be enough to guilt him into giving in.

"I...its...I'm not ready for a relationship. I want to clear my head." He takes his thumb and wipes away my tears.

"You'll be hard pushed to clear your head when there are bullets flying at it," I put my hand on his face, "I like your head." I pull him into me and pepper kisses on his forehead.

"I want to make a promise to you Eva, I will come back to you. I promise. But don't wait for me. If I come back and you have found the love of your life then I will leave you be. I promise."

I wanted to scream, 'You are the love of my life!' But I'm nearly thirty and we've danced this same dance for almost twelve years. If I can't make him stay, then maybe we aren't meant to be together. Maybe he was right after all.

"When do you leave?" I smooth away some hair thats fallen across his face, I love his perfectly sculpted pink lips so I kiss them.

His mouth twists cornering a smile, "the day after tomorrow."

"I'll come to the airport and say goodbye." A shocked look sparks across his face.

"Really?"

"Of course."

The Breakfast Club

"Where are you going?" Stone grabs my wrist pulling me back as I go to get off the floor.

I roll back around and crash my lips against his, breaking only to lose myself in his eyes, "I have to pick up Alma at the station and go to the realtors."

"Can I come with you?"

When he wants to do these simple little mundane tasks with me it stings, for five minutes we'll be happy we might even be a couple but only for five minutes. But I'm addicted to the euphoric high, and a sucker for the come down of his inevitable departure. But how could I ever say no to that beautiful face?

Alma, squeezes me tightly outside the station, "I'm going to go for coffee with Stone while you sign the papers and then we'll head to the house and pack up the study, how does that sound?"

I nod acceptingly.

"So if you sign here, here, here and here Miss Miller then you can leave your keys in the house tomorrow then we'll be done." I glance down at the papers Oliver slides to me, its all so official and emotionless for him. I wish it were like that for me.

"So whats the family like?" I sign on the first dotted line.

"I'm sorry?" He looks at me perplexed tapping the page indicating for me to date as well as sign.

"The family that bought the house, what are they like?" I ask again desperately needing to fill my head with scenarios of a loving family life.

Oliver flicks through the contract, "ah... it's an up and coming property developer, EMC properties LTD."

I instantly feel sick, a property developer. They'll

rip it apart and re build it. They'll ruin it.

I couldn't stand to be in there any longer, Oliver was so pleased about the sale. All I wanted to do was curl up into a ball and cry my eyes out.

So I leave, fruitlessly strolling around the streets trying to gather what little frayed thoughts I had left.

Back at the house we clean out the last of the boxes in dads study, I couldn't bear to do it on my own and neither could Alma. Stone carries boxes to the movers who will take it to Alma's, and soon enough its a shell. Our voices echo through its emptiness.

"Where will you stay tonight?" She flicks on the hallway light watching Stone as he closes the blinds on every window.

I can't take my eyes off him, all I want to do is drop to my knee and ask him to marry me, beg him not to go. If I had any gumption about me I would book a flight and go to Syria with him. He'd never let me. And he's not ready for me. But I'm ready for him.

I want a life with him, I want this life.

"I'll grab a room at the Marriott." I take my cell phone out ready to call and book, Stone snakes his arms around my waist pulling me back into his chest planting a kiss on top of my head.

"You'll stay with me at Griffin's tonight, I have errands to run tomorrow if you want you can join me?" He quickly drops his arms from my waist and helps Alma into her coat as she prepares to leave.

"You two...don't be strangers." She pecks us both on the cheek and disappears out of the door.

I take one final look around at the vacant hallway, memories of running through it as a child, hearing my giggles as the nameless nannies chased me around. Arguing with my dad. The infamous Christmas Day catastrophe being replayed in front of me.

It wasn't a happy home, but it was mine. And it certainly wasn't all bad. Despite everything we've gone through it lead me to him.

Maybe one day we'll make it back to each other.

Griffin was delighted to see me as always, he fussed around the lounge trying to coerce his housekeeper to return and make a huge meal, but I convinced him that some Chinese takeout would be just as delicious. I went out to collect the food leaving Stone and Griffin to spend some time alone before he departs.

When I come back they sit in silence reading next to the roaring fire, both mouths settled into the same stiff-upper-lip line but their blurry raw eyes give them away.

Stone and I sit on the floor eating out of each others tubs while Griffin is settled nicely in his chair slurping and chomping occasionally saying, "mmmm" and "very nice."

Soon after he had finished eating Griffin retired to his bedroom for the night leaving Stone and I to pick at the left overs as we lay on cushions in front of the fading embers, we watched The Breakfast Club on Stones iPad and just as Judd Nelson began his monologue about how shitty his parents were Stone paused it, "Eva...when you went for lunch that day..."

He didn't even need to finish the sentence, I knew exactly which lunch he was talking about. I replayed it over and over in my head, because if I hadn't gone to that hateful lunch with Angela Carlisle that day then maybe I would have made it home to spend a few final moments with my dad.

"With Angela, what did you two talk about?" His eyes curiously searched mine for answers, and I so badly wanted to lie to him but I couldn't.

So I told him everything I didn't leave any thing out.

But when I think back to my conversation with Louisa, I did exactly what Angela Carlisle asked me to do only I did it for free.

"She got what she wanted in the end then." He scoffs, pressing play on the screen.

It wasn't clear to me whose betrayal hurt him more, Louisa's or his mothers.

"Hey...hey you." I tap his leg as he stares blankly at the screen, "Aster Stone Carlisle."

He glances at me out of the corner of his eyes, "nuh uh...I want both your eyes on me."

He turns his full head and I grab his face capturing his lips in mine pulling away for just a second to say, "I love you. I love the man you are becoming, how hard you are working to break the cycle of narcissism—"

He juts forward taking my mouth as his own, parting my lips passionately evading my tongue with his.

Breaking the kiss abruptly, "we should watch the rest of this movie then go to bed." He takes one final taste of my lips and turns away.

This was so unlike him, which only reiterated how hurt he was under the surface.

"Okay." I slide off his lap and settle next to him, if I'm being honest with myself I'm a little bruised. But he was clear that this was not something he wanted right now. Our tumultuous relationship, if you can even call it that, has taken its toll on both of us. I start to wonder, is this break what we need?

His arm sneaks around my waist and he pulls me closer into him, I rest my head on his chest adoringly.

I feel him kiss the top of my hair, fragrant with the dwindling fire.

He didn't say he loved me too.

Pretending

♥

I keep myself busy in Griffins kitchen making coffee and pancakes, anything to stop myself from thinking that tomorrow might be the last time I ever see him.

That tomorrow might mark the end of us.

I just hope it isn't forever.

"Stone still asleep?" Griffin unwittingly sneaks up behind me grabbing a pancake from the stack at the side of the frying pan tearing into it, wincing he turns his head away spitting it into a napkin, "I pay someone to do that y'know." He fills his mouth with coffee swirling it around.

"Sit with me a minute please Eva?" He slides into the little corner booth patting the table encouragingly. But I can't stop, not for a minute.

I keep my back on him holding back sobs, "I'm sorry, I'm busy." I know I am being impolite, but I can't. I...can't.

"I understand, its difficult. I pleaded with him as I imagine you did too. I can't help be proud of the man he has become, I put it all down to you, Eva." I hear the tiniest of quivers in his voice, "I sometimes wonder what would he would have become if it weren't for you." In the reflection of the window I see him wipe away a tear.

A small smile corners his mouth when I turn my body to face him, "I don't think I made much of a difference, but thank you for saying it." I offer a sad smile in return.

"You did, I know it hasn't been easy for either of you. I believe that one day, it'll all come together." He winks at me lifting up the newspaper that sits folded next to him and starts reading it meticulously.

"Whats going on down here?" Stone saunters into the room wearing casual jeans and a cream cable knit sweater, his hair still damp from the shower but swept perfectly to the side. I look down at his feet finding myself amused at his louboutin sneakers, "what are you smirking at?" He pinches my butt playfully, "oh! Ana made pancakes I see." He grabs one from the stack shoving the entire thing into his mouth.

"Eh, no. I made them!" I smile proudly returning to the dishes. Watching in the reflection as Griffin passes Stone a napkin to spit in, "oh come on!" I spin on my heel, "they can't be that bad?" Pouting I grab one and take a bite trying to prove a point, "my god...they are terrible!" Stone stands in front of me palm facing up and I spit it into his hand.

"Have one of these instead, Griffin's favourite cookie."

The three of us sit comfortably in silence reading the paper and devouring cookies. It was an almost perfect morning

"So what is it you need from here?" I walk around the aisles of the tech store lifting cameras and snapping pictures of Stone when he wasn't looking.

"A GO PRO, a power bank for my cell aaand one of these!" He lifts some power adapters.

When we got to the counter he pulled out his own card to pay it gave me butterflies to see how far he had come, he didn't swipe Griffin's platinum card. He really was a man now.

"What are you staring at?" He looks slyly out of the corner of his eye.

"Whats next?" I clear my throat of the ball of emotion that aches there, "lunch?"

He lets out a soft laugh and slings his arm around my shoulders, "whatever you want, sweetheart." He leans in and kisses my temple.

How could he be this happy?

I mean, here I am completely dying inside and he's being chirpy and playful. But as long as I can have these last few moments of happiness with him, then sure...okay, I'll pretend.

I paid for lunch despite a strong protest from Stone, "I want to. Please...will you just let me?"

He accepted with a dissatisfied nod, growling as I placed my card on the contactless machine.

"What else is on the agenda?" I pull the list out if his pocket and begin checking things off.

"This." His big arms wrap around me as he lifts me onto his waist, I lean into him hovering my lips above his feeling the tickle of his breath on my skin.

My every nerve waits impatiently to be touched, he presses his lips to mine softly at first but as the taste of our mouths mix he deepens it.

This was out of character for us, such a public display of affection. We've only ever done it once before under the blanket of infidelity and guilt. This time it was different, it was a kiss that spoke a thousand words, when it broke we still didn't know what to say.

"Boxers..." I moan as he sets me back on the sidewalk.

His nose nuzzles into my neck, "whats that?"

"You need boxers, the store closes in half an hour."

He lets out a soft moan, "okay, can you go pick me up some? I have something to sort at the bank before it closes too."

"Are you shopping for your husband?" The nosey lady behind the counter pops the five boxes of Tom Ford boxes into the bag and I swipe the credit card Stone gave me.

"Mhmm." I answer some what ambiguously I don't know why I didn't correct her. I wanted to but the little lie made my heart flutter, and after all today was about pretending.

"Hi!" I chirp at Stone as he waits by the car, "you have expensive taste you know that right." I hand over the bag and he dips his head pecking my lips.

It was a quick kiss, like a habit he had no control over. It meant more to me than him, but I'll take whatever I can get.

The sun had set and the crisp winter breeze swirled around, I shudder suddenly the stark reality of tomorrow hits me, hard.

"Lets go." I open the car door and slide into the passenger seat, Stone places the bags in the trunk and takes his place behind the wheel.

Stone is leaving in the early hours of the morning, I decide to shower tonight because there wont be time tomorrow, and I'll leave right after him.

I turn up the temperature trying to get heat into my body, but somehow I still feel cold and empty.

I feel him press against my back snaking his big arms around my naked body, I turn around slowly in the circle of him praying that the stream of water will have disguised my tears. I stare into the contours of his bare chest, placing his finger under my chin he tilts my head up to look into his bloodshot eyes, they always were my favourite part of him. The windows to his heart.

Stones lips capture mine adoringly I moan into his mouth and he breathes it in.

Running a finger down into my velvety folds he finds that I am ready for him, I am always ready for him.

He lifts me onto his stiffened length, gliding inside me perfectly. Like our bodies were made for each other.

"Yup"

I don't even notice if the airport is busy.

Every part of my body aches.

I keep thinking of ways to make him stay, thinking of lies that I could tell. Anything to change his mind.

But I don't have it in me.

Angela sniffles as she stiffly boxes her arms around her boy, Richard pats him on the back unable to show even a fraction more emotion than his wife.

Griffin cups his face simpering proudly, this is the scene that will break me.

Thinking back to their exchange in the kitchen yesterday morning, the subtle little grandparent/grandchild bond suppressing the impending doom for one day, and now here they are saying goodbye.

He turns to me. Fuck. It's my turn.

I shake my head, "no."

I don't want to say goodbye. But he wants to, and it's all about what he wants right now.

He stands towering above me like he has done a thousand times before but this time it was different, this time it felt final.

He presses his forehead against mine, and my legs go weak. Please don't leave me.

"Can't I buy a seat on the plane? I can fly to London with you then fly home." Tears perpetually flow down my cheeks. We could have another 9 and a half hours together, what's the point in having all this money if I can't do what I want with it.

I hate that he will have to sit in the departure lounge on his own. We could have some more time.

"I could buy a seat on any plane just to sit with you till your flight boards, please Stone." He shakes his head scoffing sadly, "please." I whimper.

"You have to look after my car." He hands me the keys to his precious BMW.

"Fuck your car, I want more time with you." I choke out through strangled sobs.

He kisses the tip of my nose, "Christine will want it for Meg, and the fucking brat will ruin it." He clamps my hand over the keys.

The man standing in front of me is what I want, but I'm not what he needs. What he needs is to go and grow, and be proud if himself, to be able to look in the mirror and love the man he sees, just the way I love him. Despite everything we have done to one another, I love him.

I love him.

That's why I am letting him go.

I move away nodding my head. Offering him a sad smile as I pull myself out of his reach. I have to go, I have to leave.

I turn my back unable to watch him check in, when he disappears behind the sliding doors who knows when I'll see him again.

I savour the last kiss we had this morning, it didn't feel final, it felt normal. That's the one I will remember for the rest of my life. I walk towards the automatic doors desperately wanting to be outside, to be away from this wretched place.

"Hey! You!" He calls out jumping over the barriers leaving his passport, ticket and bags with the woman at the desk.

I ignore him continuing to walk away, "hey! I'm talking to you." Stone shouts his voice becoming louder as he chases after me.

"Don't take another step." He yells, I hear his footsteps slowing behind me as I stumble forward to the entrance, "Eva Miller, stop." He growls.

Slowly turning my body to see his blotchy red face and eyes welled with tears.

He grabs my arms pulling me into him, I melt into his chest my entirety shuddering underneath the weight of sorrow.

I can't breathe, I' am so utterly heartbroken that I think I might die.

Stone breaks our embrace cupping my soaked face in his large hands dipping his head to lock his eyes with mine, "I love you." He sobs attaching his lips to mine, the salty taste of our heartbreak leaking into our mouths.

I want to scream at the world, why is life so cruel.

Will we ever get our chance to be together?

"Look after this for me will you?" He places something in my hand and closes my fingers over it, I open my fist to see my cherry stalk dry and brittle but perfectly preserved in the little knot tied by him all those years ago. I had forgotten about it.

Stone begins his slow walk back to the check in desk, wiping his eyes on the back of his sleeve.

"Aster Stone Carlisle!" I call after him, he stops dead and turns to look at me, much to the line of waiting passenger's dismay.

I trace my cupids bow with the stalk recalling the way it made me feel back then, bringing it all those emotions back to me. I press it to my lips gently before grabbing his hand.

"Give it to me when you come back." I close his hand over it, I brush my lips on his fist.

"I love you." He breathes through broken sobs.

"I love you more, Stone."

I couldn't bring myself to watch him disappear through the sliding doors.

Instead I sat in his car by the runway sobbing for three hours, imagining that he could see me from the plane window. Wondering if he was sobbing too.

The other half of my broken heart soaring into the sky.

FROM: ASC

Landed in Syria about an hour ago, on way to base. Reception is awful. Will drop you an email when I get settled. I meant what I said. I love you.

TO: ASC

Be safe.

I love you more.

I call Griffin to let him know that Stone has made contact, he was able to breathe a sigh of relief. I don't know how. I feel like I'll hold my breath till he comes home. Six months...

How am I supposed to live like this, under this constant weight of worry?

I drum my fingers next to the mouse pad on my laptop the loading circle moving frustratingly slow.

BEEP

His face appears lighting up my screen, "h-h-hii!" Stone' voice stutters.

My body vibrates with nerves; I am just so relieved to see him for the first time in a month.

"my god Stone, you're filthy!" His face is black and so are his hands as he tries to wipe away some of the dust.

"yeah there was a bombing just outside the city, I got caught in some of the debris." His hand shakes as he takes a sip of water.

Fuck. I feel sick.

"How are you?" I try to keep the conversation light, he looks exhausted and I can see from the clock in the background that it's a little after 5am, he's been up all night.

"I'm okay, this connection is terrible." He slams his fist on a box next to the computer, "I'm sorry I keep missing your calls." He rambles fiddling with a pen looking down as he scribbles notes.

"Stone...?"

"Mhmm." he looks up into the camera,

"are you okay?" I bite my bottom lip reminding myself to stay strong, he must be terrified.

"I'm fine Eva. I uh...I have to go, I have to get these words down while they are still fresh in my head." He stands up ready to close his computer.

"Okay, talk soon. I love you." I breathe out suppressing the ball of vomit that sits heavily in my throat.

"Yup." He pops, dipping his head quickly he ends the call.

I stare at the blank screen, numb. I don't even know where to begin.

I don't know why I thought the conversation would go differently; he is in a war zone, witnessing horrific scenes and having to relive them to report them to the world. So why did I think we would discuss the weather or what we were having for dinner? I check the time stamp on the call, 2 minutes 28 seconds. I waited a month to speak to him for 2 minutes and 28 seconds, and yes, I am aware of how incredibly selfish I sound right now but I wanted longer.

Even if we had just stared at each other not saying a word, it would be better than that. Then again, would it?

I've spent the last twelve years wanting more from him, and he couldn't even tell me he loved me too.

God, I am so self-centred.

Stop it Eva, how about you worry more about the fact that a bomb could be dropped on his head at any given time. Instead of focusing on the fact that he didn't say it back.

He was in shock, the way his hand was shaking. He was frightened.

I hate that he is frightened. Why did he have to go there?

'Yup' I cannot think of a word I now loathe more than fucking, 'yup.'

Selfish, So Fucking Selfish

♥

If I'm being honest with myself, I am having a hard time adjusting, I feel like I am walking around aimlessly just going through the motions of life. Feeling completely numb. Unable to form any sort of relationship with anyone.

It's my weekly call with Stone tonight, after last weeks I felt deflated. A surge of emotions cut through me, but mostly I feel guilt.

'Yup' replays through my mind dominating me, the way he popped the 'P'.

And I know that he is in a war zone, witnessing horrific scenes. He's terrified, don't you think I know all of this? But it has taken over me. I'm consumed by the unknowing. I'm in love limbo.

"Eva?" Stones voice comes through the speakers of my computer, "I'm here, can you see me?"

I wipe away my tears trying to compose myself, "I'm here I can't see you though."

"I can see you, are you crying?" A hint of concern is hidden in voice.

"I'm just tired. Stone, are you okay?" I have an ache in my chest at not being able to see him, hearing his voice just isn't enough. I need to see that he is okay. In my head I have the image of him covered in blood and debris. I'm so selfish I know, but I need what I need.

"I'm fine, hold on...I'm going to fix this." I hear him fumbling around cursing under his breath, irritated.

His face appears on my screen a ragged sigh ripples through my lips, "Hi." I whisper holding back sobs as I stare at his face.

His blue eyes barely visible under all the dirt, he has a deep red scratch under his eye just at the top of his perfect cheek, his scruffy mousey brown hair is dusted with debris and the lower half of his face is coated in a darkening stubble, a half smile cornering his mouth.

As I lower my gaze from his lips to his shoulders I notice something, "What are you wearing?" my eyes fixated on the cream and brown camouflage.

"this?" he tugs on the Velcro removing it tossing it onto his bed, "it's just a bulletproof vest."

My shoulders jut forward, 'just' I wretch.

"Come home, come home right now." I sob out throwing my head into my hands, "a fucking bulletproof vest Stone come on..." I slam my hands against my head looking up though the break in my fingers at his face, "its enough now, please come home."

"I don't know what you are saying, Eva, what did you expect?" He snaps back, his brows furrowed so deeply a crease forms between them. He sighs heavily running his hand through his hair shaking his head incredulously.

"You could die Stone do you understand that? You are not some mercenary, you are Stone Carlisle, you are my Stone and I want you to come home before something terrible happens."

He doesn't utter a word in return, he just stares back at me through his screen.

"Listen Eva, I don't want to live my life as some spoilt brat anymore. I want to get out and make something of myself-"

"and you had to go to fucking a war zone to do that did you?" I interrupt him, my heart races in my chest with desperation. I wish I came across as desperate, but it didn't. Anger was the only emotion my body can convey at this moment.

He exhales sharply, "and what are you doing with your life Eva?"

"I can't do anything because I'm waiting for you! I can't think about anything except you! You have taken over my life Stone, and if you get hurt or worse then what will I do?" I yell back, did I mention that I was desperate not angry.

"Then you'll have wasted your life. Don't wait for me, don't call me. I think we're done." He flicks the end of his nose with his thumb I see his chest falling and rising rapidly, I can almost hear the growl deep inside.

"Stone, I-I...I guess you're right." I close the computer, throwing it across the room screaming.

How could I have been so stupid? Why did I have to hurt him like that?

I'm such a fucking idiot.

"Its great to see you in New York," I squeeze Griffin tightly, its good to see a friendly face.

"Its a god awful filthy place Eva, I wish you would come back to Boston." He chuckles sitting across from me.

I glance out of the window at the blistery street, the snow piles up at the sidewalk its crispness ruined with dirt and sludge.

I wonder what Stone is doing, we haven't made any contact in three weeks. I've been keeping up to date with the conflict via the internet and news.

I can't bring myself to watch his coverage though, its different knowing that he is over there, but physically seeing him amongst it tears me apart.

Almost as if he can read my mind Griffin reaches across the table patting the back of my hand, "he's doing well. I spoke with him last night, he asked about you."

I'm still riddled with guilt over our fight, it was my fault.

But I can't shame myself into apologising and trying to make amends because I can't wait any longer.

It's okay to wait for the one, but I can't wait for him to be the one.

When will I be allowed to start my life?

Griffin and I make small talk, we laugh over silly things and talk about books and plays.

I can tell he is tired but he insists on walking to his hotel so I walk with him, our arms linked as the winter sun disappears behind the grey clouds and night falls.

We stand in front of the St Regis, I lean up to peck him on the cheek.

"Can't you make it right with him Eva?" He pulls me into a warm embrace and I shake my head.

"I think this time it was pretty final." I push back tears, doing my best to remain strong.

"I doubt that very much." He turns around and disappears into the grand foyer.

I thought about hailing a cab but decided instead to walk.

I walked for miles in the freezing cold, and somehow found myself outside Emily's house.

I stood counting the steps just like I did all those years ago instinctively searching for his hand.

Desperately longing for our subtle 'I love you' exchange.

"Eva?" Emily calls from the front door, "come in its freezing out there." My legs carry me inside before my mind had a chance to overthink.

"Is everything okay?" She searches my face for answers looking worriedly at Robert who sets a cup of coffee in front of me.

"I'm feeling a bit lost," I begin to open up, "I don't have anyone, and I pushed Stone away." I swirl the liquid around the cup unable to stomach even a sip.

Emily leans into Robert, "I don't know what to do." She whispers in his ear fidgeting awkwardly.

"Just listen." He whispers back.

I look up at them through my soaked eyelashes, I'm still trying to figure out why I came here.

Then it hits me, "I'm lonely." I wheeze through a strangled sob.

I'm isolated and I did it to myself.

Five Stages And An Intervention, Sort Of.

To: ASC.

Stone...I'm struggling to find the right words to apologise to you. I got scared, and I know that isn't an excuse but my desperation came across as selfishness. Maybe I was just being plain selfish, but I miss you and I'm sorry.

Please forgive me.

Eva x

I press send, and as the email disappears my eyes open up their dam and expel tears down my cheeks.

Now I have to wait on his reply. Like a damn teenager waiting on a text from her school boy crush.

Please let him forgive me, I know I really fucked up this time. But he has to forgive me. He'll forgive me, he will...right?

Hours turned into days, days turned into weeks and before I know it 2 months have passed since I sent the email to Stone, with no reply.

At first I wondered if I had sent it at all, I sent emails to every one in my address book and everyone replied. I wondered if maybe his email had changed so I came right out and asked Griffin if he had a new one. Almost broke my heart when he said no.

Maybe its gotten lost amongst work emails.

Thats it, he will find it nestled between magazine subscriptions and deadlines for his articles. And when he eventually finds it he'll call me and we'll laugh and cry about it. He'll come home and we will live happily ever after.

Another day passes and still no reply, why is he doing this to me? After everything he put me through! The drugs and the cheating on his fiancee. The fight with Jake. The pregnancy scare!! And the asshole can't even reply with even a simple sarcastic thumbs up emoji?! What was all the bullshit in the airport about loving me and keeping that stupid fucking cherry stalk for all these years? I hate him. I hate his fucking guts. He is rotten, to the absolute core. And I' am better off without him.

I swear to god, I wish I had never lain eyes on him.

Its been another week and still nothing, I know he's working because I caught a snippet of his coverage. He has a fuller beard now, the blue of his eyes has darkened, I imagine he is talking directly to me, but seeing his face on my screen, the gun fire and explosions going off behind him, it tore me apart. I couldn't watch any longer. I'd give anything to bring him back, I'd lay my life down for him.

I'm begging you Stone, please come home or at the very least send me a reply.

I don't check my phone any more, I don't do anything. Because I don't feel anything. The endless black hole of hopelessness circles me threatening to consume everything in its path widens...edging closer as I close my eyes and pray to be swallowed.

"Eva?" Emilys voice comes from the other side of my apartment door, "We've been trying to call, let us in please?"

I don't need to let them in, I haven't locked that door in days. Teetering on the edge of danger hoping that maybe someone will force their way through and put me out of my misery.

"Its open." I groan turning around in my bed not even remotely ashamed enough to get out of bed and greet the almost strangers.

Robert and Emily tip toe over the threshold looking around the pristine apartment, "I don't think she's been eating." Robert hushes to Emily as she opens the fridge gawping at its emptiness.

"I'll go to the store, talk to her." I hear him whisper the door closing quietly behind him as he leaves.

Emily stands in the light of my bedroom door, "I think its time you got out of bed Eva."

I turn around facing away from her wrapping my arms around myself, just trying to hold every fibre of my being together.

I feel the bed sink a little as she sets herself down at the end, shifting her weight uncomfortably.

Its nice that she is here, but I wish she wasn't.

I want my dad.

"Okay Eva its time to get up and shower, you can't wallow forever. You missed Christmas and New Years." She opens the blinds allowing the winter sun in to expose me.

"No." I growl sliding underneath the duvet.

She pulls them back swiftly, "yes!"

"Get up now, this is enough Eva. I don't have time for this...its tough love time." She starts rummaging through my drawers yanking out clean underwear and fresh clothes.

"I suppose tough love is better than no love huh?" Reaching down for the covers I catch a glimpse of Emily wincing in the mirror.

"And whats that supposed to mean Eva?" She walks over to my closet pulling out jeans and a hoodie, "no that one!" I scream.

Its his, its Stones Hugo Boss sweatshirt. He gave it to me the morning he left for Syria...

"What the fuck is this?" I pull out a black hoodie that lies on top of his duffle bag.

He rolls his eyes at me, "incase I get cold on the plane."

My mouth hangs open as I try my best to hold back laughter, "Stone Carlisle, are you seriously telling me that you wear sweatpants now?"

"Fuck off!" He lunges towards me grabbing the sweater out of my hand and forcing it over my head.

"It looks better on you, keep it." He sweeps the hair away from my face, planting his lips on the tip of my nose.

"I'm only messing Stone...take it with you." I fumble around inside trying to get it off without falling over.

He helps me get it over my head, smoothing my hair once more.

Ripping off the price tag, "I want you to have it, and here..." he grabs a bottle from his dresser and sprays it with his aftershave.

Just as he turns away from me I grab his wrist pulling him back to me. I reach up and capture his lips occupying his mouth with my tongue, deepening our kiss trying to prolong it. Not wanting to waste a single second.

He lifts my body, I instinctively wrap my legs around him our lips never parting.

Stone leans me against the wall pinning my arms above my head as he begins to lace his tongue along my jawline, trailing it down my neck. Stopping when he gets to my favourite spot nibbling lightly. A carnal moan forces its way from my mouth, I fist his hair pulling his mouth back to mine taking his bottom lip between my teeth.

His fingers dance along the waist band of my jeans slowly sliding down, desperate to feel how ready for him I am.

"Ahem." Angela awkwardly clears her throat lingering in the doorway, "its time to leave."

"Okay...not this one," Emily puts it back, folding the jeans back on their hanger and instead pulls out some of my gym gear, "lets opt for comfort eh?"

I sit on the edge of the bathtub listening to Emily and Roberts hushed voices.

"Do you think I should have went in there, you don't think shes...shes...y'know...suicidal." Emily's voice trails off.

Fucking hell...maybe I am.

No I'm not.

I feel like I might die, but not by my own hand.

"I'm not going to kill myself!!" I walk out of the bathroom curtsying sarcastically showing the intruders that I have successfully managed to wash and get dressed without using a toaster as bath bomb.

"Happy now?" I smirk gruffly lying myself across the sofa, staring at the TV on the wall. Images of Syria flashing across the screen, scenes of death and destruction as people flee and run for their lives.

Bitter tears sting my eyes.

Robert changes the channel, "put it back!! I never turn it off." I scrambled for the remote.

"I get that Eva, I do. But Alma called and shes worried about you-"

"And so is Griffin." Emily interrupts handing me a cup of coffee.

This is an intervention, but without anyone actually attending.

Robert sits on the coffee table in front of me, "I - I mean we just think that maybe you should take a break from all of this," he holds out the articles that Stone has written which I have printed off, like some sort of obsessed stalker. "I think you need to try and move on." He pats my knee, "I'm not your father, and I'm not trying to be...but maybe we could be friends?"

He offers me a kind smile and moves away from the table heading back to the kitchen, Emily sits in front of me, "he's right you know."

"I like him...he doesn't hover." I growl at her through my eyes.

She nods respectfully.

I turn on my back and look at the ceiling fan as it spins around slowly, focusing on the blades as they disappear becoming one.

Are they right...is it time to move on?

And what does that entail exactly? I have no job, no friends. The only thing I have is a large bank balance and a hole where my heart used to be.

So explain to me how I am supposed to move on.

Which Would Hurt More?

♥

"Why are you guys here?" I ask shovelling eggs into my mouth; Emily looks around to Robert who gives her a reassuring nod and disappears into the kitchen area.

"I uh...well after you...at my..." I watch as Emily stumbles over her words, my wiser years making me soft. I see her trying to be a parent, and I can't help but wonder...is it time to cut her some slack?

A welcoming smile twitches in the corner of my mouth. I went to them, to her because I'm lonely and burdened with grudges. I'm not sure how much longer I can hold onto them.

Hesitantly I pull down my barrier and let her slide through.

"I couldn't stop thinking about you." She looks down shamefully at her feet, "I've thought about you every day, I uh just didn't know how to reach out to you." Tears form in the corners of her eyes.

A heave a guilty sigh, "I haven't been the most approachable person."

Emily pats the back of my hand gently, "we've all made mistakes. Me more than others. I can't rewrite the past but if you'll give me a chance then maybe we could be friends?"

I suppose I owe myself that.

"Okay, but don't crowd me. I'm not used to that." I get up from the sofa, scowling at them sarcastically.

"We won't, it's not our style. What I will ask is that you lock your damn door." Robert shouts over the noise of the dishwasher.

I dip my head sniffling back some stray tears, "deal."

"I don't know, I just think it's a bit soon." I hold my cell between my ear and shoulder fumbling around with my keys in the lock to my apartment, "excuse me... I have friends, well you and Robert and Griffin, that's more than enough."

Emily wants me to join her and Robert's 'gathering' tonight. They love entertaining, and I hate being a part of it. Plus it'll be all Robert's fellow firemen, and their wives. I'll just be the poor lonely spinster only there to bring down the mood with my sad eyes.

I don't need a friend; I need a pet or a job!

I fall through the door to find Emily standing in my kitchen filling out a glass of wine, "I let myself in."

"So I see, I thought we were setting boundaries?" I throw my keys into the bowl on the credenza and flick through my mail.

It's all junk mail and bills I lay them on the side of the kitchen counter, secretly hurt that there still isn't a letter with a foreign stamp on it.

He'll be home in two more months, I try my best to forget about him and move on, at least until then.

I imagine that one day he will be waiting for me outside my apartment like he did in LA and we will have fantastic make up sex and then he'll leave me like he always does, or did. Or maybe one day I will I go down to the parking lot and his car will be gone, no note, no nothing. And I'll send the spare key to Griffin and that will be the end of us, again.

I just don't know which would hurt worse.

I just don't know that I can go through it all again, there isn't an ounce of strength left in me.

The fight is gone.

On the surface that is.

Emily fills me out a glass of wine and slides it over to me, "this party, it'll be good for you."

I drop my gaze and scorn her, "I thought it was a 'gathering'.

"It's a yearly thing that we do for Robert's old squad from the firehouse, what's the middle ground of a party and a gathering?" I know exactly what this is, it's a set up. I see right through the pair of them.

I'm. Not. Ready.

"A place that Eva doesn't want to be?" I groan as she tops up my wine, she smooths away some of my stray hair.

"please Eva, it would really mean a lot to us and I do genuinely think it would be good for you."

"Ugh!" I moan like an angsty teenager, "fine!!" I gulp the rest of my wine and head for the bedroom to get myself prepped.

"I'll see you there at eight thirty, Eva!" Emily calls on her way out.

I stare at myself in the mirror noticing the little fine lines appearing in the corners of my eyes and around my mouth. My skin not as young and fresh as it once was. I've spent almost half my life chasing, Stone, or not chasing him. Being left and lost by him. And in doing so somewhere along the line I lost who I was, in fact I was never given the chance to find out who I was in the first place.

So maybe this party or gathering will be good for me.

I wasn't entirely sure what the dress code for a g-arty was, but I knew that Emily would be dressed immaculately so I opted for the safe option, a deep forest green midi dress, black court heels and a black duster coat.

Catching my reflection in the elevator mirror I smile at myself, I look good. I feel good.

I'm ready for this, I'm ready to make friends.

Maybe spark a relationship.

Somebody out there will want me?

Maybe I'll even want them.

I can do this.

My mousey hair is sun kissed with highlights and elegantly waved framing my face. I took special care doing my makeup, putting in a lot of effort to look as naturally beautiful as possible. I smile at myself again, only this time a sting in my heart shocks me. The look I gave myself was the same look my dad would give me. It's the first time I ever realised that I had a bit of him in me. I always thought I looked like Emily, but there nestled in the corner of my mouth was a little part of him.

I push back the tears not wanting to spoil my make up.

'Hi Dad.' I whisper to myself, not entirely sure why I did it. But it made me feel better all the same.

The doors slide open; I nod to the doorman as he prepares to hold the main door open for me, but it wasn't me he was holding it for.

It was Stone.

Eyelash Wishes

"Stone...wh...wha...how..." words fail me I can't tell if he's real or not.

He stands stoic looking me up and down, the slow rise and fall of his chest deepening with the passing moment.

His tawny hair is longer than I've ever seen it, lying scruffily on the top of his head, he has a few scabbed over grazes on his face, his eyes are so dark. They look exhausted.

I can barely see his lips underneath the thick dark beard that has overgrown around his face adding to his ruggedness. I miss his lips.

"We got pulled out early, it was getting too dangerous," he stares at me coldly, "you're going out, I only came for my car."

I felt as though the wind had been knocked right out of me. Not the scenario I had envisioned.

I feel a sudden urge of anger towards romantic movies for filling my head full of unrealistic reunions, where the girl runs into the guys arms, he lifts her spinning as he kisses every inch of her face. And they sob and swear to never leave each others side again.

I call bullshit on the whole fucking thing.

"Oh." I fumble through my bag searching for his key remembering that I had taken it off and put it in a drawer in my bedroom.

"It's upstairs I'll go back up and get it." I call the elevator turning my back to him allowing myself a moment to react, holding back the tears as best I can.

My chest heaves up and down as I try my best to keep some sort of composure, I can tell he is still angry with me.

"I'll come back tomorrow and get it, you've got plans. Enjoy your night." I hear him shuffle his weight close behind me.

How long has he been back, why didn't he call or write to tell me he was coming back? Does Griffin know?

Just when I thought I was ready to move on, he comes back into my life shaking everything up again.

I see him edge closer to the exit in the reflection of the tiled walls, "Wait! Stone...please wait!" I chase after him, "You didn't call or write me, why?"

He exhales deeply boring his eyes into mine, "dDdn't have anything to say." He huffs, heading down Central Park West.

"Stone...I...I-I what happens now?" I pant out, pedestrians in the street slowing to witness our demise.

He throws his hands into the air, "I guess we move on." Running them over his face and through his scruff.

"You're late," Emily sighs through a Cheshire cat grin, "Everyone this is Eva my daughter." She introduces me around the lounge area, men and women raise a glass and nod their heads acknowledging me.

I offer them an awkward smile in return.

Should I have chased Stone down the street?

Robert hands me a glass of wine pecking me lightly on the cheek, "smile Eva, its not that terrible." If only he knew.

"Got anything stronger?" I plead, he chuckles and fills me a glass of grey goose vodka, which I absolutely despise but I neck any way.

"One more and I'll be grand." This time his brow furrows, he can tell something is wrong, but he knows better than to press.

Across the crowd I see Emily trying to catch my attention, she has her arm looped with a tall sandy haired man, he rolls his eyes as he is reluctantly trailed across the living area into the kitchen, "Eva! This is Thomas." She places her hands on his shoulders.

"Tommy." He sighs, mouthing 'I'm sorry' at me.

Emily doesn't even give him an introduction, she just brought him over and abandoned the poor guy.

Tommy shifts his weight from side to side awkwardly in this intense silence, I suppose someone needs to break it. I see Emily standing on her tip toes observing us over the crowd and if we don't start talking soon, she'll come over here and do the talking for us, "Wow, I'm so sorry." I laugh out.

Tommy chuckles back offering me a friendly smile, "don't worry about it. They've been planning this for weeks." I could tell that he had already anticipated it.

My mouth inadvertently hangs open, the pair of meddling assholes. 'Not our style indeed.'

"Do you smoke?" Tommy pulls out a pack of cigarettes from his pocket, I shake my head.

"I don't but I'll come outside with you if you want." I'd do anything to get out of this 'gathering' which was quite clearly always a party. The fresh air would do me good.

I grab two beers from the ice bucket on the kitchen island and head out onto to the stoop with Tommy.

"So Boston huh?" I swig my beer watching him light his cigarette, Bostonians can always tell.

He nods taking a deep inhale, "yeah! Harvard, you?" blowing the smoke out away from my direction.

"I'm from Boston but I went to UCLA for a semester, then transferred here to Juilliard." His eyes widen as he bobs his head, he's impressed. I blush a little, chills run through my body. This feeling... is it because of Stone, or is it something else?

I feel weird, Tommy makes me feel comfortable. It's really easy to talk to him, something that I always find hard. I can go on stage and perform in front of hundreds maybe even thousands of people because it's easier to pretend to be someone else, but when it comes to meeting new people, I don't know which Eva to be.

A gust of wind blows some of Tommy's cigarette ash into his hair, I get up from the step and stand in front of him reaching up and pick it out, I allow my eyes to lock into his for a second. Taken back by the sparkle of the green, "Sorry, but I would want someone to tell me if I had something in my hair." I blush taking a step back away from him trying to calm the butterflies in my stomach.

Tommy clears his throat, "Well in that case," he dips his head brushing his finger lightly on the top of my cheek holding up a stray eyelash, "would you like to make a wish?" he holds it in front of my lips on the tip of his finger.

I shake my head softly from side to side, "Finders keepers." My mouth twisting into a coy smile watching as Tommy squints his eyes and purses his lips before blowing the lash gently away.

"What did you wish for?" My cheeks burn through my wide smile.

He smiles back, "I can't tell you that...It won't come true."

My heart flips inside my chest, it surprises me because I wasn't even sure it was still alive. For the first time in three months I had forgotten about Stone, and thought about something else. Me.

"Do you wanna get out of here, maybe go for a walk?" I simper, silently panicking incase I've come across too forward.

Oh shit.

A wide smile spreads across Tommy's face, "I'd love to."

The Ominous Knock

"Thank you for walking me home, Tommy." I hand him over the bottle of bourbon that he bought from the liquor store, we had shared it as we strolled around New York.

He bows dramatically, "It was my pleasure m'lady." Swigging the last of the bottle he throws it into the trash.

"Good Evening Miss Miller." Arthur the night door man steps out into the cold to hold open the door for me.

I nod acknowledging him slipping him a fifty dollar bill, "give us a minute, please." I whisper not quite ready for the evening to be over.

Tommy saunters over to me locking his warm, addictively green eyes with mine, "It was really nice to meet you Eva, I'd like to see you again...if that's okay with you?"

He makes my heart burst, everything about him screams good guy. I should take a chance on him, because at this point what do I have to lose?

"Sure, I'd like that." My cheeks flush as I hand him my phone.

Handing it back to me I glance at his name, Tommy Vaughn.

"I'm going to kiss you now." He dips his head tilting it to the side, leaning in softly as he cups my face between his hands, pressing his lips gently to mine.

I was soft and sweet, like all first kisses should be.

I liked it.

"Goodnight Eva." He brushes his mouth on the back of my hand, stumbling on the sidewalk as he leaves.

Arthur clears his throat, "Sorry Arty...I think I just had my first date." I giggle covering my face with my hands.

"I find that hard to believe Miss Miller, a girl as beautiful as you should have them lining up outside your door." He holds the door open for me and I slide inside the building.

As I wait on the elevator I pull out my cell phone.

TO: TOMMY VAUGHN

Thanks for the walk home
and the kiss.
Hope your wish comes true.

I step inside and wait to be taken up to my floor, just as I exit my phone pings.

FROM: TOMMY VAUGHN

Don't thank me, thank the eyelash.

This wide smile hasn't left my face the entire walk home, its one of those heart flutteringly painful smiles that hurt your ears and the back of your head. It's a feeling I haven't felt in quite some time. I'm almost too afraid to enjoy it. Just in case I get reliant on it.

I couldn't sleep I replayed the night over in my head, but not all the good parts with Tommy, the ambushed reunion with Stone, he has invaded my mind again.

I feel guilty, almost like I have cheated on him with Tommy. Which is preposterous, because Stone told me it was over, he shouted to me in the middle of the street to move on. So why do I have this awful gnawing in my stomach that I have done something wrong?

I think I must have gotten all in, about two hours sleep. My conscience never letting up, drowning my good mood in sinfulness.

After showering I sit on the kitchen stool trawling for jobs on my computer when the ominous knock comes at the door.

Fuck.

My hands begin to shake knowing that, Stone, is on the other side. When I hand him the keys to his car then the last tie I have to him will be gone and we will truly be finished.

I open the door slowly, I have to do this. It's time to do this. One way or another this has to end, because there is no road for us anymore.

I can't force him to be ready to love and accept me. He has to do that on his own, and I don't have time to wait.

I got a quick taste of what life can be like if you stop holding onto to a deadweight love, and I liked it.

Stone's s frame hangs sheepishly, his face is now clean shaven and hair slicked into his signature side shed.

His eyebrow flickers, "I'm just here for my keys."

"I kissed someone last night." I blurt out.

Why did I have to say that?

Stones eyes shoot up glancing into mine then back down to his feet, "Like I said, I'm just here for my keys."

I reach across into the bowl and pull out the keys for his precious BMW placing them in his hand.

We stand staring at each other, only for a second but it felt like an eternity.

He breaks our gaze taking a step backwards out of my door way, I close the door gently.

Just as it's about to lock Stone's boot slides into the gap.

He comes crashing through, lunging at me and I throw myself at him. He yanks my t-shirt over my head throwing it across the floor, jutting his face to mine he takes my bottom lip harshly between his teeth as I fumble with his belt sliding down his jeans.

"Are you fucking wet for me?" He purrs in my ear gliding his hand down my stomach to my heated core, dancing his fingers around the waistband.

He flips me round facing me to the wall, falling to his knees using his thumbs to pull down my yoga tights.

Getting up off the floor he kicks his jeans away pressing his naked body against mine, his strengthened length pressing into my back as he pins me against the wall.

He peppers open mouth kisses on the back of my neck, lacing them down my shoulder, his hands gripping my breast firmly as he rolls my pebbled nipples between his thumb and index finger.

He continues to work one breast, his other hand grazes my stomach as he reaches to my mound brushing the neatly trimmed curls at the top of my opening.

"Did the kiss make you feel like this?" He kicks my legs apart stretching my slit open, gliding his fingers inside, "always so fucking wet for me aren't you, Eva?" He flicks my ear with his tongue.

"Say it..." he growls lightly flicking my engorged clit, "Fucking say it!"

"I'm always wet for you, Stone." I mewl desperate for him to relieve me, "Make me cum." Begging as I inadvertently tickle my fingers down to my pulsing core.

He thrashes his fingers into my sopping folds, I throw my head back onto his chest in ecstasy, he attaches his mouth to mine inhaling my pleasured moans.

I pull myself from him turning my body around, "Fuck me." I breathe into his neck.

He hoists me up hooking my legs around his waist lining his throbbing cock up with my entrance, "Say you want me." A carnal look overcomes his eyes, and in one feral motion I roll my hips packing myself onto him.

"I said fuck me." With his length stretching me wide he walks me through to the living area, taking a seat on the sofa. I pound myself onto him, relishing in the lecherous curl of his lip as I buck him onto the cusp of orgasm.

"Stop!" He grabs my seat slowing my motion, I feel him resist inside me.

I lift myself off and fall onto my knees, lacing my tongue from the base of his cock to the tip before plunging my mouth down swallowing its entirety, the beastly gagging motion electrifying every nerve in my body.

He intertwines my hair in his fingers pulling my head back off his cock, I release him with a pop, a wild grin creeps over his face at the sight of my gaping mouth. He drags my head up to meet my mouth with his, tasting my juices and saliva as his tongue invades mine.

He lifts me off my knees savagely throwing me onto the sofa burying his steeled cock deep inside swollen mound, viciously ploughing into me as I dig my nails into his back.

I thrust my hips upwards into him curling my body as the height of my climax explodes through me hitching my breath as I hold on begging for another.

Stone slams his body into mine ruthlessly demolishing me as my walls grip on to him, milking him. Draining him. Warm ribbons pumped deep inside me, the final twitches of him expelling inside me. Our mixture dripping out of me.

"You kissed someone." Stone pants out catching his breath, "Don't fucking do that."

"Fuck you Stone." I spit at him, "I'll do what the fuck I want."

He takes his fingers and delves into the creaminess between my legs flicking over my highly sensitive clit, he curls his fingers relishing in my lewd gasp as I fight against him, "Stop!"

"You'll always be mine." He pulls out, angrily searching for his clothes whilst I lie on the sofa covering my face with my hands.

Why did I let him do this again?

Fingertips

♥

Inviting Stone over to talk was the right thing to do, we had to end whatever this was between us, the hot and cold. It was our real life toxic love trope and it had to stop.

"I really think its time we talked, Stone." I close my apartment door behind him, he shoves me against it, running his hand up the inside of my thigh, "Stop! I mean it. No sex...just talking." I reluctantly push him away, and he grabs my wrist firmly.

"Enough." I seethe.

He scoffs loosening his grip and heads towards my kitchen filling himself a glass of scotch.

"You're all dressed up." Sneering as he undresses me with his eyes.

"This," I wave my finger back and forth between us, "Is so fucking unhealthy. Honestly, Stone...you're so hot and cold." He rolls his eyes gulping the liquid in one, not even so much as flinching at the bitter taste.

He saunters over tome backing me into the couch, "Why are you dressed up?" He runs his finger up my Gucci tights running it along the seam that is lined with my covered slit. Grabbing my knees he spreads my legs open, peering down under my leather skirt, "got the sexy thong on as well..." he hums.

I snap my legs shut, trying my hardest to remain strong. Praying for the willpower to say no.

"I have a date." I press the red sole of my stiletto against his chest and push him away.

"With the kissing man?" He curls his lip as he gets to his feet.

"Fireman actually but yes, its the man I kissed." I twitch my mouth into a quick defiant smile.

His eyes widen and he burst into hysterics, "A fucking fireman? You're serious?" He clutches his chest in an attempt to steady his hearty guffaw.

"Naw, a fireman...you're joking. Tell me you're joking." He continues.

Rolling my eyes I get off the arm of the sofa, "No Stone...I'm not. And I like him, he is nice to me and he doesn't use me."

I wipe away a nervous tear.

Stone leans down catching my gaze, "But does he make you wet?" He attaches his lips to the sweet spot on my neck.

The spot that he knows I cannot resist.

I roll my head back, he swallows my lewd moans with his mouth.

"You're here to talk," I pant out breathlessly aroused, "Not fuck."

He laces his tongue around my lips flicking my cupids bow, "can't we do both?" He purrs in my ear.

"No, Tommy will be here soon."

He pulls away, "Urgh! That's his name? Fuckin' Tommy. Maaaan. Tommy the fireman. What a dick." He flails his arms in the air like a child.

"He is not a dick, he's a nice guy and I like him." I fix the makeup around my mouth in the mirror.

Stone steps in behind me trailing kisses along my shoulder, peppering up the back of my neck.

"Stop. It." I growl.

He heaves a petulant sigh, "Fine...you wanna talk...then lets talk." Throwing himself onto my sofa in a strop, covering his mouth and chin with his balled fist.

Suddenly I can't remember what I was going to say. I never expected him to give up so easily.

I inhale slowly diplomatically trying to pick my words before I spew them out. God, I wish that would have worked, "Do you love me?" my legs weaken, I sit on the coffee table across from him to stop myself from collapsing onto the floor.

He rolls his eyes removing the fist from his face his lips part as he is about to say something but he just sighs instead.

"If you have to think about it then the answer is no, Stone." I hold onto my tears as hard as I can, gulping back the painful lump in my throat.

He leans forward pressing his hands on my knees, "It's not as simple as that Eva."

"But it is Stone, for me it is. I love you. It's as simple as that. I love you." Pushing away his hands I get up from the table, I can't look at him.

I can't do this anymore. It shouldn't be this hard.

I pour myself a drink keeping my back to him.

"You have a part of me and I want it back..." I sob out unable to hold on any longer.

I don't know what else we have to say to each other, I'm ashamed of myself. I really thought he'd say he loved me too. I really thought he did.

"You knew what this was from the beginning." Walking round the other side of the kitchen he leans against the counter pouring himself a drink.

"You mean twelve years ago? Oh...okay. All of that bullshit in the airport was just some sort of what? Dramatic performance was it?" I throw my arms out exasperated, "Stone, why are you doing this to me?" I grip the counter breathlessly looking up at him doe eyed, "I love you," giving him a final chance to say it back...

His eyes drive into me but he doesn't utter a word.

"I said I love you, Stone." He stands stoic.

I shrug my shoulders at his silence, "You are it for me...anyone else is just going to fall short. But I wont wait for you to wake up and realise that you are in love with me too. Because while I may not love anyone else, I deserve to be loved by someone." My body gravitates towards him I stand right in front of him, he slips his hands into mine our fingers laced together.

My mouth hangs open a little in anticipation edging closer to his lips, readily waiting to capture them. I can taste his sweet breath tickling the top of my cupids bow.

A knock comes at the door.

He drops my hands quickly and heads to the sofa grabbing his keys, phone and wallet.

I try to steady my heartbeat.

Plastering a fake smile across my face I unlock the door, "Hi Tommy!" Trying to disguise the quiver in my voice.

"Hi." He simpers leaning in softly pressing his lips against mine in a lingering kiss.

I press my hand on his chest gently pushing him away, "I...uh...this is Stone, my oldest friend."

Tommy stands wide eyed, blushing a little before extending his hand out to Stone, "Sorry man, I'm Tommy."

I hear the familiar growl build inside Stone's chest as he sizes Tommy up, his lip curling in disgust.

"Stone." I hiss under my breath.

He grabs hold of Tommy's hand gripping it firmly.

"I was just leaving, have a good night. Eva...pleasure as always." He brushes his lips on my cheek pausing the moment, I thought he was going to say something, unspoken words left lingering on my skin like an invisible brand etched by his lips.

"So what do you do for work Eva?" Tommy leans across the restaurant table reaching for my hand, hesitantly I relax mine and allow him to take hold sweeping a gentle thumb across the back.

I look down into my wine embarrassed that I don't have to work, that I have been living off the money I inherited, "Nothing at the minute...sorta between jobs, and lives right now."

He presses his thumb on my hand getting me to look up, "There's nothing wrong with that." Reassuring me with a wink and a soft smile.

"I sent an application in to Juilliard for an assistant teaching post, its a long shot but..." I shrug my shoulders unenthusiastically, "You never know."

"Thats great!" The restaurant starts to get busier, but we sit for hours talking and eating slowly.

He's a really sweet guy, he gives me butterflies in my stomach its unsettlingly addictive.

"So that guy...Stone? I feel like I've seen him before." My heart falls into my stomach when he mentions his name.

"He went to Harvard, maybe you saw him around campus." I fill my mouth full of wine, stress drinking.

Tommy shakes his head, "Possibly, but I feel like I've seen him somewhere else." He pauses looking at my face for answers.

I gulp the wine down unintentionally making a loud glugging sound, "I mean he's a journalist too, he just got back from Syria. Maybe you caught one of his articles or saw him on CNN."

"Holy shit!" He pulls out his cell phone typing quickly, "This is him."

He holds up the screen showing me footage from CNN, its Stone surrounded by rubble and dust helping a screaming man pull a woman free from a collapsed building, she's screaming the subtitles tell us she is saying "Stop!" "Please wait!"

She reaches up out of the hole that is drastically caving in on top of her, she hands Stone a baby girl. No older than one year old, covered in dirt and scrapes screaming so uncontrollably that her face is purple. Just as he hands the baby off to the father he reaches back down to grab the woman's hand but as their fingertips brush she slips away disappearing under sand coloured bricks, Stone is thrown backwards by the force of the collapse, the camera man runs to his aid, the footage ending on the image of Stone defeated on the ground covering his audible sobs with his hands.

I hand Tommy back his phone, his eyes are filled with concern.

"Excuse me for a moment." I rush off into the bathroom staring at my tear streaked face in the mirror as my body convulses in pain.

How could I have been so selfish. Stone, my Stone has been dealing with this on his own, all of this anguish he has been carrying around in his mind, and I just had to go and pile more on him?

I slap the side of my head turning away from the mirror ashamed of myself.

Breakfast And A Little Bit Of Something Else

Tommys eyes are wide watching me come back from the bathroom, "I'm sorry, I didn't mean to upset you." I slide back into my seat unable to hide my puffy red eyes from him.

I shake my head unable to form words just yet.

Tommy reaches out for my hand and I let him have it, nodding reassuring him that I'm okay.

I'm not.

I run my tongue over my top teeth trying to compose myself swallowing the painful lump that swells in my throat.

"Its alright, I...I just didn't...we had a...we weren't talking." I breathe out, Tommy nods understandingly, signalling for the cheque.

We stand outside the door to my apartment, its so easy and light with him. I've pushed the Stone stuff to the back of my mind to deal with later. Right now in this moment I want to give him all of me, well most of me. Okay, just a little bit of me. But its better than nothing.

He brushes his the back of his fingers along my shoulder and down my arm making the hairs on my body stand on edge, every nerve electrified.

"I like you, Eva." He whispers into my ear causing me to shiver, the excitement is too much.

I feel like a teenager.

"I like you too." He hooks his finger under my chin tilting my mouth up to meet his capturing my lips softly, he tracing my bottom lip with his tongue asking for permission.

I part my mouth allowing him access which he takes with fervour, gently pushing me back against the door deepening the kiss he wraps his fingers in my hair, inhaling my moans. As he presses himself up against me I feel his hardened bulge through his pants and I run my hand over it causing his hips to buck forward into me.

"Not here..." he pants out, "Not like this." He peppers kisses on my neck.

He's right, I want this to be more than just about sex. I think.

"I have an afternoon flight to Boston tomorrow." I tease his bottom lip between my teeth, "But do you wanna come over for breakfast?"

He pulls back, a coy smile brushed across his face.

"I'd really like that. I'll bring the coffee." He kisses my pink swollen lips.

"8am okay, or is that too early?" I take his hand in mine swinging it by our side.

He pulls me closer, "perfect. I'll see you tomorrow." He waits until I get inside, and when I look through the peephole I see him punch the air and skip off down the hallway like a horny frat boy.

Now I have to do something about this pulsing ache in my core.

"Good morning!" Tommy beams leaning in to kiss me holding two coffee cups, he makes my heart warm.

"Morning." I return grinning like a cat.

I lead him into my kitchen area, "Okay so I have a confession to make..." he looks at me suspiciously, "I really suck at cooking." I bite my bottom lip nervously.

He chuckles out loud setting down the coffee on the counter, "I don't really eat breakfast, I just wanted to see you again." He looks through one of the cupboards finding two old pre wrapped croissants, he grabs two plates out of the dishwasher and places them down in front of us, "voila, breakfast."

God what is it about this man, he is so good.

My cheeks burn as my mouth twists into a painfully happy smile, sliding off of my stool I make my way to him, reaching up to bruise his lips with mine.

It started off sweet but somehow turned into something more, before I could catch my breath the plates were swiped from the counter smashing on the tiles, as Tommy lifts me up yanking down my sweatpants tossing them onto the floor, I fumble reaching for his belt, "This is about you." He whispers in my ear. Pinning my arms down by my side I let out a nervous giggle that he inhales breathing me in like I would give him life.

He drops down to his knees grabbing the dip in my thighs pulling me off the edge slightly, my legs inadvertently open. Exposing my slick slit readily waiting for him, Tommy's tongue runs from my inner thigh lacing around my mound slowly flicking at my seam.

"Fuck!" My breath hitches in anticipation, I reach for his head wanting to guide him deeper.

"Patience." He growls devilishly taking his index finger he parts my lips in an upwards motion barely brushing my clit, my body squirms desperately needing him to relieve the pressure that pulses inside me.

I throw my head back in pleasured frustration silently begging for him to delve into me.

Almost as though he read my mind, or maybe it was the buck of my hips he swipes his tongue up the length of my glistening core settling his pouted lips on my swollen clit sucking with a pop. My body jerks upwards I want his length inside my, "Fuck me." I beg panting through the cusp of orgasm.

Tommy gets off his knees standing between my thighs, "I'm not gonna fuck you. I want to make love to you first. Then I'll fuck you."

I reach again for his pants trying to undo them, "Not today baby." He glides two fingers inside my opening attaching his mouth to mine as I yelp, he drinks in my muffled moans pumping into me curling his fingers at the end. I inhale sharply as he paints my orgasm beautifully, nibbling my bottom lip as my body shudders in ecstasy.

"What time's your flight?" Tommy kisses my forehead before reaching down for my pants guiding my legs into my underwear and then again into my sweatpants.

"A little after twelve, I have to leave pretty soon." Coyly I slide off the counter and wrap my arms around his waist, "do you wanna talk to me while I get ready?" I reach up to kiss his chin.

"I'd love that." He bounces into my room after me sitting on the edge of my bed whilst I pick out an outfit for lunch.

"Have you told your friends about me?" Tommy swirls around a make up brush in some bronzer sniffing it curiously.

"I don't have any friends." I furrow my brows ashamed, "actually that's not true, Griffin's my friend and Robert." I swipe a light pink lipstick across my pouty lips and step into a short tight leather skirt tucking in a cream blouse, happy-ish with the way I look.

"And Steve.." I spin round confused.

"What?"

"Steve is your friend."

Still doesn't help.

"Tommy are you having a stroke?" He stands up off the bed chuckling.

"No...your oldest friend." He kisses my lips licking his afterwards, "I met him yesterday, the journalist?"

"OHH, Stone!" I throw my head back hysterically, "'Steve?' I was like WHAT?!" Breathing deeply trying to compose myself, "I suppose he's a friend, kind of. He's complicated."

I grab my coat and bag ready to head out the door, "Eva!" Tommy calls after me, "I guess what I'm really saying is...and I know its a little fast but I like you and I get the feeling you like me too..."

His face searches mine like he's looking for clues, "uh huh." I narrow my eyes waiting for the next line.

"I would like you to be my girlfriend like officially, life's short y'know." He shrugs leaning against the door frame waiting for an answer.

"Okay...sure." My hands shake, I'm so nervous.

I've only ever been a girlfriend twice before, I'm nearly thirty years old but I feel like I'm in high school.

"Really?" He wraps his arms around me into a bear hug picking me off the ground and spins me around.

My heart swells inside my chest.

I have a boyfriend now.

I step off the plane and make my way through to arrivals, I had assumed that Griffin would have a car for me but instead he was here in person.

It wasn't until I seen him that all of the feelings about Stone that I had suppressed came crashing back through my barrier.

It took my breath away, and suddenly I wasn't elated any more.

I had forgotten all about my beautiful morning.

All I could see was the video of Stone and his face when he ambushed me in the foyer of my building.

"My dear!" Griffin wraps his arms around me, "I wanted to collect you personally." He links his arms with mine.

"Hi, I've missed you." I grin as he leads me out to his car.

We sit in the back in silence as the driver takes us to our favourite Italian restaurant.

I finally pluck up the courage to tell him whats on my mind, "I need to talk to you about something Griffin."

"Hmmm..." he nods his head like he had been expecting it, "we will talk over wine and food. The back of a car is no place for important conversations. Its usually reserved for weather chit chat." He pats the back of my hand gently.

I adore this man truly I do.

After finishing our lunch we order a final glass of wine, "what do you need, Eva?"

I inhale slowly preparing myself for this, "Did you know he was coming back?"

Griffin looks down into his glass, "Yes."

The shooting pain I felt in my chest when he said that deflated my entire body, "Why didn't you warn me he was coming?"

He sighs heavily spinning the glass, looking up into my eyes never letting his gaze falter, "You weren't in a good place darling. You made it clear that you didn't want to talk to any one." A lone tear falls down his cheek he wipes it away, "He's not the same man that left...I didn't want to you get your hopes up."

That last sentence.

Stone went there to find himself and they broke him.

My Stone is broken.

Bad Decisions = Great Sex

♥

As soon as I knocked on the door I knew I was making a mistake, and that I should turn around and leave.

But I gravitate to bad decisions, and when it comes to, Stone, I'm like a moth to the flame.

The door opens slowly and with a heavy sigh Stone appears, "Eva." His eyes are heavy with exhaustion, he hangs in the door way.

"Can I come in?" I shove past him not waiting for an answer.

He's been staying at his parents Manhattan apartment while he works for the New York Times, Griffin said he has been surrounding himself with work, instead of dealing with his tortured mind.

I look around the pristine space, so open and light. The only part that looks touched is a dark corner where there is a small desk nestled, Stone's computer sits open next to a bottle of scotch and a half filled glass.

"I'm busy with work right now, can you make whatever this is quick." He swipes the glass from the table and drinks the entire thing before reaching for the bottle and topping himself up.

Inhaling slowly I reach for the glass taking it from him, "We need to talk and I mean really talk this time, Aster."

His eyes snap round at me his lip curled upward, "Don't call me that." He snatches his glass back, "I don't have anything to say to you." Dismissing me with a wave of his hand.

He turns away from me slowly walking over to the ceiling to floor windows that surround the apartment.

I follow him grabbing his shoulder trying to turn him around to face me, but he doesn't give up easily.

"Hey," I reach for his face pulling his gaze to me, "Stone, what happened over there?" My vision blurs with tears, his saddened blood shot eyes act like windows to his pain, that he only allows me to see for a second before closing himself off again.

Clearing his throat he finishes his drink, "I have work to do Eva, and you no doubt have a fireman to fuck." He brushes past me setting himself back down at his computer beginning to type ferociously.

I walk over standing behind him to read what he is writing but I'm distracted by three thick lines of white powder drawn on the desk next to him along with a tightly rolled hundred dollar bill.

Remember I talked about bad decisions...

I lift the bill up to my face, Stone watches out of the side of his eye, I put it to my right nostril and lean over lining it up with one of the rows. My heart thumps in my chest.

Why am I doing this?

Just as I am about to snort the cocaine up Stone grabs my hand tossing the bill across the room.

"What the fuck do you think you are doing?!" His grip tightening on my wrist as he dusts away the white lines.

"Ouch!" I pull myself away from him, "Well clearly it's been helping you so why can't I try it for myself, maybe I need help too." I rub my wrist.

Stone scoffs, "Why would you need help, Eva?" His brows furrow when he see's the reddening of where his grip had been, gently he lifts my arm to examine it guiltily.

"Maybe because the love of my life went to a war torn country, maybe he made a promise to me. And when I got scared that he wouldn't come home, I said some horrible things, and then he ignored me for weeks." I wipe my soaked face on the back of my sleeve, Stone stands detached listening to me rant.

"And then you ambushed me, Stone. You just turned up for your car and that was it. What about everything you said. You made a promise to me Stone, am I a fool for believing you'd keep it?"

Still he stands not saying a word. His facial expression never changing, but a tear trickles down his cheek.

I press myself against his body looking up at him but he just stares blankly ahead, "I know you saw gruesome stuff over there Stone, okay I get it. You're hurting...I want to make it better. Please let me make it better."

A sharp breath exits his lungs, his head dipping down. I hear a deep gulp inside his chest.

"I saw how worried you were when you saw the bulletproof vest, I didn't want you to have to deal with that so I cut you out." It was a start, and I didn't have it in me to argue for more.

I wrap my arms around him tightly breathing in his citrusy scent but he doesn't wrap his arms around me, they just hang sadly by his side.

"Stone?"

"Mhmm..."

"Do you love me?" The desperation seeps out of my words.

"You don't get to ask me that." He breaks free of my embrace leaving me feeling exposed and ashamed.

All I ever wanted was him, to be with him. To help him and to let him help me.

I know in my heart of hearts that we are supposed to be together, but that doesn't mean that we will.

Because he is a stubborn self sabotaging prick and I am so god damn sick of chasing him.

At some point I have to be the one to stop fighting for him...

I should have walked out there...I should have grabbed my bag and left.

But thats not what happened.

Bad decisions remember.

He stands staring out the window once again his back facing me. It seize the opportunity to strip off, removing every article of clothing, standing completely naked in the middle of the cold vast room.

All of my insecurities, inside and out on display.

Waiting for him.

"Do you love me?" I ask again wrapping my hair up into a messy knot on the top of my head.

"Fuck off Eva." He growls his arm raised leaning against the window.

"Aster Stone Carlisle...do you fucking love me yes or no?" He spins around in a rage stopping in his tracks at the sight of my naked frame.

"What are you doing?" He reaches down to pick up my clothes, I sashay towards him reaching out for his face placing my hands either side of, before he stands up straight his large blue eyes look up at me silently pleading for me not to do this.

I fall down to my knees slowly unbuttoning his shirt sliding it off his arms while I trail open mouth kisses along his neck and collarbone, peppering them down his chiselled chest lacing my tongue down his navel to the top of his pants. I undo his belt with one hand while I palm his solid bulge through the fabric.

Stone swiftly grabs my hands pinning them by my side, "Stop." He growls, halting my motion.

"Do you love me?" He doesn't reply, I resume my position shaking my arms free, sliding down his pants and boxers springing his length free.

"Please Eva..." he groans...I stop for a second sliding myself back from him, leaning against the back of his sofa. I bring my knees up then let them relax exposing my moist entrance, I lace my fingers from my breasts down my stomach to my folds, dancing my fingers into them watching Stone watch me as I flick my clit, swelling in tune with the brush of my fingers.

I run a finger the length of my opening swiping upwards, swirling around my clit causing my body to jerk forward.

In a blink Stone is in front of me edging his face closer to mine, his eyes lock with mine and I saw it there for a moment I think I saw it.

His lips bash against mine biting my bottom lip harshly as he lifts me off the ground, my legs wrap around his hips and he holds me in place against his desk lining his thick lustrous cock with my entrance he slams into me stretching me wide, the pleasurable pain hitches my breath, I gasp his name.

"Do you love me?" I breathe into his ear.

He plunges deeper into me rapidly, the tip of his cock grazing my cervix. Bruising my walls, and I love it. I can't get enough of it, I need more. I buck my hips harshly into his pelvis causing him to bury himself deeper, gasping carnally as I dig my nails into his back relishing as his eyes roll in to the back of his head.

I try my best to hold onto my orgasm for as long as I can, but the feeling of him inside of me brutally driving in and out of my swollen core draws it out of me and I gush so ferociously that I push him out.

I scramble down for him to guide back into me, I need more I want more.

He obliges by pummelling me into the desk lying me back across his computer, I grab out for his hand forcing it on my neck screaming for him to place pressure on.

And he does it, applying just enough to thrill me into another toe curling breath taking orgasm. My walls tighten around his cock, milking him. As I feel the twitch of him inside me as he bucks me into another primal orgasm, I beg him to answer me one last time.

"Do you love me?" I pant out.

He collapses on top of me catching his breath, "Of course I fucking love you." His lips sweep across mine. Before I can wrap my arms around him to keep him close he pulls away from me.

"I need to sort my self out." He pulls out, walking across the room to gather our strewn clothes.

"So I'll wait." I slide off the desk following him around, "I'll wait until you are sorted."

He scoffs gently simpering down at me, "No you wont Eva, go and live your life. If we're meant to be together then we'll be together."

"He's right you know." Angela Carlisle stands in the door way, "Now get fucking dressed the both of you."

My heart falls into my stomach, how long was she standing there? Did she knock?

God how much did she see.

Surely she wouldn't have watched the whole thing.

"Mother." Stone greets her whilst he pulls on his pants, I frantically scramble to pull up my underwear but cannot for the life of me locate any other garment, Stone hands me his shirt.

"How long have you been standing there, mother?" Stone asks barely fazed by her ambivalent demeanour.

"I was just in time for your dramatic exchange of 'I love you'." She lights a cigarette, "it's all very pathetic. Anyway I'm here now..."

Stone finds the rest of my clothes, I quickly run into the bathroom and get dressed.

When I open the door Angela waits for me on the other side, "when will you two learn? My boy needs professional help, unless your vagina has healing powers I suggest you leave." She seethes through her teeth.

I brush past her heading back into the living area, Stone is back at his desk typing.

"I'm leaving, Stone."

He doesn't turn around to say goodbye he just continues tapping on the keyboard, just as I reach the door he shouts after me, "Tommy called."

I look down at my cell phone guiltily glancing at the one missed call and one text message from the boyfriend I had completely forgot about.

Friends

I really wish I had told Tommy about Stone right away, because now we are a month into our relationship and I feel like its been tainted.

I should have told him that Stone and I had been more than friends, but neither myself nor Stone could ever decide what we were.

Our tumultuous on again off again relationship wasn't worth mentioning.

Except it was because it was everything to me but I had left it too late now, haven't I?

"So have you met Tommy's parents yet, Eva?" Emily hands me the salad tongs, Tommy pats my knee simpering gently as he sends me a wink, "not yet, we're going to Boston next week for a night."

Emily beams proudly it's easy to see that she is pleased with herself for setting us up.

Robert hands us both a beer and sits across from us.

"I'm taking her to meet my friends tomorrow, we're going to Ellens Star Dust diner, thought Eva would be more comfortable there."

Robert nods approvingly turning his head to look at me, he narrows his eyes.

I reassure him with a quick smile.

I don't feel like I'm in my own body, I feel like I'm above looking down at a person I barely know live my life for me...the way it should be lived.

"It'll be great." I lie.

Tommy brushes his lips on my cheek, draping his arm around my shoulder, "she hasn't introduced me to any of her friends yet."

"Unfortunately Eva doesn't have any friends." Emily's eyes sadden, "her father secluded them when she was growing up."

"Whoah!" I yell throwing my hand up, cutting her off, "lets not." Robert agrees with me calling for a change of subject.

"And for everyones information I do have friends, I have Griffin and Robert." Robert chuckles patting the back of my hand.

"You need friends your own age, ones with the same problems you have, but I am your friend." He winks at me, a little flash of pain strikes my heart.

I miss my dad.

It's a strange feeling, mourning the time I wish we could have had together, when we were too busy resenting one another. But I cherish the time we had, however short.

Tommy has work, which means he'll be gone for 72 hours and when I find myself idle and alone for too long I tend to try to contact Stone, but Angela Carlisle's words ring in my ears.

She's right he needs help and my selfish toxic behaviour is not the answer.

But I want him.

I want Tommy too.

He's so gentle and attentive and I love that I really do, but there was always something special about Stone.

He's just so... Stone.

I stare at his name on my screen desperately wanting to call or text, just to see what he is doing.

Maybe he could come over and we could talk, actually talk this time.

To: ASC
Hi,
What are you doing?

From: ASC
Nothing, what
Are you doing?

To: ASC

Going to buy
Some wine.

From: ASC
Want me to
Come over?

Always...of course I fucking do. My cell pings right away. Oh god.

From: Tommy Vaughn
Hey! Missing you, hate
these long shifts.
Get some rest before
your big interview.

Lost in my vortex of guilt I had forgotten all about my interview tomorrow afternoon.
Its only just gone 6pm, one bottle of wine wont kill me. Wine or no wine, I will probably
definitely end up telling Stone to come over. Wine will just help with the pain, the stress.
Because, wine.

My finger lingers over the call button next to his name.

I have a boyfriend now.

So I toss my cell into the bedside cabinet drawer, keeping it far away from me.

Praying that wine me doesn't remember and start drunk calling...anyone.

I walk around the aisles of the store tossing unhealthy snacks into my basket, grateful
when I find myself in the wine section.

Red wine, lets go for red wine.

No! Red wine makes me slutty, and I cant call Stone.

White wine gives me a terrible headaches.

I lift a bottle of sparkling rose down off the shelf, "eight bucks?!" I exclaim to myself
plopping it in beside the Hershey's kisses.

"Its eight bucks because it tastes like cat piss and vinegar." A short blonde reaches up to middle shelf grabbing a blush pink crystallised bottle, "this is twelve bucks and it tastes less like vinegar and more like...uh fizzy wine." The woman nods her head in a matter of fact way.

"Oh thanks!" I swap the wines over and do something that I've only ever done once before in my life, I left my comfort zone.

Turning back round I inhale deeply trying to steady my nerves, "I uh...I'm Eva."

I feel like a fucking idiot, and before she can reply or take out a restraining order on me I spin on my heel to make a quick getaway.

"Hey! Wine girl!" She calls after me.

Oh fuck oh fuck oh fuck.

I turn back slowly, my cheeks burning with embarrassment, I silently pray for the ceiling to fall in encasing me in my own mortified turmoil.

She beams walking towards me.

Oh god she thinks I'm simple.

"Bad breakup?" She peers into my basket moving bars of chocolate around with her finger, "Eva, right?"

I nod, thinking carefully about my next words.

"Sophie." She presses her hand gently on her chest a sweet smile hiding in the corners of her mouth.

"I'm sorry I was so weird." I shuffle my feet sheepishly trying to disguise my fear; shyness oh fuck who the hell knows, its all jumbled into one.

"All the best people are weird, so bad breakup orrrr..." she eyes the basket again.

"Ohh, well...no. I don't know." I pinch the bridge of my nose trying to calm my overactive brain, "just uh stress eating and drinking." That was the truth.

Sophie nods her assent.

"Well Eva if you ever want some company heres my card." I glance at it, Sophie Jones, PA.

"You got time now? My apartment is right around the corner." God way to sound like a serial killer.

"Sure!" She chirps.

"Whats the tea Eva?" She halves an Oreo licking the white centre whilst leaning over the island in my kitchen.

"Huh?" I raise my shoulders, not quite sure what she means.

"You got a boyfriend or a girlfriend...that sorta thing?" Oh!

I hesitate for a moment, "yeah I have a boyfriend Tommy, he's a fireman." He wasn't the first person I thought of though.

When she said 'boyfriend' it was *his* face appeared first in my mind, because *he's* all I think about.

"The thing is Eva, people don't introduce themselves in grocery stores...especially not in New York, what I'm getting at is...are you okay?" Her eyes study my face, slowly searching my arms.

"OH!" I gasp covering my mouth, "no no no!" I burst into hysterics, and it doesn't take long for her to join in.

Once we managed to compose ourselves I felt it was time for the truth, well some of it.

"My mom and step dad were digging at me for not having any friends...so when you were nice to me in the store I thought I'd try the meeting thing...fuck." I cover my face ashamed, "I'm so sorry, you can leave...take all the snacks and wine. I am such a dick." I hide behind my palms, cheeks burning red.

I have no social skills whatsoever, none.

And now Sophie is gonna go back to all of her friends and laugh about the weirdo she met in the wine aisle.

"Wait...you must have friends." She pulls hands away from my face uncovering me from my inner torment.

"I mean...I have Griffin but he's 83 and Robert my step dad he's-" Sophie holds up her hand shaking her head in disbelief.

"Alright alright...you realise how sad that is don't you?" She fills out two glass of sparkling wine, "well...I guess you have three friends now." She clinks my glass.

"And lucky for you Eva, I'm in between clients right now so I got some free time." She winks, "what are you doing tomorrow?"

Then I remember, fuck.

"I have a job interview at Juilliard tomorrow afternoon." The nerves start to build inside me again, I wonder why I ever applied in the first place.

I haven't worked in so long, and the only job interview I ever had was with Roger in the cafe back home.

Auditions for shows were different, they were easier. The minute I stepped on stage I could pretend to be someone else.

"Do you feel okay about it?" I shake my head no, "well I'll come with you." She flashes me a smile grabbing her bag from the back of the stool.

"You don't...we just...you...i-it's okay." I turn my back putting the empty glasses into the dishwasher.

"Nonsense, we're friends remember."

Interviews, Coffee, Fire Engines and Hypocrisy

There is only so far, a person can take you in life, your parents can only lead you to a certain point. Then you're on your own, my father didn't have the time or patience to show me anything at all, so I had to navigate myself around life, which was evident in my mistakes. I don't resent my dad for that because it's energy that I no longer wish to hang on to. Having his good name behind me was always going to open doors back in Boston, but here I had to fight for what I wanted just like everyone else, and I liked it.

I step out of the double doors, breathing deeply as I try to take it all in. The second stage interview went well...I think. My anxieties replaying every little detail over and over in my mind, thinking of the things I should have said instead of what I did say.

Scrutinising every little twitch of the interviewer's eyebrow, the shared glances between the panel.

At least when I was auditioning for a role, I was able to pretend to be someone else, somewhere else. But in there I had to be real and that was the hardest thing for me to be.

Sophie beams at me, "Well how did it go?" she stuffs her cell into her purse rushing over to me excitedly.

I'd convinced her to come with me again, afraid that if she didn't it would jinx it. She was my lucky charm. I needed her there to soften the rupture of nerves I had been feeling lately. I'd tried to convince myself that they were because of the interview, but Sophie had other ideas.

It was crazy how well we had gotten to know each other of these past three weeks, how quickly we had become friends as though we had known each other our whole lives.

Only, I hadn't told her about Stone. Guilt. That was the only explanation. I had cheated on Tommy with him and worse than that, I had ignored Stone.

"Good...I think. But you can never really tell with these things." I smile back at her, my best fake smile.

"I know that smile...what's wrong?" her eyes narrow at me.

"Nothing, nothing... really nothing. Coffee?" I shimmy my shoulders it looked like a playful movement but really, I was just trying to remind myself that I was alive.

Tommy was on shift, so I had seventy-two hours of alone time of just me and my wicked thoughts. I didn't have his soft attentive hands as a distraction from my inner turmoil.

I was silently thankful that Sophie was in between clients right now, her lack of work meant my idle hands couldn't do the devil's work. But that was short lived wasn't it.

"I'm sorry Eva, I just got a call before you came out. I have to meet a potential client, it's a big deal." She leans in whispering, "He's a big fucking movie star!"

"Oh okay, no problem! Good luck." Sophie leans in kissing both my cheeks before rushing off hailing a cab in a very aggressively Manhattan manner.

"Let me know if you hear anything!" She yells leaning over the cab door.

I take a deep breath I need to keep busy.

I stand lost in a daydream in the queue at Starbucks, I wish I knew what I was dreaming about but it was pleasant, I was acutely aware of the smile that lingered across my lips.

"What can I getcha?" The barista called me forward breaking me from my moment of solace,

"Just a flat white and a blueberry muffin please."

"Name?"

"Eva." I reach into my wallet for my card to pay when someone reaches forward scanning theirs instead.

Snapping my head around to protest the 'pay it forward' cliché, I'm faced with my turmoil.

"Hello, you." Eyebrow arched with that death of me smirk hanging out of the side of his mouth.

My knees quiver as my eyes take all of him in, "Stone."

We sit together in silence just staring, the odd flicker of a smile coming from one to the other.

He takes a sip of his coffee, his smug smile visible in the corners of his eyes. They have a little sparkle back. Not much, but it's there.

"You've been avoiding me..." he sets down his cup licking the corner of his mouth clean of the foam, I can't tear my eyes away transfixed by the subtle instinctive movement. Wishing it was my mouth he was trailing it against. Why does he make me feel this way?

"And now you're ignoring me, Eva..." His fingers brush against the back of my hand, snapping me out of my daydream.

"Hmm? Sorry, what did you say?" I stammer trying to collect myself.

What did I say about the devil's work? But was he the devil or was it me?

"I said you've been avoiding me, why?"

"It just felt like the right thing to do Stone." I look down at my hands shamefully, "and Angela said..."

"Oh fuck Angela!" He snaps harshly shaking his head, "fuck what Angela said...please don't shut me out." My eyes narrow as I curl my lip, "what?" He shuffles smugly in his seat.

"Hello pot, meet kettle. You Stone Carlisle have some nerve asking me not to shut you out, don't you think?"

I was completely taken aback by his obvious hypocrisy, and he wasn't even fazed by it. Just as he was about to argue his pathetic case my cell phone chimed. I had assumed it was Sophie or Tommy, but when I turned the cell around it was an unknown number...and I knew what that meant. I snap my eyes from the screen of my cell to Stones perplexed face.

I swipe 'answer' across the screen and put it to my ear, clearing my throat.

"Hello?...yes speaking...okay...yes...I understand...I will...and you...thank you." I hold my breath for a minute trying to process the conversation.

"I got the job." I look across the table at Stone, "I got the job Stone." I get up out of my seat and start jumping around, "I got the fucking job!!"

He gets up rushing over to me, and for just a second, I thought he was going to force me back down, but he didn't, he wrapped his big arms around me lifting me up off the ground and spun me slowly. His nose pressed softly against mine.

"What job?" He pants out brushing his lips on my forehead as he sets me down.

I was well aware that my chest was heaving up and down with elation, this was the happiest I had been in so long, and for the first time it had absolutely nothing to do with a man. It was something that I had done on my own, something that I was qualified to do with nothing but my own talent. The stage life wasn't for me, I found it hard to accept the criticism but more potent than that, I found it impossible to accept the compliments. It was praise for faking it, for pretending to be someone that I wasn't and that made it easier to do it in my day-to-day life. I wanted a real job, a real life and more than anything to be comfortable with just being me. Getting this job was the first step in finding myself, my real self.

Stone smouldered over his third cup of coffee as I explained to him about the job, I left out all the profound shit about feeling less than stellar about life, he didn't need that baggage. He had enough. When I asked about him, he changed the subject, that was okay too. He wasn't ready to talk about it, or maybe he was just not with me. I had to learn to accept that even though I loved him and always would, that didn't entitle me to have him. If we were meant to be together then we would be. Classic case of right person wrong time.

I hadn't realised our fingers had been laced together until he broke them to check his cell. "Oh! I meant to tell you; you'll never guess who is getting married?" He chuckles up his cuff trying to keep his voice hushed, its quiet in here now. I throw my hands out inviting him to continue, the suspense keeping me on the edge of my seat. I was unlike Stone to participate in gossip, he was much too cool for that. "Louisa and the gardener." Coffee flew down my nose burning the inside of my nostrils, "No! the fucking porn stars?!"

"The fucking porn stars." he sighs, the little glint in his eye dulls down.

I reach my arm across the table taking his hand in mine, "Hey, you okay?"

"Why wouldn't I be?" he clears his throat, "How's the fireman?" Swiftly changing the subject, his hand still placed in mine. "Good, all good." It would have been cruel of me to go into more detail about us, I'm just not sure who I was being cruel to, Stone or Tommy.

"I'm sorry we're closing now." The barista interrupted our silent stares. We both looked out of the window, neither of us had realised that the March sun had begun to set. "Walk you home?" Stone hands me my bag and jacket. "I'd love that." I say, smoothing down the collar of his camel dress coat, picking off the smallest piece of lint from his light blue cable knit sweater.

I don't know why we always think it's a good idea to walk around Manhattan, it's huge! We walked in comfortable silence, just enjoying each other's presence and other times we would talk about music or movies. I laughed at Stone's disgust when I purchased two hot dogs, heartily guffawing as he asked the vendor for his credentials.

"C'mon Stone!" I yelled as he held his nose taking a bite of the bun, "that's just bread! You have to eat the dog." I swear I almost peed my pants watching him wretch into the gutters. "No..." he grabbed mine out of my hands and launched it into a trash can on the sidewalk, "no." he shuddered. "Hey! I love those." I huffed, pouting at my lost snack.

I spun on my heel to scold him and when I did our eyes met, and they locked in. Lost in the deep pool of ocean blue that I held so dear to me. He inched towards me, my body shivering in the breeze. 'I love you.' I whispered under my breath barely audible to myself let alone Stone. But God I did, I really loved him.

"Fire engine." He coughed. I tilt my head in confusion, "What?"

"Eva!" Tommy roared out of his rig pulling up behind me, he jumped from the slowing vehicle halting traffic as he ran across the street, lifting me up into his arms spinning me around on the sidewalk, "I missed my girl, I had to see you. Was just about to drive to your building and run in for a kiss." He bruised his lips to mine earning an applause from his crew as they rang the sirens and flashed the lights. My cheeks burned a glowing red, guilt. "Sorry baby, I didn't mean to embarrass you!" He wrapped his arm around my shoulder tightly, "Hey man." he nodded to Stone, who sneered flicking his head upwards subtly acknowledging him. "Hey Vaughn, we gotta go!" A booming voice came from the rig. Tommy held his hand up, "I'll see you tomorrow night angel, I got a shift swap." He leans in pecking my cheek urgently before racing back across the street, the Fire Engine speeding away sirens blaring.

Stone leans in kissing my other cheek, "Bye Eva."

"Goodbye Stone."

My Someone Else

"Oh shit!" I yell out just as the plate hits the sleek black tiled kitchen floor, smashing into smithereens. I crouch down picking up the bigger pieces tossing them into the trash can at the side.

Tommy emerges from the bathroom shaking his head, letting out an exasperated giggle, "seriously woman, I have never met anyone as clumsy as you in my entire life." He grabs the vacuum cleaner from the side and starts collecting up the tiny shards.

"You said you would help by cleaning up, but you're making more of a mess," he leans down helping me off the floor, softly brushing his lips against my forehead.

"I'm sorry...it just slipped out of my hands." Tommy stands in front of the stove stirring a large pot of meat sauce he leans over to the side for the garlic powder, and I stare into the pot of deliciousness knocking the ladle onto the side splashing marinara sauce all up the white countertops.

Tommy turns around glaring at me, "That's strike two Miller, you are skating on very thin ice young lady." Leaning into the oven to check on the bruschetta I feel a pair of tongs nip at my backside.

A wave of memories washes over me, I hear Stones laugh as he chased me round my LA apartment that one thanksgiving. I try to quash the feeling of dread that suffocates my chest, Tommy hadn't brought up seeing me with Stone so neither did I.

I keep trying to tell myself everything that happened was innocent but if it was, then why did I feel this way about it?

The tongs keep pestering at my cheeks ushering me to move, "hey!" I slap them away as I try to gauge the estimated cooking time left on the starter. This is why I don't cook, because I don't have the patience to wait for it. I want it hot, fresh and delivered quickly.

Tommy hates take out, he always insists on cooking. Usually he makes it at home and brings it over, but to celebrate my new job he wanted to do it in here with me. Because he is sweet like that.

"Miller...I'm really serious..."

I hold my hands in the air, "alright...what can I do?" He hands me a tea towel pointing to the little puddle of water that has pooled by pot of pasta, I clean around the bottom of the pot and around the gas ring stopping the starchy water from crusting into the stove top.

But the flames lick the tea towel and suddenly but not surprisingly it goes up disintegrating almost immediately. I don't know what to do, I am frozen still in a panic holding the flaming tea towel as the flames work their way up towards my hand.

Tommy acts fast grabbing it from me, throwing it into the sink and quickly running the tap, he resets the smoke alarm that is blaring above my head.

"You're done." He puts his hands under my armpits and lifts me onto the island, "You are done." He checks my arm for wounds.

"I'm fine, don't worry about me." I assure him, absentmindedly wiping sweat from his brow.

The flicker of a smile twitched on his lips, his face relaxed as if he was gratefully surprised by the small intimate gesture.

Then I realised, I don't do that.

At least not with him.

The little adoring sentiments, I always reserved them for my someone else.

The knot of guilt that twists inside my stomach tightens, I try to disguise my guilt with a playful smirk but his gaze doesn't falter and his eyes continue to lock in with mine.

But I don't want him to be able to read me, afraid that if he looks long enough he'll see me.

That he'll see the guilt hidden just under the surface.

I jut my face forward to capture his mouth, closing my eyes to catch a reprieve from his stare. Our lips press together puckering and parting in unison, Tommys hands roam up my thighs and rest on my waist gently.

He pulls back with a smile, "I l-" I clamp my hand over his mouth.

"Please don't say anything." I sob out.

Why is he doing this to me?

His eyes narrow at me, hurt written across his face, he pulls my hands away holding them tightly.

"Eva...I love-" this time childishly, I clamp my hands over my ears shaking my head ferociously, my eyes screwed shut.

I can't let him say those words to me, I don't want to hear them.

"Eva Miller, I love you. I am in love with you." I hear his muffled panicked voice through the security of my hands.

"What's going on in the pretty little head of yours? I want to tell you how I feel." He pries my hands from the side if my head desperately gripping them.

"I don't want you to." I breathe weakly.

This is awful. I am awful. "You don't want me to say it or you don't want me to feel it?" His greens eyes pool with sadness.

"Both." I choke out.

He turns away from me switching off the stove, sighing heavily as he runs his hands through his hair.

"What do you want Eva, I always just feel like you've kept me at arms length."

I shrug, unable to form words.

"Fucking say something damn it!" He snaps, the change in him startling me.

I try to breathe through it, failing to calm my racing heart.

The man stood before me, Tommy. He can give me everything and more, we could have a beautiful life together with beautiful children.

But I know that I'll always be lying to myself, because when I close my eyes and envision that life; I am happy chasing after those little mousey haired children in the big yard with him.

My unattainable life.

When I try to picture that life with Tommy, the girl I see isn't me. She looks like me, but she is someone else.

I shouldn't force him to settle.

"I don't know, Tommy." I shrug again, its the only movement I can muster.

He grips the tops of my arms shaking me vigorously, "I don't know isn't an answer, I love you and I want to build a life with you but I can't just keep being a body to fill the space," he releases me, "Is it him?" Oh god.

I don't say no, and I think that is worse.

"I'm a good man Eva, great even. What does he have that I don't?" I stare ahead at him, he's right what does Stone have that he doesn't?

The answer is me.

Stone has a piece of me that will never be reclaimed.

So where does that leave us?

Where does that leave me?

Alone. Again.

The Choice

"I think you need to take some time and figure out what it is you actually want, Eva." Tommy storms around my apartment gathering his things, "and if it isn't me then let me go and find someone that will treat me right...I'm not an idiot, remember that." All I can do is bite my lip attempting to choke back tears. Tommy had known all along that something was going on with Stone, I thought that him knowing would make me feel better but somehow its worse. I've been hurting him, just stringing him along. Lying to him, lying to myself.

So what did I do when he left? I tidied the mess we made, the mess I made.

"What happened?" Sophie burst through the door of my apartment eyes widened with concern. I shrug my shoulders; I can't do anything else. "I happened." Fat tears flow freely down my cheeks, Sophie tilts her head sympathetically furrowing her brows.

I go on to explain what had happened with Tommy, Sophie strokes my knee as she continues to listen, nodding and making all the right faces at the appropriate times.

"So, what about this other guy then? What's his name?" She hands me a beer from the fridge. I shake my head, "It's not important, he's not important." There I go telling lies again.

She inhales deeply holding her breath in, "Eva if he wasn't important, you would be throwing grenades around your life, getting caught in the fallout." She raises her brows, shuffling her shoulders in a sorry not sorry sort of manner. Still, I don't tell her. I keep him to myself. "I can't tell you what to do Eva, I can't tell you to choose the other guy in case you don't and then I'll always have betrayed Tommy, and vice versa honey. The only person that can make the decision is you..."

I need someone to tell me what to do.

"Eva, come in. Is everything okay?" Robert stands sleepily rubbing his eyes. I shake my head, "No..." I slide in the doorway heading for the lounge. Sighing heavily I collapse onto the sofa burying my head in my hands shamefully. Robert sits on a footstool gently placing his hand on my knee. I sob out a string of inaudible words, my breathing comes high pitched and fast unable to be controlled.

"Hey, hey. Come on now. Whatever it is Eva, I'll help." He places both hands on my shoulders trying to hold my eye contact, "breathe slowly, in...1....2...3...4...out...2...3...4" we repeat this a couple of times and I start to calm down. We sit in silence for a few moments. I look around the living room fixating on a picture frame on the mantlepiece. Its Emily, Robert and me smiling in their kitchen the night Stone ambushed me in my foyer, the night I met Tommy. Next to it is a picture of me sitting on the edge of my dad's bed reading to him. Alma must have taken it when we weren't looking, it's a beautiful picture. How did it get here?

I walk over to the fireplace and lift it, "How did you get this?" Robert smiles, "Your mother asked Alma for a picture of you and your father, this is the one she sent." Alma. I make a quick mental note to call her. "Robert, I'm ready."

I tell him everything. Shamefully admitting to cheating on Tommy with Stone. Working through my inner conflict with him. He doesn't judge, and he doesn't make any faces. He just listens. "Tell me what to do, please." I pant out finishing my monologue. He chuckles softly, "Eva honey, I can't tell you what to do. What I will do is say this, the heart wants what the heart wants, and you should never settle for less. Even if that means hurting someone."

My heart wanted married life with a doting husband and adorable babies and Tommy could and would give me that, but I wanted that life with someone else. With Stone and being with him was a risk. I could go to him tonight and bare my soul to him, but would he do the same? Would he leave me lifeless again?

Two Days Later...

The walk to work only takes twelve minutes, but I went the long way trying to clear my head. I wanted so badly to call Tommy and apologise, I wanted so badly for him to be the man of my dreams. But the truth is, he wasn't, and he would never be. I have spent almost half of my life chasing my dream thinking that it was Stone, but I can't let the fear of being alone be the reason I settle for less than what I want and that includes Stone. I can't fight for Stone's heart anymore, and I shouldn't make Tommy fight for mine. Love shouldn't be this hard.

I called Tommy after work and asked him to meet me on the stoop of his building, this conversation was going to be one of the most difficult I'll ever have but it was a necessary one. "Hi," his solemn face appears next to me as I sit on the cool step, I turn my body to face him. I breathe deeply, "I'm sorry Tommy. I really am, but.."

He scoffs, "but you chose him."

I take his hand into mine, "No, I chose me."

Ten Years Ago Or So

♥

27th of December.

Sitting on the edge of Eva's bed I watch her as she packs an overnight bag, not quite sure why she would want to go find the woman who abandoned her.

Last night I told her I love her, and I meant it.

It's a difficult kind of love, though. When I first saw her all I wanted was sex. She intrigued me, this beautiful shy girl who never flew above the radar. I can't remember ever seeing her at school or around the estate, always undetected. But how? Now after knowing her, I can't imagine my life without her. She's engrained in the fibre of my bones.

"Why don't you want to come to Harvard with me?" I accidentally ask the question out loud.

She spins on her heel zipping up the bag, "because I want to make my own decisions." She winces through the pain of her face, pressing her hand against it almost as if she is holding it in place.

"I need to be in charge of my own life and stop letting things happen to me." Her eyes brim with tears.

I thrust my tongue to the roof of my mouth trying to stave away my emotion. Everything that's happened to her in the last twenty-four hours has been because of me.

Her swollen face, my fault because I couldn't control my temper.

I am no good for her, but without her I am miserable.

"I'm coming with you, Eva." She opens her mouth to protest, holding her hand up ready to fight me on it.

"It wasn't a request. I'm coming with you. No discussion." She exhales sharply bunching her mouth to the side, through the vacant look in her eyes I can see her mind working overtime.

I'm going to be with her, I'm going to do this for her. For us.

I will try.

New Years Eve.

We stand together at the bottom of the stone steps leading up to the grand town house, shivering in the blistering cold for what feels like forever.

Eva grabs my wrist, twisting it to check the time on my Rolex, 7:50pm.

I look down into her panicked eyes, the bruises on her face on faintly visible underneath her makeup.

She offers me a small nervous smile breaking my heart, I slide my hand into hers.

"You gonna go in?" She shakes her head frantically bringing her trembling free hand to her mouth she begins biting the skin around her nails.

Her words ask to go back to the hotel; her quivering voice practically begs.

A man pushes past us taking the steps, he hesitates for a moment before turning around, "Can I help you?"

I stand forward taking lead, she can't do this. Not now.

So I'll give her time.

"We're looking for Emily." Its only now I realise that we don't know her surname.

The man yells inside the door, "Em!"

He calls us kids.

"Fuckin' kids." I scoff under my breath stuffing my hands into my coat pocket.

He introduces himself as Robert.

"You guys lost or somethin'?" An immaculately dressed woman stands at the top of the stairs hanging in the door way, she folds her arms across her chest as the wind howls through the streets.

Evas stands stoic, eyes wide.

She moves behind my arm, remaining silent.

I can feel her tense up against me, soft little tears trickle down her cheeks.

If she can't speak then I'll be her voice.

<u>New Years Day.</u>

After last nights catastrophe we were invited back for the family party at Emily and Robert's.

Eva is flawlessly beautiful, everything she does is with effortless grace.

She lifts one leg up onto the footstool at the end of the hotel bed to smooth on some moisturiser.

I am taken over by the urge to touch her, but not in the way I normally touch her.

I want to be her hands.

She places her other leg onto the stool patting the cream into her bare skin, I run my hands up her calf and around her thigh gently massaging the comforting scent around.

I rub the excess cream onto my neck, connecting myself with the soft powdery aroma of her

I love he

We stand in front of the large varnished townhouse door.

Removing my hand from the small of her back I turn her body round to face me, "If at any time you want to leave just say the word and we'll go."

I want her to be strong enough to try.

Her hand reaches for mine, brushing her fingertips inside my palm. I take her fingers, intertwining them with mine, squeezing softly three times.

I lean down into her my lips grazing her ear, "I love you."

Before she could say anything, the door swings open.

<u>2nd Of January</u>

I know that I have had an affluent lifestyle, more money than I'll ever know what to do with.

I have had everything handed to me on a platinum platter, never having to fight for anything.

But the hardest thing I have ever done was watch Eva being treated like a parasite by her own mother.

I should have killed Emily and Robert right then and there.

I wanted to.

I actually think I was going to, when my hands had hold of her shoulders I wasn't myself. Blinded by the rage of Emily's coldness towards Eva.

But then Eva struck her across the face, and quite rightly so, and I knew instantly that she would spend her eternity regretting it.

I knew that right away she wanted to take it back, her mouth said "fucking fantastic." But her eyes were defeated by disappointment.

Emily had the audacity to ask for a third chance she wants to meet Eva for coffee.

I can't stop myself from pacing around the room, Eva actually agreed to it.

Rage builds inside my chest, my head pounding in anger.

Mostly because I know that Eva thinks that its all her fault. Shes been gaslit from the moment her mother left.

The victim of narcissistic parenting.

She wont allow me to come with her, explicitly banning me.

I watch her heartsick frame disappear behind the doors of the elevator, the false smile etched on her lips faltering just as the doors meet.

I watch through the window of the diner as Emily and Eva talk.

I couldn't let her do it alone.

I'll be here for her, even if she doesn't see me. I'll be the crutch to catch her fall.

She kisses the top of Emilys head, drying her tears on the back of her sleeve and leaves her sitting forlorn sobbing guilty into her coffee.

Eva leaves the diner walking around the side out of sight of Emily she slides down the wall crouching, crying distraughtly her head struggles to hold itself up under the weight of her anguish.

I take back what I said before...this was the hardest thing I've ever done.

Not being able to pick up Eva...my Eva.

I wait until she stands back up, dusting herself off before I leave to wait for her back at the hotel.

My heart conflicted between pride and sorrow.

A Brief Encounter

Standing on the platform at the subway station I lose myself in the sound of the underground city, I used to hate it here but now the constant noise and pollution calms me, it settles me. It reminds me of Syria. Boston is too quiet. Especially on the estate. The silence that surrounded it was like being held within a dome of seclusion. There's nothing there for me now.

My therapist diagnosed me with PTSD, whatever that means. I think that's made up shit that people use to blame their problems on, but she assures me that it's very real and I should take it seriously. Whatever, I'll take the meds because Griffin asked me to.

My mind continues to wander, I allow myself to be transported back there. Hearing the screams of women and children, the deep anguished groans of men I see them clearly. I feel it all deeply.

Two trains cross quickly my heart stops. Bringing me back into the moment.

Looking down at my wrist I check the time, it's 6:34pm. I just want to get home to sleep, then wake up and do all of this all over again.

My life has no purpose now, I work, eat, sleep and repeat.

I sleep for four hours every night my mind won't allow me any more than that.

The doctor assures me that I will sleep, eventually. These pills once they settle will stop me feeling numb. And my life will have purpose again.

My train pulls into the station and I find myself a seat, leaning my head against the cool window shutting my eyes for just a minute, allowing them to rest.

The train shudders, a mechanical chomping sound comes from underneath the carriage.

Fucking fantastic, this is all I need.

Passengers begin to look to one another panicked voices surmising about faults, everyone just waiting for information.

The train conductor rushes down the aisle towards the front of the train.

"Excuse me sir?"

My head snaps up at the familiar voice, my heart dancing around in my chest.

The conductor stops dead in his tracks, roles his eyes and turns to her. Eva stands up bashfully.

"I just wondered, well I think we all are...what's going on?" She fiddles with her hands nervously.

He sighs giving into her sweetness, "There's been a mechanical fault, I'm going to speak to the driver now. He'll make an announcement."

Eva's breathing hitches she grabs his forearm, "Please, roughly how long?" Her little panicked breaths catching everyone's attention.

He tilts his head softly, "It happened last week on my other run, won't be more than an hour two tops. Don't panic ma'am."

He turns on his heel and heads back down the train.

Eva rubs her hands over her face, I can't decide whether to make myself known or not. It's been a month since I've seen or heard from her. We almost had something outside her building, but the fireman interrupted us before we could go any further.

The way he looked at her, he loves her.

And I can't do anything about it, because even though she is my Eva...she isn't mine any more.

Almost dead set on slumping down and hiding from her the decision is taken away from me as she looks up from her hands clocking me immediately.

"Hello, you." She grabs her bag from the seat and works her way down to where I am sat.

"As I live and breathe, Aster Stone Carlisle on a train...the subway no less." She giggles tucking lose hair behind her ear as she sits in the seat across from me.

I shrug my shoulders, "Sometimes it's just quicker."

"Ain't that the truth." She bobs her head.

"I never thought I'd see you on a train not after..." I stop myself, not wanting to dredge up past emotions for her. The statement actually sort of slipped out.

I think I'm nervous.

"Well I had to get over it eventually." She sighs, releasing a sad little smile.

"No you didn't, but I'm proud of you." I watch as she pulls out her cell phone.

"One second." She mouths putting the phone to her ear.

"Hey honey, listen I'm not gonna make it tonight...the train broke down and...yeah I know...two fucking hours...I promise I'll make it up to you. Love you too." She shoves the cell back into her bag.

Hearing her talk like that to him was like a dagger in my heart. She loves him.

Those were words reserved only for me.

Now she has someone else to say them to.

I don't blame her, doesn't mean I'm not jealous though.

I miss her.

The urge to choke out those words to her is overwhelming, but she looks happy and content. So why would I want to ruin that for her?

Why would I take another thing away from her?

She begins raking through her bag pulling out two little individually wrapped mints, she holds her hand out offering me one. As I go to take the blue one I absentmindedly brush my fingertips along her palm. The flicker of a smile hides contently in the corner of her mouth.

"How's your new job?" I ask trying to break the tension.

Through the crunch of the mint she nods her head, "Really good. It's everything I thought it would be and more."

I shuffle my legs accidentally grazing her shin with my foot, "Sorry." I apologise pushing myself back into the seat.

She waves her hand dismissing it.

"How are things with you, Stone?" God I love the way she says my name.

"Good, everything's good. I'm in therapy." Fuck! Why did I tell her that? Now she is going to think I'm some sort of fucking basket case.

"Me too." She whispers back.

Everything about her settles me. Brings me back down to a rooted plain. How could I ever have hurt her the way I did?

I'm such an idiot.

But I refuse to go back to the way it was. I will not be my parents.

"Are you going back to Boston for your birthday?" I remember that she is turning thirty in two weeks.

She shakes her head, "I have plans here, then I'm going after my birthday, Griffin and I have a lunch planned. You should come?"

I love the relationship she has with Griffin.

That's all I can say on the matter, I love it.

"I'll see what my work schedule is like." My cell phone rings interrupting our conversation.

"Sorry, I have to take this."

"Yes? Right...okay. Yup...that's fine I can do that tomorrow...I know...I will take a day off next week I promise...alright pal...see you in the office tomorrow. Coffees on you this week. Bye." I look up from my cell, catching Eva's wide smile beaming at me.

"What?" I furrow my brows at her.

Shaking her head, she twists her mouth coyly.

"Nothing, you're different."

I wanted to tell her that up until I saw her face on the train I was borderline catatonic.

That it was her that made me feel different.

It was this brief encounter with Eva that pulled me out of my vortex of numbness and reminded me that I had emotions.

Jealousy being one of them.

But this little moment between us ignited something inside me.

I feel alive again.

Because of her.

The train shudders once more and begins to move. Sighs of relief echo down the carriages.

"This is my stop." She leans across smoothing my hair into a side shed, "Maybe I'll see you at lunch. If not...take care Stone."

"Eva?" I reach into my pocket.

"Mhmm?"

"Never mind."

She stands next to the doors waiting for the train to stop, the doors slide open and she walks off without so much as a glance back.

It Seems Like Everyone Knows

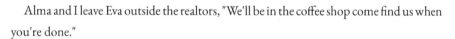

Alma and I leave Eva outside the realtors, "We'll be in the coffee shop come find us when you're done."

The streets are busy this morning, we stand together in silence while we wait for the traffic to shallow.

It's awkward with Alma, it really shouldn't be. I've known her my entire life. She's worked for Griffin for as long as I can remember.

She always silently had my back when my parents decided to come down hard on me.

Maybe I'm just on edge because I'm leaving for the Middle East the day after tomorrow.

I'm probably projecting it all on to poor, Alma.

The barista sets our coffees down in front of us Alma nods graciously arching her eyebrow at me prompting me to be mindful of my manners.

"Thanks," I grumble as he walks away.

"Do you think she's okay in there?" Alma gazes across the street the outline of Eva's frame barely visible.

I take a sip of my coffee trying my best not to think about it because I'm not convinced selling her home was something she genuinely wanted to do. I think she acted on an impulse fuelled by grief, but I know better than to voice my opinion.

Well, that's not entirely true, but this time I chose my battle wisely.

"I'm not sure how long we have without her, Stone." Alma reaches into her purse, bringing out a small leather ring box.

A sickening wave crashes around in my stomach as she slides it across the table to me.

"This was the ring Preston was going to propose to me with, I found it with his things." Her eyes are brimmed with tears, I open the box, and inside glistens a large emerald-cut diamond encased in white gold.

"Why are you giving this to me?" I snap it shut and pass it back to her.

"Because one way or another it's going to be you that puts it on her finger, it might be tomorrow it might be ten years from now, but it's you, Stone. It's always been you."

I feel my throat tightening, the sting of tears prick my eyes as I try to think of reasons to walk away.

Clearing my throat I exhale sharply trying to stave my watery eyes, "This is your ring, and besides, we're not even together."

Alma opens the box smiling softly at me, she lifts out the ring turning it around to show me the bottom of the band, and tied to it with the tiniest piece of string is our cherry stalk, "even when you weren't together, all those years you spent apart. You were still together."

This fragile little nothing will outlive us, and Eva kept it all this time.

Because it meant so much to her, it meant more to her than it did to me at the time.

But now what does it mean?

I don't deserve her.

"What do I do with it?" Nervously placing it back into the box.

Alma takes hold of my hand, "when the time is right, you give it to her."

"She's too good for me." I sigh.

"I don't believe that for a minute, I think she made you a better person without even meaning to. And I think you saved her." Alma lifts the box and places it in the palm of my hand once more clasping my fingers over it tightly, "You'll end up together. I don't doubt it."

But how can she be so sure?

When I'm not.

I don't think I've ever been sure of anything in my life. She's given me this token of love to pass on to the one person I hold deepest in my heart, this one final act of love. But I can't bring myself to burden Eva with me. All the horrible things I have done to her, all of the pain I have caused why would she even want to?

Repeatedly opening and closing the ring box I wait for the pilot to turn off the seatbelt sign.

She wanted to come with me on this flight just to spend a few extra hours with me, and now as the tears sting my eyes I wish I would have let her.

I should have given her the ring, there in front of Angela, Richard, and Griffin I should have gotten down on one knee and asked her in the middle of the airport to be mine forever. But when I reached into my pocket something stopped me.

The way her eyes lit up when she saw the cherry stalk, that may as well have been a ring to her, it was as good as.

That's when I decided that this box will never leave my pocket.

Alma said, when the time is right I'll know...

I watch as Eva pulls out her cell phone on the train platform, her smile spread from ear to ear.

She throws her head back in laughter, and I wasn't sure if I could actually hear it or if the sweet sound was encapsulated in my mind forever, replaying on a loop. The song I go to sleep to every night.

I imagine his hands roaming all over her body, the way mine used to. When she walks through the door of the apartment will he crash her against the wall touching her favourite spot with his mouth?

Images of them together flash through my mind, fuelling anger inside me.

It isn't anger, it's jealousy.

If I went to her right now would she give it all up for a moment with me?

Just a little taste?

I place my hand on the burdening ring box in my pocket, I will not inflict any more pain on her.

A Monsoon, A Typhoon, Some Really Bad Rain

♥

"This is good wine, Soph." I read the label, a little flutter in my chest takes my breath away when I realise that it's the same wine Stone ordered for me at the airport.

Sophie walks around the island in my kitchen, she takes a sip of the glass I just poured, "is it? Joshua gave it to me."

"Oh, so it's Joshua now?" I chuckle.

"Well 'he who shall not be named'," she means the movie star, he turned out to be a massive dick. She dropped him rather swiftly. The hassle wasn't worth the pay-check.

She took on a much smaller client the pay wasn't half bad and he lavished her with expensive 'thank you' gifts.

"Where was I?" She stares at the bottom of her empty glass, immediately filling it up.

"Joshua..."

"Oh yeah, so we're actually hitting it off."

I try my best to weaken the beaming smile that pains my cheeks, "oh...do you have a boyfriend now?"

She flares her nostrils at me, "You know I don't do that!" She smiles coyly at me, "But maybe."

Her cell phone chimes right on cue, "I'm sorry Eva, I gotta take this."

She disappears into my bedroom while I re-cork the wine, placing it in the fridge. I finish my wine and hers and put the glasses in the dishwasher.

I let my mind wander for a moment, thinking back to Stone on the train.

I had thought he would have texted or called, but it's been a week and there has been nothing.

That's okay though.

So long as he is happy.

I think I might be happy too, but I'm not entirely sure. Its never happened before.

"Eva, I'm so sorry. Joshua called and he needs me." She grabs her bag flustering as she throws in her keys and wallet, staring at me through apologetic eyes.

"Off you go, what kind of friend would I be if I cockblocked you?"

She grabs my face between her hands, "I love you, y'know that right?" Sophie heads towards the door, "I'll see you next Friday for birthday drinks, okay? You still haven't told me what you want for your birthdaaaaaay!" Her voice trailed off as the door closes behind her.

I sit on my sofa alone, working through some of Monday's lesson plans trying to get ahead a little. If I finish them tonight, then I can have my Sunday free.

I set the pile of papers down and put my completed lesson plan into my binder glancing up at the clock on the wall, god did it only take me an hour to finish all of this?

I take a peek through the blinds, it's a nice night. The sun is just getting a little low but it's a dry March evening which is unusual for New York, so I decide to take myself for a semi-sober-up walk. Anything to keep me busy and pass the time, I'm struggling a little with being alone sometimes. Especially in the evenings. I make it to the elevator before I realise that I didn't pick my jacket up, I tug down the sleeves of my favourite cream cable knit sweater. I should be warm enough.

I weave myself through the faceless crowds, finding myself wondering what their stories are. Making up scenarios for each of them in my head. The handsome suited man rushing for his train, he works on Wall Street. He's going home to his expensive townhouse where his pregnant wife will have dinner laid out on the table for him. I pass a young homeless girl sitting on the ground next to a parking meter, her toothless smile breaking my heart as she holds out an empty coffee cup begging for any spare change, every passer-by ignoring her. Pretending like she doesn't exist, her eyes cast downwards at the silent rejection.

But I see her.

I stuff my hand into my pocket fumbling around for whatever money I have on me. I drop a crumpled up twenty dollar bill and a few coins into the cup, "I'm sorry, it's all I have." I simper apologetically, "I have my credit card though, can I buy you some dinner?"

"No thank you." She whispers, her eyes brimming with tears.

I wanted to ask for her story, I wanted to know how she ended up here. She had to have been my age, her cheeks drawn in with hunger and possibly other things. I didn't want to make assumptions because who knows, any one of us could have ended up here. I twitch a smile and keep walking, a small prick of tears stinging my own eyes as I think of what life must have been like for her. Wondering if she ever had a loving home, or was she cast out. Was her start in life poisoned?

In the short moment where I forgot myself and thought of others, I think of my dad. I think of what he would be doing right this very moment before he was sick, he would be on some call with the Tokyo office or drinking scotch in the kitchen looking out across the grass of our old estate. When my mind wanders to the estate I wonder, did he ever see the encounters I had with Stone on the grass? Was he always so blind to the nineteen-year-old climbing the trellis on the side of his house, slipping through his daughter's window? He must have known.

"There is no way you didn't know dad, am I right?" I chuckle to myself, so lost in thought that I don't even know if I said the words out loud or not.

Just as my mind was fornicating in Massachusetts with the bad boy next door, the heavens seem to open.

I am buffeted by torrential rain like someone has turned on the sprinkler system in the sky. Was this dad's way of chastising me, again? I chuckle to myself as I search for somewhere to shelter until it dies down.

I run for Macy's awning, the warm stream of rain running from my head down the tip of my nose. My dark brown hair is drenched, and I squeeze some of the water out onto the stone tiles.

Another couple of bodies run for cover from the monsoon and huddle in beside me, I tilt my head allowing myself to stare at the soaked strangers.

But he wasn't a stranger.

The man standing directly next to me, rainwater running down his forehead as he attempted to dry it on the back of his sleeve.

Stone.

His gaze caught mine, that famous Carlisle smirk creeping across his perfect lips.

I didn't even fight back my smile, he made me feel electric.

We both burst into hysterics, amused by another chance encounter.

"Hi." I pant through my laughter.

He turns his whole body to face me, "Hello, you."

"How are you?" I ask, I wasn't sure what to say. But if I'm being honest, I would have been perfectly comfortable staring at his face, offering small smiles back and forth. We didn't need to talk, we were always better at communicating through our silence. And other things.

"I'm good, just finished at the office then this typhoon closed in on me." He puts his hand out into the rain, "How are you?"

"Same, I was just out a walk clearing my head."

He narrows his eyes, "Why, what's going on in your head?"

"Wine," I answer immediately.

"Drinking alone or...?" He lowers his gaze, shuffling his feet.

I shake my head, he didn't need to know the ins and outs of my life now. If I'm being completely honest with myself, I was afraid that if I told him anything about my life, then he would tell me about his, and selfishly...I didn't need to know if he had moved on or not. The rain stops suddenly, "Bye Stone." I step back out onto the street.

"Eva, wait!" He calls after me, "I can walk you home if you'd like?"

There is no right or wrong answer here, is there?

"I'd like that." I smile and we walk together quietly in the direction of my apartment.

"God would you look at her." I break our silence as we pass the same girl sitting on the street, only now she is completely sodden, "How much cash do you have?"

"What?" Stone asks pulling out his wallet.

I grab it from him without a second thought, "Can I give her this?"

"Three hundred and forty-seven dollars?" his mouth hangs wide waiting for my response.

I nod enthusiastically.

He sighs, "Sure why not." He shrugs.

I hand her the money, her eyes lighting up.

"I can't take this." Her gruff voice quivers.

I smile delicately, "Yes you can, please take it. Besides...he doesn't need it." I point to Stone.

The girl gets up from the wet ground, she reaches for Stone's hand taking it in hers.

Stone's eyes widen massively, "Thank you, thank you, thank you." She shakes him.

My heart warms at her happiness, and a little snigger sneaks out of my chest at Stone's uncomfortable stance.

"Don't you feel good?" I ask, pulling him away.

He shrugs, "I guess, I hope she doesn't spend it on drugs."

"Why is that what you were going to spend it on?" I counter without hesitation.

"Bitch." He scoffs, playfully shoving me into a puddle.

I grab his wrist stopping him for a moment, "I'm sorry. That was uncalled for." I apologise.

He dismisses it, "It was funny."

We arrive outside my apartment, the sun has almost completely set, and a spit of rain begins to fall from the sky again.

I stare up at Stone waiting for him to make a move, to crash his lips to mine. But he doesn't.

"Do you want to come up?" I ask, glancing quickly at Arthur as he stands holding the door open.

Stone shakes his head, "I best not." He leans down into me, kissing my damp forehead, "Have a great birthday, Eva."

I release a shuddering breath.

"Goodbye, Stone."

He winks at me before heading in the opposite direction from the way we came.

I wanted to scream after him, had we really come this far?

I think this time we are truly over.

New Beginnings

♥

Breathe...I force myself to take a second.

I must have changed my outfit a hundred times, no make that a thousand. Finally settling on my favourite black Prada leather pencil skirt paring it and an off-white low-cut silk blouse. I opted for a black, lace bralette-type thing underneath. It contained my ample bust and even made it look like I had a little extra.

I feel good, I feel sexy. "Alright, Eva! You look unbelievable." Sophie barges through my door slamming down a very expensive purse. "Treat yourself did you?" I pick it up peering inside the black padded Chanel.

She looks away sheepishly. Joshua treated her.

She hated that he bought her expensive gifts when they weren't officially an item, it made her feel like a prostitute.

Which of course she wasn't.

And why shouldn't she accept these beautiful things, if he wanted to buy them for her and spoil her then let him.

"It's beautiful, and you work hard Soph." I watch her chew her bottom lip nervously as she avoids my gaze, "are you seriously embarrassed about a bag?"

Her eyes widen with fear.

No not fear, guilt.

"Sophie Ann Jones...what have you done?"

"Nothing I promise... I didn't do anything." Her hands shake as she reaches into her purse for a vape.

"Cut the shit. Is there a stripper coming?" I flash my eyes to the door in a panic.

"Ugh no! But now I wish I had thought of that!"

I throw my arms up waiting for an explanation.

I don't think I can cope, I hate surprises.

My birthday drinks better not have turned into a surprise party with a bunch of people I don't know.

"Joshua and I are...we're finally...well...we're an item." Her mouth curls into a sort of uneasy smile.

My heart melted for her. Even though she would never admit it, she liked Joshua. A lot.

And it was clear to see that he liked her too.

"I wondered if it would be okay if he met us for drinks tonight, you can say no. It's your birthday. I just really wanted you to finally meet him. He's going out of town in few days so I-" I throw my arms around her, trying my best to ease her nerves. I hate when she rambles, her little slip of anxiety bleeding through her bubbly personality. She masks it so well, but she can be real with me. I'm her safe space, and she's mine.

"Of course! I'd love to meet him." And that was the truth. Why wouldn't I want to meet the man who has made my friend happy?

Her breath hitches a little with excitement, but the sheepish gaze still lingers.

I start to wonder, am I really that judgemental?

"Oh good!" She pants out, "this leads me to the next thing..."

Oh god.

My face falls straight as I watch her plaster a forced reassuring smile across hers.

"Sophie...?"

"He's going to bring his friend."

"Soph, is this a blind date?" I stare her down.

"No. Well, I mean...no." She backtracks.

What part of Eva Miller screams 'I would enjoy a blind date?' On my thirtieth birthday, after a somewhat painful breakup.

"Eva, I promise it's not a blind date, it's drinks with friends. He's bringing a friend and I'm bringing one. Please don't freak out. But if you really don't want to go I'll cancel." She takes her eyes up and down my body, "but please let me just say...it would be a fucking crying shame to waste those red bottom heels and that lace negligee." She offers me a wilful grin.

It's not a blind date, it's just drinks. And who knows, maybe I'll enjoy myself.

What if this is going to be my 'meet cute'?

If I keep saying no, then how will I ever find myself?

"You owe me big time." I point to her, inhaling deeply as I look into the mirror at myself, sweeping a soft nude coloured lipstick across my lips.

Don't overthink it.

It's just some fun.

It's my birthday tomorrow, and it would be a shame to waste all this effort.

I take one last glance at myself.

I can do this. I can meet new people.

God, I hate blind dates, and double dates... and setups.

This is all three rolled into one toe-curling cringe-fest.

"Ready?" She leans her chin on my shoulder.

I smirk, "As I'll ever be."

"Thank you." She chuckles, dipping her hand into her purse fumbling for her cell phone.

"Honestly, I'm a little excited," I admit, shocking myself with the outburst of honesty.

"I don't mean thank you for agreeing to come, I mean thank you for being my friend. I was kinda lost when I found you wandering aimlessly through the wine aisle. I don't know what I'd do without you, it's been a short amount of time but I really feel like we were meant to meet." She shrugs emotionally shaking off some feathering tears.

"Stop, you'll make me cry." I pull her in tightly, choking back every word.

I didn't need to tell her how much she saved me, she knew.

It was written in every text and email, and all of our giggles. We were made for each other.

The friend I had always wished for but had given up on ever finding found me instead.

"I thought you said drinks?" I whine, stepping out of the cab and onto the sidewalk.

"So its dinner and drinks, and they are already here." She grabs my wrist, pulling me into the restaurant which turns into a cocktail bar in the evenings.

So technically she didn't lie.

A wave of anxiousness starts to build from my toes, I grab onto Sophie's arm halting her for a moment.

"Whats he like, the friend?" My voice hoarse with nerves, I plead a little for some more information.

I hate meeting new people.

This whole evening was out of my comfort zone.

Sophie shrugs, "sorry babe, never met him." She continues to pull me inside the bar weaving her way to the host at the restaurant.

"Table for four, the other party is already here I believe. I think it was under 'Coates'." The tall host sneers down her nose at us.

"This way..." She leads us to a booth in a quieter back corner.

I swear my heart is going to rip through my chest, I need a drink and I need it fast.

"Hey!" Joshua jumps to his feet, he leans into Sophie whose face is beaming, lifts her chin with his finger and plants a gentle kiss on her lips.

She has good taste, I'll give her that.

Joshua is tall, dark and handsome. His chocolate brown hair textured with soft waves, his face completely clean shaven showing off his strong jaw line.

"You must be Eva." He places both hands on my shoulders, not quite as intimate as a hug but not as formal as a hand shake.

"Hi Joshua, I've heard so much about you." Sophie's cheeks redden, I throw her a cheeky grin.

Just a little bit of payback for springing this blind date double setup on me.

I haven't quite figured out what it is yet.

Sophie slides into the booth and Joshua manoeuvres himself next to her, I sit across from them glaring at Sophie bemused.

She clears her throat, "wheres your buddy?"

"Bathroom." He pecks her cheek delicately, they share a quick moment between them.

I sit awkwardly like a buckled third wheel. Deciding then and there if this 'friend' is a tool then I will leave immediately, go home and eat the pint of Ben And Jerry's Phish Food ice cream that I have been saving in my freezer for a rainy day.

"Oh there he is." Joshua grins towards then crowd.

I spin my head around watching the man weave his way through the bustle of waiters.

"The line at the mens room was longer than the woman's, when has that ever happ-"

He looks down at me through his familiar smirk.

I look up at him, my eyes disappearing in my smile.

Simultaneously, we erupt into fits hysterical laughter.

"Eva." He breathes through a lull in his giggle.

"Aster Stone Carlisle, hi."

He slides into the seat beside me his gaze never faltering from mine, he wipes away a tear from the outer corner of my eye with his thumb.

"You guys know each other?" Joshua and Sophie look around the table perplexed, "Like really know each other, because it seems like you do." The question turns to a statement as we ignore them. My hand absentmindedly searches for his, our fingers intertwine immediately like magnets that had lost their way.

"Guys what is happening right now?" Sophie taps the table.

"What are the chances, eh Stone?" I brush my fingertips on the back of his knuckles. All of these brief encounters, had it all lead to this?

"I have something for you, Eva." Stone reaches into his pocket, "I have wanted to give you this so many times, but something always stopped me. I kept waiting for the 'right moment' but there is no such thing. We've spent twelve years doing this thing that we do, the stubborn toxic on again off again bullshit. Everyone could see what we have, everyone but us. I promise you Eva Miller I wont ever hurt you again." His bright blue eyes brim with tears, "I love you." He says with such certainty, "I always loved you, and will always love you. I'll never leave you again, I promise." He opens a leather ring box, inside a large emerald cut diamond ring elegantly sparkles in front of my eyes.

"Will you marry me?"

The Elephant In The Room

Sophie's eyes hang out of her head as she watches from across the table.

"This is the most successful non-set-up, set up ever." I hear her mutter,

Joshua pats her knee lovingly, "That's why you do Soph, you get people what they need."

I can't breathe, refusing to look at the diamond that sits in front of me.

The noise of the restaurant fades into the background or is everyone just waiting for my answer to the question.

I feel like I've been transported back into the mind of the eighteen-year-old girl sitting on the roof with the 'bad boy' next door.

We sat there that night promising one another that we wouldn't fall in love.

"You can't change me," he said with such determination, declaring moments before that he didn't want me as a girlfriend.

But it was okay because I wasn't fit to be loved.

"You can't break me." the words flowed so easily from me, a little shattered girl already torn down by her own self-loathing. There was no need for anyone else to do it when I had so successfully done it all on my own.

His head whipped around, he didn't like what I said.

I didn't care.

"I don't want to break you." under his arrogance hid a quiver of desperation.

With a straight face, I replied, "you can't fix me either."

The truth was he did break me, he took all of my already broken pieces and ground them down, but by breaking me, without even realising, without meaning to he fixed me.

I'm acutely aware of how hard my heart is beating. It's like a bass drum in my ears, pretty sure the universe can hear it too.

I see the slightest of twitches in the corner of his perfect mouth. Even now he thinks he knows what I'm going to say. The arrogance of him is insufferable, but it's not, not to me. It's what drew us together at the start, when I really think about it we wouldn't have had anything if it weren't for him.

So why can't I say yes?

"This is awkward," Joshua mutters from the side of his mouth, Sophie shoots him down with a sharp hush.

Stone brushes his fingers along the palm of my hand, and for the first time in twelve years, I recoil from it.

My stomach bubbles like acid, I feel the vomit rising.

Pulling away from everyone's gaze, I force myself through the bustling bar, barely making it outside onto the busy dusk streets. I throw myself over a trash can, hurling into it. Passers-by looking on with disgust. I couldn't hold onto it any longer, every emotion surging through me, threatening to burn me out at any given second.

"Eva?" Sophie's hand comes gently on my back.

"I can't go back in there Sophie, did you know? Did you plan this?" My body shivers in the cool breeze.

Sophie grabs my hand, "I swear to you, none of us knew. I promise Eva, this is a fucking unbelievable coincidence." She hands me a cigarette but the thought of it causes me to heave.

"It's too much Sophie, I have to go home." I blink through fat tears, catching a glimpse of Stones pushing through the dense crowd.

She hails me a cab, "I think it's a mistake. The few times you have talked about him it's been-"

"Soph," I cut her off abruptly, "you don't understand." I slide into a cab before Stone can reach me.

No one understands, Stone was offering me everything I ever wanted. I'm just not sure I want it.

I don't know if I can trust him, trust us.

No, that's not it either.

I'm afraid.

The bathroom mirror fogged up with the heat pulsing from my rattled body, I wipe away some of the steam to look at myself.

I check the time on my watch, it's 00:21 am.

I stare back at the thirty-year-old woman.

'I don't recognise you.' I mumble through conflicted sobs.

This isn't anywhere near where I thought I'd be when I turned thirty. I thought I'd have so much more.

A sad knock on the door of my apartment pulls me out of my desperate trance.

I know who it is before I peer through the peephole.

Stone stands sheepishly on the other side.

"Hi," I pant out awkwardly standing aside to let him in.

His sad eyes filled me with guilt as he walks through the threshold.

"I didn't want you to be alone on your birthday," he offers me a sad smile, "And I'm sorry." his head hangs low.

"I'm the one who should be sorry. I was in shock, and I think I still am." The words were out faster than I could think.

He leans in, "Happy birthday Eva." his soft whisper makes every hair on my body stand on edge.

He brushes his lips against my cheek, I never realised how much I missed his touch, his scent until now. Except I think I did. He's been my missing piece.

"Were you just going to bed?" He rakes his eyes up and down my jade night dress.

I glance up to meet his gaze, the deep pool of blue enticing me majestically I want to dive right in.

"I was going to have some ice cream." His eyes crinkle in the corner, he nods defeatedly reaching for the door handle, "Do you want some?"

I've never seen his head snap around so quickly, his eyes widening with delight.

"Depends, what kind?" his cocky facade barely visible through the sheet of sheer joy written across his face.

I giggle inwardly at him as he throws his coat over the credenza in my hallway.

I reach into the freezer for my emergency stash of Ben and Jerry's, grabbing two spoons from the drawer before I set myself on the counter.

I struggle to peel off the lid, Stone takes it from me pulling it free with ease.

Watching me shift uncomfortably on the marble top he flicks his head to the side gesturing to the sofa.

We make small talk about the weather, glossing lightly over the old days...too embarrassed to bring anything up about our adolescent mistakes. Basically doing anything to avoid the elephant in the room.

The answer to his question.

The question itself.

If this were a movie then I would have jumped into his arms bawling "Yes! My answer is yes!" But life just isn't that simple, is it? Maybe it is and I'm just overcomplicating it.

The thing is, no one ever talks about what happens after 'happily ever after'.

If I say yes, and we get married...then what?

What happens to us? How do we end?

The uncertainty of life fills me with such fear that I think I might drown in it.

Stone takes the empty tub from the tiny space between us on the couch putting it in the trash, he washes up the spoons and places them back into the drawer. Almost as though he is hiding the evidence of him being here.

He sighs a little, grabbing his coat and keys he hovers by the door.

"Stone?"

"Mhmm."

My heart pounds again, thudding in my chest almost ready to burst through the flesh.

"I'm sorry."

His back still facing me I can only imagine his face, the corners of his mouth turned into a sad smile.

"Why are you sorry? I ambushed you." His hand reaches for the handle but he doesn't pull.

I don't know what I wanted him to say, I don't even know what I wanted to say.

All I know is I didn't want him to leave...not yet anyway.

"I'm sorry because I don't have an answer for you."

My words sparked hope inside of me, they came from my heart. My answer wasn't yes, but it wasn't no either.

But I didn't want to hurt him by keeping him on a hook.

Now what?

"Eva, I understand. I haven't been very good to you. Maybe one day soon you'll give me a chance to explain. Even then, I know that it won't make what I did right, I know that."

"Then stay." I reach my hand around him placing it on his wrist, I pull it from the handle and force him to come to me.

I want to hear what he has to say, I need to hear it.

But first...

I stand up reaching for his lips with mine, his perfectly sculpted Cupid's bow begging to be kissed I make the first move. Pressing mine lightly against them.

My hands find their way to the side of his face, I pull his head deeper down to me.

"We need to talk before we do this." He moans into me.

"We will, but I want this Stone." I flick his bottom lip with my tongue parting his mouth.

But he doesn't allow me in, "Kiss me." I plead.

"I want to." He murmurs, his body stiff.

Who knew he had this much restraint.

"I want you to, please Stone...kiss me." My pleading turned to pathetic begging.

I feel his hands grip my waist, pushing me against the wall next to my bedroom his lips brushing against my ear, "Say my name again."

My body trembles with the thrill, "Stone..." I pant out.

"No, say my full name." his hot breath tickles my cheek.

"Aster Stone Carlisle, I want you." just as the last syllable leaves my mouth he lifts me off the ground hooking my legs around his waist, bruising my lips with his.

Our tongues fight for dominance, but I give into him easily. I just wanted to be a part of him.

I hear his pants drop to the ground as I wrestle with the buttons on his shirt.

He hikes up my satin nightgown, pushing my underwear to the side he sweeps a finger along my slit, groaning when he feels how ready for him I am.

I nip the sweet spot on his neck, enthralled by the taste of his skin.

He moves deep inside me giving me a moment to adjust to him.

And as I sit on him waiting for him to thrash me, the mood changes.

He locks eyes with mine, his mouth parted slightly.

"I love you." I hear the quietest of quivers hide in his statement.

It's the most honest he's ever been.

"I love you more." slowly I move my face towards his, softly bringing our lips together.

He throbs inside me and I roll my hips slowly grinding myself on him, my arms wrapped around his neck he carries me through to my bed and lays me down never detaching.

The Answer

"What time is it?" Stone rolls over peppering open-mouth kisses along my shoulder.

I turn to look at the slatted blinds by my bed, the morning dawn peeking through.

I glance at my watch that lies on the bedside cabinet, "It's 7am!" I gasp jumping to the edge of the bed.

We spent the night talking and just being together.

It's the most intimate we've ever been.

"I have to get ready, I have my birthday lunch with Griffin."

I'm not even tired, I don't think he is either. But I'm scared to leave this bed, this room. This bubble of us that we created last night. Petrified that my answer will change us forever.

I sit on the edge of my bed looking at Stone while he rests his eyes, his chest rising slowly.

"You're staring at me." He mumbles through a grin.

I climb back into the bed beside him, he lifts his arm and I snuggle close to his body.

"Do you want to come with me? I can try and get you onto my flight." I tried not to sound too enthusiastic, knowing that he would decline the invitation, I was ready for him to make an excuse to get dressed and leave.

And when he checked his watch my heart sank.

"If we leave at eight, I could drive us?" I did my best to contain the look of shock that sat on my face, but I didn't do a very good job. Stone looked a little hurt.

"I'd really love that." I kissed his chin.

We left a little later than we had anticipated, and as soon as we got out of the busy city we stopped at a gas station for snacks and water.

"Candy?" I offer out my hand, Stone pops the luminous green hard candy into his mouth.

His face contorts almost instantly and he rolls down his window, "nope." He spits it out into the wind.

Everything he does I find endearing.

He has been all of my tropes, my right person at the wrong time. My wrong person at the right time. And I had been all of his.

But here we were sat comfortably together in his favourite possession, each other's right person at the right time. So why couldn't I say yes? What was stopping my heart from taking what I so desperately wanted, why was I so afraid? Just as I was about to self-sabotage myself he reached across and took my hand into his, pulling it to his mouth, kissing it ever so gently.

His lips lingered like a tattoo. No, not like a tattoo. Like a part of my skin, a freckle of love that was always meant to be there.

"I love you." I breathe out without a second thought.

He didn't say it back, instead, he squeezed my hand four times. And that meant more to me than anything.

But I knew I was hurting him, by not giving him an answer I was tearing his heart to shreds.

"Stone, I do you know."

"Do what?"

"Love you." He takes his eye off the winding road for a second.

"I know, I love you more."

But I didn't want him to love me more, I just wanted it all the same.

I didn't want to be splintered by love.

"How does it feel to be thirty?" Stone asks wrestling with the old radio, the static filling the car.

I shrug, "I feel different, but I'm not sure if it's because I'm older or because-" I pause hesitating, for the first time, thinking before I speak.

But as always, Stone knew what I was thinking.

"Because I barged my way back into your life." his statement stung my heart.

"You certainly made an entrance." He chuckles at my truth. There was no point in lying. We knew each other inside out.

Well maybe not, but we understood each other.

And if I couldn't be honest with him then we didn't stand a chance.

"Okay so answer me this, now that you're thirty do you have any regrets?" he stares ahead watching the road.

The answer was yes, a simple yes.

I take a deep inhale of breath, "I regret not standing up for myself against my dad, I sometimes wonder if I had then maybe we would have had a better relationship. We would have had longer together. Instead of those years spent filled with resentment."

Stone nods, he understood it.

"What's your biggest regret?" he asks.

This was a heavy conversation for a Sunday morning, but we were talking. Like friends would. And that opened me up, "not allowing myself to be open to friendship."

"Like with Sophie?"

And right on cue my cell pings.

From: Sophie
Happy Birthday, Eva!
I'm sorry about last
night. Can you
forgive me?

To: Sophie
Nothing to forgive
I'm with Stone
now. Call you
tomorrow xx

From: Sophie
Is there a ring on
your finger?

My heart falls into my stomach at the thought of the ring. It's a heavy burden weighing me down before I've even decided to wear it.

To: Sophie
Too soon. Call you
tomorrow. Xx

Stone's eyes flit from the road to my face, "yeah, like with Sophie. I regret not finding friends, because then maybe I would have had more of a sense of who I was. Then maybe we would have worked better, and life wouldn't have been so hard."

I know that I had lived a privileged life, and that's not what I'm complaining about. But I was ignored by my parent, which led me to ignore myself. Stone was the first person who saw me.

"What about you, do you have regrets?" I wanted to know.

It was my narcissistic trait, I needed to know if he had any regrets towards me, or us.

He blows through a heavy sigh, "Sure I have, more than most I'd imagine. I guess I regret being a little shit when I was younger. Not appreciating Griffin, and abusing my privileges." He drums his fingers on the thin steering wheel.

I let go of all my vices, this man had come full circle and grown so much.

I realised I didn't need to hear about his guilt. I had forgiven him for everything, just as he had forgiven me.

"I guess my biggest regret is treating you the way I did after New Year, remember?"

Oh, I remembered.

During our five-minute pregnancy scare, when in the two minutes it took for the pee to settle on the stick he had told me that I would live to serve our unplanned child, he told me that my dreams hadn't mattered because I allowed this to happen. That he would continue to live his life, and mine would be over.

I remembered, unfortunately, I'd never forget.

"Well, that's my biggest regret... I wish I hadn't been so conceited. I guess I was just scared, that's no excuse. When I replay it in my mind it's all different now because I say all the right things, and we don't break up." A sad smile sits on his lips.

I had no idea he felt this way, none.

I always assumed his arrogance kept him from seeing how wrong he was about the whole situation.

Now I felt guilty knowing that he had suffered just as much as I did.

But it made sense, he never reached out afterwards. It was radio silence from him.

Of course, that's when he met Louisa.

Curious how she hadn't been mentioned in one of his regrets, but it made me happy that he loved her or at the very least had feelings towards her.

She was his bridge. He needed to have her, even if she had hurt him.

"In the scenario, you have of us in your head, what are we doing?" I blurt out.

He grins, "We're married, we have a kid."

"Boy or girl?" My heart races.

"It varies. But we're happy, in every scenario."

My breathing slows, "Stone?"

His head turns.

"Yes." I pant out.

"Yes, what?"

"Yes is the answer to your question."

He sniggers, "what question?"

Then his jaw almost drops to the floor at the realisation.

He pulls the car to the side of the road, turning his whole body round to face me. He reaches into his pocket pulling out the leather box, he holds it in the palm of his hand.

"I'm going to ask again, no big speeches. Just you and I."

I nod. Just us, the way it should have been.

"Eva Miller, I love you. It's all I can say. Will you marry me?"

Immediately I answer, "Yes."

He pulls out the delicate ring to place on my finger, I sob out elated tears at the sight of our cherry stalk which is tied to the bottom.

He had always promised to return it.

I crawl over the seat to him, "I love you." Our lips meet, tears from both of us flowing onto them.

"I love you, Eva. Always have. Never stopped." His breath hitches with emotion.

Communication Is Key

"Eva!" Griffin pulls me deep into his chest, it's been so long I missed the smell of him. I always associated his scent with home. The smell of fire and autumn no matter the time of year.

"Happy birthday sweet girl." We walk together to our table, Alma gets up from her seat wrapping her arms around my neck, I'm a little taken back with guilt for not keeping in touch as much as I probably should have.

"Thirty...I can't quite believe it. Your dad would be so proud." My heart flutters nervously, would he be proud?

I look around at the table the place is set for four, before I can mention anything Griffin places a hand on my cheek, "I had hoped Stone would join us, but I'm afraid he is busy with work. I'm sorry."

I nod my head, "thats okay, I brought my boyfriend...he's parking the car." Met with wide stares from them both, I decide to have a little fun with them, "we have some news."

Alma claps excitedly, "I've been waiting to meet this mystery man. He's a fireman like your step father isn't he?"

I shake my head, "not quite."

Just at that Stone saunters through the door, my stomach does a somersault. Even though we just spent the last 16 hours together, every time I set eyes on him, its like I'm seeing him for the first time.

God, I love him.

"Oh Stone!" Griffin exclaims, "I didn't think you would make it. I'll have the waiter set another place." He looks down awkwardly through his glasses, "we're um waiting on Eva's partner."

"Oh really?" Stone places both hands on my shoulders, I bring my left hand up and rest it on his.

Trying my best to remain coy.

"OH MY GOD!" Alma yelps jumping up from her seat again, "I knew it!! I really knew it!"

"I'm confused." Griffin looks around the restaurant perplexed, his cheeks flushed.

Alma shakes him vigorously, "They're engaged you silly old fool!" Her sobs come out fast as she says the words out loud.

Once the screaming and tears had settled slightly, we sat around the table sipping champagne. My heart swelled when Stone declined because he was driving. He really wasn't the same reckless bad boy I had fallen in love with at the beginning, he was better.

"So when did this happen?" Griffin asked grabbing my hand taking another look at the diamond on my finger.

Stone opened his mouth to tell our story, I gripped his thigh under the table. I wanted it to be sacred, just for us.

"It was a long time coming, we had a few random encounters. Something just clicked." I simpered at them.

Alma nodded her head, her eyes still blurry with tears.

I knew she was crying because she was happy for us, but she was sad for herself. I knew this ring was meant for her, I had helped him pick it. It was part of the reason I was so shocked when I saw that Stone had it.

I wonder, how would my dad feel about me having it? How would he feel about the man who gave it to me?

He never got to see the good in Stone.

We didn't drive home, instead we decided to stay in the honeymoon suite in the Boston Harbour Hotel.

Griffin had wanted us to sleep at his place, but we had different plans.

We walked hand in hand to the elevator, giggling like teenagers reminiscent of our devious relationship with them.

I struggle with the stupid key card as I always do, Stone grabs it from my hand unlocking the door. I take off my jacket hanging it neatly in the closet.

Stone snakes his arms around my waist, I feel his lips brush against my ear.

"Spread them." He kicks my legs apart, his hands sliding up the back of my thighs, reaching for the elastic he hooks his fingers gliding them down lazily, he drops to his knees, lifting my legs to allow me to step out of the lace.

I slowly turn my body keeping my legs wide. Stone looks up at me through his thick lashes as he runs his middle finger along my seam, teetering on the cusp of my opening.

The thrill of him hitching my breath, the excitement alone building my climax.

He flicks his tongue upwards, delving between my folds the tip brushing my aching clit gently.

I want more.

I need more.

Wrapping my hand around his head I push him deeper, "I want you to fuck me Stone."

He moans against my core lapping me hungrily, he curls two fingers deep inside me.

Pulling a gasp from my lungs as I try to hold back my orgasm. Its too quick.

"Cum for me, you can do it more than once." He growls.

On his command I release myself, bucking my hips forward as he wipes my juices from his face with his thumb, relishing in my taste.

He stands towering above me, his eyes burning into mine.

I try to catch my breath, "I love you." I pant out.

My words bring out my favourite smirk, he crashes his mouth against me. His lips capturing mine like they couldn't bear to be apart.

In a flash our clothes were gone, he lifted my body onto his. Inserting himself deep inside me, he laces his tongue along my collarbone.

"I love you, I love you." His words ricochet against my skin. Piercing me with adoration.

My back presses against the closet door as he pulses inside me, the tip of him brushing my sweet spot.

Each movement more enthralling than the next. I roll my hips feeling my orgasm building again, I can tell by Stones high breaths that his is ready too.

I wanted to finish together, I wrap my hand around his neck lightly scratching the base of his skull.

Just as I feel him twitch inside me I give into the high of my climax, clenching my walls around him.

The mixture of us running down my inner thighs.

We lie in bed together, our bodies intertwined. Desperately clinging to one another, too afraid to let go just incase we lose ourselves again.

"Stone?" I'm acutely aware of how many times I've started a conversation with just his name.

He chuckles, "Eva?"

"I want to get married tomorrow."

"Why?"

I shrug, "I don't want to wait. Its taken us twelve years to get here, I can't wait any longer."

"Eva, don't you want a big wedding?" His eyes are wide with concern.

I shake my head, "I don't. I just want to be your wife."

He dips his head down kissing my forehead, "I'll do whatever you want, but I don't want you to settle for less than what you want because you're afraid."

I inhale deeply, how is it that he just knows exactly how I'm feeling?

I am afraid, I'm scared that if we don't rush then something will happen and I'll never get my happy beginning.

"I'm not going to leave you, Eva. I promise."

This time his words hit me differently, and I knew he was telling the truth.

"I'm not worried about you leaving, I'm scared that it'll be ripped from us. I just can't take any more heartbreak."

He simpers down at me, "That's just life, we can't control that. Being married wont stop it."

"I know, but I want to be your everything and I don't want to wait."

"You'll always be my everything." He presses his lips against my passionately, "I don't want you to regret not having a perfect day."

"Will I be there?"

"Yes."

"Will you be there?"

"Of course."

"Then it'll be the perfect day."

Stone's cell phone rings disturbing our moment, "Yes?...okay...yup...see you in an hour."

I look up at him, "we're going to Griffin's for dinner." He pinches the bridge of his nose, "my parents are there."

"That'll be fun." I groan pulling the sheets over my head.

"C'mon Miller, lets get cleaned up." Stone slaps my backside before scooping me up into his arms, carrying me into the bathroom.

He turns on the shower, pulling the head down so as not to wet my hair.

He begins trailing kisses down my neck, "I will do whatever you want to do, if you wanna get married tomorrow then we will."

"Stone, I want to be your wife. I want to be your family." I roll my head back inviting him to plant his lips on my throat.

He laces his tongue from my chest to my mouth in one swift ticklish motion, grazing my tongue with his.

"Okay." He pins my arms above my head with one hand, "now...stay still." He detaches the shower head bringing it between my legs, with the other.

The spray of water blowing against my nerve centre.

Reluctantly Compromising

"Fuck." I breathe out as Stone turns the car off the main road and into the estate. The gravel road crunched under his tyres, it was a sound I hadn't ever thought about. Never realising that I missed it until I heard it again.

Stone reached his hand over and rested it on my thigh, "shit, I never thought about how hard this might be for you." He stopped the car abruptly turning off the engine he turned to me, "do you want to go back? I can call and cancel."

I shake my head, "No, I can do this. It's just bricks and mortar, right?"

He simpers gently at me, squeezing my thigh.

I imagined the new owner had completely demolished the house ripping it back to bare brick leaving nothing of me and my life.

It was better to imagine it that way, because I couldn't bear to think of someone else painting over my memories.

But seeing it in the distance, almost exactly the way I had left it hurt more.

"Lets go," I pack away my feelings, "we can't keep Angela waiting." I force out a panicked smile.

"Fuck Angela, if you want to forget all of this we can."

I shake my head, this is supposed to be our happy time. I will not let my pessimistic thoughts overshadow this day.

"Well I suppose congratulations are in order." Angela circles around me without so much as a hint of delight, her eyes closing in on my hand.

Stone scoffed at her lack of enthusiasm, shaking his head. Everything about her was laughable, she just didn't have it in her to be happy, not even for her only son.

"I'll call the club and see when they next have an opening." She pulls out her cell phone and starts dialling.

I had to stop the corners of my mouth twitching as she began trying to plan our wedding, the thing is and Stone was too far gone in his disappointment to notice, that Angela did care. Just a little. It was in the small gestures. Like calling the country club.

I give Stone a little nudge, "You gonna tell her or should I?"

He rolls his eyes, "Mother, we want to get married tomorrow."

She mimics him hanging up the cell, "tomorrow? Like some sort of tacky shot gun wedding?" She snipes lighting a cigarette, "Oh god...not again!"

Alma steps forward, "I think it's romantic."

"Of course you do." Angela scoffs, "remind me why she is here?"

Stone steps forward seething, "she is Evas family...don't do this mother, you don't want to go down this road." They simultaneously pinch the bridge of their nose, puffing their chests in unison.

I can't help but smile affectionately, their similarities shining through their anger and yet somehow even through the argument it warms me.

"Down what road?" Angela throws out her arms.

"The one that would lead me to choose. Because, and I want you to really, really hear me clearly when I say this."

"Get to the point already I have a manicure at 6"

"If you push me any further; there is no doubts when I tell you I will chose Eva over you. Every. Single. Time."

I twirl the ring around my finger nervously, the argument between Stone and his mother weighing heavily on my chest. I knew that there would be some animosity, but I never expected this.

Alma reaches out for my hand, "its okay, just breathe." She whispers, smiling fondly at the sparkling diamond.

"Wheres your special?" She asks.

I knew right away that she was talking about our cherry stalk, I also knew that she was trying to take my mind off of world war three going on in the back ground, and bless her for that.

"Its in the box back at the hotel, I'm scared incase it falls apart."

Alma places her gentle hand on my cheek, "If that frail little thing can go through all of that and still be intact... then you've got nothing to worry about. When I gave it to Stone...I told him..."

"Wait!" Angela steps forward again, guns blazing, "When you gave what to Stone?"

Alma looks flustered her eyes flitting violently between the ring and Stone, it was easy to see that even after all these years she was still intimidated by Angela.

"The ring was m-mine. Eva picked it for Preston to give to me, but he died before he got the chance. It was with his things. I-I-I gave it to Stone in the hopes that one day he would give it to Eva. Its what Preston would have wanted, its what I wanted."

Angela's face falls even more stern than usual, and if I were able to get close enough I'm sure there was a tear sitting in her waterline.

But the question is, was it a sentimental tear?

Or was she hurt?

Her face reddens, filling with more rage...not a tear in sight.

"Oh! So you knew?" She burls back around to face Stone who has decided to pour himself a healthy measure of Griffins finest scotch.

"My only son...twice you have done this to me. Twice, didn't you stop to think that I would have liked to have been involved?"

Stone swallows the glass in one, "Actually, Angela. No. I didn't, because you've never shown any interest in me or Eva, unless it was to make her or us uncomfortable." He fills himself another glass, "Actually that's a lie, isn't it? There's been a lot of manipulating and meddling but for what? What did you want from us? From me? Because honestly Angela, I can't keep up."

It was at this stage in the fight that I decided to make myself scarce. I felt like I was an intruder, trespassing on this moment that wasn't meant to be seen by anyone else.

Alma slipped into the kitchen while I wandered around the mansion, trying my best to drown out the sound of the *Carlisle Twins* yelling. I just hope they don't wake Griffin, he had retired to bed for a nap before dinner. And by the sounds of it there won't be anyone left to have dinner with.

At the very top of the stairs on the third floor, tucked behind a large dusty bookshelf is a large bay window that looked out onto the grounds of the estate. I wasn't always a reader, I always preferred music to books but something about the quaintness of this little nook hidden amongst the mansion pulled me in. I grabbed a random book from one of the

shelves and settled myself on the windowsill, I glanced down at the cover to see which one
I had picked.

'The Shining.'

I open the first page.

Nope.

I look out of the window across the grass and not so far in the distance I see my house,
well no. It wasn't my house any more, it belonged to someone else. From this cosy little
place you could see right onto my roof, and into my window. It was too far away to make
anything out thankfully, but I had no idea that it was so visible.

"I used to sit here and watch Stone climb up that trellis and through your window you
know."

"FUCK! Griffin, you scared the shit out of me." I slap my hand across my mouth
forgetting my manners.

He chuckles heartily, turning his head towards the stairs as the battle continues, "I used
to watch him creep in and out of that window and wonder why he wanted to keep you
a secret. Then he brought you here that night, the night of the break in and I knew then
that he loved you."

At that time he had a funny way of showing it.

"What are the new owners like?" I hated that someone else lived there, filling it with
their own story. I wish I hadn't sold it, I had wished that from the moment I put pen to
paper and signed it all away that I hadn't done it, that I had held on and stopped being so
rash.

I told myself that the thought of it lying empty was worse than selling it, but it wasn't.

I imagine a young girl, the opposite of me laughing with her mom and dad in the
kitchen cooking dinner. I see her growing from a toddler playing hide and seek, to a
teenager dancing around the rooms, and I'm jealous of her. I wanted that. I wanted to
give someone that. And being in any other house, in any other home I would only feel
like an imposter.

But it's done now.

That house was not a house you buy to sell, that house is a forever home. It just
wouldn't be mine.

"Eva," Griffin touched my arm bringing me back, "you are being summoned."

Just at that Stone appears at the top of the staircase his cheeks flushed, he looks directly
at Griffin, "Your daughter is impossible."

He walks over to me, a sort of sorry smile peeking in the corner of his mouth, "Hi." He kisses my forehead, "we need to speak with you, and by 'we' I mean my mother. Who by the way, turns out to have at least one feeling which has been hurt." I place my hand in his and allow him to lead me back to the battle field.

"By the way, she is crying."

"What?" Griffin stops dead on the staircase.

"Yeah I know." Stone scoffs.

"Wait who is crying?" I ask.

Stone holds back a laugh, "my mother."

"I didn't know she could do that." I look to Griffin who's face is going a deep shade of purple as he holds back more laughter.

"You're as surprised as we are." Stone places his hand on my back giving me a gentle shove into the lounge, I turn to see him help his grandfather down the final step.

Stone was telling the truth, she had been crying. Her eyes were blurred, and skin blotchy. Whatever words had been exchanged between these two had really affected her. I just hope Stone had given her, her just desserts because Angela Carlisle needed to be taken down a peg or two.

"Eva, we want to run something past you." Stone places both hands on my shoulders.

Oh boy. "And you can say no at any time, and we will move on with our original plan."

But...

"But...and it pains me to say this believe me it truly does, my mother had an idea for us to get married at the lake. In two days." Stone shuffles his feet, his eyes roaming my face for a reaction, "I know it isn't what you wanted." He looks across at Angela, "but I agree with her, it would be nice. And you can have Emily and Roger, and Sophie. It'll still be small, intimate."

I nod, it's all I can do. I feel sort of ambushed.

The lake is where it all began. But two days, a lot can happen in two days.

"I will take care of everything, I know you don't like extravagance." Angela finally steps forward, "and Alma will keep me in check." She curls her lip giving poor Alma the side eye.

"If you don't want this, Eva. I will take you tomorrow and we'll get married at the court house. But I kind of agree, the lake would be perfect." I can hear in it Stones voice that it's what he wants.

I would marry him anywhere, I would do it right now, with Angela and her cigarette officiating. I just want us to be forever, something about the security of marriage it makes the relationship feel iron clad. And I need that with Stone, I know I shouldn't but I just do. We've had so many near misses that every time I have him within my grasp I always feel like I'm going to lose him. And I don't have another heartbreak in me.

"As long as I end the day with your last name, that's all that matters to me."

I pull back the curtain trying to see the lake between the trees, "only one problem though, none of us own the lake any more"

Stone presses himself behind me, snaking his arms around my waist resting his chin gently on the top of my head.

"I'll speak with the owners." His arms tighten, filling me with warmth.

"Leave it to us." Griffin bangs his cane on the wooden floor, "there's a lot of work to do." He shuffles off into his study slamming the door behind him.

"I should call Sophie, she'll be pacing." I chuckle.

Stone meets me with a huge grin, "go do bride stuff, I'll take care of everything."

Angela clears her throat abruptly, Stone rolls his eyes.

"We'll take care of everything."

I Have Loved You Since You We're Eighteen

♥

This is supposed to be the most exciting and happiest few days of my life, so why aren't I happy?

Well that's the wrong choice of words, I am happy, at least until...

"What a way to find out my daughter is engaged..." Emily storms into the dress shop, poor Sophie lagging behind her.

I stood wide eyed watching her rage, Sophie simpered at me tearing up at the sight of me in a plain silk gown, nothing fancy or over the top, just like me.

"I didn't even know you were together...you only broke up with Tommy a few weeks ago." Emily continues.

Alma fusses over me, "You're beautiful." She says trying to overshadow my mothers unwelcome intrusion.

The shop owner takes my hand helping me off the pedestal, she offers me an awkward half smile, as Emily continues ranting and raving.

Emily scoffs at the hundred and fifty dollar price tag on my dress, "After everything he put you through, all of the hurt he caused you. I'll bet he doesn't even turn up tomorrow."

I can't take much more, that was the straw that broke my back.

How dare she. She might not have known, but bringing up my worst fear while I stand in a wedding dress on the day before I say 'I do' to the man I have loved for twelve years, that broke me.

"Alright, mother! I've had enough of this!" I snap, yanking the simple veil out of my head. I hand it to Sophie who in turn passes it to the owner.

Emily holds her hands up in protest, shuffling her feet in her expensive shoes,"Why are you speaking to me like this, Eva? I'm only voicing my concern."

"I don't need your concern, Emily...I need you to be happy for me. I needed for you to come in here and say 'Oh, Eva darling. I'm so delighted. Congratulations!' But you're just so pissed because I didn't fall in love with the man that you set me up with?"

Emily doesn't say a word, answering my question with her silence

"Oh my god, that's it. You're pissed about Tommy?" I fight with the zipper on the dress trying to get out of it. I don't care who sees me, but having a fight with my mother in this perfect dress felt like a sin. Like it would be tainted with disdain.

"You embarrassed Robert. It was a disgrace what you did to that poor boy, what a life he could have given you but you threw it away for money."

I look to Sophie who's mouth hangs wide open, she looks rooted to the ground with shock. I stand in my panties covering my breasts while Alma fumbles around looking for my shirt and jeans in the changing room, I don't wait for her to bring them to me. I just keep going. Unable to stop now.

"Shut your fucking mouth, Emily. Roger was fine about it all, I asked for his advice and he...god he is such a better parent and he isn't even a parent! And as for the money, why would I need Stone's when I have plenty of my own?"

Just at that Stone and Angela burst through the door, "Eva?" His cheeks flush, embarrassed as I stand half naked shouting at my mother. They must have been running errands in town, maybe someone alerted them to the commotion. I was just glad he was here. My anchor.

He takes off his blue cable knit sweater and pulls it over my head, thankfully he had a white T-shirt on underneath, not that it would have mattered.

"Of course you're here, you have your claws in her so deep. How could she ever get away from you?" Emily scoffs jeering for Stone.

"Oh leave him alone mother!" I lunge forward trying to pull her hand back as she points at his chest banging her finger harshly on it.

"Why couldn't you just have left her alone? She could have been so much more if it weren't for you."

Stone curls his lip, "Abandon her like you did? Let's not forget that you have only recently come back into Eva's life. She is the warm, kind, loving and successful person she is today, and it isn't because of you."

"And you think it's because of you?" Emily scolds him, practically spitting her words.

Angela steps forward, "Maybe it is because of him."

Stone holds up his hand silencing his mother, "No...it's because of her. It's because she willed herself to be better, better than you, better than me, better than anyone. She fixed herself, and she doesn't owe a single person on this planet an ounce of thanks and certainly not to you."

It wasn't until the tears bounced off of my chin that I had even realised I was crying.

Sophie and Alma appeared from behind the changing curtain handing me my purse and jeans.

"You okay?" Sophie whispered pulling my frame into hers.

I didn't answer, because I didn't know how I was feeling.

Then the strangest thing happened.

"I think it's evident Emily, that you aren't welcome here. And if I were you, I'd get the fuck out of Massachusetts." Angela thrusts Emily's bag into her arms shoving her out the door.

She turns giving me that Carlisle smirk and a wink.

In her own cold way that was her seal of approval, not that I ever needed it.

I guess I always knew somewhere deep down that Emily would do this, that she wouldn't be in my life for very long. Because she never really wanted to be a mother, and certainly not to me. It never came natural to her, and she always felt hostile towards me like I had taken something precious away from her.

My sadness was overshadowed by Stones words, he absolutely could have taken credit for 'fixing' me because in a way he did. But he pushed his arrogance aside and just adored me. Without having to say those three words, everyone in that store knew that he unreservedly, loved me. Perfectly.

Looking at him in this moment I knew with every cell in my body that he loved me. And that's when I finally realised that he would never leave me. That we were finally together.

"We said no vows," Stone held my hands as we stood together in front of Griffin, Angela, Richard, Alma, Sophie and Joshua on the dock of the lake, "but...when have I ever done what I was told?" He brings my hands to his lips kissing them gently. The weeping guests chuckle lightly.

I stare into his pool blue eyes, lost in the vast beauty of them. My Stone's eyes sparkling again, after all this time.

"Eva, this is where we had our first encounter you lay here sunbathing in that tiny black bikini." I tighten the grip I have of his hands, fearful of what he might say next.

He arches his eyebrow, "I knew from that very second that while I could have lived without you, I didn't want to and that my life would have been empty. I have loved you since you were eighteen, Eva. I'm sorry it took so long for me to admit to myself."

It was short and sweet, and everything I could have wished for.

We were married under the sunset on the lake where our love story started.

But this wasn't out happily ever after, this was our perfectly imperfect beginning.

What Happens After Happily Ever After?

♥

There was no reception just drinks and food in Griffins with our guests. And honestly, I couldn't have dreamed of a more idyllic day.

Although it was bittersweet, I only wished my mother could have mended her idiotic ways and been a part of us. It was ultimately her loss.

In her own way she gave me my family, she unwittingly brought me closer to Stone, and brought me home.

"If you would all excuse me, I need to get out if this dress and into something more comfortable." Griffin smiled fondly at me as I rose from the arm of the chair.

Stone sent me a devilish wink, he and Joshua had been deep in conversation about journalism, or something like that.

Alma had called for an early night and said she would be back in the morning to help clean up.

"I'll come give you a hand." Sophie followed me out of the lounge.

Angela stopped us in the foyer, swaying inebriated with her cigarette held high.

"Where are you two going?" She hiccuped.

Seeing her like this made me giggle, she was trying so hard to maintain her harshness but the hiccup gave her away.

"Just going to get out of my dress and into some shorts, Sophie wants to catch up." Angela stares at us for a moment, "Angela, would you like to come?"

"God, if I have to." She rolls her eyes, trudging upstairs towards Stone's old room.

"I love her." Sophie's airy voice squeaks into my ear just loud enough for me to hear.

I screw up my face, "really?"

"Yeah, she's fucking fabulous."

"I still can believe you and Stone knew each other, that he was the guy you had been pining over all this time." Sophie sits on the bed folding my veil into a neat rectangle.

Angela sits on the ledge of Stones bay window lighting another cigarette, "we should have brought up some liquor." She blows smoke out of the small gap.

I reach into Stone's bedside cabinet and pull out a half drank bottle of scotch, "knock yourself out, Angela." I toss it to her.

"Now you're getting it. Now you really are a Carlisle." She unscrews the lid and takes a swig.

"Anyway..." Sophie waves her hand around motioning for me to explain.

I shrug my shoulders, "I don't know what to say, I guess it was just fate. Stone always said if we were meant to be together then we would be, and we kept running into one another and I guess the rest is history."

Sophie's smile bursts from ear to ear, "so did he come to your apartment and ask you again or...?"

"He came to my apartment but he didn't ask me again. I said yes in the car on the way here."

Sophie could sense I didn't want to keep talking about it, she was good that way.

I wanted to keep it between Stone and I, just for us. I wasn't ashamed or anything like that, the very opposite. I just wanted to keep our story close to my heart. Maybe one day I would tell, but not today.

"Can you at least tell me what happened the day you met him, the day at the lake?" Sophie saunters over to sit by Angela, taking the cigarette right out of her hand inhaling on it like it was giving her life.

"Sure, but I don't think its mother in law appropriate." I cover my mouth trying to hold back my girlish squeal.

Sophie claps, "even better! Angela doesn't mind, sure you don't Angela?"

Angela takes another gulp of the scotch, "Angela's seen and heard worse, I can assure you, Sophie." She points her long finger at me, "and it was all her." She chuckles slapping the top of Sophie's arm.

"Okay so I was lying on the wooden sun bed by the water, and then..." suddenly a hand clamps over my mouth and I'm lifted into the air.

"Aaaaand I disturbed her, told her she was very pretty and we lived happily ever after the end." Stone spins me around.

"Could we take a walk?" He wiggles his eyebrows at me.

"A walk where?"

I catch him share a glance with his mother, "Oh come on Sophie, lets leave the teenagers to consummate-"

"Mother!" Stone grumbles.

Sophie grins playfully as she closes the door behind them.

"Hi." Stone cups my face bringing his lips to mine, "I've wanted to do this all night you know."

"Well Stone, I waited in the downstairs bathroom for you and I was left there...all alone." I flick his cupids bow with my tongue.

"I knew it! I knew I should have followed you." He peppers open mouth kisses along my collarbone.

"You let the side down, Stone." I run my hands down his chest and rest my thumbs in the loops of his tux trousers, tracing my way to his belt I begin undoing it.

His hands clasp over mine halting my movements, "Wanna take that walk?"

"What did you do?" I try to contain my sobs.

We stand in the hallway of my old house, its vast emptiness was so familiar, and us being here together just felt right, "Did you buy this?"

He nods gently, wiping away my tears.

"Why?" I sob out.

"You didn't want it to go, I could tell by the sadness in your eyes. The pain in your voice when you talked. So I bought it."

This must have been what Stone and Angela were doing in town yesterday when they saw me in the bridal store. This was his wedding gift to me.

My house, the place where all my dreams began.

Which meant that our lake, was exactly that when we got married there.

He had thought of everything.

"Wait...what about the property developer? Why didn't they change anything?" I scan my eyes around looking at the untouched walls and floors. Everything exactly the way I left it.

"There never was one, Eva Miller Carlisle."

Then it dawned on me, EMC Properties LTD. It was always mine, he had thought of everything but more importantly he had always thought of me.

And all this time I had his last name, while he carried around his heart in a box.

Even when we weren't a couple, when we were so distantly stubborn, we were bound together by the subtleness of Stone's love for me. I had always thought of him as selfish, how wrong I was.

I was home.

We were home.

<u>Nineteen Years Later...</u>

I rinse the dishes in the sink placing them in the drainer to dry, a pair of hands roam around my body working their way into the waistband of my yoga tights, "Stone..." I turn around to face him.

"Good day?" He feathers kisses down my throat and as he hits my favourite spot I tug on his hair trying to stop him.

"Stop...the twins." I mumble.

He huffs out a sigh, "where are they exactly?"

"Harry is in his room playing video games with Zach Chapman, Penny...Penny was out wandering the estate, went to the lake, came home ate half a box of cookies and disappeared to her room. And hasn't been seen or heard from since." I smooth Stones greyish hair to one side.

"When do they leave for college?" He slides his hands up the inside of my shirt feeling his way inside my sports bra.

I press my lips against his, "Stop trying to get rid of my babies."

"Our babies." He corrects me, deepening the kiss. Slipping his tongue inside my mouth, fighting me for dominance.

I let him have the upper hand, the taste of him makes me lose control.

After all this time he still has the ability to make me weak at the knees.

He rolls my pebbled nipples between his thumb and finger.

"Stone...?" I pant out as his other hand dances down inside my pants.

His finger sweeps inside my slit.

"Stone..."

"Mhmm?"

"There's a boy climbing up the trellis."

He doesn't stop working his way inside my core, I throw my head back in rapture.

"Wait...what?" Stone stops, pulling his hand out.

He rushes over to the kitchen bifold door looking up at the side of the house, "that cocky little son of a bitch, and in broad daylight too!"

"Is it the Whitlow kid?" I press myself against Stones back, snaking my arms around his waist.

"I fucking knew he was trouble, from the day they moved into Griffins I just knew it." he bangs his fists against the glass.

I chuckle as Stone tries to control his unfathomed rage.

"Stop it, Eva. I'm going up there."

"No you're not. Just leave them be."

"Why should I? That's my daughter up there."

I heave a long sigh my cheeks ache as I try to contain my smile. I brush my fingertips along his knuckles, twirling his wedding band, "Because, my dear bad boy...I was some-body's daughter too."

The End.

Acknowledgments

Cover art by Brogan Murray

Made in United States
North Haven, CT
05 January 2023

30686251R00173